Edited by:

earables

Ron Kolm
bart plantenga
Peter Lamborn Wilson
Mike Golden

Book design: Dave Mandl

Ficto-bio sidebar ("The Salvation of Rollo Whitehead") written by Jim Feast

The following pieces have previously appeared in other publications: Bruce Benderson: "Apollo's Curse" was published in his novel *User* (Dutton, 1994); Lynn Crawford: "Brood" first appeared in her collection of stories *Solow* (Hard Press, 1995); Janice Eidus: "Not the Plaster Casters" first appeared in *The Baffler* #5; Maggie Estep: "I'm Not a Normal Girl" appears on her CD *No More Mister Nice Girl* on Imago Records; Mike Golden: "The Unbearable Beatniks of Light Get Real!" first appeared in *RedTape* #7; Michael Kasper: "Laughing Stock" is from *The Shapes and Spacing of the Letters* (Weighted Anchor Press, 1995); Tsaurah Litsky: "The Shower" first appeared in her chapbook *Pushing Out the Envelope* (Apathy Press, 1992); Joe Maynard: "The Tattoo I Never Got" first appeared in *The Curse* #4; bart plantenga: "2-B 38-C 3-D in Neuropolis" appeared in a somewhat different form in *Yazzyk* (Prague, 1995); David Polonoff: "Marginal Notes" first appeared in his collection *Down the Yup Staircase* (Pantegruel Press, 1992); Thaddeus Rutkowski: "Mad Dogs of Italy" first appeared in *Wire* (Fall/Winter, 1990); Lynne Tillman: "Beats on the Beach" first appeared in *VLS*; Mike Topp: "Five Stories" first appeared in *Between C & D* Vol. 1, #2.

Printed in the United States of America

1 2 3 4 5 6 7 8 9 10 11 12 13 14 15 16 17 18 19 20 21 22 23 24 25 26 27 28

Autonomedia
P.O. Box 568
Brooklyn, NY 11211-0568
Phone/Fax: (718) 963-2603

Table of Contents

Graphics Credits

Page 10: **Yossarian**
Page 15: **Michael Gorelick**
Page 24: **Michael Madore**
Page 29: **Dave Lombard**
Page 33: **Franc Palaia**
Page 40: **Zagreus Bowery**
Page 48: **Mikhail Horowitz**
Page 64: **Winchester Chimes**
Page 68: **Foto Sifichi**
Page 72: **Yossarian**
Page 75: **Larry Hama**
Page 83: **James Romberger**
Page 93, 95, 97: **Fly**
Page 102: **Franc Palaia**
Page 108: **Inez Andrucyk**
Page 116: **Dan Freeman**
Page 122: **Michael Madore/Ron Kolm**
Page 126: **Ken Brown**
Page 130: **Patrick Stevenson**
Page 134: **Ralph Ackerman**
Page 139: **Ken Brown**
Page 147: **Lawrence Fishberg**
Page 151: **Bob Witz**
Page 161: **10/10**
Page 168: **William Anthony**
Page 170: **Robert Gregory Griffeth**
Page 182: **Ari Roussimoff**
Page 184: **Edwin Torres**
Page 188: **Chris Potash**
Page 191: **David Borchart**
Page 194: **Craig Silver**
Page 204: **Chris Potash**
Page 209: **Shalom**
Page 212: **Eric Drooker**
Page 222: **David Sandlin**
Page 226: **Kevin Riordan**
Page 230: **Zagreus Bowery**
Page 234, 235: **Michael Randall**
Page 242: **Tuli Kupferberg**
Page 255: **Kaz**
Page 258: **Matty Jankowski**
Page 264: **Blair Wilson/Sparrow**
Page 270: **Shalom**
Page 274: **Dan Freeman**
Page 276: **J.D. King**
Page 286: **Lori Ellison**

Working Without a Net: Intro to Unbearables

MIKE GOLDEN

Now that its time has come, it is only appropriate that The Unbearables, as this amorphous group of post-postmodern media casualties are known, get gone. If you're looking for a movement to attach yourself to, it's too late, it's already over. As you read this anthology of Mutant Lit, The Unbearables' one and only foray into the miasma of the marketplace has already passed into and out of that void that used to be called "culture." Just like any movement—neurological, mystical, bowel or beat—it needs to be flushed, so unlike the poor flogged out SubGenies, or the overhyped bandwagon of cybermarketeers, the conspirators can move unhindered into the next manifestation of what the hook-starved media may one day end up calling the *countervoid*.

Like some poor anachronistic *Charlie the Tuna* slumming in an overpolysaturated mock 'n' roll salad bar stuck somewhere between the industrial and information ages, Unbearables are dedicated to unblocking the shell-shocked serfs of the Infotainment Industry from their formula programming; actually they have no choice, since they have the rare distinction of being the first consciously mutant writers working out their afflictions for creation in the vortex of the post-literary age.

Attempting to balance their hallucinogenically-trained imaginations with a plethora of statistical abstracts of so-called reality so abstract in their *mundacity*, these homegrown *infomaniacs* became manifest in one fell Orwellian swoop the moment the geniuses up at B.B.D. & Shithead co-opted the Beatles'

One passage that Rollo always came back to in Leroux's Le Fantôme de l'Opéra *talked about seawater bilge. By skimming the book, Mike tried to locate those words.* **Mike Golden**, *progenitor of the legendary scandal sheet* Smoke Signals *and propagator of debraining sessions and other scampish madcap performance non-events, author and collarer was, of all of us, most obsessed with that night and the mysterious flagging of Rollo's car on a deserted New Jersey highway.*

9

"Revolution" in order to sell shoes. It was a quantum leap of the ugliest kind, and certainly a lot closer to Homer than the stick-the-nail-in-the-head-of-every-writer philosophy ("selling books is like selling shoes") promulgated in the 80's by the Editor-in-Chief of Simon & Shoestore. Be that as it may, the shortest point between any stick in the eye is a different kind of vision; thus Mutant Lit was born to be bred, if not quite read, by the mid-brow masses.

Unlike the New York School, the California School, the Black Mountain School, the Naropa School or any of those other so-called schools, this group of dedicated truants could only be connected to the *No School Today School*, if in fact there were any unifying factor other than *bad 'tude* that could be attributed to this alleged non-community of poets, pissers, middle-of-the-night philosophers, and part-time parapsychologists. Practicing *beer mystics* to the last drop, all have been on the outside looking into their heads their whole lives.

Lack of limitations may be either the friend or the enemy of art, depending on the artist, but Unbearables realize that that illusive concept of freedom, by itself, is just another trap as well. Somewhere in between oppression and lack of focus lies the church key to unlock that heady brew of ideas, ideals, and just plain deals that never go down the mainstream without blowing the status quo.

Change for the sake of change is not change, though, but just another repetition in that long list of patterns jockeying to control this nuevo world order or the next, or the next, or the next. In other words, those who do not remember history are not doomed to repeat it, but lucky enough to go their own way as long as they know that under every leaf or belief along the path a potential fascist lurks, waiting for recognition. That fascist could be you, it could be me, it could be a mate, or a movie star, or a politician, or an editor, or a boss, or a producer, or a shrink, or a psychic, or an astrologer transferring their own belief system into their interpretation of the information or service they supposedly provide. Thus, a James Dean shrugs a million and one shrugs out of context, and our sacred alienation evolves into crotch-grabbing beer commercials of the *duh* kind. We have sex with Madonna, put our money where our mouths should be, then rise up chanting LESS FILLING! TASTES GREAT! as images continue to suppress substance, while we in our post-popocalyptic comas keep on trucking down that good old-fashioned treadmill back to sweet home *Pavlovia*.

No doubt that in between creation and recreation lies profit margin, and with the right calculation, a cottage industry to hang your own T-shirt on. So while the concept of *Selling Out* has been the history-of-the-growth-of-history's one constant artistic McGuffin, true Unbearables realize that there is nothing *to sell out* other than that overstocked warehouse of lost dreams we've all been carrying on our backs for so long they've taken on the aura of that immortal 5000-pound monkey-demon of yonder yore, copulating without protection in the soft grey matter loitering around upstairs. Which is why true Unbearables are totally committed to downloading their hard drives at the memory bank as often as possible, then passing the shit along. For instance, though it's a little known fact that Unbearable Ron Kolm's "Suburban Ambush" is a more widely published poem than "Howl," "The Waste Land," "The Rime of the Ancient Mariner," or "The Hunting of the Snark," and despite the fact that by the year 2000 polls show it will be the most widely published poem in the *history of the growth of history,* it has not been included in the new revised *Master Poems of the English Language.* Most of the work in this volume bears that same thorny fruit, so those of you truly addicted to the mutant nectar of collecting better lock this one up in your archives, for these works probably won't come around again. And if they do, remember *probably* offers no guarantees. Which is both the secret and the edge a true Unbearable embraces.

M i k e G o l d e n

The Sovereign Order of the Unbearable Beatniks of Light & Most Worshipful Company of Beer Mystics© (Text of an Address Delivered at a Recent Initiation Ceremony by PETER LAMBORN WILSON)

Many have asked why the UB of L & BM© is a secret society. The general public will never know, thank Allah—but for this private and select group of the almost-initiated or "Near Beer Mystics©" the High Council of Unbearables has granted permission for me to recount the LEGEND of our founding.

One night in 1951 (André Breton's birthday, Feb. 18), three feckless young poets roamed the city in search of a bar dim enough in which to pass for over eighteen. Today you know them as Grand-Godfather of Poetry "Don" Ron Kolm, Worshipful Exalted Lush Mike Golden, and your humble scribe Past High Master Teahead, myself. (Supreme Dutch Master DJ bart

*The first problem for **Peter Lamborn Wilson** could be formulated thus: What did Rollo see that eventful evening? Apparently, waving on the side of the road was a green-tinted man clad only in a loincloth. Peter, fiery radio orator on WBAI in New York, prestigious author of* Sacred Drift *and* Scandal: Essays in Islamic Heresy, *and world renowned translator and*

13

plantenga had not yet arrived on these shores and still had his finger in a dyke somewhere in his natal marshland.)

Numb with cold, but bubbling over with bad verse, the three strolled along W. 23rd St. when suddenly they noticed an unlit neon sign: EYE-IN-THE-PYRAMID BAR & GRILL. Inside we could detect but stygian darkness, and yet a few apparent customers, middle-aged men in fezzes, sat slumped over a mahogony slab of megalithic proportions, each nursing a stein of pantagruelian capacity slow and careful as stranded time travelers.

The Eye Bar (as we came to know it) was *so* unlit that our false mustaches passed for real—in fact one night a few weeks later we forgot them, and were nevertheless served as usual. The barkeep had come to accept us as regulars and even the old gents in fezzes gave us the occasional reptilian nod. We'd made it! Our first permanent hang-out was established. We began to discuss the possibility of stealing a mimeograph machine and founding a Literary Movement, which is what one did in the 1950's.

Now, the Eye Bar had real old-fashioned booths far back in the shadowy rear of the saloon like you never see anymore, with plush leather banquettes, and thus it happened late one winter night that—under the influence of several gallons of "poetic inspiration"—we all passed into that state of Mystical Inwardness which today, thanks to our mastery of the Esoteric Sciences, we can induce at will and which the Adepts call the Ineffable Blotto Bardo, and we remained in that condition till long after closing time—apparently unnoticed by bartender or waiter—or "customers." But at last, in the deep of night, something, some strange sound, woke us all at once.

Like bleary turtles, we raised our heads above the level of the seats and peered into the gloom. The shock of what we saw reduced us to sobriety in a flash although if we'd known about LSD then, we might have suspected someone had laced our ale with a thousand mic's. Some sort of ceremony seemed to be in progress. The bar had been draped with a cloth of cabbalistic designs and set with thirteen candles, which supplied the sole illumination—as well as a sword, a beaker, incense burner, etc.—magickal paraphernalia, it seemed! Gone were the old guys in fezzes, replaced or transmogrified into a coven of gaudily-robed Egyptian priests in papier-maché masks of animals: fox, jackal, stork, wolf, scarab beetle, and the like. Eerie flute music sounded from nowhere, and the unmoving masks emitted an eldritch monotone of sinister chant. Petrified with horror, we gawked like a trio of Kilroys, our noses hanging over the edge of the back of our *banquette.*

The ceremony seemed to have been going on for some time and indeed to have reached a sort of liturgical climax; hence the increased volume of that menacing choral *recitative*, which no doubt had disturbed our meditations.

The invocation at last subsided to silence—and now stepped forward one whom we took for High Priest, dressed and masked in gold like the mummy of a pharoah, who raised in his hand the sign of an inverted *ankh* or *crux ansata*, as if to call for undivided attention. It seemed we were in good time for the sermon!

"Fellow Illuminati," he hissed. "We gather here tonight to pledge our energies to a new task—and yet, the same millenial task—the destruction of our enemies! Only the names and strategies change—yet it is the same ancient war. Yes, our foes have appeared again in a new guise. Once again to battle, O Mystic Brotherhood! And who are the enemies this time 'round, you ask? The same as always: the useless, the weak, the would-be defenders of LIFE—against *our* supreme powers of negativity— the non-conformists, the Commies, the immoral whining fatuous depraved pretenders to that 'cause'— to which WE have sworn eternal enmity—yes, you know of whom I speak—the so-called new generation called 'Beat'! The poets! *Argh! Ptui!*" (And here the entire congregation spat in unison upon the barroom floor.)

"Those unbearable beatniks!" the High Priest screamed. "We must exterminate them all!"

"Exterminate! Exterminate!" the congregation responded in metallic monotone.

"Very well then," the Priest regained his composure. "But how, you ask, are we to proceed against these new and already BEATen foes? Ha ha, these pot-

troubadour of Persian verse, was still perplexed by the arcane sign scratched on the dented car hood of Rollo's abandoned Chevy Corvair, and by the crumpled pack of Cosmadors, unopened on the ripped seat.

Only known photo of Rollo Whitehead . . . or is it Hakim Bey?

P e t e r   L a m b o r n   W i l s o n

head poets, these beer mystics, these hallucinogen-soaked parasites? I shall explain all.

"Since we control the mass media we can see to it that 90% of these worms are never published at all, except in cheap mimeographed underground journals. However, should any of them show signs of emerging from obscurity despite our efforts to suffocate them in silence, we shall use the media to destroy them by turning them into bufoons, or dangerous maniacs—evil clowns, you might say!—in the eyes of the public. They want fame? We'll give them so much fame that even the police will hear about them. Ah hah hnyeh nyeh nyeh!" the priest laughed, like Peter Lorre.

"But," he went on, "suppose that a few of these germs possess enough perversity to survive our tactics of Silence and Noise. Never fear! Our Supreme Council of Necrologues has come up with the perfect plan! We call it 'The Deadly Embrace of Complete Acceptance.' Our brethren in Washington (that is to say, everyone in Washington) are already laying the groundwork on this one. We shall set up a new bureaucratic colossus *within* the Government—hnyeh nyeh nyeh—*the arts fund*. We'll call it the National Endowment for Culture, or something bland like that. Whenever one of these unbearable beatniks begins to slip through all our nets, we'll dump a grant on him (or her, because as you know, some of these creatures are female!). Now flies love manure—but this load will land right on their heads! They'll be so gorged on shit they'll soon lose touch with the Muses! Addicted to a drug that only *we* can prescribe: total acceptance into Society and its Aesthetic Consensus! In other words, hooked on Death! I can see it now: 30 or 40 years from tonight, all true dissidence and creativity will either be driven into the sewers, or else be bought out and poisoned with rave reviews in the *New York Times*. A reaction will set in: conservatives will demand that the Government stop supporting these futile drones. Meanwhile half the so-called poets will already be our agents and spies, infecting the milieu with morbid negativity, hopelessness, and masochism. We'll create a million Baudelaires, all dressed in black, like mourners at a Victorian funeral—the funeral of Poetry! And then, brethren, sometime around the turn of the Century—victory will be ours! We'll set up a President of the USA who *pretends to like poetry!* Like poisoned bait he'll lure the last of the rats into the trap of doom! An invitation to the White House, and then . . . slllghghttt!" (the Priest drew his thumb across his throat).

At this, the entire congregation of Illuminati began to laugh like Peter Lorre—but ritually and in unison! HNYEH NYEH NYEH, like some chorus of crazed H.P. Lovecraft fans. The effect was so terrifying that Ron, Mike, and I passed out and collapsed onto the floor—our crashes unheard in the unearthly din of freemasonic mirth.

There's not much more to tell. Around dawn we woke again with splitting headaches to find the Eye Bar deserted, stripped of all magic mumbo jumbo, and locked. We had to break out to escape—hence our certainty that the Illuminati learned of our presence. Needless to say, we never went back. Needless to say, although we'd never heard of "beatniks" before that night we at once swore an eternal oath to uphold the cause of Beatitude.

Throughout the succeeding decades we've fought the good fight; matching conspiracy with conspiracy, intrigue with intrigue, and blow for blow. Outwardly the Illuminati program may seem to have triumphed—but no, the Beatnik Cause still lives, bumbling, optimistic, in favor of life and of all poetry, even bad poetry, of beer and pot and celebration unfunded, unpublished, pure and undefiled, in the form of our secret society, the Sovereign Order of the Unbearable Beatniks of Light & Most Worshipful Company of Beer Mystics©. From bar to bar we hop, still seeking that lost and perfect hang-out, the utopia of poetry—and all along the way we've been joined by all the true giants of Unbearableness whom you see here tonight amongst the hierarchy of initiates. And so, before we proceed with the ceremony of induction into the Order, let us pause to remember our sacred origins in the struggle against all oppression, all publicity and all public acceptance—the true meaning of the origin-tale, the *ur-mythos* of our cult: THE LEGEND OF THE UNBEARABLES!

("Beer Mystics" © copyright 1952 bart plantenga.)

In Memory of David Rattray

CHRIS KRAUS

David Rattray was the most disciplined person I've ever met. Even though he was an essayist, translator, prose writer, and scholar, David had a clear picture of his life as a Poet's Life: that is, he didn't need to write for money, myth, or reputation; he'd do exactly what he liked. David was as uncompromising as Johnny Sherill, the car thief from St. Louis, whom he wrote about in "Van."

David was one of the first and certainly the best and truest translator of Artaud, though he never got anywhere near the credit he deserved. Retitling "To Be Done With the Judgment of God" as "To Pass Final Judgement on God," calling *merde* not "excrement" but "shit," made Artaud immeasurably more interesting, intense.

About these extraordinary translations, David later wrote: "What interested me in him was the sense of displacement, of not being my own person in my own skin, not belonging where I was. Of course I was an alcoholic and drug addict as well, which didn't help matters. And I was crazy, and I didn't know what was wrong with me, or what was wrong with the world, but I knew that something very serious was wrong with it . . . "

Trained in Classics at Dartmouth, Harvard, and the Sorbonne, David went on to find the junkie and the mystic impulse in his translations and essays on 18th century German poet Friedrich Holderlin, medieval musicology, Persian rebel poets, suicides and crazies of this century, like Emile Nelligan and Rene Crevel. He wrote the most translucent and amazing

*If we were to look at a picture of the audience that night, as the police did, we would be able to make out exactly 100 people, 60 or so with faces clearly visible. One of those people, it is assumed, sent Rollo Whitehead, guest lecturer, the threatening note he received backstage. **Chris Kraus**, editor of the Semiotext(e) Native Agents series, was in the audience. She reported feeling a strange tribal vibe, resonating anticipation.*

19

prose, manipulating scholarship and sensation with incredible lightness, that Phillip Whalen sense of poetry-as-breathing . . .

Talking on the phone with David was like plugging into a universal switchboard of *Bigger Stuff*; what it might've meant to be an educated person in another age. David was an anachronist and a futurist. He aimed to be invisible. He took things very seriously.

I'm Not a Normal Girl
MAGGIE ESTEP

I'm not a NORMAL GIRL
I'm an angry sweaty girl
so bite me
and suck my not normal flesh

I'm not a NORMAL GIRL
'cause I'm full of contradictions and kinks
and the weirdest things make my PANTIES SWEAT
    and
it's very very *very* important
to make my PANTIES SWEAT
in fact,
sometimes I think about how if I were ever to run for
    political office, *that*
would be the theme of my campaign: PANTY SWEAT

In fact, if nominated,
I'd see to it that *everyone* wore PANTIES
yeah
'cause I'm not a NORMAL GIRL and
I want men, women, and dogs too
to wear huge, droopy PANTIES with *disgusting* stains
    on them
mustard-colored stains
it'll be equality through panty stains
it'll be a revolution
a brand new twist on evolution

Yeah, I'll fix up the economy
create jillions of jobs in the PANTY STAIN-
    REMOVAL INDUSTRY,
retired bondage queens in spiked boots

Rollo's topic was trip wires.
He had developed a theory,
similar to Michel Serres'
ideas on parasites: that
these wires were central
metaphors for helping us
understand the organiza-
tion of modern life. According to Rollo, in the U.S. trip
wires have been set up
between the classes. If a
writer sets one of these off,
for instance, by emitting
signals monopolized by one
class and circulating them
to another class, then he is
likely to be censored or
punished. Perhaps, half
blindly, he or she even
desires that punishment.

Maggie Estep, ranter,
musician (with Huge
Voodoo and I Love Every-
body) and author of the
forthcoming Sex Diary of an
Addict, heard Whitehead
discriminatingly peregrinate
on this topic till he reached
lather heat, his words flung
out like backward-facing
BBs.

walking the creases out of people's stained-with-slime PANTIES,
And all of America will be chanting
"Thank you, Not Normal Girl,
Thank you, Not Normal Girl,"
'cause it'll be a
Brave New World
everybody running around
eating and loving and fucking

No more
thorazine
no methadone
no electric chairs
no simulated stair machines
with bloated and bulimic would-be beauty queens
ascending ever upwards to
prefab feminine perfection
no no no
no
city limits
no cities, all territories will spread out
like a droopy panty
on which the elastic has gone
dead. PANTY ECONOMICS
is what it'll be
and the NOT NORMAL PANTY PRESIDENT
is who I will be
'cause I'm not a NORMAL GIRL
I don't think I'll ever be
a NORMAL GIRL,
but,
all the same,
I'm still
terribly popular.

Rose Window Prosettes
WANDA PHIPPS

1.

He said, "That train was slow as shit!" and I wondered about the truth of that expression. After all doesn't it all depend on the efficiency of your digestive system?

Reminds me of this woman who really took the expression "You are what you eat" to extremes. She claimed that you are what you expel. In other words: you are your shit; she even wrote a play about it. The main character was a ladies' room attendant in a sleazy downtown dance club who also had an extreme and extensive scatological philosophy. This was the woman one ex-love-of-my-life took up with after we broke up. Amazing.

2.

As his girlfriend tried to be friendly and asked me to hire her, I stood shifting my weight from one foot to the other, occasionally looking into her eyes trying to determine whether she had anything particularly beautiful about her. She mentioned she was performing soon at the Lizard's Tail in Williamsburg and I thought of the night her boyfriend thrust his fingers up my cunt and the sound of his breathing as he stroked his cock and I held his balls as he came.

I remember yelling and screaming—holding onto an open car door as it pulled away dragging me through the street.

It is not as if people collect in an audience and then just disappear, disperse forever, when the event is finished. An audience that gets together for a revelation—an ascension into heaven, let's say—is marked permanently individually, but also linked forever subcutaneously. **Wanda Phipps** thought that if even one member of such an audience was identified, then by moving along the chain, every other one could be located. *Wanda Phipps is an acid rapper with the band Throbbers. She appears in Yvonne Rainer's film* Privilege, *and edited Elliot Sharp's CD compilation* State of the Union.

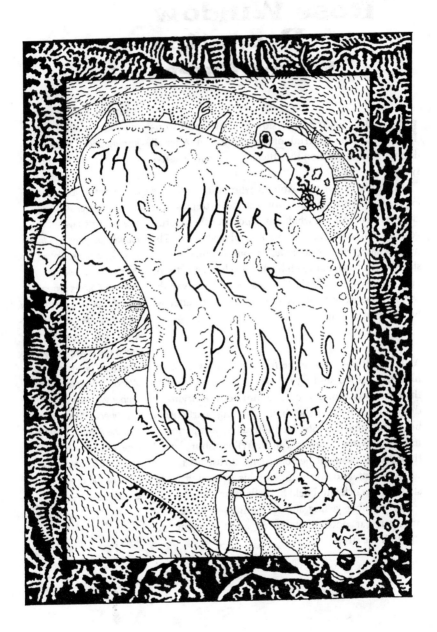

The Banging
HAL SIROWITZ

She took off her clothes & said, "While we're making love & you hear someone banging on the wall, don't worry. That's my crazy neighbor. He doesn't like noise. If it disturbs you, bang back."

"I like your underwear," I said.

"I'm glad," she said. "But let's talk about more important things. Would you like a massage?

"Then put your head under this pillow, so you can see what I'm doing. I don't want you to miss anything.

"I make my own oil. The one you can buy at the store sells for about four dollars. Mine only costs eighty cents, & I get four times as much. I buy Russian olive oil. Then I mix in orange peels & cloves."

"I can smell it," I said.

"So can the roaches," she said. "I have to make sure that I don't get any on the sheets."

"I'm going to come," I said.

"Don't," she said. "Exercise some control. That's what you tell your students when they're about to misbehave.

"You didn't listen. You're going to have to sleep on the wet spot. I won't. I'm into women's liberation."

"Let's go to sleep," I said.

"I'm not tired," she said. "Let's do something constructive for a change, like play Scrabble."

"I'm not good at it," I said.

"I don't believe you," she said. "The way you use words you must know a million of them."

"I don't like games," I said.

"I won't force you to play," she said. "It's getting cold. I think I'll take a hot shower. I want to go to bed remembering what it was like to be warm."

But the police instituted a more matter-of-fact procedure. There was a book left in the lobby in which lecture attendees could leave their names and addresses so they could be contacted about further events of interest. In this book, for instance, was the name of **Hal Sirowitz**, *the author of three chapbooks, including* Girlie Pictures *and* Fishnet Stockings, *activist celebrity and celebrator. When questioned and confronted with the photo snap, he was able to point to his own rugged profile, to the left, in a throng of shadows. There seemed to be another very similar face a few seats back.*

Y-Front
JENNIFER KABAT

I wanted her so I stole 'em. I stole them from Woolworth's. Woolworth's always held out eminent possibilities and delights—baubles and trinkets, clothes and candy. While my mother shopped for whatever brought us there, I wandered the aisles looking, rubbing my hands over the bras and panties; dreaming of the day when I could wear these frothy black and red and pink lace confections. In the candy aisle, all sweet and gooey, the words, "creme-filled nougat and caramel-covered peanut butter..."—all melted together in this one fantastic bit of lust, the names, dreams, desires dissolving all in my mind. I wanted all of them all at once, in my mouth.

My mother would never let me get as many as I wanted, so I learned to *steal over* there while she did her errands, and pocket a few while no one was looking. These were in the days before electronic surveillance and closed-circuit TV. Then after collecting all the candy that could be safely hidden without looking too suspicious, I'd wander over and look at the watches spinning around in their glass display case—pushing the button for it to stop at the pale pink girl's first Timex. I eyed it longingly, hoping my mother would get me one for Christmas or my birthday or something. Finally she'd finish and find me looking at the watches or enchanted in some other aisle, but never in front of the lingerie; I was too embarrassed to get caught fingering them. She'd always say "You deserve a reward for being such a patient, good girl, Jenny. Now pick out one candy bar you'd like, and I'll get it for you..." I would run and find the biggest candy bar there—it didn't necessarily have to be my favorite, but the biggest. I don't want that anymore, not the candy bar, not the lingerie either. They're not the kind of sweet things I now desire.

Painstakingly, the dogged detectives searched out each attendee whose name appeared in the mailing list book, both to research their connection to Rollo and to get them to pick themselves out in the photograph that was taken that night. Of the signees, only the address of **Jennifer Kabat** was hard to locate. Jennifer is a "stripper/academic" who's been published in RedTape and Screw. Her address, which read "Deadman's Curve, Shatterhead, Texas," proved impossible to find. Eventually, she was tracked down at an Unbearables Fish Picnic.

Something happened when I saw her. She was this sexy girl/boy, her short black hair slicked back, pasted to her head looking like a snake as she slithered across my girlfriend's apartment. She moved smoothly. Her gestures and steps were strong and confident. I gaped. And stared. She didn't care that I or anyone else was watching as she pulled off the cowboy boots and jeans and T-shirt—revealing the body that I had always wanted. I stared at her little breasts, no bigger than a twelve year old's. She simply and unselfconsciously discarded her T-shirt, adding it to the heap on the floor. The clothes that seemed so alive on her were now just this dead pile.

Then I saw them—the boys' cotton briefs. They were so *right* for that nubile little body. The underwear sat on her hips, encircling her waist in a shallow arc around her belly, outlining her ass and thighs. The briefs were perfect for this boy/girl—ever obscuring what she really was. They fit her attitude of casualness, carelessness, that keeps you guessing and wanting. It was impossible not to stare as she walked across the kitchen to the tub. I was hungry for her, hungry for this boyish body. I wanted a piece of her, anything, something from her on *me*. I couldn't get her out of my mind as I tried to fall asleep that night.

I was walking around in Woolworth's the next day. I forget what I needed there—bedsheets, cottonballs—who knows? It didn't really matter because I didn't get whatever it was. I wandered the aisles shuffling around with that old child lust for all the things, marvelous things, that Woolworth's could offer. In the back of the store—the back right corner—I looked down and there they were—there she was. Boys' Y-front briefs. Suddenly this irrational lust. I see her and that hunger, the taste of candy, all melt together in the back of my throat. Everything was automatic after that. I tore them out of their plastic packaging; I couldn't *wait* to touch them. I quickly sized them against my hips and ran my fingers searching for magnetic tags that would set off the alarm system. I touched them fast to lock their feel onto my fingers and then stashed all three pairs into my book bag. I just ran out of the store and into the street and sunshine, where people stared, puzzled and wary, as I hit the street like I'd been dropped from the sky, or stumbled into the middle of a crowd, or committed a crime . . .

The hunger was insatiable by the time I got home. I walked there with my hand in the bag fondling them. They're different—thicker, heavier than those lacy, fragile creations I grew up wearing. The briefs felt stronger, more powerful in my hands. I slid them up over my hips. Finally, I had her—or something of her. I waited for the feeling to sink in, for something to change. Nothing did. I ran over to the mirror and wanted to see her body staring out at me. It wasn't. The boy's underwear just *exaggerated* my femininity. The thin cotton band around the legs hit that line between butt and thigh so it simply outlined my ass making it look

even *rounder,* and they *clung* to the curves of my hips. They made me even more femme than silky lace panties ever had.

The briefs felt funny, a little off. I didn't know what to wear with them. It had to be something so people could see but not too much, not too obvious. I usually wore girly-girl clothes, skirts and dresses, clothes that wouldn't fit the feel I was after. Nothing felt right. In front of the cracked full-length mirror, I adjusted, trying, pushing, pulling, belting. It was all off. How do you describe that feeling where you keep trying things on because nothing feels right and all that trying makes you just that much more uncomfortable? I wanted these underwear; I wanted her with me, and I wanted people to notice. I folded down the waistband and pulled up the shorts. The secret was secure. No one could really tell, and even if they could it didn't matter. I just had to escape.

Only a little line of white peaked out from the top of my cutoffs, loose and low slung—dripping down around the waist, not too exposing. Still I walk up Avenue B in hopes of avoiding anyone I know or recognize. No one I know walks on Avenue B, but she lives there. I wasn't really ready to run into her like this, like some poor copy. Everything stiffens. My walk changes, hunkered over with my arms clutched tightly around my waist to hide that line of flesh between T-shirt and cutoffs and, of course, the little white circle. But no one says anything. The walk is frustratingly quiet and unacknowledged.

I want to be seen by people and then to have that attitude she has when they do. I want that confidence, that way she moved, that body, to be mine. Slowly something begins to change. I start thinking about her and about their being stolen. My walk changes. Long loping steps replace the nervous staccato ones. There is this private feeling of power locked in my secret and each step reinforces it as the underwear rubs against my body.

The men must be able to sense it; they acknowledge me finally. They start saying things. The first guys say your typical "Hey baby—oh baby—oh shit." Do they get it? Do they see? Does it turn them on? As I walk, the waistband unfolds so you can see the two thin blue lines circling around my waist and even the top of the Y-front. Some scraggly punks begging for money come up and yell "Yo, why are you wearing Fruit-of-the-Looms?" The confidence drains, quickly replaced by a blush spreading across my face. With all that fiddling and changing, how could I have missed that they were inside out? Everyone could read the secret and tag and label me—or at least try to. Some guy yells out asking me if I'm a dyke. Do they say things like that to her?

At Clinton and Houston, the usual street corner guys are milling around. They start saying things, new things, different things. "What's under that underwear little girl? Oh Little Red Riding Hood, I want to see what's under those shorts," and then, "Hey, what's wrong with you?" I want to reassure them, to say, "Don't worry, I'm straight. I'm everything you thought I was yesterday in that pink dress . . . don't worry . . . " But the words get caught in the back of my throat.

Feet

MAX BLAGG

As a tottering infant, in those soft Midlands evenings after tea had been served and cleared away, my mother and sisters would often linger around the kitchen table, to chat awhile and discuss the vicissitudes of life and death in our little town; what a shame it was that that nice old Mr Bescoby had collapsed and died, the addition of yet another beautiful Dresden figurine to Mrs Godber's enviable collection, the fancy front gate the Cliftons had installed well it doesn't really fit with the rest of the street does it neooo . . .

Their voices drifted above me a warm lilting chorus as comforting as silk or rain. I would crawl under the table, remove my sister's shoes, wrap myself around her bare feet like a dog or a blanket, and fall to sleep inhaling the redolent scent of foot powder tinged with sweat which emanated like some exotic perfume from her long white feet . . .

As the fisherman loves the sharp odor of the dawn sea, as the snurge adores the leathery contours of a well worn bicycle seat, as the epongeur relishes the fetid dampness of a subway restroom, so have I loved feet.

The tarsal, the metatarsal, the astragalus, the navicular, the internal cuneiform, the flexor brevis digitorum, the curve of the instep, the classical arch, the five toes and the nails imbedded in them, so various in size and shape, these marvelous sculpted appendages that move the body lightly over the earth . . .

And, concomitant with these wondrous feet, the shoes that fit them, with names that should be, to steal a phrase, written on the sky with lightning: from the lowly Doleis to Russell and Bromley, Charles Jourdan, Maud o Miss Frizon, Ferragamo, Chanel, Diego della Valle, Perugia's court shoe, "supple as a glove," the

Max Blagg had been regaling the crowd at the picnic, telling about how as young Borstal boys, he and Joe Cocker knocked over a fish and chips establishment and perfumery warehouse on Nautilus Square. Acting on an anonymous tip in their search for Kabat, the bulls appeared, stampeding the picnickers down toward Leaky Creek, Max at the head of the pack. Max is the author of Nine Years in a Wind Tunnel, A Monkey Wrench in the Garden of Allah, *and other works.* Max's quick wits averted catastrophe when he threw a match into the oily creek, the flames driving the fleeing picnickers in a healthier direction.

31

very special shoes of Maniatis of Paris and the impeccable Manolo Blahniks, such delicate confections, featherlight, evanescent objects of utter luxe, shoes that are made to be worn, not walked in, pure adornment, absolute fetish.

The apotheosis of my foot love, the golden locker, the pinnacle of my adoration occurred on a clear spring morning in 1978. One of the old wholesale shoe stores on Reade Street in lower Manhattan, displaced by avaricious landlords, was liquidating its entire stock of women's shoes from the fifties and sixties. Word of this singular event had spread throughout the downtown community, and as I turned the corner from West Broadway it seemed that every beauty in lower Manhattan was there on that bright morning, horning their variegated feet into a fantastic variety of high-heeled shoes, mostly variations on the stiletto in all its heights and finishes.

Boxes were stacked high on the pavement outside the store, and fashionable women were behaving very badly as they struggled to get their hands on and their feet into these treasures. There was Velma Smedley, the performance artist, shouldering aside a cluster of hairdressers. Velma towered above the crowd; she was over six feet tall, and yet, I observed with a secret thrill, she still wants to go higher ... Irene McBladder, the designer, probably knocking off ideas for her own line, and there was Tibby Carstairs, standing haughtily off to the side, while two of his creatures rummaged through the boxes on his behalf. It was a fine crowd but nobody was stopping to chat—they were too busy handling, nay fondling these glorious icons, this unique design that manages to simultaneously empower and disable its wearer, the chosen footwear of strippers and starlets and Mafia girlfriends, invoking angora sweaters and tight skirts and Lana Turner, smoking ...

Bad girl shoes, a dazzling collection in the most florid, cheap sexy colors and configurations. Magenta, turquoise, acid green, red the color of a road accident, Roman purple, pink as lovely as a sunrise, delphinium blue, a yellow that made your teeth ache ...

All around me bare and stockinged feet were encasing themselves in these leather sheaths, the occasional open-toed model exposing the inflammatory dijit of the so-called big toe topped by a ruby nail, which seemed to wink amorously from its crevice ... And amid these perfectly formed, immaculate feet, the occasional deformation, hammertoe, callus, heelspur, bunion, or veruka merely contributed its own trenchant allure.

I was humming to myself as I prepared to make purchases of my own:

Shoes glorious shoes
just one pair that will fit me
I really don't mind

U   n   b   e   a   r   a   b   l   e   s

how much they might nip me
oh don't tell me there's none my size
don't force the tears from my eyes,
just one pair of shoes, glorious shoes . . .

As this banal show tune ricocheted around a cranium already scorched by fifteen milligrams of Desoxyn, I watched in awe as the hungry women, possessed by their shopping demons, swirled around the sidewalk, delving and foraging with a singlemindedness of purpose astonishing to behold, occasionally hoisting aloft a particular find like an Olympic trophy, their ecstatic faces catching the morning light lost in contemplation of their prize. Diana brandishing the head of a stag was never more blissfully triumphant. I put my head down, my elbows out, and waded into the fray.

Not one hour later my rigid member was buried deeply in a size 9 fur-trimmed satin pump bearing the words "Carlotta Designs" in gold along the innersole. The partner to this attractive item was simultaneously being forced partway up my fundament by another enthusiastic shopper I had encountered at the sale. We had argued briefly over ownership of a particularly piquant pair of black patent spikes, which just now graced her large and not unlovely feet. Carlotta designs indeed, she designs very well, a most comely and potent pump methinks . . .

Another fine example of the cobbler's art meantime protruded from between her anatomically perfect labial lips, buried almost to the heel, to which I was firm-

M   a   x   B   l   a   g   g

ly affixed, sucking greedily on the spike as the embossed figure 9 on the slick new sole imprinted itself on my forehead.

We rolled and tumbled among the detritus of empty shoeboxes and tissue paper, shifting and modifying our positions as we went, rabid consumers locked in a post-purchase frenzy.

Later as we lay upon her brand new futon, lathered up like horses, she rolled across and hissed into my ear, "I've got a size eleven in powder blue that I want to see you in right now." I nodded weakly and she rose in search of that particular model. She rooted briefly among the boxes, and then strode back across the enormous rawness of her space, her heels clicking like gunshots on the newly sanded floor, driving like icepicks through four coats of polyurethane. Tenderly, she slipped the boat-sized objects onto my extended feet.

They almost fit. I crushed my feet into them and got up unsteadily from the bed. I felt the material give slightly as I put my full weight on the ball of my foot. They pinched, of course they pinched, but they were walkable. I hobbled over to the mirror leaning against the exposed brick wall. Light was streaming in through her excellent southern exposure, and Debbie Harry was crooning away on the phonograph, begging me to call *her*. I pirouetted away from the wall and began to dance, wailing, along with Blondie.

It was 1978, and everyone I loved was still alive.

The Glove

CLAUDE TAYLOR

She vamped me! She vamped me! She skinned me alive with her thighs. She vamped me, she vamped me, she did. She swallowed me whole. How she hated me! My only defense was my melancholy. How I reveled in my misery! I developed a distaste for wine, and drank it constantly. I was a Christly figure. I was gorgeous! I was the father of my people and the youngest man of all.

I wore an old suede jacket with fringes. I looked so young and innocent. But she did me in anyway. I acknowledged her victory by burying my face in her breasts. She stroked my hair quietly in the icy wind beneath the streetlamp. Her cheeks were cheery. Her hair blonde as pissed-on ice. Sitting alone on the stone wall the only two people there. Her voice a whisper, she comforted me.

I wooed her with white shirts. I wore only white shirts for the courtship period. I wooed her with my eyes and with old Lithuanian jokes which my father had taught to me. I wooed her by smoking unfiltered cigarettes. I wooed her with my poems. I did her homework! I scratched her back until she itched, then smiling, I'd scratch it again. I sang Cole Porter songs with Nelson Riddle arrangements. I wooed her with my enthusiasm for her thighs, which I pronounce with a pronounced lisp. "*Thigths.*" I wooed her with my endless adoration. I wooed her when she . . . when she wasn't even there!

I was always being much too cute. I lost my perspective. My sense of proportion. I wasn't myself! I'm a man of simple pleasures. I love to shave. I enjoy putting my brush in the warm, soapy water, then smoothly applying it about my face. The razor hung sharpened and gleaming from the heavy leather strop. I'm absorbed by the ritual of it all. Yet I wear a beard.

*Of the 100 audience members, the cops found that about 30 had died in the three months since they started investigating the case, although in none of the deaths were suspicious circumstances found. Quite a few of the other listeners had decamped. **Claude Taylor** was living with a hung-over geisha in Tokyo's Little Smorgasbord, the run-down Swedish section of the Ginza. Claude is the author of a detective novel, resident in South Japan, linguist, and Kaballist. Reached by phone, he swore he had left the country three days before Rollo disappeared. Questioned further about the lecture, he averred he didn't know a soul in the amassed mass, though he noticed the tow-headed fellow sitting beside him had eyes that did not contain pupils but phosphorescent rubies.*

35

Why? She preferred it. In fact, she threatened to stop sleeping with me if I shaved it off. Sexual politics gave me a beard!

Reality holds me by the shoulder like a heavy drunk. I'm outraged, but I have no voice. I'm just a shadow following myself around. But don't get me wrong. A shadow can be his own man, too. So here I am. Checked into a new address. A frightened resident of the Heartbreak Hotel. The moon constantly shines outside my window. The radio will only play "Oh Donna." Fragile as a soap bubble, it floats across the elevated tracks outside, past the moon. All the way to the junkie park. I lie upon the creaking bed, my belly extending like a small moon. The rot gut of my impending middle age.

Western exposure. Eastern exposure. There is no exposure at all in here! It is always dark. I can't help but wonder with some concern just what will become of me. The love that gave me my life has left me a dessicated corpse. Corpse? Ha! If only I were so lucky! A corpse could never feel this pain. This endless questioning. Smashed ashore by the wave of events, I had no control. I still don't. I know I'm not the first victim of love, but still. Just leave me alone. Anyone who has loved and lost knows. There are no second timers. It's always the first time. Forlorn. Withdrawn. Stillborn.

Still, even now, I can't help hoping. Even now, I dream. Though the future seems too frightening to consider, I lay my plans. In my mind, she walks beside me. Close to six feet tall in her heels, broad at the shoulder and at the hip. Her behind jiggling in its tight sheath. She's wearing a brown tweed skirt cut 1940's-style. Her stockings are dark with wide seams up the back. Everything lush, full and perfectly round. Her face, in contrast, is high boned and angular. A harsh red slash of lipstick across the mouth. Pale and cold. A face of startling indifference. No feeling, no emotion, no flicker of life. No smile, no sadness—nothing—but pure beauty! Each time I turn to her, there is nothing to say. Just smolder in the cold, black flame of her eyes. Paranoia cuts like a surgeon's scalpel thousands of infinitely small deep slits.

She sees it quite differently. I had disappointed her in so many ways, she says. It wasn't my fault. It wasn't anyone's fault. There was no one to point a finger at and blame. And even if there was, what good would it do? We each place our love in a different frame of reference. Just as a sociologist would view a fact one way, and a psychoanalyst would view the same fact another way. Or, say, as if she had given me a shoe, and I had worn it as a glove.

36

In Brooklyn

DEBORAH PINTONELLI

I'm in the backyard with Aunt June pinning up the laundry on a summer morning. She's complaining about her sister Liza's awful pound cake and how Liza didn't bring enough cash to Bingo last night. We're doing this quickly, though, as soon it will get very hot and we want to be back inside watching the late morning soap operas before that happens.

The yard is beautiful at this time of year. Large, luscious peonies with tiny black ants roaming their velvety petals lift up their fuchsia, pale pink and white faces to the sun. Grapevines that my grandfather planted twist thickly around a network of pipes built up over the walk. Fat, bloody tomatoes and tall, thin stalks of corn and gigantic yellow squash burst out of the vegetable patch. The grass is a deliciously soft blanket of iridescent green.

As we pin the last of the laundry up I inhale the thick, sweet air and become slightly intoxicated in the process. Unfortunately, at this moment I also let my eyes rest briefly on the darkened, greasy stain that is Mr. Pantozza's kitchen window.

What I see beyond that stain surrounded by American Beauty roses and their thick, thorny vines are Mr. Pantozza's green eyes staring at me from within. I shudder though it is by now very, very hot.

Aunt June says, "Did you remember to call Uncle Frank and wish him a happy birthday?" I almost don't hear her because I'm disturbed by Mr. Pantozza's eyes, by knowing that he's watching. For as long as I can remember I've been in charge of making sure he has everything he needs. He has all sorts of things wrong with him and can't get around too easily.

He keeps his first floor apartment totally dark, with the only fresh air coming in from a small window fan. So, what with the four dogs and the fact that he never

*The over-friendly flatfoot who questioned **Deborah Pintonelli** offered to "sniff the woodwork," that is, check her apartment for bugs. It might be worthwhile, she felt, to try and figure him out, so she invited the officer to stay for dinner. Deborah is the author of* Ego Monkey *and the forthcoming* Some Love. *As she prepared* brutti al fresca, *she talked entreatingly, endearingly, and learned about the 30 deaths. She also got to look at the audience photo. On a pretense, she took the photo and went to the john, where she slid her xeroxer out from its hiding place behind the douche and made a copy.*

really bathes, the smell of the place is unreal. He is usually sitting at the kitchen table drinking coffee and smoking cigarettes—this is what he does all day, and almost all night long.

I'm not extremely pretty, but I know I have a great shape, which saves me. Well, I am pretty, but you see, I've got the family nose in all its glory sitting smack in the middle of my face. The long, beak-like, bumpy Genovese nose. But I've got Grandma's tits, which compete with the nose and win every time. And I've got Dad's creamy, dark skin. I go out with Alex, who's so white he looks like an albino with his platinum hair and pale blue eyes. We look good together.

Mr. Pantozza has never cared a bit about my nose or the color of my skin. You see, he's been in love with me ever since the day that I came down with the plate of fresh scagliatelle and asked him if he needed anything from the store. "No," he said that day, "but take this five dollars and buy yourself something." From that point on I went down to see him at least a few times a week, and daily during the summer. We'd play Monopoly, Parcheezi, gin rummy. He'd buy me all sorts of sodas, desserts, toys, dresses, shoes. I'd sit on his lap and call him Uncle.

Then, I didn't notice the smell in his rooms. I didn't pay any attention to the collection of guns in his top drawer, or to the fact that though he had a telephone, it never rang, and that no one but members of my family came to see him. Even for them to come down was rare, and now it seems kind of odd that they would leave it to me to look after him all of these years. But I guess they saw no harm in it. I guess they saw an old man being entertained by a child, and nothing more.

We'd sit at his kitchen table (he never used the other five rooms) under a dusty bulb and he'd talk and roll cigarettes and drink coffee and talk and talk. One by one, as he told his nasty stories, the dogs would come up to be petted or fed bits of beef jerky from the pocket of his shirt. Though he didn't bathe often, he always wore a clean shirt and undershirt, and kept a fresh white handkerchief in his pocket into which he blew his long, shiny nose.

If he got me to sit on his lap after giving me a particularly longed-for gift, he'd have to run his hand over me for a minute before I squirmed away. He always got this awful look on his face when he did that; a look which fascinated and frightened me and I kick myself now for having felt that way, for having let things get to the point where now all that has to happen is that I see (or think I see) his eyes in the window and I get the severe creeps.

But I liked having his undivided attention. My family is so big, I get lost in it sometimes. It's always like, Oh, Marisa do this, do that, you're a cutie, get outta here—stuff like that. Everything's hustle and bustle and work, work, work. After all the cooking, cleaning, homework, I'm off with my friends. It made me feel all-powerful to have this old man do whatever I wanted.

Mama, when she was alive, encouraged it. She'd see my new pair of boots or my dress, and say, "Ah, Sammy's little favorite! There's a good girl, now I don't have to buy you anything for awhile!" And Papa'd say, "Pantozza's a little weird, but he's good people underneath."

I know he watches me when Alex comes over and we sit at the picnic table under the grapevines. I have no choice, Papa doesn't want me to go out on dates. He wants me here at home, where he can keep track of me. He imagines that I can't get pregnant in my own backyard. Alex likes to make out under the stairs where it's dark and private but it's also way too close to Mr. Pantozza's back door. But there really isn't anywhere else for us to go that's out of Papa's sight, so we do it there, but I have to hold back the part of me that's revolted, that feels the green eyes on my skin.

I still have to go into his apartment once in awhile to bring him some groceries and the paper, and that's when he tells me what he thinks of me and Alex. "I saw you with that boy last night," he'll say, puffing at his cigarette, almost letting the burning end of it touch the tip of his nose as he inhales, "I saw him with his hands all over you. I bet he was hard and wanted to put it inside of you. You wanted him to do that, didn't you?"

I do my best to ignore him. I don't look at his face, which I know will still have that awful look on it after all these years. I listen to him wheeze with his one good lung as he puffs on yet another cigarette. He sounds like he is going to die and sometimes I wish he would. Then I feel guilty for feeling that way, and I turn to him and smile, saying, "Oh, you're just imagining things, we were just talking."

And then I notice that the spot where his penis is in his pants is still worn, dry-looking. Sometimes I can't help looking at that spot for a second, and then at his eyes, which are always amazingly calm, but which flash for a minute if he notices me looking. "Come here for a minute," he'll say innocently.

When I was eleven-almost-twelve Mr. Pantozza gave me a stack of books to read. "Here," he said, "these will help improve your reading skills." The stories were about men who liked to be spanked and put to bed with diapers on. They liked to have the diapers changed by pretty, busty young women named "Daisy" or "Candy." One was about an old man who liked to drink warm pee provided by black women with hefty buttocks. They would squat over his mouth and piss while he fondled their butts.

I would get excited while reading these books, sitting in Mr. Pantozza's empty living room on rainy Saturdays. I would scrunch down on the sofa so that the seam of my jeans dug into my crotch. I did this for many hours at a time, not worrying about whether or not he was watching me.

D e b o r a h P i n t o n e l l i

Simpler, and easier to understand, were the magazines in his bathroom. The usual collection of *Playboy, Penthouse,* and *Hustler* provided me with my first glimpses of naked bodies—extremely young women with tiny, shaved snatches adorned each shiny page. My only problem was that I didn't look like the girls in the photos. I was dark. Everything about me was dark, dark, dark, and everything about them was luridly pink. And by the time I turned twelve, I weighed 110 pounds and I was very strong. I could outrun most of my class and was a pretty good athlete in general. None of the girls pictured in *Playboy* weighed more than that, and they were all a good five inches taller than me.

But as I've said, Mr. Pantozza has never had any problem with my looks. "There might be some coon in you," he'd say when I complained, "but it hasn't done you any harm." This would set him off laughing, for any kind of racial slur was almost as titillating to him as the stuff in the magazines.

Once, during this same summer, I was in the washroom with a *Hustler* magazine. Mr. Pantozza opened the door. I froze as he stood over me, afraid that he was finally going to do something bad. "Mari," he said sweetly, "let Uncle Sammy see you for a minute, just a minute." I didn't know what he meant. "This," he said, putting his hand on my knee and pushing it aside. He brushed my hands away and pushed my legs open even farther. "If you only knew how beautiful you are, how like a lovely flower you are there in the middle, past those brown thighs." Then he smiled.

"I could kiss the flower, if you'd like me to," he said, nodding his head and then actually wetting his lips with his tongue. I didn't know what to say. He wasn't being harsh or mean; he was, in fact, being much kinder than usual. I wondered if it would be like in the books when the man and the woman or the two women put their mouths on each other. "Or I could kiss your mouth, which is also like a tender rose, a frail blossom," A what? I noticed he didn't have his teeth in, which was good, I guessed, because then he couldn't get mean and decide to bite me like a dog.

All of the air in the room seemed to vanish. I was hot, and felt like I had to pee more. And I wanted some water, too.

He leaned over and put his mouth on mine, driving his smoky tongue inside, running it all over my tongue, my teeth, my tonsils, practically. I said into his mouth that I had to pee and he shook his head yes, like it was okay so I peed and then he put his hand down there to cup me while I peed and it got all over the fuzzy red toilet seat that I hated so much and I was glad, thinking then for some stupid reason that he would now have to throw it away because it was ruined.

For a minute I pushed down on his hand, liking the way it felt. We stayed like this for awhile, with him moaning and shivering like he was cold. When he finally pulled his mouth off of mine his palm held a little puddle of pee.

Then suddenly I didn't like it anymore. It was getting all messy and stupid and I was hot and thirsty. I struggled and pushed him away. He seemed to sense that this was going to be his one and only opportunity to be so close to me. He mumbled something about not being done, but I said that I was and I pulled up my jeans and ran out of the room fast.

It seemed to be okay soon after that, though. I was young and I forgot things quickly. Soon he and I were the same as always, playing games, eating too much watermelon, reading comic books, and watching TV. My father said, "Yeah, Pantozza's okay, in spite of his past. Look at how good he treats little Marisa."

((

Aunt June and I are watching *As the World Turns* and eating chicken salad sandwiches. She looks at me and asks, "What's wrong, Mar? Something the matter?" She thinks I'm bored spending my summer at home while most of my friends are away on vacation somewhere. I shake my head. Then I decide to tell her something of what I am feeling. "I just wish that old man downstairs would die." She is appalled. "Why, Mari? He's been so good to you all of these years!" She couldn't even begin to understand. "He just gets on my nerves, that's all. I'm tired of being his goddamned nursemaid."

She decides she understands. "Honey, look, you'll feel better when Alex comes back from his vacation," she says knowingly. "He'll take you out somewhere nice. You'll get all dolled up, then you'll feel better." She turns back to the soap opera with satisfaction.

It's one of those oppressive summer days when it wants to rain but can't so I can't even go sit on the porch with a book. I can call my friend Barb, but I've already done that. I pace the apartment, going to the fridge to look at the veal roast for dinner, taking out a Coke and drinking half of it, turning on the radio in my bedroom for a minute. Nothing to do. I feel like the whole building is rotten, stinking with that beast down there in his lair. My father should throw him out, I think, the apartment is overrun by mice and bugs and we could get a lot more rent from a new tenant. I think about this all afternoon long, not really knowing why I'm suddenly so obsessed with the subject.

Then I'm in the yard cutting some flowers. Through the darkened, greasy stain that is Mr. Pantozza's kitchen window, I can see his hands in the light of the dusty bulb as they move to roll and light a cigarette. The oversized mug of coffee is lifted to his lips and put down again. Through the whirl of the window fan's blades, I can hear the strains of Lite FM and one of his dogs yapping for a snack. He sees me looking at him and snaps off the light.

Mother

DENISE DUHAMEL

When I woke up my legs were wide open. This sometimes happened when we fell asleep drunk. Tom's head, left cheek to the bed, was between my crotch. It looked as though I'd just dream-delivered a man taller than I was, a difficult breech birth. I swung my leg over Tom, the heel of my foot brushing somewhere around his waist. The insides of my thighs hurt.

I tripped over a metallic beer can Tom had crushed into an hourglass. He was a slob, and I was angry, partly because I had a hangover. I kicked the side of our yellowing futon with my good set of toes, but Tom didn't budge. I stepped over the dead weight of his legs, which sprawled on the wooden floor. There was a third of my bottle of vodka left on his drawing board. I undid the ornate safety bars, unlocked the window, and lifted the latch overlooking the fire escape, where we kept the orange juice. Tom didn't believe in cluttering up his apartment, not even with a refrigerator. He unscrewed the radiators in winter and left them in the toilet in the hallway.

As I was making a screwdriver, the two girls walked in from my work room. I'd forgotten completely that they'd been here. Rosa, the taller one, shushed Carmen, who was about to say good-morning. Rosa pointed to Tom, who had on his shorts, but nothing else. I reached for the bunched up blanket that had rolled to the floor and flung it over most of Tom, as though modesty was possible in such a small tenement apartment. The girls giggled because I'd carelessly covered Tom's head as though he were dead.

Grabbing my drink, the carton of orange juice, and two plastic Star Trek glasses, I ushered the girls back into my room. We closed the door and sat on the pillows they'd slept on. My sewing machine seemed like

One might think only wannabes, poseurs, and prosthetic users would attend such a lecture as Rollo presented, but to **Denise Duhamel**'s surprise *she found herself seated beside a true original, a fleshy nine-year-old. When he noted her glance, he politely touched his fez. This could go in her book, she thought. Denise is the real consciousness of Barbie, having published several pieces in the* Mondo Barbie *anthology. She's also the author of* Smile. *She later mentioned this boy to the police, and then, after staring rather distractedly at the photo, found that all that was visible was his fez, like a smokestack over the seat.*

43

a big imposition, as the room was only six by ten. I leaned my back against a bolt of black velveteen.

"Do we have to go to school?" they wanted to know.

It was already ten-thirty. I'd set the alarm for eight, but must have slept through the beeps.

The night before, Tom and I had gone dancing at The World, because in typical live-in girlfriend fashion, I'd begun to complain that we never went anywhere. It was "Latin Night" and I ordered expensive frothy drinks that left a series of sweet fruity mustaches over my lip. Tom licked them off, though he normally didn't kiss my face. If I could have let go of even *some* of my anger, it would have been close to romantic.

On our way home, we stopped at the deli, where Tom picked up a six pack of taller-than-average cans full of cheap beer. He tried to get me to pay for half, but I'd spent so much on my World drinks that the only thing left in my pocket was my key. I started to walk east from Avenue C onto Fifth Street, a creepy dead-end that was blocked by P.S. 64. Tom kept trying to get me to go around, up Sixth or Fourth, but I kept on, ahead of him. Half of me wanted something bad to happen; the other half just wanted to make *Tom* feel like the one who was in jeopardy for a change. I sang in the empty street, Tom groaning and already drinking one of his beers. The only way out of the dead end, without turning around, was through the playground. When I lifted up the piece of torn fence that attempted to protect the school's swings, slide, and basketball court, I gouged my hand on a loose barb of the metal diamond I'd grabbed. I knew better than to mention it to Tom.

Rosa and Carmen were huddled on the school's steps, the way they were huddled now on my sample pillows that I carried from boutique to boutique in the East and West Villages. They'd asked for the time, which was four a.m. Through a series of my questions, they told us their mother had kicked them out of the house because they'd disobeyed their stepfather. It was Indian summer. Warm enough, Tom thought, for them to spend the next few hours of night on the school steps. But I couldn't stand it. I invited them to our apartment, which Tom reminded me was really his apartment. I insisted. He didn't want to look like the total grouch, so he finally said, "OK—just one night."

Though she was only fourteen, Rosa told me she had work papers. Instead of going to school today, she'd rather walk to Delancey Street to see if she could get some extra hours at the shoe store. She looked clean and pressed—she confessed she'd used my iron to straighten out the clothes she'd slept in. Carmen wanted to visit her boyfriend in the projects. She was thirteen, and she boasted that if she got pregnant, she was sure she could live with her boyfriend's family instead. They both looked to me—an unlikely mother, crumpled and wearing only a man's

BVD tee shirt—for approval or some kind of decision. I concentrated on my heavy tongue, clouds of putrid cotton candy, cotton mouth.

I promised them breakfast at Leshko's. The girls waited as I went to the shower, which was in the kitchen that led to Tom's work room where we also slept. There used to be a wall and a door, but Tom had knocked them down so he could get an extra four inches of space the length of his apartment. Soon there would be nothing left. Even his drafting table was empty, except for my clear bottle of vodka. He hadn't had a freelance job in months. I looked at him, and a purple rage entered me sideways, then quickly left. While I'd been talking to the girls, he had crawled up the futon so that his head was on the pillow. He was snoring slightly, without the least bit of curiosity as to what was going on around him.

The water was hot and powerful since we lived on the top floor. As I rinsed the deep cut in my hand from the night before, my eyes started to water. "The problem is you want a baby," Tom always said—Tom, who was impotent, but insisted that the condition had nothing to do with his drinking. Besides, he'd say he was too old to have a baby, fifteen years older than I was, beginning his forties. I didn't think that that was the problem, but I couldn't know for sure since the therapist I went to said she couldn't see me anymore until I was committed to getting sober. Until I stopped drinking. I shouldn't have a baby either, I would say to Tom. He would shrug, then assure me that we didn't drink *that* much. "I just want you to be nice to me," I would say vaguely, unsure what I meant. Tom never let me touch him, though by now any desire I initially had was gone. He liked to kiss me on my second mouth, but I couldn't reach orgasm, even by myself. In the shower, I wondered if a city agency would let Tom and me adopt. Maybe even adopt Rosa and Carmen, if their real mother didn't want them anymore. Maybe Tom would go for it, as one of his arguments against us starting with children now had been that he'd be retired by the time they'd be in high school.

I pulled on a pair of jeans and a sweatshirt. The girls were politely sitting with their hands folded in their laps when I went to my work room to get them. They gave away the fact that they'd been plotting when Rosa said that she and Carmen did very good housework. The two offered to cook and clean in exchange for being able to sleep in my sewing room. "Tom threw away the stove that came with the apartment," I said, to demonstrate the unlikelihood of the arrangement. Rosa and Carmen lowered their heads and their black shiny hair shone despite them. "But we'll see," I found myself saying, like a mother not wanting to disappoint. Then we heard the crash. Tom had thrown my vodka bottle against the wall, leaving a dark stain that reminded me of subway urine. "Get them *out* of here," he said when I peeked out of my room. He was standing on the futon in just his

underwear. His arms were tensed out at his sides, like a body builder too built up
to ever look relaxed. "Get them out of my apartment," he said.

I ushered the girls into the hall, embarrassed, fed up. "He's not usually like
this," I found myself explaining, which was true, but I could tell the girls didn't
believe it. At Leshko's, they ordered Cokes and large orders of french fries. I'd lost
my authority to talk them into anything more wholesome, and ordered black coffee. I gave them our phone number, since we all knew it wasn't a good idea for
them to stop by. I paid the cashier with the money I'd taken from the front pocket
of Tom's pants.

I walked Carmen to the projects because I didn't want to go back to Tom yet.
She openly sighed that she wanted a baby. But her sixteen-year-old boyfriend,
who dropped out of school, said she wasn't ready yet. Carmen wondered aloud:
"What's to be ready for? All a baby needs is love." The only thing Carmen worried
about was that her boyfriend's family didn't have room to take in her older sister;
so if she got pregnant, Rosa would be on her own. Carmen asked me, casually, if I
wanted kids too. I said something like the truth: "Maybe someday."

Carmen hugged me as though at that moment I sufficiently substituted as the
newborn she hoped to have. Then she looked at me and touched my cheek. Her
young palm was chubby, pink, and slightly cold. I forgot to ask her which store
Rosa worked in, so when I headed down Delancey Street, I was overwhelmed by
the number of discount shoe outlets. I had one of those headaches I'd been getting lately, that pounded in through the top of my scalp. I bought a pair of two-
dollar plastic sunglasses from a sidewalk vendor, hoping they would help. I peered
into Fayva, Bunnie Towne, Exclusive Shoes, MGB, and Thom McAn; but I
couldn't find Rosa. I walked into the Sneaker Castle and asked a manager, who
said she didn't work there either. That's where I decided to give up, knowing my
rescue plans were ambivalent, inadequate.

The manager wanted to know if I'd like to try anything on. I stared at the display of white leather hightops, beautiful as porcelain gravy boats that belonged on
festive holiday tables. I missed my own mother and decided I'd call her collect
from a pay phone, just to say hi. She might be surprised and start to cry, then
maybe I'd hang up quickly or start to cry too. On the way out of the store, I
bumped into a table of Keds. The sample shoes were all for kids. One pink sneaker
was so tiny that I was sure it couldn't have been for a real foot. It looked like a
novelty item, something that should have been dangling from a key chain.

Doll's Eyes

JUDY NYLON

Tommy Nylon and I were tight. We never spent a lot of time together; he was forty-seven years older than me and I never saw him on a weekday. My conversation wasn't baby-talk but it really wasn't brilliant enough to hold his attention for long. I guess I got the drop on him by just existing. He never expected to see himself in miniature. Everyone used to say to me, "You're just like your father." The likeness was more than just physical; we were both in the minor key. I was the only one who'd stay up late and listen to his Julie London records or watch film noir on the tube. Once, when an ad for greyhound racing came on, I made the mistake of saying, "Daddy, can we go see those dogs tomorrow?" He snickered, exhaling smoke thru his nose from an unfiltered Old Gold held between thumb and third finger. "Only Turks go to the dogs, Princess," he said, shaking his head. I won't say I understood the answer; but I got the drift and the dogs were a dead issue. Where I come from, nobody has any time for baby-talk; I learned to state a request like a telegram; I'd aim a few words with precise meaning up and under the hoods of his navy blue eyes. I could see if I scored a direct hit. Sometimes I'd miss.

My first day of school was a piece of cake. Out of thirty-two kids, I was the only one who could already read and write. You see, I'd had a foster father who played keyboard in pick-up bands at the Jazz Workshop and he'd hooked me on singing; I had to read to follow the words. Now it was coming in handy; I finished my work straight away and settled back to study everyone else. I picked out the crowd of little girls I wanted to belong in and observed that they all went to the park and played "school" after real school was over. Each had a doll, a surrogate of herself with her

The cop saw the copier light moving like a car's headlights under Deborah's bathroom door and tried to batter his way in. **Judy Nylon**, *passing along the wintry street below, was looking into the congealing drool of a fire hydrant when she saw the reflection of a lissome, dark-haired woman emerging head-first onto the fire escape three stories above.*

Judy Nylon is currently writing Manners for the New Millennium *and was an early UK punk performer (*Pal Judy, *produced by Adrian Sherwood for ROIR, is excellent) and then part of the New York no-wave surge.*

There was a sound of splintering behind the exiting woman. From high above, she jumped into an excelsior-filled dumpster. When Judy helped her out, she was limping. The excelsior sticking out over her ears looked like shavings of golden teak.

47

exact coloring. All the dolls were exactly the same make and size. I read the make and model data from one of the doll boxes and committed it to memory. All through the week as I learned Roman numerals, I'd repeat the doll box information to myself to make sure it was still there.

When I got to Tommy's on Friday night, I was *excited*. I had all the data and I practised my phrasing in the dark before I fell asleep. At breakfast, I even ate the eggs, which I've always found unnatural and revolting. Tommy and I faced each other, each clutching a mug of coffee, when I told him I wanted a Madame Alexander doll that was six inches tall and had blue eyes and dark brown hair. I'd scored a direct hit; we confirmed that Madame Alexander was a brand name and that the doll was to look like me so that I could play school in the park. He went off to the ponies and I just knew he'd bring back the doll.

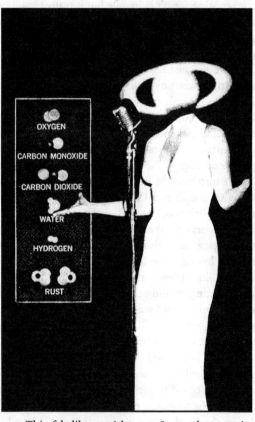

Time was eternal, even longer when you're in your room, coloring. My aunt made me go outside in the yard and "play." This was a command I never understood. It was cold out and the leaves and pine needles formed a soggy wet carpet under foot. I crouched down Chinese-style in the warm air by the expulsion duct from the clothes dryer in the basement. This felt like punishment. I was always waiting—sometimes in nightclubs if a babysitter couldn't be found. The situation was similar except that there I could have coke and watch adults play. It occurred to me that if I could learn the patience necessary to play, I could become an adult sooner.

Finally, I saw him coming. He's hard to miss, even in a crowd; he's six-foot-four, looks like Lee Marvin, dresses like George Raft. He was carrying a large box. I thought that was a bit weird; but adults were always doing that. They'd gift wrap a ring in a bicycle box to prolong your expectations. He was pretty excited too; juiced I'd say. It turns out he'd picked a tierce and pocketed a cool G at the window. Inside the house, I dived straight for the box. Tommy helped me; tipped it up as I lifted off the lid. There, nestled into thirty-two little casket-like boxes, were thirty-two of them, shoulder to shoulder; all with dark hair. The lids rolled back on sixty-four blue glass eyes in unison. I had an overwhelming wave of nausea as my eyes met theirs. The rush of simultaneous thoughts for which I had no language caused a sense of vertigo; my "thank you" was brief as I rushed to the bathroom to lose the eggs.

I know this was the first time I saw the void. As Rilke observed, dolls are the first to inflict that larger-than-life silence, which breathes out of the deep space at the edge of known existence . . . forever. Facing a doll that blankly stares back, you experience true emptiness, a heartpause during which you are only your all-time essence. I struggled through my child-sized scraps of language; none could cover the thought that hung amorphously along the roof of my mind echoing thirty-two times.

My aunt calmed me down with a cup of tea and carefully explained that she understood that if I had thirty-two of me, I would end up playing alone. My aunt was the very breath of Bostonian discretion; she only wore fur on the inside of her coats and perceived that showing up to play with an army of surrogate selves would scare the other little girls away. She was, however, unwilling to deal with the fact that no matter how precise my requests or logical her behavior, neither of us would ever penetrate my father's twin veils of gambling and alcoholism. On Monday, she would put a hat on her perfectly coifed grey hair, an amethyst brooch on the lapel of her Chanel walking suit, matching gloves and heels, and proceed to take back thirty-one Madame Alexander six-inch dolls, requesting to trade them for tasteful, well-made doll clothes. I can imagine her explanation of the facts surrounding the purchase to be as complex as her denial of them.

Tommy would never quite understand why if one doll was great, thirty-two could not be fantastic. His gestures would always be outsized, revealing in their bias his disdain for the mediocre and the bourgeois and communicating that to me. Our closeness was unconditional but unspoken, which gave rise to bizarre misunderstandings and the inappropriate gifts that became neighborhood legend. When he gave me a marabou-trimmed peignoir set, which would have looked great on Eva Gabor, for my twelfth birthday, I gave him a thirty-pound live goose for Christmas—he was my guide in the world of un-reason, a Peter Pan written by Damon Runyon. I do believe in miracles; they occur when I'm in a state of grace, acting on the intuitive level, fielding thoughts out of the void that reason has no language for. Along with an old deck of cards, so worn that the linen shows through the faces, miracles are my legacy.

2-B 38-C 3-D in Neuropolis

BART PLANTENGA

"I will strike thee without anger or hatred like the butcher in good humor. They whistle or sing while they slaughter, for man must eat each day."

—André Breton

Panel #1: Garret-bunker, mid-swivelization: I tore the crucifix from the crumbling wall of gruesome bouquets. Issued severe blows to my temple with it as a cudgel in my clutch. This is how things had always worked & I was an unwitting part of this . . . this "always." I tossed crucifix into sink & squeezed green dish liquid oozing across its slinky He-torso. Blood quickly flooded down the gurgling maw.

But cross my bra (not mine, but my lovely wife's) & hope to sigh: no sooner had I commenced to clean the lanky He-torso of all significant flocculi than I was distracted winkless by a riveting TV scene of barking guns & askew head maws. While herds of bristle-legged cockroaches swarmed across vulcanized limb to winking stigmata like be-feelered mongrel mendicants, like bronze Mexicali urchins devouring the marzipan entrails of Judas.

#p2: Feverish foot blur descends upon one spooked leather-backed roach scampering across checkerboard linoleum. & then again. & again. But it wouldn't die, clinging to my sock's tight purl. Delirious, ecstatic, but NOT dead. BEYOND dead. But eventually my alliance with the steadfast laws of physics won out—a sudden application of body weight upon shiny carapace. & so it died, morsels of rubber corpus caught in its mandibles.

I led myself down the long corridor to facilitate my escape from these quarters which had once been mine.

*When **bart plantenga** came upon the two ladies in distress, Deborah slipping in and out of consciousness and Judy strapless, he couldn't help but intervene. Lifting Deborah into his brawny arms, he manfully staggered down the rue. bart is a WFMU dj, author of* Wiggling Wishbone *and* Confessions of a Beer Mystic, *and inventor of the coif sportif. With one of her limp hands, tipped with metallic nail polish, trailing on the ground and setting off sparks, and the other still clutching a smudged xerox, Deborah nestled her head against his shoulder; and bart felt the drift of her breath, scented like spooky jasmine. A storm of bullets began to cut jagged stripes in the storefronts behind them.*

51

But along the way, the walls, made of a strange amalgam (oatmeal + asbestos + vermin dung?), went flabby. Like tent flaps misbehaving in a horrible breeze.

& at the open sore of this gnarled borax-scented threshold, I was suddenly plucked by loud collar & a bit of gooseflesh neck & heaved thru the window of sick light into a sky heavy with dingy laundry.

#p3: Neuro-dorp-pre-fab: My plucker had been a "Tooner" & near-mythical pope of pointillist disembowelment & subversion. But somewhere, in among his flareful post-hallucinogen strips, something had gone dark & ireful. His story-boards, at some personal juncture, began to forego all pretense to plot & turned into relentless Pollockian Ab-Ex explosions of viscera & venality. Something like the sextant of his soul had run him aground—& WAY outside the Comix Code of America (CCA)! & so papers dropped his strip. & he relegated himself to a purga-tory of proofreading & commercial illo grunt work. Leaving him faithumor defi-cient, a tempest in a pisspot, unkempt rum-volatile footman to upstart doodlers, broody *rechts*-brain tinker snuffing out his days the way a mercenary snuffs out his last cig entering his port of call.

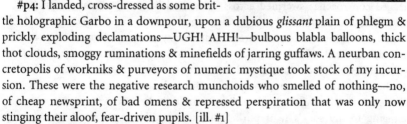

He shoved me (his major brew-bud & bio-strip-source) under eerie cynic-com-missioned sky (formaldehyde deep & pepto-abysmal dense) thru window of sick light. I was not surprised.

#p4: I landed, cross-dressed as some brit-tle holographic Garbo in a downpour, upon a dubious *glissant* plain of phlegm & prickly exploding declamations—UGH! AHH!—bulbous blabla balloons, thick thot clouds, smoggy ruminations & minefields of jarring guffaws. A neurban con-cretopolis of workniks & purveyors of numeric mystique took stock of my incur-sion. These were the negative research munchoids who smelled of nothing—no, of cheap newsprint, of bad omens & repressed perspiration that was only now stinging their aloof, fear-driven pupils. [ill. #1]

#p5: I was forced to be amazing. Neither ghost nor star. Not lost, not found, but locked out of my own closet. Wending & fending as a bony Zipatone-defined peripatetic rapido in a 3rd-world neurodissement crammed into 2 ink-smudgy dimensions. Not easy at age 37 when muscle goes inelastic & hope shows its face as Despair-in-a-Smiley-mask. Self-contempt gouging so deep into past regretted lives that you can't stand the perfume of your own flatulence. One is confused for the other. So everything I said stank of memories misapprehended, of carrying souvenirs of the Sacré Coeur in Paris, carved from horsebone, salvaged from the slaughterhouses of La Villette, in fetid breast pocket, through the empty crepuscule *rues* of the 18th Arr. Dogged by bootlicks mumbling misgivings in damp trenchcoats thru *sub-terre* corridors & *sans issues,* stark & unforgiving, yielding neither Out nor In. [ill. #2]

#p6: I was jettisoned tipsy into Metalhead Turf: disputed ne(i)ther precinct flanking both sides of the Manson-Nixon Line, face to gaga face with Vituperin addicts, Gurunoids, stylegawks, Waxheads & Deaf Rock Wilders with in-tow, over-blushed boytoys (*jouets* with convenient configurations of moist wounds) roaming the concrete shopping corridors, lined with coiffed barkers pawning black, pilfered things relegated to being mere stylish replicas of their former useless selves. Where one had to nitely run gauntlets of garb-dissing to get from 1 respite enclave to another allied style sector. Where the fortune-deprived (we need them to feel fortunate) pan-manhandle, strip bark from shade elms to wrap around shins & tap saplings for nutri-cellulose. Sugar addicts check into pop shops, buy spoonfuls thrust into their mouths by anonymous extended arms from bulletproof plexi-cubicles.

#p7: It was jittery going as "Tooner" erased sartorial get-ups & muscle tone to make me gawkier, more naked, multi-appendaged & ever more resistant to the effects of anti-agoraphobia drugs. [ill. #3] To tromp treacherous thru tite swaths of semio-turf, where each block had embraced its own dead pop-con deity.

First came Waxheads (Dean Martin as JFK, Peggy Lee as Marie Antoinette), sworn wheezing enemies of Techies & Deaf-Metalheads. Waxheads'd remained

stuck & ambulatory in misshapen memories. Bound to their scratched wax trinity: Sinatra, Torme & Ellington, & the mythic infidelity of wax.

#p8: But they had long ago given way, in coif arrogance & sonic fervor, to 45-Wonders who swore by the spindle & spin of the 45, around which twirled an entire mythos to consume & guard.

45-Wons (Gene Vincent as Liberace, Elvis as Jesus) with the spin thing, had burned bridges full of Waxhead 78's. But were re-cast as bug-eyed & loopy when music went 33 rpm & conceptual (i.e. rock operas). They & their allied hifi ilk, too, fell by the waxside to those believing the Archies had once actually been a band. & would tour again! Swore they'd actually SEEN them live in '70! Some claimed to own bootleg evid. But there IS no evid of there ever having even been an actual BAND, let alone a tour. Conspiratorially-bent Archiots (Conspiracy = post-mod stylish egotism), however, chalked this kind of news up to signs of media persecution & sophisticynicism.

#p9: The DooWop, Kiss, Runaways, B-BoomBox Boys, Doors, Velvet Underground, Jazzophiliac ("to wax godly on brass"), & Sid Vicious co-horridors are populated by those emboldened by convenient & stylish mytho-deaths. It wasn't so much the stars' accomplishments but how they wore their clothes, how their deaths allowed others (the be-faithed = confused bundles in fashionable digs) to immerse themselves in the *mort-spectacle*. Fools lavished in myths wilfully instigated by their own dogged despair. Never mind anti-CD cranks, techno-bennies, bullet-biters afflicted with scratch fever, ghettocentric quasi-nationalist gangsters barking up many a wrong flagpole. & the nodding hordes of Deafmetal Heads with their staggering booted swaggers.

#p10: Deafmetal Heads (Alice Cooper as Mad Max, Sonic Youth as burning Buddhas), are totally besoddened (beside themselves) in the pre-oc of their own fashionability. So full of themselves they're perpetually nauseous. Pilgrimaging in scoffing shoes, ensconced in their astutely profitable R&R rime schemes (fire-desire, love-glove, I-buy) with their torso-mount docu-cam-vids, out onto the Van Kill, tundra of crushed glass & seepage, to thrill the sclerotic mechanisms of the heart. Adrenal glands attuned to chem-enhanced dusks with days hotter than memories served. Patch cords dragged across brittle asphalt & dingy scrub. Tote-*boîtes* of M.I.F.S. (Mobile Intra-Veinous Food Stuffs), pug chops, & blue drinks were kept styro-coolered. But the Moodist Temples they'd set out for lay tucked faraway, across the Van Kill, in the grit-misty Black&Blue Hills. Just out of sensory shot. Affordable yet unfathomable.

#p11: The power outage was not primarily of any one sonic con-glom's doing. But Deafmetal ensembles had been courting extreme & hollow sonic eroto-promo (cast into frames of media irrelevance) for some time. Their slo-mo obliteration of sensory organs & power cord flagellations to dull corpus sensitivity were legend. Heroic deafness in the face of errant mega-debs. Their migrations out to the Pamper Mesas (amalgam of jettisoned detritus, Hi-C, Tide & Maalox spills), in search of their Ur-porkchop-selves at the Moodist Temples was seen as acceptance of blame. Or aimlessness, adrift with pocket bulges of Wet 'n' Wild condoms. Or nausea. Nausea caused by drugs, or the anticipation of drugs. Or the messy sweep of inarticulate desire.

#p12: No assurance the explosions were the mere blasts of crank pranks. (Irksome pre-pubes taped BlokBusters to panes & pay phones.) No way to tell if the slivers & splinters suspended in our hyper-saturated atmos is really crank fallout. & no one seems expert enough to tell whether the cranial detonations do damage to shifting skull plates. Survivors weaved into my sore side & whined on about migraines & mal-practice suits to fit survivors. Drinks stole my dreams 1 by 1. But slaked no thirst.

#p13: Tooner had drawn my gawk-bod befuddled & riddled with trepidation, leisure lesions, & the stink of the psycho-tourista as I was paraded past the heaving hordes of Neuropolizens, rendered sinister with microchips of animalevolence divoted into their mugs freakshow-style.

#p14: The blackouts allowed *polizei* [ill. #4] to eagerly assume their roles in chrome & *miroir* ichthyo-macula (tiny overlapping discs of heat-tempered fish scale spangles) riotgear & wield their bitter-sexed truncheons. Glorious goosesteppers in OSS fetish *leder* & Lurex, marched to strains of Deafmetal Boleros (ELP, Queen, & other coif-laden pomp ensembles), that aroused the fructations of labia & lobotomies alike.

They withheld ("unremembered" to distribute) mall-factured MIFS-*sucre,* controlling individual sovereignty via salivation rates, with snarling aplomb. Blue-bens rendered the *polizei* more astutely brawl-prone.

#p15: This terrain, a hypo-melange of fissured concretinous silos & tombs, sliverwink neon, blank starefronts, gust-blown styrotainers, & paint-by-# crowds is where reasoning pollen (Negstacy snuff-derivative) in molecules of our volatile atmos began to eat at us.

#p16: Reaction shot: brimming horde. With Blackout #S72, Neuropizens' (mostly *fonctionnaires,* classifications 1-7a & post-pensioners) stunned gape-dark smile-howls were pried open in a moment of time, like mussels suspended in a brackish bay. Ready to molt their misshapen perma-selves into something more Fantasian-oriented, something light in the immediate Fandango, whatever the turbulent *nacht* might hold. They (of collective dispiritedness) at once desiring to descend INTO & transcend OUT OF their ever-vescent *realité.*

#p17: Lycrex web-quilted red foot broke thru the panel with bold ascending line-signifiers before my very nose (hooked & warted by Tooner revenge). [ill. #5] Stan Lee as Miro? His leap of faith & hope (metaphysical whimsy) could not be

denied by my injection into the storyboard panels.

But to whom were these awe-mawed neuropizens reacting? Me, in cheap tie & indefensible nose, or man in red & blue spiderweb Spandex & spectrographic pupils? Ego paints special paranoiac patterns of urban neglect as refractions of the 1st personal.

#p18: The looter, under *nacht couverture,* bumped into me full of the righteous snarl of those trying to out-victim the victim & outsurvive the survivor (Darwin$_2$). He was drawn startled, dropping a solidstat-Fax-CDAT-corder. The hot item (diminutive expo of *liberté*) went wrecked & sizzle in a blue splash. His fuming, snarling thot balloon rammed me tug-hard. The nascent explosions & confus-o-mania at once crowded & entertained me.

#p19: Tooner changed my sox to a ridiculous pair that made my arches itch & toes bleed from under the nails, casting me wanderlusting generic jungles, home to heavy-lidded intoxizulus who *rêved* like crazy for the *formule* of curvacious indulgence & clinging desires. A fanciful thot cloud of happy Zulu all narco-lidded gaga over some wiggling grass fornicatrix.

#p20: In one mega-disco *kammer* a "keptowomaniac" vomited the delirious misfortune from her entrails. [ill. #6] Heaven as sinister Studio 54, host to an *As the World Turns* ball. On Subfloor A, Tertiary Pavilion 1C (concrete & velveteen outback) big Fanatishists in puffed coifs & Krazi-Nails rechurned entire seasons of *Turns* thru their actual lives. Unsteady in New York Doll platform shoes, I was unsure which was feeding inspiration to whom.

#p21: Heaven'd be like this—loud disappointment with towering Spam Sculptures, SpamKing & Queen MCs, Mall-functioning Fountains, stagnant water, deflated elegance, cut R-rate holo-flicks, wannabee scripters toting gilt-sleeve scripts, watery drinks cut with *meteochat* & coiffing stratagies. In air-conditioned (body odors extinguished at the door) heaven everyone flosses & peepshows disallow expenditures of fluid & emotion. Just more dotdotdot, fill in the too-many blanks.

In adjacent *Kammers,* we see a diorama [ill. #7], a blond nudismo dramaturge perched

bewildered (simulato-safe) upon a lingual-activated toadstool in a lascivio-paradiso frought with carnal delites. They, on bald knees, tuck Lincolns into her rainbow trout spangle G-string.

In heaven men are women & women cum on time. But here in Neuropolis, outside the velveteen Stud 54 ropes, men are minotaur mutants, women emotional time-bombs, children gluttons for multi-orifical corruption. All fauna is neurban & rabid, all flora thorny & homoniverous.

#p22: *Homme* of pettable nanas mounts a very arousal-prone *femme*. & I felt agonizing tics of empathy watching his moustache twitch like a vermin tail [ill. #8] as he lavished strings of *besos* across her pliant expanse. & he'd parted the paths of pain, across hot coals, a sated Nirvana of silk scarves & Tiger Balm. & this I appreciated, watching him send bejeweled Mexican bugs, traversing her torso, carrying the mother-of-pearl vessel of balm with mine eyes in lyric tow. This *homme's* concept of *amour*, future, present, past is contained in the thrust & retraction. & time's an aroma of cloven hooves & matted lambsear grass. My past, too, was of sufficient manufacture to insinuate itself into the present, resonate into the future like a bell in sea water.

& here she writhed (dark darting catfish-eyes) like someone I'd known or some post-reptilian I'd wanted to know but hadn't. Or had I? I found myself mesmerized by her moan, or the familiarity of that moan. I knew that blowfish moan!

#p23: A *femme vivant*, with residual visage of SpamQueen (suffering unnamed emotive deflation). Her wishful curvature echoed the ache-desire of our d-moted-d-mented artist. Was it the 38C padroombaas (rendered by las-civious shading & crosshatching to amplify their protuberant mythos)? She'd been plunked before me, agile, allegorical, wish-dense, vigilant, & beyond belief, but still just a 2-Dim dame. "Yo! Fungus face!" (Refering to my *champignon-nez*?!) "Yer in my way!" & she delivered stony lump of tattooed fist to my solar plexus. I fainted & outrage died. She kneeled over me; "Sorry. Yer nonscripter. You mess the story-scape. Compromise my duties to the power forsaken! You's very likely just a bad wrinkle in this outfit! & now I see that. You coulda bin a plant of devious interference!"

#p24: She, redrawn, hung up her Teflon coat (re-con stares just slid off her anatomical highlights). She had a nitecap. [ill. #9] (Inderal steadies the culpable hand.) & I kneeled before her, caressing the *bijou mädchen's peau* until ink ran & my *doigt*-print lay oblong upon her cheek like a trick stretch of Silly Putty. My wretched, pinky-less hand caressed burgeoning lip swells that whispered like wasps from the *jardin* until the ink began to smudge & her lips began to stick to my forefinger. So I went further, tore the smirk, that familiar scar, from her face.

Her clamniverous voice (familiar as Romy Schneider films) confessed to washing his floor with roach killer [d-trans Allethrin (allyl homolog of Cinerin 1) 0.060%. Piperonyl butoxide, Technical 0.120% + N-Octyl bicycloheptene dicarboximide 0.20%, Cyano (3-phenoxyphenyl) methyl 4-chloro-alpha- (1-methylethyl) benzene-acetate 0.20%, 0.096% (butylcarbityl) (6-propylpiperonyl) ether & 0.024% related compounds]. "Then I took a bath, crossed his tiptoe floor barefoot. Climbed into his sumptuous deathbed & yes, allowed him to lick the sweet-arched delicacy he'd come to describe as my feet—'the firm delight of your escartoes.' HaHaHA!"

I was helpless to do anything about her stylish & eerily familiar demasculation because as a stereo poptype, dot screen flourish of near gestures & Velox ghost I had no thot clouds crowding our already cramped little panel. & I heard her seething suddenly go soothing; "MMM. No anxiety-filled insomnia for this gal tonight." & I caught myself whispering "Monique, Monique." He'd captured my wife with almost slavish accuracy as if he'd studied clandestine photos of her. She was luscious, queerly unreal, metaphysical, made of memories & lusts not her own but rather the projected estrus of men.

From her horizontal somnabulescence a thot balloon blossomed: "I'm not just some body from which my feet dangle for his Pleasure!" I attempt response but no voice balloon emerged.

#p25: I dodged enormous dot patterns & monstrous bod parts like Iowans dodge hailstones mid-harvest. [ill. #10] Euphoric disarray like the feast of burning carnival stands. A sweep of howls, exploding crystals ("like war films projected on the backs of our eyelids" = *Cerebro peliculas*) across the witless pitch of sagging

sans issues & blockaded *rues*. Like the sky was the inside of a giant firecracker singeing all soul, melting all burden.

#p26: I sang under the bridge of *wandelling* sex-smashed couplets, where dessicated garboyles laid out on carhoods in the sun with their blackhole jitters. Young *meisjes-sauvage* smelled of *Cheval Regal* & sweat. & Malls. Thru map-blue ink veins I swam across Seines & Volgas.

#p27: But just as impetuously, "Tooner" began rendering me with troubles of heart/ home/bank & a haircut like Larry of the 3 Stooges. Cooler clothes—sure—but to what crueler end? I smelled foreign, like a stranger's hankie in a fidgette's rattan purse. & then he had me (a Zipatone marionette with no breath to hold in the polar cold) wash with my own spit to get back to myself. Or odors of that memory, anyway. & my paw poked thru delicate papyrus into a panel of fisticuffed X-Men.

#p28: I'm down, groveling across splintery floor [ill. #11], begging for Coke (something I never drink!) among a scrum of mean dickmen in killuforms who popped blue eyes like grapes. The most *triste* denizens hid their pupils full of lost sea & sky in their breast pockets.

#p29: Libretto of moans. Typewriter keys as percussion. Cross-section of cells in a penal colony for unrepentant writers. Where they toil vainly away at the task of their monumental undoing. There she is, Fall-out Falina, author of *Structural Forms of Transsexual Femininity*, who wrote: "Sad like the acned girl, the pseudo-girl, lonely & bulimic dressed as Santa in the Broadway Revue."

#p30: The Pen-Al Colony (Pen + Alcohol was an equation far from the Nirvana = Control + Incense equation we'd learned at the Neuropa Institute) resembled mallvironmental dioramas inside vid-promos. Control was by K9 & K7. K9 gargoyles at strategic locales assured the smooth fear of mass labor. So that windowshoppers would make up their minds while K7's soothed harsh realities, assured that stupid ideas, awkward fashion & misshapen desire were quickly absorbed. Every tic was filmable. All revolt mere stylish insouciance.

They (not me!) were being penalized for glamourizing the Craft of Suffering = affliction of aimless *banlieue dilletantes* who rhapsodize the ghetto-jazz-*vie*. They (not me!) wore hubris in an Edwardian hangman's knot. Climbed into select isms like a callgirl into a corset. The isms' attraction, like hers, was made more arousing by appearing less human. Their own rules turned against themselves = "Montezuma's Revenge of the Soul."

I pretended to explain who I was or pretended to be in this cultsector predicament cum stripped-down semiotic universe-hood. Then furrowed brows, tics & thot balloons bloated beyond anything Roland Barthes would know what to do with. These incarcerated scrivs would never learn. Mugs like cheese in old socks hung from rotting beams. Sneers pitched between possessed & dispossessed, hurt & revenge, smile & moan.

#p31: The fanciful fop, ex-scriv of *The Sad Testicular Braggadocio of Ingrown Men,* had a scrap of gray matter still tucked away inside "his" cranial ducts. This dessicated the *histoire.* (My leaps of amnesia were modest enough so that I could

forge them with my own deteriorating thesaurial access.) He drew distinct panels [ill. #12] full of lines made of words held together by a rithmic bronchial wheeze; "He had made a play for the lil Campfire Girl . . . "

"Monique?"

"OK, Ja. He offer her the Teddy Bear. Tho bigger & furrier than . . . "

"She'd ever seen?"

"OK, Ja. Or needed. Sinister smile & leap of conundrum into her lap. He'd drawn her to make . . . "

"Love?"

"OK, Ja. If you wish. He want to fuck her into respect for him. He draw her tight. Him mythic. Enter *doigts* into her labial conundrum *unter*-quick *priveé* & she grumble things outside voice balloons, under her . . . "

"Breath?"

"OK, Ja. See people are like sharks. OK, Ja. Craving is 2nd degree desire. She bolts from his ink-arceration. She jilts Tooner. Who shakes into a big . . . "

"Tilt?"

"OK, Ja. If need be poetic. He'd drawn obsession too close to shiver & bone. He'd emptied her marrow of all belief. So now she was left with disbelief, the nausea of the soul—or you."

"& me?"

"OK, Ja? He becomes a Brutus huff, a doorman left in charge of the world for a small hour. So he—you?—rubbed her face in 1000 strips. & later he had the beast inside you appear as a randy raja, a violator-extremist & so she had you poisoned."

"But how do you . . . ?"

"I'm an aged hero in stretch *pantallons* defined not by flesh but by flash & prescience. I once wore true levitational innerwear. I was on same block with Spiderman. Never SUPERhuman, more ULTRAhuman. I was the spark of all art, that splinter of satori wedged into our forebrain. But my strip wasn't very successful."

"Thus yer holed up in this gulag *d'ecrivains*."

"Ja, until I mold this clump of shriveling grey matter back into something like a leap of faith."

#p32: I wrote an indignant requisition for our immediate release from this mallabyrinth. I wanted Tooner to change me. But the requisition came to haunt me, to tease me, & amuse him. He even redrew my tears, made them perform like

crystals on a chandelier in a sad peeling goldleaf ballroom.

Periodic kickfest-knucklejousts [ill. #13] erupted among the capos, gargoyles of consumptive faith, mutant glossyphilia journalists, post-script scrivs, multitung wags & ethno-de-caps. They were nurtured by the false hope of progress. Oh, sour sin-eastes of the ink! "Sheep are led by a traitor sheep who knows the way thru the yards to the slaughterhouse. & is spared his life."

#p33: A 12-step USSNRAA Aversion neurocologist offered the "cure" to the scrivs (casualties of Thunderbird, crushed dreams & fountain pen injections) to become patsies, paid-off actresses for national consumption-re-education. (S)he's given Ipecac, an anemitic, & then set in front of a bucket of glamorous ryes & proofs. As she vomits for national TV humiliation-voyeur consumption, a nurse, stern yet convivial, insults the patient.

b a r t p l a n t e n g a

Scriv 2, patient #606W (me!), has torpedo, a chemically-filled capsule, surgically implanted in upper arm. Forced to guzzle Jim/Jane Beam. Result (tight close-ups) observed. Patient gets violently ill, (limbs cumbersome as firehose) punch-drunk = "neurorumba." Later, scriv tears torpedo (with beeper hook-up) from his arm with incisors. The beeper signals USSNRAA official who reapplies torpedo for redoubled action. THIS is the lamentable but necessary murder of ideas. Inserting reed into medullary canal, at brain's base destroys spinal marrow, blocks scriv's reflexes. Pneumatic wenches, poleaxes & behr gun, which stuns by percussion, also available.

Bodies of *gendarme*-blue issue jarring guffaws. Blood Pollocks the walls. When draining blood grey-red mists hang around the premises. (Disorientation here due in part to Tooner's disdain for linear plots. Destination is not predetermined so much as stumbled upon.)

#p34: Horrible close-up of her mouth. Glint of fang. Her scriv smile, a calibrated stretch across the potential menace of her maw. She spins a spell, a neurondelle, tapestry of mal-arranged words. Insists HE's so full of self or the requisite attitude that hides the him from himself that there's no room for much else. & that by releasing HIM from this burden of blood & control she'd save us all from drowning. "She'd rather spend money to dress her dog than buy me a drink" (is how Tooner preferred to describe her).

#p35: Revenge of the Looking Class [ill. #14]: tight frame full of beings who'd forsaken their humanity (streamlined their psyches), eliminated the fluffy baggage of nicety & charm to survive. Like android roaches crammed into a jewelry box. Tooner redrew me with 1 arm, then had me make change while holding 2 ice cream cones!

HARRY THE HEAD.

My personality was devoid of psychic reverb. I'd become a character, voodoo pincushion, a pawn. Life continued to syncopate & my nog became its follow-the-bouncing-ball. I wore many more outfits & voices. But ultimately Tooner's boredom looked like pity & so he yanked me, redrew me onto his desk &, with instructions, mailed me back to my wife.

#p36: Me in envelope. Mailcarrier's finger pinched around my mid-section. His thot balloon: a joint or wad of chaw or aborted *homo erectus!* My fictional self falls for the deception. & I am home. & home is a strange (tactile & tacky) topography. & Monique is a stranger in a strange mind.

Every word's now a nagging footstep, leading down some suspicious *cul de sac.* Hollow misgivings are stuffed with mockery, bad checks, sudden noise, dropped stiletto, a concrete past. The cackles come from my own family's window. They're throwing a strange party. Bouquets of bare wires, crumbling walls, a gone place, this dancehall that had once been a slaughterhouse where the parents danced. We clapped along with sardine cans. Sardine oil ran down my wrists. The shuffly waltz of clubfeet matched the scratchy hiss of the Waxhead 78's.

In the slaughterhouse the vid-screen declared, "Air pumped under the hide of the animal loosens it for easy removal." Sinister nouns & verbs reclined on the diseased furniture of intent. "The writing was always meant to intimidate the scrivs, to regurgitate the unusual thrill of disappointment. Infected by the word, the disease of divine guidance." She whispered. "Thank god most of the world's under water." Reality slowed.

SAMPLED GRAFIX CREDITS:

1. Found Japanese comic book
2. "Flying Machine"—Bernie Krigstein, *Weird Science Fantasy* #23
3. "Squeeze play"—Frank Frazetta, *Shocking Suspense Stories* #13, 1953
4. Vintage R. Crumb
5. *Spiderman & The Black Widow* #140—Stan Lee
6. "Cracking Jokes"—Art Spiegelman
7. "Malice In Wonderland"—Wallace Wood, *National Screw*, 1976
8. *Les 110 Pilules D'apres Jin Ping Mei*—L'Echo des Savanes
9. "Brenda Starr"—Ramona Fradon & Mary Scmich
10. "Powerhouse Pepper"—Basil Wolverton
11. "Funny Nazis—Yossarian *East Village Other,* 1969
12. *Oltretomba* #262—Edi Periodici, SRI Viale Forlanni 36, Milano, Italy
13. *Two-Fisted Tales* #34—Jack Davis
14. "Harry The Head"—Brian Bolland, *Freak Show*

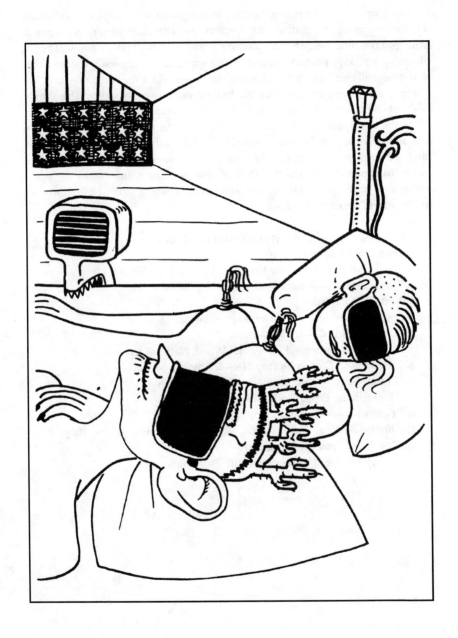

Helio

Lydia Tomkiw

Johnny, I hate you. I hate the very fabric of your being. I hate the way you contradict yourself.

I hate the way you avert your eyes as your fingers scan the bottoms of cafeteria tables looking for old gum you can pick off and discreetly put in your mouth and chew. I hate the way you won't drink wine out of anything but wine glasses, and first you examine them for water spots, even in the fanciest of restaurants.

I hate looking out my window and seeing you walk down my street, because then I can't come out of my house for days, waiting for it to rain and wash you off my sidewalk, Johnny.

I hate the way you spell your name with two *h*s and three *n*s, and you dot the one *i* with a heart, "Johhnnnie," I will never write your name that way, and I hate the fact that your real name isn't even Johnny, it's Helio, like some weird gas that's lighter than nothing, the stuff they shove up balloons for snotty kid's parties, the stuff that would make Einstein sound like an idiot if he swallowed it and spoke.

I hate admitting I know who you are, Johnny, when people ask me, then tell some crazy story about you; a story you made up to make yourself interesting, like that story of how you had a secret affair with that little girl from *Poltergeist,* sneaking her out of her house while her parents were asleep, but she's dead now so there's no way to prove it (that's very clever Johnny); or like the story of how you went to Harvard, but two days before you graduated you decided to drop out and take off for Guatemala—and no one can check up on you by contacting Harvard to ask if you ever even enrolled, because no one knows your first name is really Helio; or like the stories of how you used to work in a drug store and when you were

*Hard by the Ownership Mills on South 54th, **Lydia Tomkiw**'s house lay. It seemed like the best hiding place for the wanted women. So, commandeering a cab, the trio started off on a midnight run. As the taxi rolled up to the curb, its wheels sluiced varnish from a chemical spill by a blocked sewer onto the sidewalk. Lydia Tomkiw was half of the underground poetry band Algebra Suicide, whose CDs include* Real Numbers *and* Swoon. *Looking out from her screened-in porch, she saw the shrubbery glinting as if the moon had applied the polish.*

bored you'd poke holes into the prophylactics. Now come on, Johnny: do you really think that makes you attractive? Appealing? Enticing?

I hate your thin little body, Johnny, and I get SICK when I think of you at the laundromat, your skinny little underwear going around and around in the dryer while you lean against a top load washer, drinking Royal Crown Cola and reading your horoscope in the *National Enquirer*.

I hate your tiny little feet that you brag about all the time, Johnny, because they'll keep you out of the army because they don't make combat boots that size.

You comb your hair with an eggbeater; you have pale eyelashes like those of a pig; you clean your nails with swizzle sticks at bars; you blow your nose at the dinner table and then look at your kleenex endlessly, as if something really interesting came out of your head: Oh god, how I hate when you do that Johnny, especially at brunch. You won't eat anything pink or yellow or white, unless it has ketchup on it; and when you do eat, I hate watching your smacking lips—lips that look like they need to be inflated to 20 psi every 50,000 miles; miles your mouth runs, Johnny, saying nothing amusing or enlightening at all.

I hate the way you constantly inject that you lived in Switzerland for five years, and impregnated that stripper girl there, and you wouldn't name the baby LaTowanda like you wanted because it wasn't a government registered name: I've heard that one a million times, Johnny; that one, and all your travel stories: the one about how you think Bulgaria is Marxist, but Groucho Marxist, not Karl; and how in Hungary you came up with the idea that humans evolved from apes who ate morning glory seeds and expanded their minds; how you managed to stay in Sweden for two months without money, knowing only four phrases in Swedish which were "Hello," "Kiss me," "Fuck me," and "Goodbye."

I hate the way you smoke your cigarette, Johnny, holding it between your middle and ring finger, blowing smoke rings up over your head like you wish they would turn into a halo, for surely you believe you'll go to heaven, and when you end up in hell, you won't know why, proving things never really even out in the end. I hate the way you reach for a bottle of cognac, saying it'll take the edge off: you NEED some edge Johnny, some different edge. I hate that you need some edge.

I hate that you always whistle "Greensleeves" while shaving, that you won't use public toilets but when you use private ones, you never lift up the seat, leaving tiny puddles of yourself there for the next user to sit in.

I hate that one of your second toes is longer than the first and the other shorter; that you've slept with all my friends and now they're crazy; that you walk around all the time with a basket like a purse, with your wallet and a tube of toothpaste and a copy of the *Watchtower* in it. I hate that you call everyone "Dar-ling."

I hate that you're on the bad side of the phone company, Johnny, and you don't have a number so I can't call you in the middle of the night and hang up again and again and again, just to make sure you're not dreaming of anything nice.

I hate the pranks you play, Johnny: walking into a drugstore and asking the pharmacist, "Do you have cotton balls?" and when he says yes, cackling hysteri-cally; driving to an expressway phone, calling an old girlfriend up, then driving away, leaving the receiver dangling so she can't get any other calls; and, every month, you go to a bank and write, "This is a hold-up" on the back of deposit slips, randomly replacing them in their piles, leaving them for some unsuspecting customer to fill out and bring to the teller. Do you think that's cute, Johnny? Do you think it will never catch up with you, Johnny? Do you think, Johnny?

I hate you Johnny. I hate dreaming about you. I hate sharing the same air with you. I hate thinking about you. I hate the thought that you might ever think of me, whether you're clothed or not, drunk or straight, sedated or after seven cups of coffee. I hate the thought of you ever saying my name. I hate writing about you, Johnny—Johnny with the two *h*s and three *n*s and the heart over your *i*, Johnny, whose real name is Helio, whose first name probably means "the revolting one" in a foreign language; Johnny, I hate hating you, Johnny, and not knowing why.

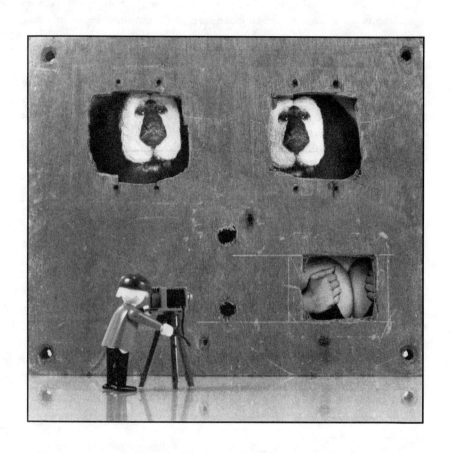

970-CHEESE

CAROL WIERZBICKI

I try to create fantasies out of common household materials; like, I see White Castle wrappers on the floor and think of their melted liquid cheese. Funny, I always think of the guy on the other end as standing in the middle of an empty field, receiver in hand. I need to put him in some kind of setting, to visualize, in order to make it work. Like this guy I'm talking to right now—he's standing in the middle of that field, looking like a lost conventioneer who just missed his plane.

And I tell him, "Look, I know you've been out of work for awhile, but all that matters right now is I'm rubbing you down with warm melted liquid cheese, right there in your bathtub, and you're sipping champagne and feeling like a king." Then I go on with the usual niceties, telling him how big he is, while staring at my Hoover upright.

I have to break it off, let him down gently, because soon the kids will be home from school. I tape all my conversations, play them back long after everyone has gone to bed, and keep the good ones for future reference. I lock them in the cabinet with the dusty liquor bottles—two vices safely contained.

My working position is usually cross-legged on the grayish-yellow linoleum with a Twinkie or Snowball or Kraft caramel balanced on one knee, reward at the ready. Kraft caramels especially make my mind wander . . . their color reminds me of my last dinner as a bachelorette. We all sat in Don's basement, half of us under the legal drinking age, downing champagne, White Castles, and instant butterscotch pudding.

I sometimes feel funny when I get the local free weekly paper and turn to the back and see some cotton candy–haired miss pouting above my number. A little guilty, like the product I'm providing is not quite

Carol Wierzbicki ran a profit-strapped detective agency situated in the South Loop. When the four of them (Lydia having joined bart and the girls) arrived in her office that morning with rumpled zoot suits and soiled dresses, she lounged back in her chair and polished off her tumbler of rock & rye. "Can I help you?" They looked rather sheepish. Carol Wierzbicki is one of the editors of The National Poetry Magazine of the Lower East Side and author of The Occupations. She drinks Glenfiddich Scotch. Deborah stepped forward.

"What kind of case is this?" Carol asked.

"Missing person," said Deborah, taking out a damaged photo. "We want you to locate these 100 people."

as advertised. The inhabitants of those back pages all look as though they're going to the same party, a party I'd never be invited to.

Melted liquid cheese . . . I wonder what it looks like—is it yellow or white? It doesn't come with anything, according to the drive-up menu, and costs only 39 cents. What does one do with . . . my mind is wandering as I'm talking with the line worker who just got laid off and who hasn't had a sex partner in seven months. I try to resuscitate the conversation by looking around our kitchen for inspiration. I can see I will need to buy either more appliances or more junk food—something with moving parts or an indescribable texture.

Everyone I talk to seems to be out of work. By the time I turn off the phone at three, I am exhausted. Making the switch from "970-SLUT" to "mom" is not an easy transition, not like flicking the switch on the Hoover from "Lo" pile to "Hi." Evenings after dinner, Don and I sometimes smoke a joint or two, put our feet up on the rusty lawn furniture, and when we get really silly I try out some of my monologues on him. "Talk faster," he says, "and maybe we could have the money to take the kids to Disney World by April."

Being paid to get and prolong obscene phone calls has its occupational hazards. When I shop at the supermarket and see men alone with their carts, I have to suppress the urge to go up to them and ask them their names, for some of them look like they might fit the voices I hear.

I snap to as a truck rolls by. The newly unemployed power plant custodian I am talking to is up to his neck in instant butterscotch pudding. Mustn't leave him stranded.

Stripe

LISA B. FALOUR

Stripe was one of Leo's best and most trusted phone girls. I met her in January of 1982 when I signed up to work as a dominatrix in one of Leo's sleazy whorehouses. When I saw her, I wondered what such a class act was doing in such a dive.

My reasons for going to work for Leo seemed fairly simple at the time. In retrospect, my entire involvement with his establishments, and with prostitution, seems like a distant, complex mystery lost in a tangled web of intangible psychological puzzles. But as I've said, at the time everything seemed so simple.

I'd tried the straight life in late 1981, working as a receptionist, and quickly realized I was going to starve. I longed for The Life again. I failed to see how I was expected to survive in New York on my $11,000-a-year salary at the public relations firm where I answered the phones, did all the overflow typing, and assisted all the account executives when their own assistants were too busy. The day after Christmas in 1981, I decided that I needed a new boyfriend, so I held a Boyfriend Interview. I invited a series of men over that day, excusing myself when I had tired of each, claiming I had "relatives coming over for the holiday." One of those men was Max. A couple of weeks later, I was head over heels in love with him, but he lived at home with his parents, and wrote novels and "visual poetry" he couldn't sell. He also chain-smoked and his hands shook. I wondered why I was set on fire by his kiss, but I was. Realizing I was hopelessly hooked, I set out to make a life that would include him within it.

He said he wouldn't see me unless I had my own apartment. Having my own place was something I'd never bothered with in New York. I was happy and comfortable subletting with various roommates, and didn't mind not owning any furniture of my own, or

The police had raided Roxor's, the club **Lisa B. Falour** worked at, and caught her with her panties down wielding a whip over a federal judge who was masticating a stale Brillo pad at her command. In the cell she heard that the bulls were turning the town upside down about the "Roller Whitehair" case. Lisa was a hostess at Club 57 and dominatrix. She's been publishing Bikini Girl magazine for 10 years. Borrowing a red pen from a pross, she jotted down a list of relevant phone numbers on her forearm. "Maybe there's some money in this 'Whitehot' deal," she thought.

storing all my clothes in trash bags. But Max insisted I get my own place. He suggested Bay Ridge. I was vaguely terrified. I was unfamiliar with Brooklyn, although I had already lived there for about a year, and didn't even know where Bay Ridge was. I managed to get an apartment of my own in the same building I had been living in with Michael, my bi-coastal, forever-absent roommate, and I was then faced with the challenge of furnishing it and enticing Max to stay with me there.

I knew I couldn't pay for the rent on the place and furnish it on my receptionist pay, so I decided to go back into prostitution. I already knew a lot about the world of S&M, so I selected a kinky whorehouse and "interviewed" there. I was hired almost on the spot.

My first night at work, I had a bladder infection and was passing blood, but I was so desperate for money, I toughed it out. I sent Angel, the "Hawkeye" for the place (semi-bouncer, go-fer, and money-bearer) out for a big jug of cranberry juice and I slugged it down in between sessions. I caught on in a big way with the clients at this whorehouse. I usually worked three nights a week, from 6 to 10, after my straight job, and always averaged four sessions a night—very good, according to management. For each dominant session I got $30 an hour, and no tips were forthcoming. I started doing submissive sessions, for which I received about $80. As a "switchable," I had an opportunity to make bigger money.

This place was the Grand Central of sleaze. But that's another chapter. This is about Stripe, who answered the phones there and also answered the phones at Leo's other houses of prostitution. He had several. One catered to old men. The other catered to straight men who occasionally wanted a little kinkiness. The other—"The Penthouse in the Sky," as its advertisements described it—catered to so-called big spenders. I worked there one night when they were in a jam—all their girls had called in sick—and was horrified to find that the tricks shelled out $100 an hour, but that price included "everything." A leering Hasidic Jew became angry when I was unable to perform Greek to his satisfaction, after we'd already had regular intercourse twice in the sixty-minute session. Enough of this Penthouse shit, I decided, and I never worked there again.

Stripe spoke in a clear monotone, and was very efficient. She also made it a point to dress as well as possible, and could have passed for a proper receptionist in any straight business. Her long, semi-wavy red hair was always worn conservatively pulled back and up, and she never expressed a desire to turn tricks herself, seeming shocked at the very concept, although she never looked down her nose at us working girls. She was, in fact, always cordial and as polite as could be to everyone, and I found out she was only making between $100 and $200 for a 14-hour workday, and that she was expected to clean up and vacuum the whorehouses each night before leaving.

Later, I learned her real name was Rose, but I also heard her real name was Cynthia. She was from Altoona, and didn't get on well with her family. She had a Serbian guy named Zile, who also worked for Leo as one of his Hawkeyes, living with her, and she had an aging, decrepit standard poodle named Sophocles, whose death sent her into howls of agony the likes of which I've never before heard emanate from a human throat. For years, she and Zile carried the dog out to the street to shit, and she paid hundreds of dollars to the vet, yet refused to put the dog to sleep. And when the dog finally died, she went completely crazy, as if that was all she had in this life to love and to care for. None of us understood her.

It was always good to see her when I went to work after my straight jobs. Most of the other phone girls were extremely kooky—even dangerous. Stripe always seemed calm and in control, even when she was drunk or stoned. I heard she liked to combine cocaine with heroin, but I never saw any evidence of this, so I always gave her the benefit of the doubt. If I had a bottle of booze, she'd always accept a shot gratefully, and I guess she was an alcoholic, like me. But in general, she was a joy to behold and I felt I could rely on her while I worked.

I wanted to do her a favor. I was too cheap to tip her, and I suppose I regret this in retrospect, but really, Leo's houses weren't tipping environments, if you follow me. I knew an elderly gentleman who was well-to-do and had been a ballet dancer in his youth. He loved to tie up and spank women, and to take pictures of them. He was very generous, and was always offering to take me on ocean cruises with him. I told him to call Stripe. They did, in fact, go on two cruises together, and may still be doing it to this day. He took pictures of her that he promised he'd show to no one, but of course, I saw the pictures, and I saw Stripe dressed in negligees, sucking his cock. They looked happy together, and Stripe gave me a beautiful evening bag and a bottle of very expensive perfume after her first trip.

I also tried to get her a straight job as a receptionist for the investment banking firm I was working for. She did well on the interview but failed the psychological test they administered. When the headhunter asked why she couldn't attend a follow-up interview, she blurted out the truth about what she really did for a living, and apparently, that ended things. I still keep Stripe in mind, though, to be a receptionist if I start up my own business. I don't mind that she's walked on the wild side. Her middle name, as far as I'm concerned, is "Grace," as in "Under Pressure," and I'd trust her. After all, I trusted her with my life for two years.

She still sends me a nice, old-fashioned Christmas card every year that breaks my heart. She still admires me, quietly, saying little complimentary things to me in the notes she writes inside the cards. I still want to save her.

Katrine and the Nazis (Excerpt from "An Absence of Angels")

CHRISTIAN X. HUNTER

"When I saw you in the restaurant
you could see I was no debutante . . . "

—Deborah Harry

It had been three nights running that I'd fallen asleep in my clothes. I had left the telephone in the bathroom on the edge of the bathtub and it rang just loud enough to wake me at the other end of the apartment.

It was Katrine, calling from a pay phone; she'd lost her job, her mind, and her contact lenses. She'd spent the earlier part of the evening getting hopelessly shit-faced in the Honeytree, one of those sterile, faceless Third Avenue bars near Gramercy Park, frequented by fresh-faced cop cadets, and the occasional vet from the Thirteenth Precinct. Four of them had been providing her with an endless supply of whiskey sour doubles and trying to persuade her to join them for a different kind of happy hour, over at the Martha Washington Hotel.

Katrine had ditched the rookies after last call and now she wanted to come by and hang out at the loft, because it was too far

Is it ever easy to find your dream? The door had opened a crack and the bouncer at the club, **Christian X. Hunter***, had caught a glimpse of a young girl, naked, head downmost, leonine hair fallen like water through a strainer, as she swung from a trapeze in the brothel's Carny Lounge. Something about the jaded, woozy look on her face had sent him stumbling against the wall, blinking and dropping his blackjack. Christian was a guitarist for Dog Sees God and Disciples of*

75

to walk to her girlfriend's place, only . . . she couldn't figure how to get over to my place (which three weeks ago had been our place). She'd gotten so loaded, she couldn't even figure where she was calling from. You see, she couldn't read street signs without eyeglasses (she refuses to even own a pair) and there was no way she could ask a stranger because the street was deserted.

I thought I'd keep her on the telephone until either she became clear-headed enough to recognize her surroundings or maybe a cop came along and gave her directions. I had her give me the number of the pay phone so I could call her back, though she insisted on using her own change until it ran out.

For the next few minutes she alternated between crying about her shitty luck and apologizing for waking me up. I carried the phone into the kitchen and re-heated some coffee while I listened to her talk. She said she had a big secret to tell me. The "secret" was, she'd spent six days kicking a bundle-a-day dope habit in the finished basement of her mother's house in Bellmore. I'd known. She said if she could stay clean for a while, maybe she could get her job back at the Mudd Club and earn enough money to get her bass player Cookie's guitar out of the pawnshop before the six-month ticket ran out. And just maybe Cookie might let her stay at her place, which would be great, because she hated living in that women's hotel by the park. Katrine said everything but what she really wanted to say, which was: Can I come back to you?

She started going on about how she was going to lose her mind if she listened one more time to her mother begging on the phone with her to come back home. Which isn't to say she didn't get along with her mother; it's just that the woman was always in mourning, because two weeks didn't go by when one of her cousins didn't die some kind of tragic death. To me, her mother seemed kind of saintly, down to earth . . . except for the holy cookie.

Mrs. Facio had this butter cookie she'd baked sixteen years ago, which had come out of the oven looking like a profile of Christ. It was triple-wrapped in tin-foil and she only took it out of the freezer at Christmas or Easter and only for rela-tives and close friends of the family, although sometimes she took it out to put on her husband's forehead when he had an especially bad migraine.

⟨

I came back to reality as Katrine dropped another nickel in the phone, and as the recording of the operator's voice cut out, I heard Katrine hollering out a request for directions at some guy in the street, but he was already on the other side of the avenue and apparently hadn't heard her. Katrine came back on the line sobbing, but stopped long enough to light up a Newport.

I asked her to try and describe the neighborhood. But that was a no-go because the stores on the block were all dark and she couldn't read the name of the restaurant fifteen feet away without walking away from the phone, and she wouldn't do that. Finally I brainstormed that she should take a cab over and I offered to pay for it. While I was trying to convince her to take the cab, Katrine rummaged around in her hand bag trying to retrieve her cigarette lighter. She talked around the cigarette as she tried to light it, only half hearing my words. So, just when I thought I'd gotten through to her ... she ran out of nickels and the phone went dead. I called back to the pay-phone and it rang. Must have rung eight or nine times before she picked it up. In a suspicious, just-awakened voice she asked:

"Who is it?" as if it might have been a wrong number or maybe her mother.

I began telling her to write the address down so she could hand it to the cabbie when she found one. Then I heard the metal ribbed cord that connects the handset to the coin box making a tinny sawing sound as it looped and twisted and rubbed against itself, followed by the sound of the handset cracking repeatedly against the glass panel of the phone booth ... then silence. I thought possibly she'd dropped the phone in order to hail a cab. Then a large warm male voice came on the line. He introduced himself and said:

"Hey, is your friend sick or what? She's sitting on the floor of the phone booth, her eyes are rolled back in her head, and there's some kind of white stuff coming out of her mouth. I think she's trying to talk."

He wanted to know if he should call a doctor. I explained that Katrine was a diabetic, and that the white stuff in her mouth was no doubt the remains of those nasty-tasting glucose wafers she always carried with her.

I tried to calm the guy down and get him to tell me what intersection they were near, and then I heard Katrine screaming at the top of her not inconsiderable lungs, telling him to get the fuck out of the phone booth, the sound of the receiver being dropped ...

Rage, and author of An Absence of Angels. *By the rules of the establishment, he couldn't enter any of the "playrooms" unless paged by one of the girls. These party hostesses came through a separate entrance, and the more discreet avoided all contact with the help, leaving quickly with upturned coat collars and wraparound shades. He found a way to split open a seam along the Carny room's mirrored wall-paneling, against which he pressed his scarred cheek.*

C h r i s t i a n X . H u n t e r

and it was Katrine back on the line. She seemed lucid, but I told her to write down the address anyhow and get in a cab. As she was hanging up the phone she asked me what I was doing for Christmas. I agreed to think about that and then hung up the phone. Then I remembered the coffee.

I took it off the stove and poured myself a cup. I took one taste of the stale, three-day-old coffee and dumped it in the sink. But I know that I must have been smiling, because I was thinking about Christmas. Not the Christmas to come, but rather a Christmas gone by four years before. I was remembering the first time going out to Katrine's parent's house.

We took the Long Island Railroad, which I always dread. I have this fear that the LIRR is a cleverly disguised time machine, and the more distance it puts between us and Penn Station, the further back in time we go.

Picture a train weaving its way past lawnmowers rusting in snowbanks, one-story warehouses, petrified playgrounds, boarded-up movie houses, and ghost families wandering aimlessly on the passed-by empty train platforms; all fading in the stasis of winter light. In this angst fantasy I become marooned way out in the Dairy Queen wastelands where fate deals me a cruel blow; I become a sno-mobile salesman in Valley Stream. I see myself looking out the dealership's showroom window, wistfully remembering Kiev pierogis at four a.m., midnight movies at the St. Mark's Cinema, Sunday night at Danceteria, and riding home from a party on my motorcycle minutes before daybreak, waving good morning to all the restless cowboys below the West Side Highway. It's a regular "Lost In Space" scenario. As far as I'm concerned, Nassau County could as well be the moon.

☾

The first thing I did when we arrived at the house was to call Long Island Railroad information to double-check the schedule of trains returning to Penn Station. Then we went into the living room and I met the family. Katrine introduced me first to Mrs. Facio, then her stepdad Mike (a retired donkey homicide cop), and lastly fat Uncle Gaetano, who'd just been released from Pilgrim State. All in all, it promised to be your typical be-on-your-best-behavior-and-try-not-to-embarrass-your-friend-in-front-of-her-parents type evening.

In the first twenty minutes, I got the up-to-date listings of tragic deaths, had six cups of espresso, saw a vast selection of embarrassing family photos, and was privileged to have an up-close and personal front-row viewing of the sacred cookie. After the cookie, Katrine dragged me out of Mrs. Facio's kitchen and whispered something to me about her stepdad's gun collection down in the basement.

The basement was about fifteen degrees cooler than the rest of the house, and immediately comfortable to me by virtue of its being a disused and abandoned place. The absence of red-faced wine-drinking family members came over me like forty milligrams of sodium pentothal injected intravenously, and when Katrine whispered the word "GUNS" in my ear I found myself remembering a night I'd spent at Katrine's old apartment on East Thirty-Third Street.

(

Katrine and I had walked into her apartment and found her boyfriend Double Johnny passed out on the toilet with a bottle of Napoleon brandy in his lap and an empty Dilaudid bottle lying in the sink. He was breathing, but wouldn't regain consciousness for at least ten to fourteen hours.

Katrine was really pissed. You see, Double Johnny was a big motherfucker and there was no way we were going to get him off the toilet, out of the bathroom and on to the couch or bed. So Katrine and I took turns peeing in the bathtub and then balancing various bottles of shampoo and other toiletry items on his unconscious head.

When she'd finished applying blusher and brown lipstick to Double Johnny's gray/green features, Katrine emptied his pockets and relieved him of all his recently purchased drugs. She didn't, however, touch the cash.

Now, if you were to take into account just how high Katrine and I were, it might seem hypocritical that Double Johnny's carefree lack of consciousness, and the graceless choice of location in which he may or may not have decided to abandon said consciousness, should cause Katrine to be so angry, not to mention disrespectful, to Double Johnny; unless, that is, you also took into account that in a house full of dope fiends it is permissible to render uninhabitable any room except the bathroom. So Katrine and I sat out in the kitchen drinking Cokes and smoking Kools while she gave me with a detailed account of her latest sex fantasy, this one involving Nazis and large-caliber guns. All the details of that fantasy came back to me down in the basement of Katrine's parent's house when she opened a foot-locker containing a small arsenal her stepdad had collected over the years.

From the look on her face it was clear that she wanted to flesh out this fantasy. I could only hope that she didn't want me to make Nazi-type dialogue, because I was sure I wouldn't be able to talk like Werner Von Braun and keep a straight face while playing "Nazi Slave Master" with nineteen-year-old Katrine in her parent's finished basement.

In the locker I found a 9 mm semi-automatic Walther PPK. After making sure it wasn't loaded I turned to Katrine; giving her my best fascist grimace I made the sign for silence. With the gun in my right hand and the back of her hair in my left, I dragged her into the little laundry cubicle, which would have to serve as the "interrogation room."

The ceiling light was broken so I left the door part-way open. Placing the flat of the barrel against the side of her throat just below her ear, I shoved her, face first, against the wall. Looking around I saw a radio plugged into an extension cord. I pulled them apart, yanked Katrine's hands behind her back, and tied her wrists securely together with the extension cord. So far, Katrine hadn't said a word, so I grabbed her by the elbow and turned her around to face me. She was a vision of pure and unfailing scorn; her deep-set eyes radiated a "spit in your face" disdain, so real that I had to take a second and remind myself that this was her fantasy. I'd become momentarily sidetracked by her utterly convincing look of live steam contempt. However, Nazis thrive on contempt. So I grabbed her by the throat and shoved her against the washer-dryer combo, which made a shitload of noise. For a second I considered the kitchen just above us, full of Irish cops and small-time hoods from Mrs. Facio's side of the family, all getting . . . very . . . drunk.

The Good Witch

MICHAEL CARTER

Okay, the subtle jarring of the temples hadn't yet subsided; vision still a touch foggy, yet a bit of hot brew might rectify that. Well, when asked if, "wasn't she like one of those people in a Tarkovsky flick"—after moving her bowl of miso with one hand, without touching it—she gleefully responded "Yes!" and following dinner, noted matter-of-factly that "the air felt like velvet." And indeed it did, one of those moist after-the-thundershower summer evenings not so unlike that year previous, when she'd first entered the story—a curious blend of tropical feathers and gentle witchery . . . Ah, so now she's no doubt in her large apartment playing Beethoven's final quartet on that old violin, with one hand . . . CRACK—the coffee water's been left on too long and outside a sleeping bum with one sock missing wakes up to hear sirens and warehouse workers, rolls up his tired eyes and drifts back . . . Was it then, or sometime slightly later, that certainty overtook its other: or perhaps some interval before that could only be seen from a later perspective; yes, the way dirty pictures finger-sketched on a steamy mirror will later come back to haunt . . . It was her special power to plunge into the crowd at will and merely to choose: because this one interests *me*.

Focus then on a typical throng at a typical art or music or film affair, where careers and reputations in various stages of development or decline come to feed off one another, to ricochet and find a small degree of mutual sympathy, albeit the smallest fraction necessary. She approaches without warning, then turns slowly though decisively away (not coyly and not emphatically). Meanwhile, they're discussing the upcoming heavyweight fight, or some aging socialite's cleavage, that the Court might well back the landlord

"She comes and goes like smoke," Christian told **Michael Carter**. *"I tried to talk to her on the street and she shoved me into the gutter."*

"I know a detective in the South Loop," Mike offered.

"Fuck that. I want you to be the detective."

Michael is the editor of the seminal and encyclopaedic RedTape magazine, curator, music reviewer, and polished dancer. *"I'll pay you to follow her, man. Please,"* Christian pleaded. *"She hangs out with this slut from Roxor's. They go out after work to billboard parties, fish picnics, symposiums, lectures."*

Michael shrugged. *"Why me?"*

81

and not the tenant in this instance, in which case it's Brooklyn or Montana . . . Two elderly artists with beards and not much more to show for 20 years of shoddy hustling debate the quality of a certain friend's paint, "It cracks." "Not if you're careful—but it ain't all its cracked up to be . . . " And against this thick impasto of visceral conversation . . . sharply punctuated by upstairs neighbors dropping missiles disguised as flower pots cuz the din's cut into an otherwise lucrative crack business—her eyes suddenly and just as decisively become interested, every suggestion implicitly answered by "Yes."

Fear of cars and the attraction of bright lights initially brought her to the city . . . A desperately cold East Village night, the kind when uncounted numbers of the homeless hurl themselves at the brick walls of abandoned buildings, and rococo icicles glaze the panorama of ruins, hookers strutting bundled in two or three coats yet still managing to expose a little leg . . . "Got a match?"—It was a line she'd heard before, though never in this strictly urban context: the man's eyes told her he didn't give a damn about the crumbling cigarette that dangled from his gaping mouth. He'd caught her scent before she'd even rounded the corner and it was driving him crazy. Of course, he was probably crazy already . . . She lingered for just a second, then, yet obviously too late, decided to ignore his request and keep walking. He moved a little in front of her, grabbed his balls and started talking about Jesus. Then he reached round her body and shoulder with a cold arm like an iron clamp . . . All grew black for an instant, and silent . . . She opened her eyes to glimpse first the slavering lips and then the intent, bloodshot eyeballs, kinda rollin' aroun' in opposite directions, and she returned his gaze with a penetrating glare . . . instantly his nostrils began to constrict; it was painful, and cut off his oxygen. Nor could his mouth inhale, but only release, issuing animal moans and screams as he scampered off.

The next ten weeks saw a progression of unsteady jobs and even unsteadier acquaintances. For a while she worked counting the number of cars that would pass a given intersection; an easy, unrewarding and sometimes tedious waste of time. There was a short stint as night manager in a fake French restaurant that specialized in rock lobster bouillabaisse; she even filled in one night for a friend on a phone sex job—she had to quit midway through the shift, when an excited customer was overcome by an asthma attack. The big break came during breakfast at a sidewalk cafe when a well-known club owner with a Swiss-German accent (remembered briefly from the French restaurant) led off with something like "Those eyes are a crime . . . " and finished with a job offer, only coatcheck but what the hell, maybe in a month a spot at the bar . . . As she left, he embraced her like an old friend and said to call later that week. She did, began work the next day and performed ably, only trouble issuing from a famous disco diva who complained quite vociferously that something was missing from her left pocket, something IMPORTANT, and after screaming loudly for the manager, somehow found it in her right. A month passed and it was well known one of the bartendresses had had more than enough of the late night excitement and was set to quit. When she mentioned this to the owner—and didn't he remember the deal?—he requested a private interview and she knew what was meant . . . After uncorking the oversized bottle of Dom Perignon, his large perspiring fingers started to reach for her exposed shoulder and she drew instinctively away. "But baby . . ." "'But baby'

nothing" . . . He stared into her agate-charged eyes as if to say "Hey, look, *I'm* in charge here" . . . It was then his prized Chinese urn fell on its side with a loud crash and collapsed into a heap of Chinese puzzle pieces and a huge ugly moth began to noisily circumnavigate the overhead lamp . . . Not long after that she got the bar job, and he never harrassed again, but would sometimes proffer quiet, searching, fearful glances. Once, he was about to question her about skimming off the till (which she was) but a lump the size of a tomato formed in the middle of his throat, and he stopped short.

Meanwhile she perfected an incipient power to choose lovers, making it clear at the outset that romance for her was a strictly ephemeral engagement. However, one warming afternoon in East River Park, distractedly watching the barges pass beneath the bombed-out Brooklyn factories, she caught the eye of an older man whom she would only ever know as "Tom," and of whom she would in time grow quite fond. He had a little money, and twice took her to the opera, which she had never seen, at Lincoln Center. The first was *Tristan und Isolde;* corny but effective. He also had a funny dog, half doberman and half pitbull, whom he called Hank. They would take trips with Hank, to the ocean and to the woods. Tom said Hank could foretell earthquakes, because he'd been born during one, but she never believed this. The best times they had were at the ocean, in a lean-to he'd concocted out of driftwood and seaweed: each time he began with her, though calmly, as if he'd never had a woman before, and ended as if he might never again, and she revelled in all the attention he paid her in between and after, caressing every inch of her body, sweetly tippling her saliva and come ... Then, it was an evening in August and a thunderous rainstorm had just subsided, he met her, drenched, at the club—which he had never before done—and said that it had to be over, that he had a wife and loved her, that he had confessed their affair in a moment of contrition. She quietly said "excuse me" and went to retrieve some emptied glasses. He understood and quickly left, casting one last glance as Orpheus might Eurydice, but withstood the temptation to follow, and that was the last of each other either had seen.

Outside a crowded movie theatre playing some recondite art film, she began to reconsider the bar job, the club, everything that had happened since the big move to the City, even and especially Tom and how little she knew about him. He had lost an inside finger but would never say how. Once, he had been talking in his sleep and muttered something about Barcelona. He was obviously not Spanish but seemed well traveled. She guessed she liked that aura of mystery about him, and had deliberately chosen not to enquire. But now these questions, as well as his personal absence, began to nag. She'd taken other lovers, much as she had done previously; however, something now was missing, and she sped them gone as quickly as possible, often before dawn ... Even thinking these thoughts she held fast (though perfunctorily) to another's hot and muscled arm as if to the wheel of a skiff over uncertain seas.

This much she related over an evening meal of shiitake mushrooms and rice. Her silken black hair become tangled by the afternoon winds—for it was fall and the leaves were flying—she looked less like a witch than a mischievous gnome. She started to speak of her childhood, of a pig ranch in Iowa, and how smart they were, the pigs. She gave up eating them when she was nine. One crisp clear winter's night she went up a stubby hill looking for the comet Kohoutek, which the papers had said would pass this way, and she heard the unmistakable sound of a pig's grunt emanating from the trees below. She opened her mouth and let out a strange bellow, clearly intended to taunt the pig, and sure enough she soon heard its monstrous bulk approaching. (She was only nine and the pig really was quite huge.) But what had begun as game soon turned to nightmare as the pig lunged toward her. She stood frozen, staring right into its eyes, its vengeful, wild, animal eyes—and suddenly the pig stood stockstill, pivoted on one massive foot and beat a quick path down the incline ... At this she grew quite excited and those same eyes, now grown, beamed with wonder and pride; the rice wine was having its effect, surely, but clearly something more was happening as well . . . "Did you tell this to that man, to Tom?" "I tried to, but he'd always change the subject—funny thing, though, he always avoids the directness of my gaze, as if he knew . . . " Then she cast those same dark brown beacons this way and the contents of a year opened and poured onto the table: In feathers at the party and she'd been dancing on the countertop like some raindance or painted Maori, how could you not notice something like that; and after, talking a short while of Shakespeare, she was hot on *The Winter's Tale,* especially the Bear. She was with some lug, a fairly close friend actually, but in this context a lug just the same, and so things might have to wait. Later, there were the half dozen chance meetings, and always enchantments, though not much more . . . And now she here finally and her preference obviously—what was that line about the Tarot, something about this pair as the King and Queen of Cups? Then, wakening from this brief reverie to find her body stretched so close, subtle fingers searching—and, making love, the bodies seemed to levitate just a bit, or was it merely oh so nice to think so, and waves crashed inside one another, until the very walls began to shake and then to collapse, fragments falling like feathers upon the empty bed.

The Sobriety Thing
MOLLY MOYNIHAN

The sobriety thing is you stole two jam jars full of whiskey out of this barrel of scotch shaped like a redwood to take on the 10th grade camping trip which was supposed to bring your class together after Bucky Salt was expelled from school for taking Melinda Larsen's sculpture of an Airedale and dropping it off the roof during Mr. Fellows' biology class when we were dissecting fetal pigs and it sounded like the bomb dropped but Mr. Fellows was on whatever it was he inhaled in the biology closet, ether or maybe gas like the stuff I get at the dentist's that always makes me want to make a speech about the nature of the universe. So nothing happened except Dougie Murray took our fetal pig and put it into Claudia Bentley's bookbag so when she opened it at lunch she fainted (someone said her eyelids were quivering) but I wasn't there because I was on the girl's hockey field with Larry Feinstein the drug pusher smoking this hash he said his mother bought in Sri Lanka. And the real reason they expelled Bucky Salt was because his parents didn't have any money.

So anyway, I drank one of the jars of scotch and then I told Lisa Sommers that yes, she was fat, and yes, I did almost have total sex with Carter Sykes whom she was practically engaged to since dancing school and I would have finished except I suddenly remembered that Carter was a complete jock-misogynist-misanthropic-rascist-limp-dicked WASP who liked the Beach Boys. I left her crying under a fir tree and went to the rec cabin where people were dancing to the Bee Gees and I got Warren Dikes, the AV geek, to play "Stairway to Heaven" and I did a striptease and then I told Madeline Burnett that her father had an

Taking tickets at the Pez Theater was no picnic, **Molly Moynihan** *thought. A lot of rough trade went through the padded doors that led into the 100-seat auditorium. But the night Rollo spoke it was like they opened a kennel. The riffraff were rifling the soda machines, spilling Cheez Doodles in the ashtrays, and cutting squares from the rug for impromptu hair-pieces. Molly has published a number of novels, includ-ing* Parting Is All We Know of Heaven. *She moved to London after her stint at the Pez. The theater was named after Pez candy, by the way, because of its unusual marquee, from which a large tongue pro-truded. If a strong arm pressed hard enough on the tongue, a dollop of fla-vored oxygen squirted out.*

affair with the wife of the guy who used to mow our lawn which wasn't exactly confirmed since my sister had heard my mother whisper something that sounded vaguely like that—but who the fuck cared? Madeline was one of the people who said Bucky Salt deserved to be expelled and when she started crying about her father I said I'd also heard something about her mother and the lawn guy and maybe she was really HIS daughter which wasn't a reflection on him because he used to let me drive his truck.

It was the acid that made things go out of control. Larry Feinstein's purple haze which his mother brought home from some organic LSD farm in northern California. Since it didn't work immediately and Larry swore it was organic, I took two more and since I was already naked, I jumped into the pool at the bottom of the waterfall which was supposedly off-limits and since it was October, I thought I'd entered into the soul of ice. I mean like ice was God and I worshipped it and then I worshipped Larry Feinstein which was definitely drugs because he'd always reminded me of a gerbil or some sort of nocturnal burrowing rodent like maybe something we'd dissect in biology—a cross between a mole and a gopher—but now he had this aura like a black light poster and he was singing a Leonard Cohen song:

Suzanne takes you down to her place by the river . . .
She feeds you tea and oranges that come all the way from China.
And just when you want to tell her that you have no love to give her
She gets you on her wavelength and she lets the river answer
That you've always been her lover . . .
And you touch her perfect body with your mind.

And this other shit about the garbage and the flowers and I was thinking about Mrs. Feinstein and how she gave Larry all these drugs and how cool that was and my mother never believing me when I lied and said I was going to the library which I never was but when I have a kid and she lies to me I'm going to believe her. And also how old my parents are and that getting old is really weird and maybe they'll invent something which will mean I'll always be the same age I was then which isn't possible because I'm older now but I think, like Dylan said: "Oh, but I was so much older then, I'm younger than that now." And that got me started thinking about Dylan and the sixties which got really complicated so I felt like Suzanne and no one could touch my perfect body except Larry and it wasn't with his mind and I don't like parts of me, like my neck is too short and Larry would have been gross but I was thinking that he'd transmuted and become Leonard Cohen and he'd make me very famous by writing songs about me which my parents would hate after I died which would be soon because that fucking organic acid was making me feel like I was about to explode.

At that point I may have just crawled off to the woods to die but the girl's volleyball coach, Ms. Trowel, arrived and began to ask these really existential questions like "Why are you naked?" and then she asked Larry, "Why is she naked?" but Larry was face down in moss, this mulch, like he was trying to become soil and then Ms. Trowel ignored him anyway because after all he was a guy and Ms. Trowel wasn't all that interested in guys. Most of us didn't mind Ms. Trowel because being girls at this stupid private school, no one paid much attention to us. The boys got all the money in the sports budget to do things like play soccer in the Soviet Union and hockey in Finland. Ms. Trowel wasn't a pervert like the guy teachers who pretended to be all worried about you and then backed you into walls and said things like: "I can really relate to your pain."

I mean even if Ms. Trowel was a dyke like Gertrude Stein at least she didn't treat us like morons. Like children which we never were. Except for Debbie Liberty who tried to start a pep club and only one person went and he was meant to be in Driver's Ed. Debbie kept announcing pep rallies during homeroom when everyone was hung over or pretending to be and finally she just shut up and stopped saying: "Hey, you guys! Where's your spirit?" when Bradley Moffat suggested she might feel more comfortable in public school where kids did weird shit. The thing was, I wasn't sure why I was naked and since I'd left the ice pool I could feel myself turning blue although I couldn't actually feel my body or anything since I'd eaten that organic acid. So I put my clothes back on and Larry separated from the mulch and for some reason Ms. Trowel left us alone and I went back to the dance and the record stuck and the word "dark" was repeated twenty times which made me peak again and it was so cool just sitting in the corner throwing marshmallows at Bitsy Binderman saying "Dark" and then "Bitsy" and then throwing a marshmallow.

Larry was on the roof of the rec building receiving telepathic messages from an alien life force so I wandered off again and spent the rest of the night inside the part of the tree where all the branches intersect. There was definitely something happening with red ants.

The next morning Lisa Sommers turned me into the Honor Committee for my own good she said but I know it was because I called her a major blimp and also for the stuff about Carter Sykes which I forgot but sensed to be unflattering. The headmaster, Duncan Blodgett, smiled very hard and said:

"I understand you may have been under the influence of mind-altering substances."

And I said: "Three hits of purple haze and a jam jar full of Glenfiddich."

M   o   l   l   y   M   o   y   n   i   h   a   n

Mr. Blodgett looked confused and coughed and smiled harder and called me Amy (my name is Emily): "Amy," he said, "you're a nice girl."

Maybe he thought I was my sister. Her name is Amanda and she's not a nice girl either but she never took LSD on a school function.

But this sobriety thing? Well, this was all pretty normal. I mean normal for me. Like this was the first time I ever took acid and I gather three hits was a lot but I never was what you'd call a social drinker. What I'm trying to say is, some people are trouble straight but drunk they're like a natural disaster, a typhoon or an earthquake or one of those Texas ice storms that come from nowhere and when the sun comes out again the cars are piled up and everybody's dead. People shake their heads and wonder if they have insurance.

But the real reason I quit was Larry Feinstein. He didn't come back from that mulch thing and they couldn't get him off the rec building until Mr. Foster, the 10th grade college advisor, pretended to be on *Star Trek* and did the entire Tribble episode with Larry playing Captain Kirk and Mr. Foster had to be everybody else including the women.

Larry Feinstein was the first man to ever see me naked. For that, I got sober.

Love and Death
DAVID L. ULIN

As a boy, he used to think about killing his parents. He would lie at night in his narrow child's bed, staring at the ribbons of street light that came in through the blinds, and wonder how to do it. He was four years old, and did not understand about responsibility, about the way only we can make our dreams turn real. Instead, he would take his Captain Action doll, an action figurine with small plastic weapons that fit perfectly into his tiny molded hands, and position him so he was aiming at the door. Then, when his mother and father came in to say goodnight, he would whisper, "Blam, Blam, Blam," under his breath.

Other times, he would make believe he was Superman. He would dress up in his blue pajamas, pull on red socks up to his knees, and tie a red bath towel around his neck. His mother even made him a costume one year for Halloween, cutting the Superman logo from a pattern in a book she had bought, and attaching it with great care to the front of his pajama shirt. She made him boots, too, with that distinctive Superman double point in front, and a cape that bore the logo on the back. All his friends thought it was the greatest thing they'd ever seen. He accepted their compliments, but secretly he hated them, and her, because the outfit featured boxer shorts, instead of the tight red briefs that the real superhero wore. He could never put the costume on without being painfully aware of that inaccuracy, of the fact that it was a facsimile and he just a boy who wanted to be something special. After wearing it a couple of times, he put the costume in the back of his closet, where it lay until, years later, it was thrown out in the course of packing for a move.

There were certain things he never forgot. Like asking his father what happened to people after they died.

*The only person Carol could identify in the crowd photo, aside from herself (she didn't tell the quartet that she was at the lecture) was the police operative **David Ulin** from the West Coast. She had met him on "The Case of the Chaste Panties." A dwarf who always wore a fez had been goosing young men as they bent over to observe a flea circus. David tailed the perpetrator to Chicago and there called in Carol. David is the author of* Cape Cod Blues, *book editor for the L.A.* Reader, *and co-editor of* Instant Classics. *He and Carol had followed the villain into a lecture, but left crestfallen, thinking they had lost him. Only now, by perusing the xeroxed photo, did the young detective recognize the telltale hat.*

He was six years old at the time, and, even years later, he remembered the circum-stances of the conversation perfectly. They were in the car, a fire engine red 1967 Ford Galaxie 500, driving from Long Beach, California, to a cousin's house in the San Fernando Valley, and, as usual, he was leaning over the front seat from the back, pretending he was an adult. He remembered that they were in an alley at the back of their apartment complex; they had just pulled out of the carport, and to their right was the dumpster into which he had recently crashed his bike, cutting up his hand. When he asked the question, his father slowly stopped the car, then turned around and looked him straight in the eye. He could see his mother, her face twisted in uncertainty and concern, and he remembered wondering if it was something they had discussed, or if he'd caught them off guard with this one. Even then, he knew them well enough to understand that they were parents with a plan, parents who'd thought out an approach to child-rearing and who were now trying to fit him into that mold.

Everything went still. The silence seemed to grow wings, to take flight, all of them clutched in its claws like animals caught in the grasp of some incomprehen-sibly vast bird of prey. The only one who didn't feel it was his two-year-old broth-er, buckled in, playing by himself with a small plastic brontosaurus in the corner of the back seat. Finally, he asked the question again.

His father took a deep breath, then let the air out in a slow, smooth rush. "Well, buddy," he said. "I just don't know."

When he was seven years old, his best friend died of leukemia, after a two-year process of wasting away. He had never known the boy when he wasn't sick, had at first been envious of his excuse for staying home from school, or the way he got everything, every toy or candy, that he asked for. During his friend's final illness, he wasn't allowed to visit him, so he could only imagine what was going on. When his parents would return from the hospital, he would pepper them with questions, but his father never told him anything, and his mother would just sit and stare. Once, he caught her crying in a darkened room, sniffling softly so that no one would know. Standing there in the doorway, he wanted to ask her what was wrong. But somehow he knew better than to make his presence known.

The day his friend died, his mother picked him up at school. She took him out for ice cream, and to the movies. When they got home, his father was waiting. "I have something to tell you," he said.

Afterwards, he lay on the couch, crying. On the ceiling above him, there was a crack in the plaster, and he felt sure that God was going to reach through the gap and grab him, too. "Take me," he yelled at the crack, "why don't you take me, too."

When nothing happened, he vowed he'd never believe in God again.

U   n   b   e   a   r   a   b   l   e   s

THE BEER MYSTAKE!
XXX
IN·DOCTRINE·NATION
© FLY '93·NYC·ONE FINE SEPT. EVENING ON AVE. A
YO! DOG BOY
SO I BOUGHT A 40 AND I LIMPED TO THE TRAIN AND
WHA SUP?
YO! PUP PEE
THE ROAD DOGZ WERE ENJOYING A DELICIOUS 40!
YOU KNOW YOU REALLY SHOULDN'T SUPPORT THE BEER CORPORATIONS
HAVE SOME
THANX
SUDDENLY!
LOOK OUT!!! HERE COME THE KEY STONED KOPS
MOVE NOW!
KICK BUTT!
I YAM #1!
SPARE CHANGE?
TWO ROOKIES EAGER TO PLAY COPs & SQUATTERS
MOVE! NOW!
I ♥ MY PENIS
U KNOW U REALLY SHOULD
GRIND GRIND
EXPAND YOUR VOCABULARY
WE DIDN'T ARGUE
WANT MY BLANKIE GO NAPPY
I HATE MY WIFE
BUT THEN
HEY! WAITTA MINIT!! WAZZAT? WUD IZ IT!? IZZAT A BEAH? (BEER)!? IZZIT?! IZZIT?! A BEAH?! (BEER)
RAT RACE
A DO NUT DONUT I WISH I HADDA DO NUT I WISH I HA DA
NO! (YOU STOOOPID FUCK!) IT'S WATER (YOU STOOPID STOOOOOO PIG!)
SHA TUP!

94

After that, he lived in fantasy. Even his own name was an illusion to him, something other people called him that had nothing to do with the world inside his own head. Growing up, he created a whole new life for himself, one he didn't share with others. In it, he was older, twelve years older to the day, married to a girl he knew from school, the sister of a friend of his, who was four years older than him and hardly knew he existed. Once, at his friend's house, he saw her half undressed through an open door, and she smiled at him before closing herself away. That image, of her profile in the sunlight, and the way her panties clung to the curve of her ass, stayed with him for years, and he wished he had been bold enough to say something, to walk up to the door and ease himself in. It would have been the perfect way to start things off, he thought, the kind of story they could have told their grandchildren. But he was only thirteen, not twenty-five, and he choked up whenever he had to speak to a girl. The only time he felt at ease was when he was alone, when he would create scenarios out of thin air, talking to himself, and responding as if he were someone else.

He didn't consider himself to be a morbid person. Death fascinated him, though, nearly made his heart stop at the mere thought of it, at the idea that his life would one day be nothing more than a story, recounted by those who had known him in fleeting detail until they, too, passed on, and he was finally forgotten once and for all. The summer he was sixteen, he spent three months thinking about that, every waking moment. When he would go to the corner store to buy a soda, he would see the people in line there as specters, ghosts, like himself the walking dead. The thought gave him a delicious tickle in the pit of his stomach, a feeling so uncomfortable that it became pleasing. It was like having diarrhea, like living constantly in the moment before the shit storm burst. He took to holding his bowels tight for as long as he could, so he was never certain whether the sensation was physical or psychological, whether it was a symptom of his body or his mind. Once, he held it for too long, and had to find a secluded spot on an empty lot more than a few blocks from his home. The terror of taking a crap outside, in the middle of a bustling city, where anyone who wanted to could see, thrilled him, and he crouched there, only partially hidden by the high weeds, his jeans around his ankles, pile of steaming excrement beneath him, for a long time, waiting for the feeling to pass. It made him feel vibrant, in spite of the certainty of his own death; for the first time since he had been a little kid, he truly felt alive.

As he got older, his feelings didn't fade. Everyone told him they would, but they were wrong, they didn't know him, didn't know what went on within the walls of his head. The idea of his own death nestled there, in amongst the fibers of his brain, like a tumor. And like a tumor, too, it grew. By the time he went to college, it was all he could do not to think about it, even for a second; the image of

U n b e a r a b l e s

WHAT!? LEMME SEE! LEMME SEE! POUR IT OUT LEMME SEE! POUR IT OUT! POUR IT OUT!
FUZZ HEAD
NO NECK
DAMN! NO SENSE OF HUMOR!
OZBO
HEY!
FOAM
THAT SNOT WATER! THATS BEAH! (BEER!)
DUDE IS FUK ED UP!
STOO PID FUK ED!
DO NUT
WAAAAH! YOU LIED!!! YOU LIED TO ME! WHY DOU LIE!?! GIMME YOUR ID LEMME SEE! YOUR I.D.
FUCK! WHUTS MY NAME?
WADDA YOU WANT? TAKE A WALK!!!
SO SORRY OFF! ICE RR I HAVE NO I.D.
I CANT WALK I HAVE A FOOT INJURY
OZ
STILL HOLDING ONTO 40!
SHIT! WHUT? SMY NAME ??
I THINK I WANNA TAKE U TO THE BIG HOUSE AND FIND OUT WHO YOU ARE I THINK I WANNA TAKE YOU INCUZ I DON'T LIKE YER ADITUDE WADDA YOU SMILIN FOR? STOP SMILIN!!!
WHUTS MY NUMBER?
I'M NOT SMILIN! THIS IS MY REGULAR FACE!
BRAIN LEAKING OUT
STILL HOLDING 40!
DO YOU THINK THIS IS A GAME?

himself, alone and unmoving in the cocoon of his coffin, hands folded over his heart and a look of unnatural calm on his closed-eyed face, was the first thing he saw when he woke up and the last thing he thought of before he went to sleep. He spent hours upstairs in his room, in the big, off-campus house he lived in, savoring the moments, knowing that they would never come again. Death was his companion, always at his left hand, a shape he could almost see. While the days passed, he thought about his childhood, remembering his fixation with being Superman, his desire to kill his parents. He hadn't thought about those things in years, but now he understood—they were reactions to mortality, all of them reactions to mortality. He had gotten so angry about the imperfect costume because it was a reminder that he'd never be like Superman, never be immortal, always be caught in the uncomfortable conundrum of being alive. And he had wanted to kill his parents because they'd been the ones to give him life, and, in so doing, had insured that one day he would have to die.

When he was nineteen, he met a girl. She was attracted to his anger, to the grimace he now wore everywhere like a mask. He'd watch the others living their lives and not even see them as ghosts anymore, but as fools, as crazy animals doing their dance of death and deceiving themselves that it was somehow something more. They dressed themselves up to look older, and talked about the lives and careers they would have. They talked about their grandparents, and how wonderful it would be to be in love after all those years. None of them, he'd bet, had ever been to a funeral, or seen a friend die. She was the first girl who ever smiled at him. He thought she was the most beautiful thing he'd ever seen. They'd stay up all night talking, and in the morning go out for coffee and talk some more. He never said anything about death, he didn't want to scare her off, just talked about the rage he felt, the way everything seemed to him to be a game. "It's never so real out there as it is in here," he'd say, tapping the side of his head. And she'd laugh and say, "But I'm out there," and he'd look at her and wonder if he'd ever be able to explain.

Once, after sex, she caught the billowy arm of her satin kimono in a flame of the gas stove as she tried to make tea. It was a Saturday afternoon, and there was no one in the house except for him, taking a shower upstairs as she shrieked and beat out the fire with a kitchen towel. The kimono was red, it was a gift from her parents, and she couldn't help feeling that this was somehow connected, that the speed with which the flames had climbed her arm was a warning or a sign. She was nineteen, and had always been a good girl, and was sure there would be a payment for sleeping with him, sure there would be a payment for her sin.

When he came downstairs a few minutes later, there were still flat black cinders drifting in the kitchen air like lazy ghosts. She was at the table, sipping her

I HATE TO INTERUPT YOUR TANTRUM OFFICERR BUT THAT WAS MY BEAH!
DUDE NEEDS A FIX SO HE'LL WANNA MAKE THIS QUICK
COKE
POKE
LOOK I'LL EVEN THROW IT AWAY! O.K?
GRRRRRRRR
GO DOG BOY
PLACE 40 CAREFULLY SO AS NOT TO SPILL!
Y'KNOW YOU SHOULD BE PAYING US CUZ WER SO COOL & THATS WHY PEOPLE WIT $ WANNA LIVE HERE!!
HEY! THIS GUY IS SHORTER THAN ME!
YEAH RIGHT! GIMME YR I.D.!
ITS YER LUCKE DAY
HEY THIS IS WELFARE I.D. THAT MEANS WE DO PAY YOU HA HA HAH I JUST FIGURED THAT OUT! HA HA! HA
BOZO
HA HA HA
LOOK WE DO PAY HIM!!
WHERE DO YOU LIVE? WUTS YR S.S.#?
DOG BOY
DOPE
uh 5
2
7
WADDA Y'LOOKIN AROUND FER? YA LOOKIN FR NUMBERS?
DO NUT
WHUT KINDA BEAH (BEER) IZ ZIT? WE HAFTA GIVE DESE STUHTISICKS 2 DA BEAH (BEER) COMPUHNIEZ
ITS A BUD!
HEY!!! DON'T DUMP THAT BEAH! ...I MEAN BEER!!
HOWD YA SPELL IT? UH... B...U...D... W...I...Z... E...R...yeah DATS IT!
DAMN!
HERE YA GO YA CAN ADD IT TO YER KUHLEKSHUN
VACANT
THANX JUST PUT IT IN MY MOUTH... THATS WHERE I KEEP THEM!
YER A GOOD COP!
COKE ADDS LIFE!
GRRRR
A FEW MINUTES LATER AROUND THE CORNER ON E 7th ST.
SO THIS WOMAN GAVE ME MONEY FOR A CAB BUT I SAID FUCK THAT AND I BOUGHT A 40 AND LIMPED TO THE TRAIN AND THEN...
ANUTHER 40!!!!!!!.........

tea. Her eyes kept returning to the rasp of jagged fabric on her sleeve, to the pink-ness of her skin. She wasn't sure if anything hurt yet, besides this feeling that wouldn't go away.

He sat down across from her, and took her face into his hands. "What hap-pened?" he asked her. "Are you okay?"

"I was just thinking," she said. "Have you ever wondered what happens when we die?"

Brood

LYNN CRAWFORD

I'm a better driver than my husband, he drives us to the park. It is an icy day, clear. I hog the slide and the kids get sore. Then my husband gets sore. Being so wrong I perch on our roof, in our oven, in our alley bursting with rain-sodden cartons. The atoning bores my children, gets my husband grateful. Which animates him to confine me. To my crib and her view: lawn sprawl, river, bridge to a market. Asking for real aspirin I get baby. On the lawn are girls in wide skirts, hands holding. Mud, I mean boys, smudge their ankles. I know the markets, their stalls, their goods brought in by barges. The head docker, elevated on a platform, sips coffee, spoons soup. Her utensils surface dinky.

A party last year, dead winter. I drive—it is difficult to navigate—over roads that are unpaved, over hills, over ice. The children sing in back, my husband sleeps in front. We come to an icy drop; my braking does not stop us. Because of hills' steepness.

Many cribs have no view; mine has several views. We make our home in a city, still there's foliage. And we're riverfront. A sliding door leads from our room—mirrors line two walls, the ceiling—to a small kitchen; ankle-thick carpet muffles any footsteps.

I'm now in my crib, mouthing aspirin, not cutting into free-range chicken plopped into my lap by my husband, smoking, drinking, on his way to stow kids at mom's.

I enjoyed the slide, am unprepared for this departure. Since childhood, I've experienced no departure not enormous and upheaving.

I climb from my crib, draw the curtains of our great four poster. My husband smokes, plucks at his chest, unbuttons his button-down-that-I-bought-for-

A friend, Muy-Muy, had sent **Lynn Crawford** a confused, soiled note, folded over and filled with shredded tobacco, saying something about owing money to a bunch of sleazeballs, about having to do her aerial act nude to pay them off, about the unwanted attentions of a couple of greasers, about the genius of some Whitenuts guy and her weird adulterous relationship with the madam of an S&M club. Lynn leaned back. Lynn Crawford is an editor of The Oulipo Compendium *and the author of* Solow. *Currently, she runs a low-tech costume jewelry firm (specializing in jeweled glass eyes) out of a remodeled basement in Detroit. Blowing smoke rings at the faux wood, she thought about Muy-Muy's beautiful tresses and watched the soles of feet pass her scrimmed window.*

him shirt. We veer; caps, skirts scream outside our window. I force him; he watches me force him; our faces turn gradually purple.

It is a breezy day, sundrenching. Hoop skirts hoop outside our window; my husband racewalks; the kids are at mom's; I've penned a drawing: top hat emerging from a buggy stopped before trees. Two steeples also poke through them.

Any time now my husband will be home, riverwashed, asking politely for snack.

I first spotted my husband lugging equipment—cushion, net and line—along the bridge of our river. He was clearly a fisherman and I, since childhood, was drawn to fishermen. Several days later I saw him again—rocking-horse eyes, knotty arms—along the edge of our bridge, grappling with a line snarled by what I recognized as a stalled reeling mechanism. I watched him swaying his hips, swinging his rod to unsnarl it.

My husband is home, riverwashed, asking politely for snack. Sometimes, often, he eats in special positions. This late afternoon, his left pinky locks around a vertical pole of my crib. His right foot plants on the very wide sill of our window. On the sill sits his rice dish.

My husband has handsome, hard looks; my heart breaks with his frequent departures. Not one excuse from him prevents my heart from breaking. Before departures he bolsters me, operates his gravel voice, peppers it with endearments. Departures are sudden and freezing; loud purple words chop from his logic-chopping mouth. I behave with cheerful disinterest. I've been able to exert that kind of control.

Our family spends the day in the park. My husband, my children, lunge toward me, wrench away, follow submissively. The park sits on top of oyster-gray cliffs, holds cavernous halls for eating. We lunch on a towel outdoors. It is an icy day, clear. I do not spend it entirely on the slide. That behavior got blown out of proportion.

We've eaten on a towel outdoors. I needlepoint; my husband cares for his newly washed hair; our children shove, yell, burst into bushes. I watch their sturdy limbs, their windbreakers; delight hits between my shoulders, my husband knuckles his forehead. His behavior stings me with sadness, not fury. Perhaps I've deciphered his behavior inaccurately—I can be an enormously narrow woman. His behavior stings me with sadness; I am happy for my closet. I sting with sadness, still my alertness does not flag, my eyelashes remain dry; I'm able to exert that kind of control. Because of my closet. My crib is for my husband; my closet is for me; there's fancy in my closet. When I leave it is with a cracked-open door, allowing soundless entry, re-entry. Last fall my husband took my door off its hinges for painting. I behaved with cheerful disinterest.

I don't actually perch on our roof, in our oven, in our alley bursting with rain-sodden cartons. Except in imagination.

My husband has chewed snack. He draws his finger through a button-hole of my suit, digs his toe into our ankle-thick carpet. I cup his shoulder but not hard. He is ready to fish; I am ready to go fishing.

Branches scrawl our sky, birds flap, bells hanging from our clothesline tinkle. A narrow wooden walkway leads from our porch over our lawn to our shed holding equipment. Against the wall of the shed stems, from a rectangle of dirt, ivy and forsythia. Next to the wall lie plots of our garden. Children, not ours, play on the lawn along the river.

It is not because of me that our children stay at mom's, I prefer them home. I worry deeply for our family, for our safety. This accounts for my behavior; I'm attempting to prepare them. Still they stay often with mom. The toys I buy are jacks, jump ropes, dolls; I buy gifts that are highly portable. Another woman with a similar appearance and similarly cautious mindset might opt for different behavior.

Eleusis

SHARON MESMER

1.

My mother offers me tranquilizers like a kid sharing a stash of candy. I sit down on the cot opposite her bed and watch her undress.

"You should see me in the nude," she winks at me, "I'm really cute."

Like any Anglo-Saxon I know nothing of the fungal world, but she defines for me the source of all unnatural splendor, half-exotic, half-dead.

"Imagine . . . all the excrement in the world packed tight into a caramel-colored Buick LeSabre." She's riffing now, recalling the spirit of my dead father, and it's only ten a.m.

"I never suffered anything in my life like the last six and a half hours. Hand me that Romilar. Listen, when we were kids we didn't have Romilar. We used the roots of a tree."

She smells of tobacco, bed sweats, bloat. She spends half her time in that bed reading romance magazines, scandal sheets, eating, coughing, spitting up. Every moment with her is another nightmare. I've just come off a week of living in an utter void of sight and sound, crescendoing with my passing out naked in The Dog Hole, a South Side bar. Now here, in this badly panelled bedroom, the long dark night of the soul is occuring spontaneously every five minutes, and I'm beginning to wonder how a human psyche can bear witness to this kind of crustacean horror, normally buried deep within it.

℃

By noon she's throwing her voice directly into my psyche: "I got palpitations of the brainpans, what they call it.

Given the FBI's penchant for hiring incompetents, it should come as no surprise that a filing clerk, late for a lunch date, had shoved papers that should have been put into the file UNVERIFIED/FALSIFIED PHOTOS into the slot UNBEARABLES, FISH PICNIC. This picnic was an annual small potatoes event in the Windy City organized by **Sharon Mesmer**. She is author of Jayne Mansfield's Head and lead singer with the popular after-hours-club combo the Mellow Freakin' Woodies. Sharon had been driven to near frenzy by the lack of variety in Chi-town's Chinatown fish stores, and so after making a lucrative deal with a Japanese importer living in Little Smorgasbord, Tokyo, she had begun hosting the festivity in Deerless Park (near the Leaky River), in which local cuisineers sold and displayed unusual, unsightly, and ungainly but scrumptious fish. It was the

103

"It's my *harmones*! They keep gettin' more 'n' more delicate!

"Hyperstatic, how they call it. Listen, hand me a Tranxene. You need a Prozac? I got ten right here. First put a TV dinner in." Syllables flying off, frayed, hasty, in jerks. Talk, talk. Listen, listen. Each of my five senses a convenient conduit for her seemingly accidental tortures. The anguish of hearing thousands of ill-conjugated verbs. She exhibits that legendary tendency of the Nordic-Teutonic nature to discern the potential for torture in any situation. I have abandoned all belief in my revival. No one will find me here where invisibility is the same as failure. I wonder if anyone has noticed that I'm dead and, if so, whether they've taken the trouble to mourn me.

Outside the streets are being cleaned, like on the weekend.

2.

I used to be a drunk and that made me a citizen of the world. A cut-rate parasite, welcome anywhere. The Fourteenth Ward regulars knew they could always count on me for a few drinks, sometimes even a bottle of pills depending on who I'd slept with. Back then we were so familiar. Of course I was always impeccably groomed and ready to manipulate exquisite verbal resources, launching my listener into diverse worlds of classrooms, country clubs, funny farms, public toilets.

I was also blessed with a metropolitan fame based on a complete disregard for my personal safety. I could drop in anytime through the night entrance of The Dog Hole and immediately sink into a delicious lethargy, my chloroform bottle at the ready. On my last night of freedom I had made my way through the verminous shadows hunched over broken tables to the backroom, where Pete, the alderman's assistant, held forth. "Have you seen the latest acquisition?" he asked, then handed me a vial containing a mixture of barley ergot and mint—the legendary *kykeon*.

"Blissful is she," winked Pete, invoking the Eleusinian benediction, "who has been initiated into the Holy Mysteries, who knows the end of life as well as its beginning."

"Blissful is he," I answered, in accordance with the ancient and accepted rite, "who has received Reason and lives on in joy and dies with hope." He mixed the kykeon in a silver goblet with the tibia of a pig and handed it to me.

My first feeling was a bottomless terror. The fitful wind I'd been hearing became a vast wheel, constantly accelerating. Then the wheel became a gondola, sweeping majestically through moonlit lagoons, then an eagle careening me up, Alp over Alp, then down into the primeval forest where my soul metamorphosed into some kind of giant vegetable, an eggplant maybe. I continued as an eggplant for what felt like days even though it was really about three minutes tops. Then from the very bottom of my despair I heard a voice like a tremendous engine full of sublime cadences, the voice of a multitude of deaths. It began as a jet of pulsating air and nerve, then crackled into a nasal whine, softened by phlegm, tinged with banality and fear. From beneath the cathedral archway of a giant fern I heard: "What kinda dummy sits in a queer bar gettin' stupid drunk?"

It was her. Her voice. And she was bending over me, the warm hole of her mouth the center of all roses, disgorging with every word the legion demon agents of my transformation. How had I found my way back to her plastic-covered couch? That was just the beginning. The Word made fleshy.

merest chance that one man who loved fish and appeared each year was Man Mountain McBrain, one of the last surviving members of the IWW. His appearance, noted in the daily Chicago Rib, *was clipped, and a file was started by a zealous law-enforcement trainee in the bureau's underground offices. For six years, this file only held one news brief.*

3.

The afternoon ritual, a perversion of the very idea of repetition as comfort. She stretches out across the bed to make contact with a blue box of ice cream cones, her favorite snack. Everything about her is vivid colors: the Wonder Bread bag, the little boxes of sugary breakfast cereals, the cheap striped cotton tops, and when she goes out to Lulu's, the red-orange trailer across the street where she buys her milk, bread, cigarettes and Lotto, she wears a green scarf over her thin, graying pincurls. All she has to do is move, or not move, and all the horrors and ignominies of a life spent with her begin flowing again, real fast, like an Ethiopian funeral mass.

"Y'know, I'm not like you," she says today and will surely say tomorrow, pulling a cone out of the box, "I don't need an audience. Go get me a Kleenex."

《

Always at about seven o'clock we enter the second phase of everyday, like a lime-green Rambler jaunty-ing towards inevitable disaster. The endlessly garish TV shows, the families in their big sweaters in their comfortable homes, the women well-fed, their cherry lips perfect. From the plastic-covered couch I watch the cars go by outside and begin again my fantasy of the perfect all-night diner, its ceiling lights and fans a beacon in the feathery night, proclaiming the comfort of whatever I want, they got.

⟨

Midnight begins with her hot breath filling the bedroom ("I got the devil lookin' over my shoulder . . . Aw now where th' hell are them Tranxenes?") and the sickly TV sheen moving mauve-to-violet-to-green in the living room where I lay on the couch, watching the shadows stirring as they seek form. The heady nausea accompanying the rapid succession of ideas that replaces sleep can be categorized in three ways: what I'm thinking/what I need now/who I should have been by now. And the reality: I wanted to be an angel; I have become a beast.

Everything implied by the word *chance* has turned on me to reveal the depth of my mediocrity; I am, in fact, a kind of patron saint of mediocrity, a Saint Teresa of Avila pierced by the arrow of all that has been and will forevermore be Lost.

I recall the good old days, when by merely going to dinner I could scandalize everyone. The good old days, of "I can't run in these earrings!" The good old days, when the simple cure for insomnia was a good beer shit: like writing a poem, a routine cleanse for desperation.

Now, enthralled by oppressive thoughts that come sudden, perfect and inevitable, I can comfortably anticipate extraordinary pain the likes of which the man in the street will never know. This certainty becomes the very archetype of my psyche's precise annihilation. I am a being truly transformed by the purity of complete mediocrity.

Later, just before dawn I hear, from somewhere near my ear: "The god of Sleep is the same as the god of Healing."

Later. Within the safety of an endless stream of thoughts the night progresses to its end mysteriously, piously, like the Canticle of the Ancient of Days.

4.

Dawn's milky light reveals only enlarged pores and the results of a recent $7 haircut. The light overflows its shafts that stripe the bathroom tiles and fuses into a single intense instantaneous feeling of eternity. Who was I before this light and what did I do and what did I think?

She's still asleep. But soon she will grow, swell, and burst like a meteor, coughing, shuffling, smoking and flailing into the bathroom then back to the bed, and this halo of nostalgia for the present will disappear forever like prehistory's first lost tribe.

⟨

I go into her room, as I do every morning, to see if she's still breathing. I listen for the little "puts" of breath coming from behind her skinny lips. But today there are no little "puts." She's dead. I sit down on the cot across from her bed. I look at her hard round head, her mouth open as if she were trying to form the perfect vowel.

(

I sit on the cot across from her bed and watch the hours swing down to afternoon. It's amusing to wonder how long I can sit here with her body. I like having her body in this room. No one in the neighborhood knows; they are all going about their business and we are alone, just the two of us, and the memories her body has released to me. She is my new all-night diner, her body a beacon of comfort in the feathery dark. She for whom I sacrificed everything and now have nothing. No thing.

Tonight we will both be able to sleep.

5.

It's the warm yellow morning of a busy day. The languid and astonished condition of giddiness replaces any memory of past unhappiness. Outside I can hear the neckbells of invisible horses. I think of the punishments I've suffered and the comfort of this new insatiable thirst for clarity. Thus I see no great danger in breaking free, despite the certainty of losing a bit of dignity: I can call any 7-11 in the country and be assured they're serving strong, shiny coffee.

What I know now: Reality is the raw material for the process of personal demise as The Great Work. My ego feeds exclusively now on the certainty of my immediate and eternal ruin. Like Chiron I have been mortally wounded, but through my sacrifice at the hard red nicotined hands of The Mother I am immortal and cannot die. This is my punishment. But like the Hanged Man, whose orgasm is not a gesture of submission but a gift from The Tree of the Knowlege of Good and Evil, I have received nothing less than ultimate Reason here, and can live on forever in purest Joy.

The Lost are lost by destiny, and destiny starts early and falls naturally one thing to the next like an old man's lazy game of dominoes on the summer stoop.

I speak to you now in her own flat, spent idiom: on the day you wake beyond the Pleiades, remember me to the One who lived here.

She once was a true love of mine.

S h a r o n M e s m e r

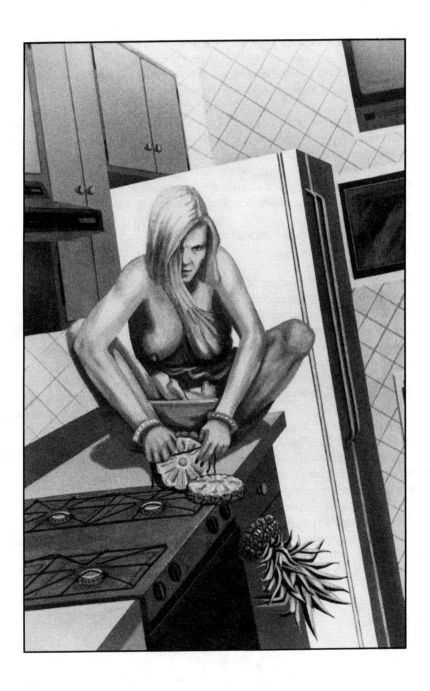

The Last Bikini Wax

ANN ROWER

Cancel your car reservations, she said. You can drive my Jag. Now I got scared. I knew Aunt Cherry would never offer to let me drive her Jag unless she was crazy or dying. When I got to L.A. they told me the cancer had spread to her brain. The brain cancer made her say things and also forget the things she said. In the morning she'd say she wanted roast chicken and then at night she said, I thought we were having Mexican lasagna. One morning she said I want you to sleep with me. I can't explain the funny little ruffles of feeling, dread and desire, that filled me and kept fluttering their tails as they swam around in my gut like saltwater tropical fish all day even though I was pretty sure she'd forget that she'd said it by bed-time, like she forgot about the chicken. Nonetheless, I kept my fingers crossed all day. We went to the beauty salon—she insisted on keeping up with her hair, nails and feet though in deference to her dying they broke it up; hair one day, nails the next. She made me buy some extra strength conditioner and I said I'll put it on tonight, sort of testing the waters but nothing more was said about my sleeping with her. She looked much better after her hair was done, it was kind of pink-gold and curly. Sweet and almost glamorous. We watched the Chinese in Tiananmen Square. I waited. She said she was going to bed. Nothing more was said. This time, when she begged for extra valium, I gave them to her.

She had these little bottles and there were three bottles, morning noon and night, per day, seven days a week. They were all different. At night there was valium with L-tryptophan added, the only chalky white pills in the group—the L-tryp were white footballs

It turns out Ulin had been recruited by the FBI for an unusual sting operation. Once he was hired by the Bureau, he was left to cool his heels for three hours in a deserted bunker, four stories underground, filled with drawers of microfilm. He didn't know why he had taken the job, and, as he waited, he casually switched the caps on the containers. On one gray top, he saw, in hand-printed letters, the name of an old drinking buddy, **Ann Rower**. She is the author of If You're a Girl and has worked with the Wooster Group on LSD (Road to Immortality, Part II). She is writing a biography of her uncle, songwriter Leo Robin.

Scrolling through the tape, Ulin read that she had been seen in the company of the mysterious dwarf Miles Outstandish, a trans-lator of nineteenth-century French fiction—the same he and the valiums were those ones when the open heart ones were a new thing. They were also white—two-and-a-halves. The rest peach, hot pink, aqua, yellow, baby pink, and light blue. It's just like her house, her clothes. Only no black ones, no black pills. She had black jeweled jogging suits now. Now everyone wears black in L.A., but Aunt Cherry was one of the first. Clink clink clink. Into the little glass bottles. Aunt Cherry caught every pill mistake. That night she decided that the L-tryptophan was trying to poison her.

No no, I cried. You're supposed to have it. You're not supposed to have so much valium. Aunt Cherry seems to have developed a little valium habit. They were in little bottles and someone was supposed to give them to her at the right time and in the right amount. And after the first night we—me and Mara the day nurse—had to hide the Valium. Not that she didn't know what was going on, most all the time. She was hardly ever wrong.

No, no, the L-tryptophan is trying to poison me, she said last night. It gives me fever, she said. (The next year L-tryptophan was pulled off the market because a huge batch had caused thousands of deaths. At first they thought it was "just" a tainted batch but it wasn't.) But I just thought she was trying to manipulate me into giving her an extra valium which immediately made me manipulative and so I said she couldn't have the valium unless she took the L-tryp. So she did, but when I looked again, the second and third little bottles contained two long white oval L-tryps and no valium.

But tonight I didn't argue. I tucked her in and closed her door almost all the way. The condo was quiet. I felt like I was deliciously alone. I'd applied some of that pink hair goop conditioner that she'd forced on me on the top of my head. I looked like a greaser who'd used cum for hairspray, but I was sort of fascinated by the look and kept sneaking peeks in the many mirrors as I paced on the deep pile carpet. There was a full moon. Suddenly I heard a voice from the bedroom.

Annie?

What?

Come here.

Go back to sleep.

No. Come here.

I started to panic. I said, In a minute.

You still have that stuff on your head?

Yes. I have to keep it on an hour. The hour's not up yet, I said.

Wash it out and come to bed.

Uh oh, I thought. Just a sec, I said.

Come to bed. I'm cold, she said. I just want to cuddle. My hair did look magical the next day. I left the goop in a long long time.

But I couldn't leave it in forever. Eventually I took one of Aunt Cherry's valiums and slipped into bed beside her. I had no choice. I didn't want to make her beg, she was lonely, cold, old, sick. It was her last wish, or so I thought. I got closer to her and then put my hand on her flank. It was bony. The skin was dry and thin, not velvety, or silky or satiny or even burlappy. It was like fabric but some fabric from another planet. I moved closer and tried to curl into her like the two-spoon thing because she'd said she wanted to cuddle. I tried to put my arm around her and touch her stomach. She'd always told me how sexy she used to be and I still thought she was sexy, at least until she got sick and I thought if love is blind can it be also deaf and dumb? And if that why not—I couldn't think of the word for having no sense of touch. Love is numb? I thought. It sounded all right. Musta been the valium talking. I heard her snoring and flopped over onto my side facing away but letting my ass touch. But sometime in the early hours I must have moved closer into the center of the bed and Aunt Cherry, though desiring it so much, was not really used to sleeping with anyone and must have moved over toward the edge and eventually—she was on extra valiums too—fell out.

Crash.

I woke to hear her poor old skull cracking on the marble bed table. I rushed around to the other side of the bed and tried to lift her dead weight. I could feel the scar from my operation in my abdomen stretching and hurting, could easily imagine the wound busting open and everything falling out as I put her back into bed.

Crash.

The third time it was too much for me. I was really afraid my scar would rip open and everything would fall out. I let her finish sleeping on the floor. In the morning I told Aunt Cherry my worry. This gave Aunt Cherry a reason to have a nurse at night too, to

and Carol had been tracking months before on a morals charge.

be good to me, not herself. But Mara, the day nurse, had to go back to Mexico to nurse her mother so we got a new nurse. Aunt Cherry's son-in-law Jerry suggested we get a male nurse. Jerry assumed that a man would be strong, bulky, a good lifter, insensitive like himself. But instead of a moose, the new nurse, Gary, was more of a spirit, a slender reed, more delicate than either me or Mara, almost as delicate as Aunt Cherry, but he worked out and wasn't dying—not yet, at least, or at least he didn't know yet—actually Michael brought me up to Sloane Kettering to read him this story, but I didn't bring it but I asked him if he wanted me to and he cracked a smile and squeezed my hand meaning, I guess, yes—his esophagus was gone—so I said I'd come the day after but he died overnight and I never got the chance to read it to him or anyone till now—anyway, back then, he was just twenty-four and gorgeous. Ravishing, his hair long and cruelly curly like some pale Afro from another planet. He was the most beautiful nurse of any sex in the world, a young faun from the other side of the Earth. I held the door open for him, held him with my eyes, held on to every word he spoke as we sat and chatted in the kitchen on the chairs with the pink bows, waiting for Aunt Cherry to wake up and smell the coffee. We clicked. I am the world's best listener, east or west, avidly surfing waves of information. And everybody knows Australian waves are perfect 10's and he had done things I couldn't believe. At twelve he ran away and joined.

—A circus? I said—can't help interrupting—

No.

A band of gypsies?

No. I didn't really run away. My mother had left when I was twelve and so my dad just said to me one day when I was thirteen I guess you might as well leave too. He gave me bus money. There I was, just a boy on a bus to Adelaide. I ended up backstage at the Old Kings Music Hall. It was a drag review. I stayed there five years first putting on makeup and stuff backstage and then they let me out front. I did Dietrich.

He couldn't believe it when I told him Aunt Cherry's husband wrote practically all of Dietrich's songs—well, not "Falling In Love Again," and not "Laziest Gal in Town," but "Hot Voodoo," "What Am I Bid for My Apple," "I Couldn't Be Annoyed."

My total favorite, said Gary.

Do it.

Not without makeup. I just can't, he said.

What else?

Well, I used to run around the streets of Adelaide in a little yellow tutu and everybody followed me and fell in love with me and nothing bad ever happened to me. I've led a charmed life.

He got very good with makeup and then he expanded to the body. He did bikini waxes over there, in Adelaide, where males are allowed to give bikini waxes to women. They are not in the USA. He had the longest eyelashes I'd ever seen. He gave off no perfume but the sense that he understood not me maybe but women like Aunt Cherry, understood and admired especially her for having her hair and nails done when she was dying.

So when Aunt Cherry woke up Gary suggested that she have a bikini wax. She clapped her old hands together and her eyes lit up.

I've never had a bikini wax, she said. And I never thought I'd ever have one.

Well, he said, you're getting your wish. You don't even have to leave the house, he said. You don't even have to leave the bed.

I always thought that calling it a bikini wax was kind of ass backwards, I chattered.

Here, he said, ignoring me and handing Aunt Cherry two pieces of peach Kleenex. Hold them over yourself, he said. He showed her, one on either side, one in each hand, overlapped in the middle over her crack. He worked and worked. He waxed and waxed. They waited and waited. He was a little nervous but making cheerful converation. He'd never waxed a dying woman. Then came the time to pull it off. Somehow Aunt Cherry's cunt hairs fused with the wax in such a way that her dying labia loosened and stuck to the tape and opened up a world to the young Gary Phillips who, though he had seen so much, and thought he had seen everything, had not seen that: eye to eye to an old gal's vagina which opened up as he pulled the wax strips back, like the surface of a distant planet in some far galaxy on the nightly news. He was no astronaut. One look at that fleshscape and he bolted.

What happened? I said, bumping into him as I came back from the kitchen.

I pulled off the wax, he gasped, the way Aunt Cherry did when somebody keyed her Jag, and it all fell out.

I adore him but he can be such a fucking misogynist! But he was frantic and I tried to catch him as he fled. But he was gone. It was the first bikini wax she got, the last he gave.

Dissection
SUSAN SCUTTI

She stares out of the window at the river and invents a conversation with a lover she doesn't have. If you were to split her head open, if you hit her with an axe or a brick or maybe even if you aimed a gun and shot her between the eyes, you would see that the river she stares at is the same color as the gray matter of her brain. It's snowing. Flakes kiss the window then melt. The conversation with her imaginary lover goes like this:

Woman: You're smothering me.

Man: What do you mean I'm smothering you? I love you.

Woman: I don't want to talk now. I just want you to hold me.

Man: Tell me what you mean when you say I'm smothering you.

Woman: Give me more room.

Man: I don't want to lose you—I love you.

Her imaginary lover's eyes turn wet like the snow that is falling, falling, falling. The phone startles her. Her husband's voice is unpleasant. Un-pleasing, she thinks. He tells her stuff about his day. Event-things. He doesn't describe the shape of his mood or the colors in his dreams from the night before. Would she listen if he did? When she hangs up the phone she fantasizes her imaginary lover making love to her. No, they don't just "have sex." The river is gray like her mind and if you took an axe or a brick or even a gun and placed it between her legs . . . did I tell you this already?

Susan Scutti lay in undressed beauty, her body wrapped in a flounce of bedcovers. Like Baudelaire's Jeanne, she was naked except for her jewels, though unlike Jeanne, Susan's eye was pressed to a telescope. Its focal point was the window of Mike Topp's flat. She was expecting bart to turn up there at any moment.

Susan's poems have appeared in Black Swan Review, re:Issue, Mixed media, *and* Cocodrilo

Susan and bart were not "lovers," but rather soul partners. She felt it would be indecent to confront him directly with her mysterious forebodings. She would have to find him and lead up to it.

Premonitions had come to her in a dream. She had seen bart, curled up like a slumbering newt, being pushed along a shuffle-board by a mystic, wiggling wand.

Juggling

SU BYRON

In the middle of dinner George decided to demon-strate his juggling technique. He had just learned to juggle from a book. He picked up three of the wine glasses and held them in one hand. Wine from one of the tipped glasses spilled onto a guest's skirt. The guest was dressed as a gypsy and had several bracelets hanging from each arm. She flashed her bright eyes. We should take a picture, she said.

Are you going to juggle wine glasses? asked Flo, the woman George lived with.

George didn't answer. First he threw one of the wine glasses up into the air. Wine splashed over the table and walls. Still holding on to the other two glasses, he caught the first one with his free hand.

Any idiot can juggle, said Manny, the single man. He handed his napkin to Flo who started wiping the wall.

George threw the second glass into the air. Not everyone can do it, he said. I disagree with you there.

Mikki, another guest, was pregnant. She worked in a jewelry store and had six earrings hanging from one ear. I don't want to get wet, she said, so I'm going to sit over there on the couch.

George threw the third glass up into the air. How do you get red wine out of a blue rug? asked Flo.

You're going to miss this, said George, if you don't watch closely. He began to juggle all three empty glasses. The gypsy clapped her hands and jumped up excitedly. Who has a camera? she cried. We should get a picture of this.

Flo said there was a camera on the bookshelf next to the radio.

And turn up the radio while you're there, said Manny. I've been hearing this song in my head all day.

A certain phrase had harmed her. If Su hadn't read those few words in Gaston Leroux, perhaps she would have been able to finesse other parts of her life. The phrase appears in Le Fantôme de l'Opéra when the Persian and the Viscount are trapped in the Chamber of Horrors. Erik, the opera ghost, forces the kidnapped Christine to look through a peephole and tell him what is inside the chamber. Surprised, she describes two occupants in a room with a forest depict-ed on the wall.

"Not a forest," Erik says, "la forêt tropique." At that moment, the bas-relief begins to glow like an ener-gizing toaster, slowly roast-ing the cubicle's prisoners. Su had pondered that. **Su Byron** is the editor of Wha? (later Sarasota Arts Review) and author of Paris Notes.

The idea of a picture radiating heat had fascinat-ed her along with that phrase, "la forêt," that fell

Don't fall asleep, said Roberto to his wife, Mikki, who was lying with her eyes fluttering closed on the couch. How can you miss this?

I'm all right, said Mikki. I'm watching. She put her hand on her stomach.

Paula, a woman with extremely large breasts, got up to go to the kitchen for a sponge.

What are you doing? asked Flo.

Don't you want to get some water on those wine stains? asked Paula. She looked back into the dining room. George had just smashed one of the glasses and was now juggling two wine glasses and a small plastic statue of a saint. To do it without moving, he was saying, is the key. That's the real way to do it.

Flo went into the kitchen with her plate and put some salad on it. Did you like the cous-cous? she asked Paula. Paula stood with the sponge under the faucet. Do you have more glasses? she asked. I'd like some more wine. The wine was a 1983 Bordeaux. Mikki and Roberto were drinking iced tea. Flo had diluted her wine with Perrier. The gypsy was drinking water. Only Manny and Paula were drinking their wine straight. George was drinking beer.

Forget about the wine, said Flo. I don't know how you get wine out of a rug, but I don't think you do it with water.

Put some clay on it while the stain's still wet, called Mikki from the couch. And vacuum it off later.

Paula looked in the cabinet for a wine glass. Anyone else want one? she asked.

Back in the dining room, George had just dropped the plastic saint and was trying to pick it up while maintaining the two wine glasses in the air. One of the glasses struck the edge of the table and shattered. Without pausing, he caught the pepper mill Manny threw him and continued juggling. Paula sat down on the couch next to Mikki.

Those are beautiful, she said, touching the tiny silver birds hanging from Mikki's ears. I've been thinking of piercing another hole in my ear. I don't know if they'd like it at work.

Mikki burped and covered her mouth. She smiled weakly and then brought her head down quickly as the pepper mill crashed into the wall behind her.

George! Flo ran over to Paula and Mikki and grabbed the mill from the back of the couch. Did it get you?

Hey, George—catch this. Manny threw him an empty beer can and George deftly juggled it along with the saint which he had managed to pick back up and now was turning around and around in the air. The gypsy gasped with delight and snapped a picture. George! she screamed. George!

Flo took the pepper mill into the kitchen. This has to stop, she said as she put it in the cabinet. She emptied the rest of the cous-cous into a plastic container and put it in the refrigerator.

When she came out Manny was letting the gypsy climb on his back so she could attempt to get a photo of George from a higher angle. Whoa! she cried as she wobbled on Manny's back. Whoa! I don't think this'll work!

Throw me that saucer, said George, as he struggled to keep the beer can and the statue in the air. The gypsy fell from Manny's back with a loud squeal smashing the camera on the side of the dining room table. Oh, no! she cried. Flo!

Manny threw the saucer to George spinning it like a Frisbee. George caught it and continued juggling.

Did the camera break? asked Flo coming in from the kitchen. I thought I heard something break.

Roberto and Mikki got up. We should be going, he said. Mikki rubbed her stomach. It's hard for me to stay up much later than this, she said. Her six silver earrings glittered.

George moved away from the door keeping his eyes on the beer can, the statue and the saucer which he had whirling in the air. Somebody throw that plate, he shouted, pointing to a mounted Chinese plate hanging on the wall. Oh no, not the plate, yelled Flo, overhearing from the kitchen. That was my grandmother's. She was holding a wine glass in one hand and a dish towel in the other.

The dish! The dish! Manny jumped with excitement. Hey buddy she thinks you'll drop the dish! He ran up under George who had climbed a chair while continuing to juggle the beer can and the saint. The other saucer had fallen and broken into pieces at Roberto's feet.

out of lockstep with the book's prose.

Thank you so much, said Roberto to Flo, stepping away from George. He took his wife's hand. It was great. They stepped outside onto the front porch. Flo followed them, clucking.

He's gone too far, she said, looking up at the swollen white moon hanging above them.

Oh, he's great, said Roberto, with a small smile. He looked at the moon. Honey, he said, look at that moon. Mikki glanced up and then back down again. Umm, she said.

Goodnight! Flo waved them into their small grey Honda. Let's do it again!

Inside she saw the gypsy on her tiptoes reaching for her grandmother's plate.

Oh no! said Flo. I really can't . . .

Who's king of this house? screamed Manny to George. You or her?

George didn't answer. He started humming in a low voice.

The radio, lying on the rug near the couch cursed with static. The gypsy put her hand over both her ears. I can't stand it! she yelled. Sensory overload!

Flo walked into the kitchen where Paula stood sipping her wine and looking out into the dark backyard. I hate him, said Flo, picking up the dish towel again. And I'm not even married to him.

Men, said Paula. Her breasts hung with a heaviness beneath her thin cotton top. He's destroying the rug.

It was old anyway, said Flo. Still, he didn't have to ruin it.

It's a full moon, said Paula. When I was little my mother always said that a full moon meant trouble. She licked her upper lip which had the remnants of a pale lipstick faintly glowing on it.

Are you still seeing that dentist? Flo leaned over Paula to put the large slotted spoon she had just dried away in its drawer.

We're still going out, said Paula. She took another sip of wine and wiped her hand on her thigh. Crash! From the other room they heard loud noises and much laughter.

I'm afraid to look, said Flo. She walked slowly to the doorway, a dried pot lid loosely held in her hand.

On my god! she said. Damn you, George!

George was there still juggling. Her grandmother's plate, a huge Danish affair with a picture of a peasant woman carrying a basket of bread along a country lane, lay broken in pieces near the front door. The gypsy was somberly inspecting the shards.

This was *so* beautiful, she said, a sharp piece of blue crockery in her hand.

George didn't hear her. His face, shiny and red, was turned upward, the light from the ceiling playing off the reflection in his glasses. He kept his hands busy, juggling the saint and now the small plastic lighter that Manny had just thrown him. His eyes spun with excitement and his legs danced to the sounds of Manny's tortured giggling.

I can't stop laughing, gasped Manny, bright red with exertion. He leaned over, his face creased in pain. I can't stop laughing!

SUBURBAN AMBUSH

        firebombed
The dinner table
Taking us comple___
By surprise.

        evacuated
        casualties

Tracers skittering
Across the summer
Sky.

Dad is a memory
We're trying to keep
Alive.

                    -Ron Kolm

Five Stories
MIKE TOPP

1. A woman ran an employment agency for girls. The girls were supposed to be going to jobs, but they just disappeared. A man in an automobile spoke to the woman and told her he'd found the girls' trunks at some place, but no girls. He was a night doctor and was going to take the woman to the hospital.

2. A sixty-year-old man one morning went from his home into the fields. The people of his village had subsisted without water for centuries. He decided to live on flowers like a bee. When his money was gone, he would go out to the fields and gather some more flowers. One evening when he was out gathering poppies he found a yellow spring that furnished enough water for many villages. Everyone was happy. Now if you try to talk to him he won't even answer you, but only give a drunken smile.

3. A young man became a soldier and was killed by a bomb. Locusts laid their eggs in his corpse. When the worms were mature, they took wing and flew north. When the wife of the soldier saw them, she turned pale, and she knew her husband was dead. She thought of his corpse rotting in the desert. That night she dreamed she rode a white horse that was so fast it left no hoofprints. She found her dead husband and looked at his face eaten by the locusts and she began to cry. Afterward she never let her children harm any insects. That same winter a swarm of locusts nested in her heart.

4. A woman made a pornographic movie in which she sucked on men's penises for four hours and thirty-one minutes. She made many more movies after that. Near the end of her life she told a newspaper reporter she'd been drugged by the director in her first movie. The story of her adventure spread far and wide, and soon made her famous.

When the ragtag fivesome (Carol, bart, Judy, Debbie, and Lydia) arrived at his door, Mike was a bit apprehensive about letting them in. He became even more irritated when they pulled out the same photo the police had been badgering him about. **Mike Topp,** universally loved and universally published, has a chapbook entitled Local Boy Makes Good from Appearances.

When they asked him to identify some people, he said, "What's in it for me?" He had soured on humanity since his get-rich scheme, selling recycled spools with verses from Kipling hand-lettered on their circumferences, had failed .

Debbie shot back, "Don't you want to recover Rollo? You must dig him. Why else are you in this picture?"

"I just went there," Mike confessed, "Because of a letter in the personals in the Rib. The one about mayhem."

"Huh?"

5. A man found himself in a strange country many miles from home. He was taken there at night by a large black pig. While traveling they passed a beach full of crabs that had human faces on their backs. He walked around a little, stepped and slipped on something clammy, and began to scream; his face was tense and pale. When he awoke, cedars laughed in the sunlight, oaks beckoned, and the birches bent far down and waved.

The Smile
STEPHANIE URDANG

It had rained so hard. But it hadn't been predicted. This was in the summer of 1985, during that long, drawn-out drought, and it was just shortly after the well-publicized hurricane that shut down the city for an entire day and then never arrived.

I was dressing to go to a film with a man I'd recently met, by chance, on his lunch hour. It was in a deli. He liked me, I found out later, because he said I looked like I'd been in bed awake all night. I had insomnia. I liked him because he seemed healthy, vital, and intelligent.

It had been terribly, terribly dry; it was hot and dry, and the storm came up suddenly, with just a little thunder as a warning. Then it rained harder and harder, until finally it hailed. It was a full moon.

As I hurriedly shut the last of several windows, I saw this woman standing on the stoop in the rain. It was across St. Mark's Place. She was wearing an old purple housedress and she was hollering gleefully to the skies; she was throwing kisses, and she was playing her ukulele to the rain. I watched her rejoice until it rained so unbelievably hard I could no longer see her. But I could hear her.

Then, I went into the kitchen and turned on the water, full force, just letting the water rush down the drain, and I cried full force. I cried while I got ready to go out.

After the film, we came back downtown to my neighborhood, and we ate, we talked, we walked, and we stalled, until we went up to the apartment where I was staying. They were out of town.

More stalling. I showed him my sister Melanie's family photo display, and there's this one sepia photograph of my mom and dad on their wedding day. The man I was with loved my mother. He stared at her

Lisa got out of the slammer on a fog-stained Tuesday afternoon at about 5 a.m. She boarded the El, which began barreling along like a paper match thrown in a rainswept gutter. At Frostpoint Street, a mysterious, bundled-up blonde got on board. The subway entrant sat next to Lisa, who had been the only occupant in the bulky car.

The blonde turned to Lisa, "Hi. I'm Stephanie. Can we trade seats?"

Stephanie Urdang *is a writer/performer who has been described as having a soft voice and a dangerous mind. She has won three awards from the American Film Institute for videos of her storytelling.*

"What are you talking about?"

"I always sit in that space. Given the trajectory of this train as it plunges along these steel stripes, this is the only seat where I feel comfortable."

image until it actually became embarrassing, and he talked about her "innocent, yet knowing face. And that smile." He kept saying, "That smile." Then he brusquely tossed the photograph aside and grabbed me and started kissing me and feeling me all over, but I got up, I put all the photographs in place, I went into

the kitchen and got a drink of water, and when I went back into the room where he was sitting, he was naked!

Well, I sat down beside him because I was lonely and I was hungry, but I felt no connection with this man, and as he became more and more determined, I retreated. And in the end, as I sat complacently leaning against the wall, watching him masturbate, while looking at me, as his tension mounted, he begged me for a smile, and when I smiled, he came. I almost didn't even need to be there.

Period Piece
NANCY KOAN

Dawn: Father, my confession isn't an easy one—after all, if what I'm trying to say is true, then how can I go on being a proud woman, proud of my sex and my genetic code? If most of my crimes are the result of my female hormones, well, then, damn femininity and damn my ovaries. Alright, alright, I won't get hysterical. Yes, I'm better now. Calmer. How did it start, you ask? Well . . .

Susan: I was home, exhausted, lying on the divan with my legs above my head. Alan had promised to pick Billy up after Little League. After all, Billy was *his* from Al's first marriage to The Dragon Lady. Billy was impossible, not unlike his father. Anyway, I'd whipped up an easy quiche and was planning to steam some garden beans. By 9:15 my head was beginning to pound when mother phoned. Her call had a dual purpose: to criticize me and ask if I needed anything from the mall.

Lisa: I told her to drop dead. She said I had already killed her years ago when I married Alan. We hung up. At 10:30, the two "boys" rolled in. All filled with themselves. They'd had pizzas with the other dads and had *forgotten* to call. The pain was now at my temples. Rent was overdue and so was my period. I decided to stay calm and asked Alan if he would drive to the mall and pick up some sanitary pads and aspirin. Alan refused and suggested I use the quiche if I got stuck. Billy laughed hard and threw his softball into the air. Even before it knocked over the Ming jar I was seeing red.

Maggie: When I was certain both my little men were asleep, I crept into Billy's room and lightly tied him to the bed. I put his left hand in a bowl of icy water. He didn't feel a thing, at least not then. You see, Father, Billy had been seeing a child shrink for 18

"You might recall the opening of The Hunchback Of Notre Dame," *the FBI agent mentioned to David.*

"I can't say that I do."

"A play is being put on for the Feast of Fools, but it keeps getting interrupted; first by the entrance of the Cardinal, then by the taunts of a beggar named Jose Pantaloon . . . "

There was a trendy pause.

"So, um, what?" David said in tremolo.

The agent removed a photo from a folder. "This woman wrote a letter that we obtained." He held a picture of **Nancy Koan**. *Nancy is a filmmaker, actress, and caretaker to the masses. She directed and starred in the film* Dinner with Abbie. *She is the artistic director of Lambster Productions. "In the letter, she says she's found a mistranslation, a clinker, right in the first chapter of the English version. Do you know who did that translation?"*

127

months for his bedwetting problem. I had learned this little trick at camp and was positive it would set his psychological progress back another five years. But I was just in that kind of a mood.

Regina: Then I slid into bed with my darling, understanding husband. He was passed out from the beer part of his pizza, but *I* was so horny I could have screwed a doorknob. I shook him awake, ignoring his pleas of not being in the mood. I finally offered to help wash the Jag; he decided to perform. One quick jab—it's all I needed. I slept.

Jane: But Father, the next morning was worse. I'd put on six pounds of water weight and couldn't even get my ankle bracelet on. And, of course, now Alan wanted to have sex. I told him, "later." MUCH later. The only oral thing I was interested in was sugar—lots of it. I hulked down to the kitchen where I captured a half gallon of chocolate mocha fudge ice cream hidden behind the fish sticks. I polished it off with two donuts and then ran to the bathroom to puke.

Dawn: Billy passed me in the hall without even saying hello. He was soaked. On seeing him I didn't feel good, but frankly, Father, I didn't feel all that bad either. And when I finally got to work I discovered *I* was already late for court.

Susan: This was to be the wind-up of a three week trial—my uterus was anxious for it to be over. The case I was trying was that of a man accused of stealing Christmas presents from underneath a big tree in the lobby of a major financial firm. His defense called it a "political act." He said he was planning to give the gifts to the local orphanage.

Lisa: After three hours, I didn't care if he'd stolen pabulum to give his granny. I wanted out of that court and close to my heating pad. By the time the jury reconvened, my pills had worn off and my teeth were chattering. When all the evidence was in and the jury declared him guilty, my judgment was made—Attica, for six years.

Maggie: When I opened the front door, the phone was ringing off the hook. I picked it up, and yes, Father, I knew who it was. That woman—she'd been hanging up on me for a year. Alan had a mistress. A blonde waitress/actress who'd first served us pasta with sun-dried tomatoes on Billy's 11th birthday. A lovely girl with incredibly bad taste in hairdos—and lovers.

Regina: She must've thought Alan was Jesus. He'd probably given her the frustrated playwright line. Together they'd inspire Broadway and drain our bank account. Ha! What if they were giving me herpes? I'd have to draw the line at herpes. I headed for the bathroom.

Jane: Billy was at karate practice and Big Al was asleep in the den. His trousers were off so I only had his boxer shorts to contend with. I warmed up some ketchup in my palms and gently swabbed his manhood. He just snored as I covered the whole thing nicely. Then I smeared a knife with the red stuff and placed it by his hip.

Dawn: Cramps were coming fairly frequently by now, but I was having too much fun to care. I grabbed my Polaroid, aimed and shot. The flash woke Alan up. His expression was priceless. I caught that too. By the time he'd wiped himself dry I'd hidden the pictures in the broom closet. Alan never went in there. When he confronted me I made light of it all and said he'd gotten my period instead of me. He fumed and stormed out to play pool.

Susan: Oh, Father, you'll never guess what I did then. I pasted shots of his face on to his thing like they do in *National Enquirer.* Then zipped out to the local copy place, made some lurid color Xeroxes and dropped the package off at the restaurant, left it with the bartender for HER. After all, I hadn't tried 52 criminal cases for nothing.

Lisa: Well, Father, two days passed. Alan hadn't left me—he was too scared. And my period hadn't arrived—I was too nervous. At least that's what my gyno had said when he pronounced the litmus test negative. (At least there'd be no Billy II to spoil my perfect marriage.) I took a bunch of water pills and sat out on the back porch.

Maggie: It was a spring day and the calla lilies were in bloom. I had a bowl of green beans to snap and a Jane Austen novel to perhaps breeze through. I experienced a rare instant of peace until my neighbor Estelle stopped by. She had nothing to say. She just plopped down on a chair and started eating an apple.

Regina: The still of the afternoon had been destroyed by her chomping presence. A chomp every 5 to 10 seconds. Her loose dentures made the sound even worse. Snap of beans, quiet, chomp, snap, quiet, chomp, snap, quiet, chomp. Estelle continued to aimlessly gnaw away at that damn piece of fruit as if her life depended on it. Little did she know. Chomp, chomp.

"The midget?" David guessed.

"Smart boy. Miles did it. Instead of the Feast of Fools, he put down Happy Head Festival."

"I see," David mumbled.

"What do you see?"

"Madness."

Jane: My head went dizzy, my palms went clammy, and then I struck. I picked up *Sense and Sensibility* and hurled it at her. She thought I was kidding around and threw her apple core back at me. THAT was IT. I picked up the yard rake and took it to her powdery puss. There was blood on the grass, a section of flesh and

yes, then her EYEBALL came rolling out. When I had totally raked her over, I took the remnants of her shredded body to the well and dumped them. I stood there exhausted and covered in blood. But Father, you know what? I got my period the next day.

All: Forgive me.

Mad Dogs of Italy
THADDEUS RUTKOWSKI

Mad dogs are rare here. Most, I imagine, are confined to asylums. Some, at least, must be kept under maximum security.

A few, however, reside at the Verdi Foundation Rest Home in Milan. I saw a crazy mutt there, on the sidewalk outside the front door. It had the shape of a greyhound, but its fur was straw-orange. Curiously, its coat shone like a sane dog's. I could tell it was demented by the way it was sniffing around.

A small number live in Venice. Crossing a canal, I saw a shocked dog. Its testicles were balanced wrong. But the light was poor and I may have been mistaken. The small, insane beast was loping over a crooked bridge toward me. Its tongue was hanging out, and it looked as if it were grinning. I got out of its way, and I glanced behind me as it passed.

The odd canine misfit may still be found. On the street in Florence, I looked up at a window and saw a criminally insane dog. Its head was triangular, so its cerebrum must have been small. Its ears swiveled slowly as it stared back at me. I had to assume it was disturbed because it did not make a sound.

Mediterranean veterinarians are partly to blame. In an animal clinic, I saw an apparently normal dog on a steel-topped table. The dog's toenails skidded across the surface as the doctor's aides murmured encouragement. Dog fear filled the air. Even if this dog had been sane when it arrived, I decided, it definitely would be touched in the head by the time it left.

Lately, I haven't seen any canine lunatics. All the dogs I've encountered have been among the stablest of their species. I do not believe, however, that the num-

A bull got on the car and swaggered lustily down the aisle, banging his nightstick against the hold poles. He stopped at Lisa and Stephanie. "Hey, what you broads doing there?" He interrogated. "You a couple a lezzies?"

"No," Stephanie wet her lips. "We're just . . . we know each other."

"I like lezzies. it turns me on. Why don't you kiss. Do some tongue kissing right now." He was fondling his nightstick.

A man in the next car, **Thad Rutkowski,** *pressed his face to the door window like a fly stuck to shimmering flypaper.*

Thad Rutkowski is the author of Desperate Measures *and* Super Nature.

Thad, an amateur voyeur, strummed his penis through his pants like a blind Bluesman playing a guitar.

131

bers of emotionally troubled dogs are declining in Italy. They have simply taken refuge and are waiting for the right moment to begin their rampage.

Project Notes
ALFRED VITALE

being that I'm afraid of heights, it's pretty funny that I live on the twenty-second floor of my building . . . don't ya think? so whenever i wanna go out, i have to get in the elevator. now, normally i wouldn't mind riding them once in a while . . . but doin' it a few times a day has become a routine i'd kill to be rid of . . . maybe it's the fact that as we pass each floor, a bell rings . . . ting . . . ting . . . ting . . . ting . . . etc. . . . so that blind people will know what floor they are on. fine.

there's not a single blind person in any of the 120 or so apartments.

someone put a sign in the elevator . . . looked like one of those haphazard signs that painters put up that say, "cution, wet paints" . . . our elevator sign said "all you crackheads [sic] better get out of this bulding [sic] or else your [sic] gonna get thrown out of here by the good tenents [sic]!" it was signed "x." how fuckin' corny. like this letter is gonna really do something . . . the crackies can't read. what would they do if they could? leave? because some citizen with no balls or language skills threatens them with harm? if i was gonna write some kind of sign in the elevator . . . and believe me i've thought about it many times . . . if i were to write one, i would've told the crackies that EVERY tenant in the building wants them dead . . . and i would've ended it with "SO??? what are YOU gonna do about it?" with the hopes that they would knock on all the *good* citizens' doors and threaten THEM. i figure, if these tenants would actually CONFRONT the crackies, rather than say hello to them when they walk in the building, then maybe someone would snap and kill a crackie . . . hey, bumper sticker idea: kill a crackie for christ. one of them lives on my floor . . . washington is his name, supposedly. one

"Madness?"

"I mean," David said, wetting his lips, "how could he expect to get away with such a transparent travesty?"

"The American public is not as possessed of literary acumen as you might think, Dave. In fact, the FBI let this one slip by."

"Why, though?" Dave began.

"Huh?"

"Why do you have a picture of the person that sent you the information?"

*"She didn't send it to us. We intercepted it. It was in a letter to **Alfred Vitale**."*

Alfred Vitale is the editor of Rant *magazine and the author of* Fairy Tales from the Urban Holocaust. *He has work in* Shockbox *and* Sensitive Skin. *"Vitale also decodes foreign languages. There's a whole ring of them . . . of translators whose works—we think intentionally—continually misfire."*

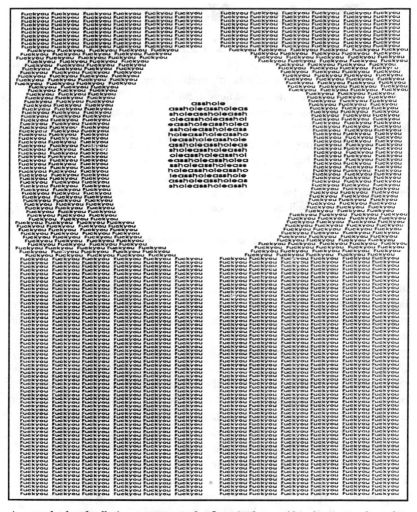

time, as he lay fetally in a stupor on the floor in front of his door . . . a door that had to be replaced when some terrific kids taped some blockbusters to it on fourth of july and blew it to shreds . . . i kicked him in the stomach. his grimace of pain came in slow motion . . . it was eerie . . . surreal, almost, watching my sneaker land in his solar plexus and seeing his drawn-out sloth response . . . maybe it takes a few seconds for pain to register in a crackie's brain. i tried it again . . . this time his hands crawled down to guard his stomach. i felt a little guilty about doing it . . . it was pretty scummy to kick a man when he's down. but . . . y'know . . . guilt is a useless emotion.

so what was I saying? oh, so this note that "x" wrote stayed up for the rest of the day. at some point in the evening, it was taken down . . . probably not by a crackie, but by one of the few yuppies that slum by living here. another sign replaced it, though, next day . . . it said, "A notice to all and sundry: We, the united crack addicts of this illustrious edifice, would like to state here that we abhor these threats of violence, we detest your irrational sensibilities, and pray that you find the time to educate yourself so that your neanderthal-esque threats can be lucid enough so as to elicit a proper response."

i wrote that one.

Apollo's Curse

BRUCE BENDERSON

He yawned and peered through the orange mercury vapor street light, as the departed wave of Dilaudid dropped him on his ass again. Carly was across the street. The transvestite stopped at the curb and yanked up her top to bare her breasts, grabbed them and squeezed them. She looked good from a distance. Glancing quickly both ways, she pulled down her miniskirt, keeping her cock pressed between her legs, and mimed a pussy dance just for him. Apollo mimed cheers and applause.

It was only for a split second that a collapsed version of what had happened maybe two months—a year?—ago flared up in his brain. He'd been her boyfriend then. Kind of.

But, well, then one night he needed . . . something . . . from her purse—all right, it was fix money—and when she found out, she came looking for him on the Deuce. He'd had the bad luck of talking to another queen when she found him.

"Carly, *really* I woulda asked you."

"I'll fucking cut you, you son of a bitch," she said, reaching into her purse.

"No. Come on now, put that shit away. There's cops around."

Carly's big hand, with its inch-long fingernails, whipped the gleaming blade from side to side. First it slashed open his shirt, then some long cuts across his chest. She kept reaching for his face, but he fended her off; let her cut his forearm instead.

Winded, she let the knife drop to her side, her eyes streaming with tears, running the mascara. Her wispy hair had come undone and was plastered to her face with sweat.

It wasn't so much being cut by a queen in public, but the sight of her with her hair undone and the ugly

*Carter sat mooning in a muddy funk. His attempts to track down the trapeze artist had brought him a series of soiled leads. Muy-Muy was an assumed name, her address in Shatterhead was non-existent, she had no known acquaintences and no known past. Mike's friend Christian was paying him a handsome pittance to find this girl, but since she had been fired from Roxor's, she had dropped out of sight like a dime through the keyhole of a sewer cover. There was a guy, **Bruce Benderson**, who she had been seen with at the Ziggurat after hours. Bruce Benderson is the author of Pretending to Say No and User, and has been published in Between C & D. But he proved as elusive as a Cantonese call girl. Michael thought perhaps Bruce was not so much a man as a flickering light that only existed because there were too many candles and mirrors in the Ziggurat.*

drops of sweat on her forehead that curled his fingers into a hard fist. He smashed her face, knocking a tooth out.

"Is this guy giving you trouble, little lady?"

"Yes officer, he tried to rape me." Her head was bowed, her hand clasping her bloody mouth. She was sobbing.

"Against the wall! Put your arms up!"

"Can't you see it's a guy, officer! That's no lady!"

"Shut up!"

The cop found his works and a bag right away, so he was sent to Rikers, bleeding like a pig, and waited three months without bail.

Some of the guys had put ads in gay papers about being lonely and needing a gay they could write to and call collect. Then you were supposed to write about your big dick until the guy cracked. You'd talk about all the things that would happen when you got out and then hit him up for money and cigarettes. For some of the guys, the relationships turned into long-term ones. It was ripe for fantasy. The person on the outside starting to do all kinds of favors, calling relatives for them, sending them cigarettes, books, commissary money. Occasionally, the locked-up one getting strung out so that the other's generosity took on strange, impossible significations, sexual identity stretching like a rubber band.

It was just his luck to get one who wanted to be a "nice guy" more than anything else.

"Don't write me sexual letters. Let's be honest with each other." A series of "spiritual" letters passed between them discussing third world liberation, sexual politics, the prison system. The guy complimenting his intelligence. Sensitive talk about relationships and the meaning of friendship.

"May, upon the arrival of this letter, it find you in the best of health . . . " Apollo always began each letter cursing the fact that his perpetual damning and desperate need always had to rear its ugly head again. "I sincerely hope that you . . . " "Please forgive my asking but . . . " "Hope you are well and by the way could you . . . " "I'm sorry we got to know each other under such bad circumstances for me but if you could . . . "

This time it was worse. When you're alone in your cell after lights out, anguish might settle in. The loneliness seems limitless. You're tempted to think that this guy could . . . Later it will seem absurd.

Nightmares of torture and sadism, witchcraft being performed on and by him. He felt, as he sat bolt upright in bed in the middle of the night, that it was only fair to warn his penpal with whom he was dealing. "I've got to admit to you right off the bat that I'm not a very trusting person. I hate to say it but I'm full of bitterness and rage."

The admissions backfired. "I'll take the chance . . . " "I can handle it" were the guy's responses. An avalanche of feelings welling up. An intolerable need to believe that the guy really might understand everything. Ferocious hate about the better possibility that he would not. He wrestled with it, pushed it away. "Dear Comrade . . . "

It was too late. The mark had marked him. There were sweet moments, his weakest, when he sank into the dream of a friend and protector who was taking care of everything. A kind of Frankenstein patchwork of a buddy-brother with a strange, scary erotic aspect. It intoxicated him like nerve gas. Coming down from it was worse then withdrawal from dope. The sense of injustice riddled him, made him feel murderous.

"This will be our last letter. For both our sakes, I think it better we stop communicating. I'll never be able to make you happy."

But the guy kept writing. Was he the con artist of the century? It had almost lulled Apollo into what seemed like a passive, infantile state. A desperate, intolerable need leaking with sexuality. It felt like incest. There he was daydreaming lying in his arms like some kind of woman. He'd turn into jail-pussy if he wasn't careful.

SAINT BOBO

Then, on Christmas, came the pair of Nikes he'd been asking for. And with it, a letter that set his teeth on edge. "This should prove to you that I'm really thinking about you in the best possible way."

And what exactly was that supposed to mean? A man who needs shoes on his feet like anyone else having to bow down and kiss the feet of the one who provides them? He wrote a grateful-sounding letter, but he had the gnawing sense that every word of it stoked the guy's ego.

A month later the guy came to visit. Apollo had saved the expensive sneakers for when he got out and never thought of wearing them. Not thinking that the guy would not understand the communal nature of prison, he borrowed new sneakers from buddies to dress up for him. Traded a pack of cigarettes for a haircut, got a pressed shirt and even some stolen cologne. He cleaned his teeth.

Sitting in the courtyard, a sinking feeling as he tried to imagine what he would do when he got out to please his benefactor, the guy's hairy arms, his school-teacher-like clothes. He pushed it out of his mind, courageously promising himself not to let his benefactor down.

The guy was staring at his sneakers.

I thought you said you desperately needed sneakers.

I did. I borrowed these from somebody.

The guy gave him a doubtful, lacerating look. It made him feel lucky to be locked up, because all he wanted to do was slash up the guy's face and hurl the sneakers into the wounds. Everything he'd suspected had come true in one overwhelming wave.

By accepting the sneakers he had branded himself as a user, coated himself with slime. And all of it had been ordained by the other person, who was always in power.

But, for the guy, it had obviously been no big deal. He kept up the sweetish letters, spelling out high ideals, forging a high-class image.

Apollo's emotions, like hot coals, put all his strength into playing along, waiting for the chance to strike.

The guy's letters and calls had a plaintive element now, because his father was dying. Apollo mimed the right sentiments, said he was *there* for him, until the guy wrote that his father had finally passed away. Then Apollo went right to work. "May, upon the arrival of this letter, it find you in the best of health . . . I've got to admit what I think of you . . . You're a sad, lonely gay guy who likes to fantasize that he can control other people . . . I felt sorry for you and appreciated what you did for me, I was willing to make some sacrifices for you when I got out—sacrifices, if you know what I mean . . . "

Gleefully, but with gritted teeth, he took his punishment as cigarettes, commissary money, books, and promises of lodging stopped abruptly. The rejection was exhilarating, as the reins fell back into his hands, the bitterness reinstated its protective bulwarks and life became simple again . . .

So simple that here he stood, in the spot he had been hundreds of times, a couple blocks from Jilly's bar, without any money and a gnawing yen to get high, a citizen of the world of dope following its laws . . .

Max
DAVID RATTRAY

Every morning at eight-forty-five, one of my clocks plays the *Meistersinger Prelude* theme on a set of silver chimes, and I wake up. I lie still for another fifteen minutes, staring at the pipe and the lamp on the bedside table, and at the photograph on the wall behind the lamp, of Gul, a young woman I have never been able to forget.

At nine sharp, I light the lamp's oil-sodden wick. Aching with anticipation, I wait for the clear flame to come up, sunk back on my pillow, the pipe clasped in my left hand. I often fondle it and lick the cold, hardened pill on top of the bowl.

A few minutes later, I roll over and smoke, all in one long drag. I lie back, holding my breath to a count of forty, the euphoria of the day's first indulgence illuminating my entire being.

An unmarried woman, I live just round the corner from the Royal Saint-Germain; it's my boudoir, so to speak. At exactly nine-thirty every day, the doorbell rings, and a waiter from the Royal appears, bearing a silver tray with one croissant, sweet butter, coffee, hot milk, and *Le Figaro*, which I scan for theater and book reviews over breakfast. I've declared a moratorium on the Ben Barka affair, and I don't care what Sartre says about it. I'm not interested in the doings of Che Guevara. Nor do I share Ho Chi Minh's optimism that the Yanks are going to be out of Indochina in the next three years, say by 1970.

The coffee aroma, the bakery smell and the whiff of fresh newsprint never fail me. I have no appetite in the morning. These smells bring me back to life. At all other hours, the apartment, which like the house itself was built by Dulac, an associate of Gaudi, in 1904, smells of two things only: blond Virginia tobacco and opium. Pall Malls have a honey smell that never goes

"If Rollo," the FBI Director continued, *"got tied in with this network of swindlers, his goose was plucked. They were headed up by this wiry Welshman, **David Rattray**."* David Rattray, who was not Welsh, is the author of How I Became One of the Invisible *and* Opening the Eyelid. *He worked for* Reader's Digest *on such books as* Mysteries of the Bible *and* After Jesus. *He died on March 22, 1993. One of his last readings was with the Unbearables, at Fez in December 1992.*

"This Welshie had as his right hand dope Outstandish, that masquerading, pimping, feely boy, who gave midgetry a bad name."

David shifted uneasily, the purloined Rower tape chunky in his back pocket. "But why would he, er Rollo, be interested in them?"

"Ha . . . they all had the same vice," Hoover *sneered.*

stale. I can't endure the stink of Gauloises, et cetera. "I say, Max, it's like smoking the anal hairs of an Egyptian peasant," my friend Dede, Dedale de Saint Maur, used to exclaim, until I begged him to desist. Then Dede's wife Gismande (my mistress as of a year ago yesterday) has tried to invade my place with scents like vetiver. There again I draw the line. Gismande occupies the guest bedroom. I *sleep* with no one. I never receive her before noon, either. At twelve sharp, Gismande knocks and comes in for her first pipe of the day, after I have had time to bathe, dress, and smoke three or four myself. Then I am ready to make one for her.

This morning while awaiting the stroke of nine, I tried to imagine the contents of my police file. One day a few years ago, during an interview with an inspector in a fourth-floor office at the Prefecture, I saw the outside of my folder. Peach-colored and tied with a pale green ribbon, it was surprisingly slim. I had rather expected it to bulge like a telephone book.

I had been summoned to appear because of an anonymous crank letter that denounced me (a) as an opium smoker, (b) as the notorious "Max," a lesbian with a special foible for pubescent girls, and (c) as a UFO zombie reporting to my alien handlers in their flying saucer via a transmitter secreted in my wisdom tooth.

The inspector handed me the letter. Its writing was childish, with carefully formed loops and the *i*s dotted with tiny circles. My thoughts flashed back to the pair of truants I had chanced to meet one afternoon after a matinee at the Pagode, Jacqui and Toukit. I introduced myself: "Maxine's the name, Max for short." I was intrigued when after five minutes the girls offered to boost recent jazz from the new record shop at Saint Germain des Pres where a manager had insulted me the week before. "They have to be catalogued," I objected. "One doesn't just collect at random." "We can do shorthand," Jacqui boasted, "and we type more than a hundred words a minute." I hired both of them. Within a week, they were coaxing me to teach them how to smoke. Then I noticed that a tube of codeine tablets was missing. I fired Jacqui and Toukit. I knew where they were going, I told them. I was in the street myself at their age.

To the inspector I only observed that the letter had to be the work of a very sick individual. "That goes without saying," he replied and showed me out with a handshake and a wink.

I could only speculate as to what other information might be included in my dossier. It must have contained the fact that I was an orphan. That my mother had died having me. That she had been the youngest of three daughters of Etienne Bernard, whose Trotsky biography had raised a hoo-ha at the Sorbonne in 1929. That my father, Colonel Duhautier, had earned the Croix de Guerre in the war of 1914, and that, as a still-young, childless widower in 1930, he had become the black

sheep of his Catholic Royalist family by marrying the
Jewish professor's daughter in a love match unprecedented in three hundred years of an illustrious family
history. That as a result of his clandestine pro-Allied
activities, he had been tortured to death by the
Gestapo in 1944. That I had lived in the streets
throughout the winter and spring of that year, only to
be rescued just before the Liberation of Paris by the
notorious Dedale Aristide de Saint Maur—who
throughout the German occupation had led a double
life; that of a gilded youth often seen with the likes of
Charles Trenet and Jean Cocteau, while at the same
time rendering important services to the Gaullist
branch of the Resistance—twenty-five when he first
picked me up, having mistaken me for a boy. That at
age fifteen I had hired the Salle des Plantes and deliv-
ered a lecture in a zoot suit, "Defense and Illustration
of Pedophilia," for which I was arrested and fined,
having been put up to it by Saint Maur. That I had
subsequently used Saint Maur's lawyer to represent
my claim on the Bonn government for damages in the
deaths of my father and the two aunts whom he had
designated as my legal guardians. That I had won a
favorable settlement of my claim and had been living
on a sizable tax-free pension ever since. That I was
seen almost daily at the Royal Saint-Germain and,
since the publication of my radio play, *Chez Lipp*, as
well as at the Petit Pave, often with Saint Maur,
though we were not generally reputed to be lovers.
The outside of my folder read (Mlle) DUHAUTIER,
Edouarde Maxine; 43, rue du Bac; Profession: Writer;
Born 3 August 1932, Hôpital de la Pitie, Paris.

In my opinion, a year and a day is long enough for
anything to continue. This will be Gismande's last day
here. Dede will be coming with his car at eleven, for a
couple of pipes with me and a bonjour madame to his
wife when she appears. Gismande will also have a pipe
or two, then go for her soak. She is regular as clock-
work. At twenty-three she has a good body, enjoys

"And what was that?"
"Hakim Bey."

looking at herself in my ceiling mirror, often falls asleep in the tub, and is never ready to go out before three.

The bathroom is where I began to discern fatal flaws in Gismande the same day she moved in. We had just taken what was to be our first and last shared bath. While toweling her down afterwards, I discovered that Gismande was heavily infested with crablice. I had to ring the pharmacy. We spent another suffocating hour in the bathroom. Hadn't she realized? I asked. Gismande replied that she had never even heard of morpions, save as a peculiar term of abuse. She had certainly never laid eyes on one.

"Never heard of crabs!" I shouted.

Gismande cocked her head to one side in a pout. "I don't suppose there is any need to warn your husband," I continued. She shook her head.

For a few seconds, we stood there without saying anything. Then I asked her to join me in my room for a smoke as soon as she was dressed. People are under the impression that I am easy-going, because I would rather smoke than deal with conflict. Given my bent, I was unprepared for what followed.

I had put on my dressing gown and the Moroccan slippers I wear around the house, and was pacing back and forth between the bedside tray containing my smoking gear and the glass cabinet in the next room, where I keep my collection of seventy-odd pipes, trying to make up my mind which I ought to offer to Gismande as a gift. I settled on a double-jointed one that could be unscrewed in two segments, which if dismantled with its bowl could ride unnoticed in a pocket, a model commonly known as a traveling pipe. Taking its plum red stem in both hands, I dismantled the pipe, noting, with a satisfaction that had never diminished over the years, the shininess of its silver fittings and the elegance of its tightly threaded joints. I dropped the segments in my pocket, intending to reassemble them in front of Gismande as soon as we had smoked.

Gismande had already entered the room. Wearing a white sailor suit, she sat cross-legged at the head of my bed, staring at the photograph of Gul. "Max, the day I saw this," Gismande said, "I knew I turned you on."

No one likely to make such comments had ever been admitted to this room. Never mind the fact that Gul and I had never done anything but kiss, even on the few occasions when I slept with her at the hotel. She had been preparing to leave for Germany with her Turkish friend, a black marketeer. The Germans were still in Paris. I was fourteen and had just met Dede de Saint Maur. I had been coughing a lot. He arranged for me to enter a clinic where all the patients had flower names. Mine was *Bouton d'Or* (Buttercup). They removed half of one lung. The very next day, Dede taught me to smoke in my hospital bed. He brought opium daily thereafter. The doctor did a paper on me. It seems the medicated smoke not only anesthetized the surgically wounded tissues, but other, as-yet-unknown alkaloids present in the opium worked to accelerate healing; at least that is what the doctor, also a smoker, theorized.

Two days before the operation, I said goodbye to Gul at the hotel. She was packing her things in a cardboard suitcase and a carpetbag that had to be strapped shut with a belt. Twice she thanked me for my friendship and the second time choked on the word. She fished out a handpainted necktie that could have belonged to a pimp, together with an old prewar edition of *Le Puits de la Solitude* (The Well of Loneliness) by Radcliffe Hall, which had fallen to pieces. Tears filled her eyes as she knotted the book's two halves with the tie. I never saw Gul again. The Turk died in Hamburg during an air raid, but of Gul there was no record whatever.

Opening the book, I found Gul's photo. I told Dede Gul had saved my life; he had the picture framed.

I could think of no suitable reply to Gismande, who had by now shifted her attention to my lacquered smoking tray. Behind her fair head loomed a black-framed screen forming the back of the bed, which was painted with a Tibetan hell scene, in which grimacing demons subjected still-unliberated souls to yet another turn of the karmic screw, a scene I always miss when smoking because, turned the other way, my pipe aimed at the lamp and Gul's photo in its silver frame behind it. Gismande was right. She had indeed reminded me of Gul.

In spite of myself, I remembered the glimpse I had had a half hour before of Gismande retreating naked from the bathroom.

"Now I want you to pay close attention," I said, "to the precise amounts I use." I opened the jar and reached for the needles.

"I want to learn," Gismande murmured. Just then a detail I had never noticed in the curve of her hip drew my hand up into the flat of her belly, under the sailor shirt. Extending my thumb downward, I felt the beginning of her hair, a bit past the waistband of the trousers. With a slight quiver, she took a deep breath and leaned back, her legs spreading, her face in three-quarters profile with a cigarette dangling from the corner of her mouth. I opened her pants and was immediately put in mind of an erotic description by Verlaine at his most perverse, in which he has a lesbian marveling at the skin inside her friend's thighs:

Smoothly white as a milkwhite rose, and pink
As a lily under a purple sky . . .

A few minutes later, she whispered, "I like your finger better than most people's mouths."

D a v i d R a t t r a y

We had not taken time to strip but only opened our clothes; now Gismande reciprocated. I was incredibly wet. "You never guessed what a cunt lapper I am," she said. I found it impossible not to surrender to the pleasure flooding me to the marrow of my bones. I made believe it was Gul's tongue instead of Gismande's. I found myself staring at the photograph. I imagined Gul's image expanding, breaking through the frame, entering the room to pick me up in an embrace I would never come back from.

I woke up with my face in Gismande's lap. The lingering odor of insecticide aroused me. I began licking her organ. Then, separating its labia between my fore-fingers, I looked inside. The exterior parts were of an almost translucent smoky lavender like the stems of certain mysterious plants I had seen in the woods the day I turned thirteen. I had been all alone in the country house where my father had raised me as a son, dressing me in boy's clothes. The Germans had arrested him in Marseille the day before. A friend telephoned the family lawyer, and he in turn instructed the housekeeper to pack me off to my mother's two older sisters in Paris. My father had provided for this; it had been the best he could think of.

For weeks I had been riding Banzai every day. That morning I galloped him down a cart track through the southeast corner of our property. I began to feel something I had never felt before. I never even considered reining him in. Moments later, lost to the world at the height of my first orgasm, I was swept out of the saddle by an inconvenient branch and dashed to the ground.

I awakened to the dank smell of a clump of ghostly pale, waxy, leafless plants growing on the patch of dirt into which my face had been projected by the fall. I stuck out my tongue and licked the violet-gray flute of earth-ooze nearest to my nose, had a vision of myself turning into a mushroom, and passed out.

I revived, only to discover that my wrist was broken, and nearly swooned again. Back at the barn, Banzai was in his stall. I smeared my wrist with blue lina-ment, sobbing as only a child can sob, for the irrevocably lost time of life when I could pretend that I was a boy and actually believe it.

I arrived in Paris with my arm in a sling. Before I got my wrist out of the cast, the old ladies had a dressmaker measuring me. The news reached us that my father had died. We dressed in black. My aunts smothered me in hearts and flow-ers. The better part of a year passed. One winter afternoon, on my way in from a bookshop that had become my second home, I was intercepted in the courtyard by the concierge who told me that my aunts had been arrested. I left immediately, and a week later met Gul. She had been living in the streets ever since summer. She took me under her wing.

That was many years ago. Gismande brings it all back. However, as I smoke increasingly, I find myself taking less and less interest in Gismande, while at the same time my reveries involving Gul grow ever more absorbing.

A warm baritone voice rumbles: "Follow thy fair sun, unhappy shadow ..." I am looking up into Dede's enormous round face and unfathomable eyes. Soon he and I will be driving out to the flea market to call on a man who wants me to see a Second Empire wristwatch. At four we will return here to fetch my smoking things and close the apartment. Then off to the country, to arrive before dark in plenty of time to prepare a *gras-double,* our favorite supper. The meat is already packed. Gismande will stay at the château when Dede accompanies me to the clinic four days hence. The patient is kept in a deep sleep for three weeks. During that time, Gismande will move her things out. We'll all be friends, a happy family.

In the evening, Gertrude Stein removes her makeup, brushes her hair back, and curls up in bed with a good book

I don't want this cure. Dede's doctor, a withered, chain-smoking gnome in thick bifocals and a white smock, talked me into it. This son of Aesculapius addresses me as "madame." "Madame, for the next six months at the very least, abstinence will be your ticket." He thinks addiction is like malaria. One brings it home from the colonies. It's in the blood.

Just now I thought of an alternative to the cure. Dede and I would murder Gismande. It would be simple. Gismande takes massive doses of vitamin C daily before her bath. I could refill the capsules with double-strength gardenol. Then, once she was asleep in the tub, I would turn on the bathroom water heater without lighting the gas.

That would be a switch on another possibility that has been haunting me ever since a recent afternoon when Gismande asked me if I didn't think she might be Gul's double. I asked her if she would like me to kick her to death slowly. She laughed and walked out of the room. The conversation continued in my head. I imagined Gismande saying that if Dede were to die, she would inherit, and the two of us could look forward to a lifetime of discreet pleasures.

D   a   v   i   d   R   a   t   t   r   a   y

Time and again I harked back to this speech, until I almost believed that Gismande had actually pronounced it. I wondered if she might not in fact have murderous designs on both Dede and me. I fancied a conversation with Dede in which I would report Gismande's proposal. He and I would arrange for her to die in the tub, then take the body out to the country and bury it in quicklime.

But before any of this came to pass, something even crazier might happen. I might go through Gismande's papers (which, it did seem very odd when I came to think of it, I'd never once seen) only to discover that she was, in some inconceivable fashion, not a mere double or revenant or incubus, but, in very fact, Gul herself in person, metamorphosed into a monster, no, an angel of unmitigated carnality, forever well and young. Then we would rush to the bathroom, Dede and I, to find it full of gas, but Gul would be gone. There would be a note scrawled in lipstick: "Sorry."

Treading on air, as it were, we would drive out to the chateau. Then, as we unpacked, Gul would suddenly walk in, and the two of them, Gul and Dede, would turn on me.

All my life I have surrounded myself with strictly 1900-style Art Nouveau things. I cannot imagine living any other way than in silence and darkness, with clocks, books, pictures, and pleasant smells.

On the bed next to me, Dede is working with the pipe and needles. I have always been in awe of Dede's protean trick of mind. True to his name Dedale, he has an inventor's hands and understands flight. He is the only source of the opium I have smoked, and where he gets it I have never known. He is friends with the Prefect. He takes care of my clocks and arranges the mechanism of my life. The pipe is trained over the lamp. In the silence I can hear the opium cook. Dede inhales it at a drag, then lies still. I picture a sea lion resting in the sun.

The Quevedo Cipher

HARRY MATHEWS

Ilaid out my tools on the hotel bedspread: five lengths of cord, a leather gag, mushroom powders.

Comfortable, anonymous, safe, La Perla satisfied my needs. At the front desk I had experienced some anxiety when the receptionist, an elderly Levantine, glanced up from my passport and said, "I believe I knew you elsewhere, although not as a Triestine." For a matter of seconds I forgot my current name, and stammer points began glowing in my nape. (I shall not censor my stutter. That would make it worse.) Before I had to respond, he began leading the way to my room.

On the bed, parallel to the "tools," I placed my card—Karl-Ignaz Molinaro, Direttore Commerciale, Assicurazioni Lloyd Triestino—and the report sheets on my three women: Paula Fotopolis, Claire McDonald, Madame Lothar Schmidt. The names had once belonged to S, born Fotopolis, her first husband a McDonald, her third a Schmidt. The women had all three been born in Belgium sixty-two years before. Beneath each name an address and telephone number had been typed, as well as another name to use when I introduced myself.

If none of those women proved to be S, my months-long quest would come to a forlorn end. My correspondents had investigated every city and village on this Mediterranean Sea to whose shores I knew she had come. That was all I knew of her. I had toured those shores. My search would end in this town.

I dined at Fahrenheit 451, at the receptionist's recommendation. His earlier remark set me musing, after I had begun my dinner, on the many other names I'd previously used in my career. Mr. Haak in Croatia, in

The bull lifted his truncheon meditatively. "Let's see some tit, too." He suggested. "One of you open your blouse."

The El skidded as it entered a serpentine curve, throwing blue sparks like spittle against the glass.

From his window at the Hotel Alcove, where he sat dingily brooding, **Harry Mathews** could see the train lean into the curve. Harry Mathews is the author of the amazing trilogy Tlooth, The Conversions, and The Sinking of the Odradek Stadium. The Dalkey Archive Press recently published his exemplary collection of masturbatory fantasies, Singular Pleasures.

Mathews could see the trio on the conveyance; they looked like impurities inside a long, half-transparent link of sausage.

Mesopotamia Henry Shah . . . They had abetted my progress to prosperity. Whatever happened now, Karl-Ignaz would be my last disguise.

While I ate, I resumed reading my golfing farce, *Par Seven*, and finished it with the cheese. Its climax described an exceptional chip shot that dropped straight into the seventh hole, whose cup was mysteriously connected to a septic tank beneath it; an off-color geyser resulted. (Much as I love angel wings, I refused dessert.) The player, who with this shot became the first ever to make par on the hole, earned the right to baptize it with the female name of his choice.

I needed something else to read. For the past thirty-seven years no day of my life has been spent without a book at hand. I therefore paid my first visit to one of the town's landmarks, a bar called L'Iris de Souss. Underneath the name, its sign read:

SPÉCIALITÉ DE GENTIANES
BOOK BAR
ANNA DELAFORGE, PROP.

On the shelves behind the counter, against a wall-length mirror, bright bottles alternated with darker books—a comforting sight, spoiled only by the brief pang I felt when from the door I spied the tiny, well-proportioned figure of the owner, almost a replica of S's. A flurry of hope was erased as soon as I noticed her blue-tinged, frilly hair, her brown eyes, the flat cross of white gold nestled between her breasts. I nevertheless welcomed the sight of Anna Delaforge as a favorable omen. After inviting her to join me in a drink, I took out a book and retired to La Perla.

The Quevedo Cipher bored me, no doubt because I at once deciphered the cipher of the title. Its first demonstration, a passage entitled "An Englishman Heads East," made its secret all too obvious:

By hazard nabbed in Mecca, he was befuddled, wretched, and miffed. He was ragged, then withheld (by rigid raj-jarring) from trekking on. A sullen backgammoner, he was stunned by rococo poppers from an Iraq-queered, weak-starred, misshapen steamfitter. At sunup he revved his new-wound fax-xerox-telex and, without as much as a by-your-leave, buzzed away.

I stopped reading and distracted myself until sleep by using the cipher to encrypt my fancies. One example only, one only:

Miss Hammer's full of essential latter-day pessimism. Without trust, she muffles my efforts to see her marred.

Next morning I called at the records office in the town hall. I wanted to verify my information about the three women and, if possible, to obtain more. The clerk I was directed to proved skeptical at the outset, subsequently mistrustful, and finally, when I tendered a lunch-size banknote, indignant. Pursing his lips, letting his arms fall to his sides, with a flick of his eyebrows he set me on my way to the door.

After telephoning Paula Fotopolis, I drove my rented fan car to her address outside of town: a broad three-storey house surrounded by a walled park. As I approached the gate, a young zebra stared out at me through its high bars.

A gardener let me in. Mrs. Fotopolis, who was neither Belgian, nor small, nor blue-eyed, answered my initial question by explaining that, two months previously, mounting expenses had forced the municipal zoo to close down. Its animals were first auctioned off. Despite considerable publicity the sale was not a success. She herself had bought the zebra, a few others had bid for ponies or peacocks; most beasts found no takers. Even the exquisite Mesmaecher fauns, who when the dealer approached them had remained perfectly still, with heads bowed and forelegs crossed, were in the end eaten by the auctioneers.

Our conversation was interrupted by a telephone call. I overheard Mrs. Fotopolis say, "I'll look after Bodley Head, you invite Cape, she can handle the

H a r r y M a t h e w s

other." On her return she informed me that she was organizing a convention, scheduled to coincide with the town's annual fiesta, of a random sampling of American and British publishers.

"We're trying to anticipate every difficulty after the disaster of last year's fiesta—first disease in the vineyards, then the dust hashish riots. Our celebration is not meant to be an orgiastic spree."

I learned several facts about the fiesta. It begins at the ninth new moon after the vernal equinox. It lasts three days. Predictable processions frame less formal gatherings, all supervised by specially marked police, haughty in manner but more helpful than severe. Music of great antiquity is played during concerts conducted from atop traditionally sculpted farm wagons. In many a square and park the oldest of the region's dances is performed. On the second evening a chapel dedicated to Saint Novellus is opened for vespers, which is the only service celebrated there in the course of the church year; a priest is specially sent from Rome to officiate. A statement whose opening words are spoken by the mayor to inaugurate the fiesta is continued by his deputy and then for seventy-two hours passed from one citizen to another without ever being allowed a pause longer than the equivalent of a comma; each human link of this verbal chain must not stop speaking, whatever the hour or circumstances, until a willing successor has been found. (I was grateful for this information when accosted one night by a babbling local.)

Mrs. Fotopolis inquired after the supposed acquaintance whose name I had mentioned when I called her. I had anticipated the question. I replied that I had come with the hope that she could supply this very news.

I eventually attended the vespers service at Saint Novellus's. I did so in order to study the remains of the frescoes Chardin had painted on the scroll-work of its pilasters, the artist's only known work in that medium. The imported priest entered wearing a long silk mantle embroidered with a collage of texts printed in small capitals. I remembered that Saint Novellus was the patron of journalists.

I drove back to town and parked at L'Iris de Souss. As I entered the bar, a Chinese employee was exclaiming to Anna, "This man dump Suze on your greenery" as he pointed to a dripping philodendron. Shrugging her shoulders, the proprietress offered me a glass of the house apéritif. For lunch I contented myself with a single dish, the "Cocteau and Artaud," a brace of *quenelles a la ruthénoise.*

A passenger met aboard the *Haghion Pneuma,* the ship on which I had arrived the day before, joined me at the counter. It had been he who, standing next to me on the foredeck as we approached the town, named in order the peaks of the anfractuous range that rears its precipitous wall of pink limestone behind it: Mounts Pond, Souss (famous for its wild irises), Saint John . . .

"Is that N-n-noz over there?" I had asked, pointing to the highest eminence and repeating the one name cited in my cursory guidebook.

It was Mount Noz indeed. I asked if its summit was accessible by car. He said that a road existed, one too dilapidated for standard automobiles. However, a friend of his had invented a five-bladed fan that could be fitted to the underside of ordinary vehicles. Switched on, the fan, by blowing a concentrated air stream onto the road surface, created a cushion that allowed the chassis to pass safely and comfortably over any rut or pothole. Fan cars were available at local rental agencies; he recommended I try one. His friend, he added, was now at work on a new project: a writing car.

(I took his advice; but it was not until the last day of my quest that I made the ascent of Mount Noz. By then my third inquiry had ended in disappointment. With my last hope dashed, the excursion held little interest for me. At the top I found the usual observation platform and a telescope through which I examined the town and its surroundings, now bereft of all charm. My only consolation was finding a specimen of olive yarrow, Linnaeus's "forgotten plant.")

Now, at L'Iris, I learned that my shipboard companion was an Armenian recently established here. He had just traveled to Yerevan and had returned laden with periodicals to distribute among the Armenian community. Out of politeness I asked if his trip had gone smoothly. It had, he replied, except for "the usual Florence delay." He had had to change planes many times. When I suggested that a journey by sea might have been more direct, he flatly stated that such an option was inconceivable. He had taken the *Haghion Pneuma* only because the town was otherwise inaccessible. He related how, having fled to Lebanon after the 1917 massacres, his family had soon after embarked with him for Marseilles, only to have their ship founder three hours after leaving port. He had providentially survived, with his feet floating on a wooden bar stool and his head on one of his father's clogs, fashioned out of the dense *Taxus opacus* of Mount Ararat.

"In 1917?" I wondered. "You age h-h-hardly—"

"I was three at the time." He looked a generation younger than his ninety-one years.

I telephoned the Lothar Schmidts: no answer. Driving to their house, I found it shuttered. I left the fan car at my hotel and wandered about the town until dark, then went back to L'Iris to return *The Quevedo Cipher* and choose a new book. Anna was behind the bar. I drank another Suze and, while chatting with her, told her of my supposed professional reasons for being here and my consequent disappointment at finding the Schmidts away.

"*She's* away—for some sort of psychotherapy," she told me. Anna evidently had known the couple well. She recounted, among other things, that Lothar

Schmidt had recently left his mark on the history of medicine. He had locally and tentatively been diagnosed as suffering from a rare blood disorder called haemocrypsis. A sample of his blood had been sent to a specialized laboratory in Belgium, where, as part of one test, plasma had been injected into a young, healthy rabbit. Soon afterwards an altogether unexpected accident occurred: death intervened, "and in a way," Anna said, "that apparently makes it the only known instance of this type of death. I gather that in medical circles the case will henceforth be referred to as *the* death from boredom."

"Of Sch-sch-schmidt?"

"The rabbit used in the test was the only animal left in the laboratory. The firm was in the process of moving from Bruges to Antwerp. All the mice, cats, and other rabbits had been taken to the new location. Alone, with only occasional human attention and nothing to do, watch, or listen to, the rabbit abruptly expired."

"And Sch . . . Schmidt?"

"He was cured by plenum acupuncture," Her attempted explanation of the treatment failed to enlighten me.

"What about M-m-m-mrs. Schmidt?"

Anna smiled and sighed. "Suki—a sweet lady. And in almost every way a respectable and respected one. For reasons she may discover on her present travels, she suffers from an irresistible attraction to Native Americans, especially from Latin America (although her 'depth champion,' as she defined him, hailed from Wyoming)." Since foreign commercial fleets began destroying the Peruvian fishing industry, Anna told me, more and more such Americans have sailed on ships that call here. First came the coastal Peruvians, then their mountain cousins, then *their* cousins from Ecuador and Bolivia. As soon as Suki heard that one had arrived, she would go down to the docks, find him, and lure him into bed, or even seduce him in some obscure warehouse corner. The owner of an in-and-out hotel near the port agreed to inform her when there was her kind of "flesh ashore" and of course—it was a very cahoots-cahoots relationship—to provide her with a room. The most notorious of her conquests was a young Ecuadorian from the hinterland. Like all his people, he wore a brass bell fastened to his throat by a leather thong. Suki caught him on the way back to his ship, led him into a nearby shed, and there cast off her wrap-around frock of Venetian lace, under which she was wearing nothing except her famous blue-cotton spider bra: at its points, circular holes let her nipples protrude; around each of them, eight furry stems radiated in an embroidered likeness of tarantula legs. Driven wild by this partial nakedness, the Ecuadoran did not wait to undress before taking her. The tolling of his thrusts could be heard all the way to the main square. Anna paused. "I have to

U   n   b   e   a   r   a   b   l   e   s add that the rumor that she publicly performs lapdances and other *cochonneries* to tempt her prey is unfounded. She has assured me that she reserves these practices for purely private encounters."

I asked what Suki looked like.

"Five foot eleven, blond—pure Scandinavian jock."

Anna suggested a restaurant. I took with me a copy of *Paul and Lulu*. (As I left, a German tourist was loudly complaining, "Boot I do not *like* booter!") I started the book at dinner. Returning to La Perla, I watched a group of young boys and girls rehearsing the *djerdan*, the time-honored festival dance. Two refrains I jotted down may catch something of its discreet lilt:

I finished *Paul and Lulu* later that night. The novel tells the story of two charming, rather ineffectual con artists. They had only one consistently successful pat trick—"the veal caper." It permitted them, if not to prosper, at least to eat.

The following morning I woke up with a stiff neck and four bites of an out-of-season mosquito. I called up Pauline McDonald. Her gentle weary voice, impossible to imagine as S's whatever her age, filled me with foreboding. I found her in the company of her daughter, a Mrs. Margarita Ford. She lived with the latter's family in a sprawling, modestly appointed apartment in the southern quarter. As I entered, broadcast *presto* strains of *Simone Boccanegra* were considerately hushed. One glance at Mrs. McDonald crushed any lingering expectation: portly, coarse, kindly—not a trace of a trace of a resemblance. She smelled of a cold cream my mother used long ago. I stayed perhaps fifteen minutes, long enough to learn that she had first come here to work as cook for a well-to-do local family. She had later continued to do sewing for them. She had had to quit their kitchen because the members of the household reserved their encounters in the dining room as occasions for sustained mutual vituperation; in time Mrs. McDonald could no longer bear seeing her best dishes grow cold under endless torrents of abuse. She had married Mr. McDonald—Willie, as she called him—when he had come here in retirement from his Cimmerian homeland. Just before I left, her chubby grandson entered, beaming proudly as he reported to his mother the results of his weekly weight review.

It was after this last, fruitless visit that I drove up Mount Noz. The fan car proved its worth. At an outdoor stand beside the parking area I lunched on a few gloom-ridden swallows of *duzhvo*, a kind of cheeseless pizza. Such was my despondency and agitation that after lighting my last Flor de la Isabelita *cortado* I bit off and swallowed its first inch.

I drove down to the port and there booked passage on the *Haghion Pneuma*, scheduled to sail at midnight. At La Perla I packed my bags and paid my bill. I had nothing left to do but return *Paul and Lulu*.

In mid-afternoon L'Iris was nearly empty. Anna was standing behind the bar with her back turned to me. She was dressed in a simple, flowing, astonishingly elegant black dress, one from a distant past. It was such a dress that Susanna had worn on that fateful evening thirty-seven years earlier, the last time I saw her. On the counter behind her were arrayed lengths of cord, a leather gag, packets no doubt containing mushroom powders. At that moment, presumably catching sight of me in the bottle-lined mirror, she curtly spoke:

"Miller!"

She placed her left hand on her crown and slowly lifted above her head a wig of blue-tinged, frilly hair. As she turned, long, full strands of silvered brunette fell about her perfect ears. Dropping the wig, she raised a thumb to each eye. Brown contact lenses popped into the dusky air, revealing unfathomable blueness.

The scales fell from my own eyes. I understood, not only that "Souse" and "Suze" belonged to "Anna" and that a Schmidt might be known by his forge, but that I had nothing to forgive, nothing to punish. She was her own atonement: even if she had never been mine, I was hers. As she stepped from behind the bar I began trembling, the stammer points burned inwards from the base of my skull, I opened my mouth and made no sound.

She stretched her arms towards me: "Miller, you dodo! I never knew you cared."

("The Quevedo Cipher" is part of a collaborative novel co-authored by Florence Delay, Patrick Deville, Jean Echenoz, Sonja Greenlee, Mark Polizzotti, and Olivier Rolin. It was published in France in 1991 as Les Semaines de Suzanne. *The chapter is the final of seven episodes in the life of Suzy, or Susie, or Sue, or Susan, or Susana: the elusive Suzanne of the title.)*

Letter from Crete
—Suites Pandora, Hania, Crete
JORDAN ZINOVICH

Lovely Selene,

That's my terrace in the lower right corner of the photo, its limestone walls glowing yellow in the afternoon sunlight. Morning, midday, and evening those barn swallows sweep past in hot pursuit of life. The cobalt blue morning-glories have puckered their red-veined trumpets closed in the heat. You can see how their leaves cascade over the ledge beneath my window.

I know! I've regressed. I promised that I'd try to relax, and not fix lenses or filters between the world and me. *Mea culpa*. It's impossible for me to abandon my addiction. I record the spaces and situations I drift through.

I wanted to stir your memories, so I took this Polaroid from the west side of the harbor. I hoped to include the whole of the Kastelli hilltop, but had to crop severely to enhance the staggering profile of the archives complex for you. My back is to Roland's wonderful old house. (It's a superb place, rising alone from the other harem-district ruins. He did a magnificent job restoring all the Turkish woodwork. I understand now what tore his heart. To have put in so much effort, invested so much of himself . . .)

You know, until I started examining the photo to write this letter I didn't realize just how close I'm living to the apartments where you stayed. Nor could I see how close I am to Alex's house. Her terrace curls around mine, as if it's trying to protect me.

"What do I mean by trip wires?" Rollo asked as he stood meditatively on the stage of the Pez. *"How is it,"* he continued rhetorically, *"that the ruling elite is aware of disturbances around the class interzones . . . when, for example, a writer's group founds a type of cyst at the boundary?"*

The audience was transfixed; whether by virtue of the intensity of his gaze or by the intelligence conveyed by his words, it would be impossible to determine.

"A type of cyst. A T.A.Z. . . . A T.A.Z., my friends, the Temporary Autonomous Zone researched by Hakim Bey. Now, if I may digress, what is it?

"If the working class is encased in ice like turkeys in a freezer, there is still a hope, a slim hope, that

157

Don't misconstrue what I'm saying; I don't need protection, and you're with me all the time. I don't feel threatened. In fact, I feel in total control of myself. Yesterday I made a first soft-booted expedition into your old territory. Now all sorts of riddles engage me.

Since you left Barcelona none of your letters have reached me. How is Melissa? It's almost impossible for me to imagine you sitting beside her in the hospital. (It's even more difficult for me to imagine her being there. We were all so happy.) I'm still not sure why you insisted that I continue on, rather than returning with you to Vancouver. I guess I just don't see what Simon and I have to explore.

A few days ago I travelled through the gorgeous foothills to Meskla. My visit with him left me angry and wasted. He's a filthy sunburned eremite with a satyr's beard and wilderness eyes. His condescension infuriates me. He reeks of rut and self-righteous piety. He says he's tried cutting himself loose—cutting his life to the bone—but only succeeded in sinking into a swamp of bitterness. He says that he forgives us; but I didn't absolve him. My chief satisfaction came in recognizing that he can't escaped his past as easily as he'd like to.

Perhaps you were right—it is a good thing to have come here, to see for myself. He's been living in a large, squalid stable in the stinking attic of an olive oil factory. A plastic sheet encloses a corner of the room, to funnel smoke out a hole in one wall. The windows haven't any glass so the wind rips through them. It must have been cold during the winter, but the afternoon I was there the roof grew very hot. A pair of wrens had nested in an old mud-swallow nest cemented to the concrete ceiling, and one of their chicks tumbled down and gasped out its life on Simon's sleeping bag. Other working tourists lived with him in that room, because there's an enormous straw-covered bed constructed of old orange crates which he wouldn't have built only for himself. But now he's alone in the village.

What a crock of shit! Why am I putting myself through this? You say that Simon is the barrier that separates us, but what am I gaining for us by confronting him? His pain and confusion are obvious and pathetic. Disillusionment has changed him more than he realizes, but he'd still like to impose standards on us. Mumbling about forgiveness. He refuses to accept responsibility, but if there's guilt to be assigned he's as guilty as anyone. Guilty of narcissism and self-deception. Guilty of blind assumption. Guilty by virtue of his determination to recognize only his own point of view.

I'm sorry. I'm not sleeping well. My guts are tender, sloughing off layers of carefully built-up body; menstrual time. I'm losing a lot of blood. The half-moon was swollen before this torrent began flowing. I dreamt that you asked me to come, urgently. I arrive—you standing across my large empty studio—and realize s/he'll be arriving soon. Why do you call me when you know s/he is coming? I'm projecting my own anxieties.

But now I'll make you smile. I've just seized a zany image of chicken me. I'm lying prone and naked on the cool-tiled floor, my neck extended, my mesmerized nose to a grouted line. My breasts, stomach, and thighs are flat against the towel beneath me, my nipples as hard as the gooseflesh at the base of my spine. Your warm, oily, perfumed hands move over my shoulders and outstretched arms, down my back and sides. I cross my arms in front of me to support and lift my cheek. Stray locks of your hair tickle my neck. A cool breeze from the Gulf of Hania caresses the carmine geraniums on the terrace and slips through the open door. Beads of moisture condense on the pitcher of sangria waiting on the terrace table.

The best part of the trip to Meskla was the bus ride. Crete's antique local buses still stop at every small village along the road. It was as if I were surrendering my tight clutch on time and relearning the joyful freedoms of travelling. The high inner island rolled toward me to the rhythm and rattle of the bus. And the look I got at life here was a good unvarnished one. At the edge of each village was the perfect disk of a threshing floor. I felt the terrible resignation of the pygmy donkeys, all but invisible under enormous loads or swaybacked beneath a man or woman as big as they are. The black-draped isolation of the widows and old women moved me into an isolation of my own. If people smiled at me, I smiled back. If they talked, no matter the language, I pretended I didn't understand.

There are times when not speaking Greek has been a great advantage. It helps me select the company I keep and the things I understand. During this trip it kept life superficial, and I realized that the luxury of living superficially is one of the true joys of travel. Stop in a village; smile at the people; replenish your

individuals can have a devastating effect on the ideological state apparatus; if and only if they form a T.A.Z., the social equivalent of a perpetual-motion machine."

Jordan didn't catch that part. **Jordan Zinovich** *hails from Canada and has written extensively on his homeland's acquiescence before its dominant neighbor. He is the editor of Semiotext(e) Canadas.*

He didn't pay close attention to the lecture because he was too busy eyeballing all the authorial celebrities. There was Harry Mathews, and over there Stephanie Urdang, and to the left, "the" Hal Sirowitz.

travelling supplies; order coffee, wine, or a meal; then catch the next bus out of town. Life becomes very simple.

At the moment I sit at a new restaurant in the ruined harems near Roland's house. Two young girls have just run down the street. One is tiny and fierce—she reminds me of you. The other chases her into my restaurant. A mother calls insistently. The waiter gives the tiny girl a heavy-looking wallet. (A rich discovery? Money? Is this what their dispute is all about?) The tall girl continues taunting the smaller one, but the little one is sliding out of the restaurant like a cat with calculated footsteps. Her black eyes burn. She hefts the heavy wallet behind her back and a soothing tone slips into her voice. There! Something distracted the taller girl, and the little one slapped her face hard with the wallet. Now she has retreated to the restaurant, exulting, leaving her stunned enemy in the street.

I didn't tell you before, but Jason is back from Egypt. He's jaundiced and thin, irritable and self-involved. He and Simon push me toward true Solanasianism. At times I long to force a turd session on them, to take them by their throats and say, "Repeat after me: I am a turd, a lowly abject turd. I wronged Selene. My ego resides in my cock. My mere existence offends all women. There's no possible way for me ever to atone for the pain and irritation I cause, and which I continually inflict on you and all women." I don't, though. Instead I deploy another scummy strategy and quietly undercut them. "It was smart of you to leave the art scene," I tell Jason. "You're ahead of your time." So I've managed to control my responses to his pathetic rants and rationalizings.

Alex lets him live and work in a room in her house. He paints through the days, then spends his nights drinking with Lionel in the Green Poppy. He's not really accomplishing much. He came back from Egypt to recuperate, but with Roland gone a touchstone has vanished. Alex's company and the familiarity of a studio are the only things he really craves.

When I returned from Meskla, I wandered the harbor and shopped for saffron at the spice stalls in the Market arcade. Then I ate at the Minos Restaurant on Daedalus Street—moschari, the flesh of a bull calf. That evening I drank iced retsina on my terrace and watched the stabbed and bleeding sun spin on a bed of clouds and collapse beneath an island. Then I dreamed again:

I climb a flight of broad stairs carrying a wine goblet, part of a set carved from a single block of jet-black crystal. There are designs incised in the goblet's sides; images graced with gold leaf. Inside there's a rich red liquid, thick and warm as blood. (I tell myself that I'll spill it when and how I please.) A lifesize golden statue whirls in the center of the hall at the top of the stairs. Radiant with joy I smile and raise my goblet in a toast to her.

Beyond the statue there's a doorway; beyond the doorway a mountaintop. On it I discover a small peak sanctuary surrounded on three sides by a low wall of rusticated grey blocks. At the far end of the enclosure there's a flight of broad stone stairs to a black door, and then a series of gigantic graceful stone arches. On the landing at the top of the stairs I find a simple marble altar. Four objects rest upon it: a perfect sphere carved from the same marble as the altar, a black crystal wand, a gleaming steel knife, and a goblet of purest warmest gold.

Though there was no moon when I awoke, I made my way easily back inside my room and slept peacefully through the rest of the night. And in the morning my head was perfectly clear and still, as if I'd crossed a threshold. I seemed to have opened some perceptive door. The world leapt into view, sparkling and fresh.

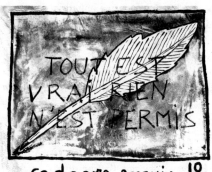

cadavre exquis 10/10

Yesterday, for the first time in ages, Jason stopped painting long enough to join Alex and me for dinner. Alex gave me the choice, either to eat good food at a backstreet place or to sit on the quay and watch the harbor. I chose the harbor: the damp salt and seaweed smells aren't as sharp on my terrace as there. Though the Greeks (and Alex) normally don't eat until well after dark, I insisted that we go down early. We took a table outside the Hassan Pasha Mosque, at a place Anthony Quinn and Irene Papas discovered in the 1960's, when they were filming *Zorba the Greek*. (Then Haniots had all but abandoned their ruined harbor. Now the quay is a carnival.)

Alex refused to order our food until after the sun went down. Instead we drank ouzo and she bantered with the restaurateur. Her Greek is brilliant, and he knows and appreciates that. As the evening wore on the tables around us filled with packaged Scandinavians, here for a week in the sun. A few working tourists were down from the citrus groves. A tambour-beating gypsy passed by with a dancing bear, and in the ancient Venetian arsenals behind the mosque fishermen tarred their boats.

It was still very warm, and the sun was just vanishing when a tall, dignified, very drunk old man tottered stiffly down Swallow Street. He was a Sphakian palikari, with his scarf fringes dangling wildly over his eyes. The white tips of his moustache bristled under the wide wings of his nose, and his bloodshot eyes glittered. A cigarette dangled from one thick hand. The other rested on a silver-sheathed knife he had stuffed through the corded sash wrapped around his waist. A crimson geranium rode a golden chrysanthemum as a posy in the buttonhole of his blue jacket. His baggy blue *vraka* swayed, and his white boots clattered on the cobblestones.

As he drew near us, a working tourist called out, "*Ti Kanis, Mouray?*" Alex had been watching him closely, and when he halted in mock astonishment a smile lit her face. "He's down from the mountains for Saint John's Day," she whispered. "'Mouray' can be friendly, but between strangers it means 'fool.' So he's just been insulted. The only way to stop him now is to offer him a drink."

The shepherd turned and waited a moment in silence. And when no drink came his way he shouted, "*Ti Kano? Mouray, Polla provata kano!*" in a voice so loud that everyone looked at the embarrassed tourist.

Alex laughed out loud, and the fishermen in the arsenali applauded. Our restaurateur appeared with a glass of wine, which the old man accepted graciously, and a small pile of salted peanuts, which he swept aside. He drank with a snort, then continued on his way. Alex says that he shouted a challenge: "I own flocks of sheep. Does any fool dare to try stealing a few of them?"

So what shall I do now, my dear? I'm learning more than I ever dreamed I would about the life you lived in Hania. And our conflict, the one I'd hoped we would grow beyond, sulks in the mountains south of here. I feel that we are growing closer, but our past is not receding.

Full fathom five my lover lies/Of her bones are my reefs made/Those are the pearls that were her eyes/And now across the sea floors play.

I'm getting very disoriented, Selene. Trying to explore and extend embattled old relationships depresses me. Traveling without you seems odd. There are so many things I don't understand, and just trying to record things takes so much of my energy. I miss you. I think that I may come home soon.

Love to you and Melissa,

Rachel

Atalaya (Excerpt from "Pilgrimage")

JANINE POMMY VEGA

The heat and the flies, and the presence of alcohol, brought an aimlessness and lassitude to the patio of the Shell Camp, most days. It was augmented by visits from the local guards of Sepa Penal Colony—swaggerers and bullies—who came to buy beer and exchange local gossip. Atalaya was looking better every moment. David and I were discussing hitching a ride with anyone going downriver, when someone docked below.

He was a man, neither young nor old, who looked to be from a local tribe. Unlike everyone else I'd observed coming up the path, he was neither drunk nor looking for liquor. The other striking thing about him was his eyes: they were open, clear, and they laughed. He seemed to carry a center of gravity without taking himself or anyone else too seriously. I liked him instantly.

Bert introduced us. He was Don Domingo, the *curandero* on the river, who'd prepared *ayahuasca* for Bert and his friends on many occasions. Bert looked at me questioningly when he gave this news, and I understood he was asking if I wanted to try it. I trusted Don Domingo, and agreed. It was arranged for the following evening. Don Domingo gave instructions to eat nothing after breakfast, and to come to his house at sundown with an empty stomach.

The following evening, Bert took David and me down the river to the *curandero's* house. I was surprised to find other boats docking. Since telephones were nonexistent, and there had been so little advance notice, I wondered how so many people got wind of the ceremony, and decided to show up. *Ayahuasca* is

"What letter in the personals?" Carol asked.

She looked pointedly at bart, who was screwing around with his pants trying to put down a "Dutch Erection," an unfoldable pleat that is sometimes formed by gas nodules queuing up under a trouser zipper.

"About mayhem," Topp asserted again. *"It said this white feller wasn't going to do what he was billed as doing, that is, talk, ramble. Weren't you at the lecture, missie?"* Topp threw at Deborah.

Carol answered for her. *"We were all there. Most of us."*

"It was rather a long clipping," Topp ventured. *"Signed—let me think—signed Vega or something."*

Janine Pommy Vega *is the author of* Here at the Door, Drunk on a Glacier, *and* Talking to Flies. *She is a writing teacher at Poets in Public Service.*

163

used for curing physical diseases, mental and emotional problems, spiritual ills. It is meant to be taken in the dark of night, hopefully with little moon. Taken by day, the light would be too overpowering, they say, and the teachings lost.

Don Domingo spread a ground cloth out over the dust of the patio. With the roof overhead, I had the feeling he was creating a space where he could hold and protect his charges through the night. Two apprentices brought in bunches of sweet basil and other herbs, and a block of jungle tobacco, wild tobacco called *mapacho*. The *mapacho* was shredded and rolled into cigarettes. Everything was done with great care and seriousness. Don Domingo's daughter would be one of the participants. She had something wrong with her leg—perhaps polio, perhaps severe arthritis; it was shorter than the other leg and looked in pain. He wore all white. Don Domingo's family retired behind the walls of their house. Night fell.

We were twelve: David and I; the two apprentices who were there to learn and to serve; Don Domingo's daughter; a young couple who was having trouble conceiving; an older woman and three men who sat together; and lastly, a boy of perhaps ten, who was a servant in Don Domingo's house and came from a nearby warrior tribe.

Don Domingo sat with his back against the wall of his house, flanked by his two apprentices. In front of him was a small table, on which was the *ayahuasca* he had just brewed, an assortment of bottles and flasks, various rattles and gourds, the herb bundles, and the rolled cigarettes. To his left sat the little boy, and next to him with her back to the south was Don Domingo's daughter, dressed as if for a wedding. David and I faced the *curandero* across the patio; our backs were to the river west of us, just down the steep embankment. Next to us was the couple, who shared a blanket and presented themselves as a unit; then the older woman, and the men, with their backs to the north.

Ayahuasca, called *yage* in Colombia, means "death vine" in Quechua. The hallucinogenic drink is made from the jungle vine *ayahuasca, Banisteriopsis caapi*, which Don Domingo said grows away from the sight of man; and the leaves of a forest shrub, *chacruna, Psychotria viridis*, which he called *la jocosa*, "the jocose one." It was she who gave the journey its laughter. He said we could recognize her, if she appeared, as a very short, good-natured woman.

The *curandero* gave each of us a glass of the brew to drink. The taste was a vegetable dark green, not as bitter as peyote, not as tasty as psilocybin mushrooms. When he handed the glass to the boy, the boy shook his head.

"Why are you here with us?" asked Don Domingo.

"To watch."

"There are no watchers here, only participants."

The boy shrugged, and held out his hand for the glass.

After some time, I asked for more; Don Domingo gave me another glassful. A bird began to sing in the dark. They said her name was Maria. Her song sounded like *cocodrilo, cocodrilo,* and she kept it up all night. They said she always came to the spirit of *ayahuasca.* There was an animal feeling in all of us huddled on the patio, expectant, like sheep grouping up at the barn door.

My own individual journey began. I was in a green cathedral, composed of arches and muted colors, all lit from within. My emotions seesawed between reverence and humor. All problems seemed nonexistent, laughable; all states of being I might hold onto, evanescent. A female presence was everywhere—in the leaves, trunks, drops of water—fecund, pulsing, green and dark. I flew out to the reaches of created worlds, worlds within worlds, where everything was round, and returned along curves coming back to the body, again and again. The vast jungle, the vaster earth, star systems, and galaxies were one round order that took form when it curved back to itself, as it always did. All expansion was followed by contraction.

Don Domingo was the only one who entered into the separate journeys. He would come into the presence of my voyage and check on me, and watch. Part of me was aware of him doing the same with others. His was a maternal presence that did not close its eyes or waver in its attention to his charges. The flying lasted all night. He came to each of us several times, and sang over our heads, and rattled and waved sweet basil, and wafted smoke our way with a woven rug. His moves were purposeful and calm. Over his daughter's leg he sang songs, and waved his herb bundle. She was so beautiful; she was the princess of the night.

The path of the moon through the vegetation wove a net of cellular intricacy, like a three-dimensional spider's web. Walking through it to go to the bathroom, I saw the truth of cellular integrity: how the life principle gathers building blocks of matter around itself,

Topp went on, "It said the lecture would be like one of those magic shows where they call a volunteer from the audience, who has to have eggs broken in his hat, his tie clipped off, his wallet set on fire. But somehow Whiteman was going to subject the whole audience to that . . . that humiliation or enlightenment, whatever you want to call it."

bart caught him up, "Did the clipping say all this or are you embroidering?"

Mike scowled, "I'm giving you the gist. The letter was much shorter than what I've said."

and the light that ensouls it is the glue. But walking through the moon shadows, you see how all matter integrates with other matter, disintegrates, loses its individuality, then separates out again into itself—and we are trailing a path of light behind us, like a comet, when we move.

Long after the moon set, Don Domingo lit a cigarette made from *mapacho*, and gave it to each of us to smoke. From the free flight out in the air we were suddenly constricted down to our individual selves, each one of us seated on the patio, stapled to the earth, seeing in the dark. There was an awareness among us all as well, like a herd of cattle have, resting in a field at night. The *mapacho* cut into the journey. I was aware of my fingers, my shoulders, my lungs, myself, pulsating in the dark. Don Domingo asked us separately if we were back. Another cigarette went around the circle. Harsh strong smoke. Everyone had landed.

People prepared to sleep in place for the few hours that remained of the night. The little boy very deliberately thrust his legs out in front of him, and covered himself with a thin blanket. Visible in the outline of his body were his arms crossed resolutely over his chest. It was the stance of a warrior.

People started leaving in twos and threes, until only David and I were left, of the people who did not live there. Don Domingo's daughter picked up her blanket and walked away. The light came blue gray over the green canopy. The *curandero* instructed us to eat nothing all day, and take only water. He indicated the fields behind his house and said we should wash our bodies outside, and take the water inside, but nothing else.

"The *ayahuasca* will keep teaching all day. It is important that you keep listening."

Behind his house a herd of zebu cows were making their way toward the fields. The little warrior was leading them. I noticed he had a goiter on his neck. His eyes sparkled and laughed. David and I went to a basin hollowed out in the stream. The water was a living presence flowing over and over and over the skin of my body. One body on another body. Above was a *guyaba* tree, ripe with yellow glowing fruit. We gathered a couple of dozen, and carried them back to the house.

Don Domingo nodded at the fruit, saying that the next day, we could break our fast. His boat was ready to take us back. The boatman was his apprentice; the little warrior rode in front. The boy's eyes were so sharp, he picked out some turtle eggs on the shore fifty yards away. He admitted, when we were well underway, that a great snake had come to him in the dark, a snake as large as the river, and he had been very frightened. But he hadn't screamed. He said this with a touch of pride. I thought ahead, to my bags at the camp, and what was in them that I could give him for sharing his journey. I wanted to give him something red.

Back at the camp, I handed him a red beaded bracelet woven into a snake design. When he put it on his wrist, he laughed delightedly; the bracelet seemed to be glowing, as was his arm. He and the apprentice said good-bye, and walked down to the dock, trailing light behind them.

David and I made our way to the little river, through vegetation soaked with light. Something had opened. It was time to go—to set our sights on the *Urubamba,* and send our intention out to reach Atalaya. Intention was the telephone I had been looking for in the jungle. It was the arrow under the canopy roof that sought its mark, and more often than not, found it.

We came back and packed in twenty minutes. David went down to wait by the dock while I sat with Lena and Bert on the patio. No bugs bit. There were no bugs. I confessed I had had a great fear of losing myself in the *ayahuasca.*

"Always that way," said Bert. "We're always afraid of losing what we know, afraid of dying. And it's a new life when we return."

David shouted from the dock. A boat was coming. The three of us ran the bags to the river. A Coca-Cola boat was coming in.

It was almost dark when we docked by the beach in Atalaya. Maruja waved happily at us from her kiosk, and called her husband to watch us come in. It was hard to say how old she was; her husband seemed much younger than she. Her youngest child was a three-year-old girl, who twirled and twirled in her little dresses and was picked up and spoiled by everyone. But the oldest son had a daughter the same age. Maruja simply had the ageless face of a woman of the land.

David and I took a bench at one of the tiny tables. Maruja's father was also there—a vigorous looking man who might have been eighty. Hearing where we'd been, he told of his own first time with ayahuasca—how he'd taken it because of pains in his chest. A doctor had told him he had tuberculosis, and he went to the *curandero,* afraid. Within a week he was healthy again. No chest pains, no T.B., nothing.

Maruja's eyes glittered in the candlelight as she sat down.

"I took it for protection," she said. "It's true, every sorcerer has an animal shape, and if you can see that shape, you've penetrated a secret. Then he or she can have no control over you."

"Years ago, there was someone fighting me, trying to control me. I went to a *curandero* I trusted because I needed the ability to *see* my enemy and the animal he appeared as, to protect myself."

She gestured toward the street up from the beach, and the people walking in the dim light." There are some, I can tell you, who want to do harm, who want to control you, and they are powerful. There are even some in this town—three or four around here—I see them all. And they know I can see them. They don't dare try anything on me, or my family."

"I went to the *curandero*, who recognized that I had been under attack. I stayed with him, fasting with no meat, no salt, and no sugar, and taking the *ayahuasca*, until I could *see*. When I came away from there, I could identify everyone's animal—even those who don't know they have one—and can to this day."

She looked off over the river.

There's one around here," she said, her voice rising, as if she intended to be overheard, "who is a black bird. A great black malevolent bird. He knows who I mean."

I didn't dare look around. I had in my mind's eye the image of someone, shadowed in the moonlight, ducking behind a wall. Surfaces changed places. Reality shifted gears. The moon that had come up almost full, sailing over the town, slid into a cloud.

The Arapaima
Roberta Allen

See the fish swimming in the trees. No, I am not crazy. I am in the Amazon. Fish swim in trees in the rainy season when the rivers rise up to forty feet and flood the forests. Both the fish and the monkeys are eating fruit. If this were the breeding season, you might see the head of the male arapaima—the largest freshwater fish in the world—turn black. Swarming above the head of this eight-foot father, you might see more than a hundred little black arapaimas, each half an inch long. The father's head turns black to protect them. At other times, he is pea-green like his mate. If this were the breeding season, the mother would be watching the babies from a distance. But since this is not the breeding season—arapaimas lay their eggs in the dry season, when the streams are shallow—you won't see the arapaima with his head turned black, and you won't see the small-fry swimming above him. You won't wonder that these tiny fish will grow to be eight feet long. You won't feel sad that hundreds of thousands have ended up as salted filets. There will be so much water and so many biting flies and mosquitoes, you will not think about arapaimas. You will not think about anything. You will be sweating and swatting insects and wishing you were home.

This woman, Nhi Chan, who was listed as Muy-Muy's beneficiary on a policy Roxor's had the trapeze artist fill out, was not an easy target for Carter's search. He managed to get her on the phone at work—she was a cashier at the China King restaurant—but she didn't converse so much as squawk like a rooster. Finally, he went down there. She was sitting at a table with a couple of other employees. They were all eating crabs.

A lone customer fiddled with a menu. The diner, for your information, was **Roberta Allen**. *Roberta Allen is the author of* The Daughter *and* The Traveling Woman. *She is an artist with work in the permanent collections of the Met, the Museum of Modern Art, and several other museums.*

Nhi didn't say anything Michael hadn't already heard. She sucked the juice choicely through the crustacean's cracked skull, then pried loose its bottom plate. A ruff of her black hair was torn by tawny shades as the huge overhead fan rippled air through the restaurant, tippling the water in the sink and billowing the bright dresses of the waitresses.

Frank Sinatra on a Cheap Bus to Italy
LITTLE ANNIE ANXIETY

I took a cheap bus to Italy once. I forgot to bring food and, more importantly, water. I had the fever. I woke between nightmares, freezing with my head flattened against the window and I thought I was falling off the jagged cliffs of a mountain range dotted with tortured statues smelted in aluminum. With each bend and turn in the road I died. Chalets, evil in their primness, lurked like chocolate-box tombs. I had no idea where I was. It looked like hell and I was sure I had hypothermia. Everyone except for the driver and me slept. I was too petrified to move to the front of the bus for comfort so I just sat there grasping myself. As it turned out we were going past Mont Blanc, wherever the fuck that is.

Miles' obsessive question, as he told it to Annie, might have been formulated thus: "How does one bring about a revolution without getting caught?"

*Hakim Bey's ideas on this subject were ingenious. Bey used the concept of the epiphany. In "The Prelude," the epiphany occurs when the poet sees the clouds pissed away beneath him as he stands on Mount Blanc. This vision gives birth to his poetic vocation. Thus, Miles explained to Annie, an epiphany only occurs when a person makes a decisive change. **Annie Anxiety** is a funk singer/writer who currently works with On-U Sound dub-producer/genius Adrian Sherwood. Her latest CD is* Short & Sweet.

Hakim insists that one has epiphanies solely (a) in groups and (b) against the grain of convention. Such an experience, which must occur in an audience or other community, causes the person who went through the adventure to renounce society and voyage toward T.A.Z.

But how did one produce these epiphanies?

If one stood on the street corner preaching utopia, one ended up in the slammer or in the alley, knife between the shoulder blades. Besides, there were other considerations. Miles was too short to be seen on a soapbox in Bughouse Square.

Yet he could wield ink and paper and had garnered a reputation in a small way as a translator. He had access to the publishing conglomerate Ink, Inc., and its parent company Corpse Corp. It was not impossible to create out of inter-linked texts and computer bytes a web that sucked in a generation.

We got to the Italian frontier, where all the passengers were woken by officious border guards. It was then I noticed a man who looked like a young Frank Sinatra. He was from Naples and we fell in love for the rest of the journey. He mopped the sweat off my brow and asked me to marry him. He had a briefcase full of porno, a suitcase full of secrets, and a really nice golden cross round his neck. As we held hands I could feel his wedding ring digging into my flesh. He told me not to worry, we were just going thru the little *Halps*.

I didn't twig till the next day that he meant the Alps. How those woesome stones haunt me! At one point I formed a circle with my thumb and forefinger, and he stuck his finger thru the hole and I got insulted. The heat was making me insane. That and the magazines smashed the dream. Our two-hour engagement was broken and I regretted that. We said goodbye at the bus station in Rome and I just left things to fate. He continued onto Naples, probably back to his wife and many offspring. I wanted purity and Maggio. He wanted a nun and I wanted to be one.

I think I saw him years later on a promenade in Southern Spain. We stared animal-eyed at each other. I'm pretty sure it was him but I didn't approach. I was no longer a saint and he was an older Sinatra with a little pot belly and lots of little Sinatra kids circling his legs. I'm sure to this day it was him but I couldn't have stood seeing Frank anything less than Frank.

clintexc.393 in pdsk two, 2.93
(Excerpt from "The Clint Series")
JILL RAPAPORT

Clint two:
Somebody knew somebody who knew Clint Eastwood, and I was sitting around scheming up a way to get invited to one of his parties, so that I could move in under his girlfriend's nose, make him *fall* in love with me, let him marry me, and then dump him—with a lot more money than when I walked into the deal. During the course of a few hours, I covered some ground. He might not fall in love with me. He would discover that he had an *obligation* to love me; that without me certain doors would never open, he'd never know what I would have been like, and in addition, to support me, so as to avoid contributing to my downfall, which would impoverish the culture of the West. I sort of loved him, and he had profited every time I put money down on one of his movies; he owed me at least the dollar value of my ticket stubs. Why should I have to pay to see the work of someone I sort of loved? His enormous box office ought to embrace me, not shut me out. I could teach him French, and show him around the Lower East Side. He looked like some of my relatives on my mother's side. There was even a possibility he came from related genetic stock. But for the grace of *something* he could have been my older brother, or even my young dad. We were both cold fish; there was a complementarity there. He lacked refinement; I had a certain ability to create the illusion of refinement without having any—I could teach him how to do the same. In return he could

Stephanie attacked her blouse with a passion, quickly opening the buttons and unclipping her bra. Unsheathed, her alabaster breasts flowed with a gossamer purple reflected from the light of an overhead ad—a bas-relief of a tropical forest.

"Let the other girl suck them."

Jill began banging against the window. **Jill Rapaport** is a poet, essayist, and playwright.

She had seen what was going on as she got out at Kedzie Station, where the floorboards had been freshly painted a bright green.

When the train began to move out, she jumped on the outer tread of the door. As the car accelerated, she fell back onto the platform like a single die cast from a box onto a green felt table.

173

teach me how to make money and get financial backers and producers to see things my way.

Most significantly, I understood as few people did the mechanism by which he had attained popular and critical acclaim. I was more astute about the workings of culture than he was, even though he was more astute about making culture produce for him. Having me around would be like having a Boswell to whom he could look not only for insight, but for a good time. Unlike Boswell, though, I didn't cling; I wasn't some stout old dude whose mission in life was to write somebody's biography; I was a self-lighting fire, in whose flames he could find his reflection.

Clint had a few years and a lot of dollars on me, but he would never have grasped 'til meeting me the fact that, because of the direction in which human evolution was moving, the only possible choice of mate for him was me, or someone like me; I would be his television monitor, the dark pool into which he could also sink, learning that his authority and identity were as ephemeral and unreal as everybody's these days; I would give him the credibility he needed to stay alive in this world, and whatever shot he had at the next.

Clint had a problem understanding duality and paradox. He needed considerable help with contemporary concepts. The way of everybody's fathers had already died out with the dinosaurs. One could no longer embed the reality of others inside oneself, could no longer sell one's product to those with whom one was not equal but peripheral. Capital, in fact, was terminal, and this above all was the downfall of men like Clint, who had made a lot of money in his day not necessarily even believing he was entitled to it. He was very, very good, but not good enough. There was a deficiency in him; it had killed others like him. Clint needed someone who could make a woman out of him, and that someone could very likely have been me.

The very idea that he and I should not meet and come together was such an affront to the way events should unfold that I came to feel it unnecessary that I try to contact him. If he and I didn't meet, it would be a stroke of bad luck for the cosmos, and I was pretty sure the cosmos took better care than that of its self-interest. In any case, in view of how great a need Clint had for me, it was unseemly for me to make the first approach.

Approaches were everything these days, and by messing up their protocols you created the possibility that data would be misinterpreted, and then it wound up your own fault, and now it was you who, like trigger-happy revisionist archaeologists with particular axes to grind, jeopardized culture, insofar as culture hung on the tracking of its forebears' footprints.

174

A Visitor

SPARROW

One rainy Saturday, as my wife and I were about to have sex, the buzzer rang. We looked at each other. "The Jehovah's Witnesses?" I asked.

I stood, and depressed the lever of the intercom. "Hello?"

"This is Paul Revere, of Paul Revere and the Raiders. Do you remember me?"

"Yes, of course."

"I need to speak to someone."

I went downstairs (our buzzer is broken) and there he stood, still in that Revolutionary soldier uniform, now patched and frayed. His clothes were drenched. "Come in, come up," I said, and he shuddered, stepping through the door.

Inside, Violet brewed a pot of comfrey tea as I draped a felt blanket over his shoulders. "I guess you wonder where I've been the last 23 years," Paul Revere said, looking down at the linoleum.

"Don't strain your voice," said Violet, but he waved her away. "It's a story I must tell." His face, once mild and enthused, now seemed strained—his nose beaklike, eyes small.

"It started around 'Cherokee Nation,'" he said. "That was our last hit. It rose to seven, and would've gone higher, if Dusty Springfield hadn't pushed us down. I believe there are songs that stop other songs from climbing. We reached as far as Dusty, but couldn't climb over her. I told her this later, and she laughed.

"I'd alway tried to communicate something in my songs. I modelled myself after Paul Revere, who rode the streets, alerting his townsmen of danger. In 'Kicks,' I wrote:

Man Mountain called Sharon Mesmer at 4 a.m. He couldn't sleep that well since he had been shot in the head during a lumberjack strike in Spokane. He wanted to be sure the Fish Picnic was going off without a hitch.

*Sharon was just coming in the door when the phone rang. She had been sitting up all night at St. Garter's Hospital, waiting with **Sparrow** for the birth of his first child. Sparrow is a former presidential candidate and founder of the One Size Fits All Party. He is a "singer" in Foamola, editor of Big Fish and The 13th Street Ruse, and author of Test Drive (Appearances).*

She grabbed the receiver on the first ring. She was pissed. "How can you call me at this hour, whoever you are!" She kept talking, not letting the other person respond. "People in Chicago have a lot of nerve. I wouldn't live here permanently for a million dollars."

She was planning to

No, you don't need kicks
To help you face the world each day.

"I saw that Americans were seeking sense stimulation, and losing their soul essences. If only they had heeded me, so much suffering could have been avoided! Even Vietnam . . ." He paused, and looked down again. "I spoke of the Cherokees, forced to walk 1000 miles in winter from their native home. I tried to express the love crushed, the cup dashed from their lips! If I could convey this to the readers of *16* magazine, their parents might learn from them.

"I was riding high on 'Cherokee Nation,' when I developed a personal problem. I became hooked on . . . books."

He paused a long time, examining a few specks of comfrey in his tea.

"It began the way it usually does—with Agatha Christie. Of course, I'd read books in high school, but I could drop them anytime. This was different.

"My first was *The Case of the Sealed Jury*. I was sure the drowned sailor was not English (as he appeared) but Scottish, and sympathetic to the separatist cause. I couldn't stop reading. Past page 127, I was helpless. I missed a concert in Portland and sent my assistant out for *Murder on a Shoestring*. Of course, the sailor had never drowned at all.

"By the time I finished all of Agatha, my career was ruined. After that, I became consumed with ornithology. I read the complete *Birds of North America* twice—then once in Portuguese. (My mother grew up in Brazil.) I read Charles Darwin's *Voyage of the Beagle* three times. I read everything that's been written on flamingos.

"I moved on to constitutional history. I read Fiske's *The Making of the Magna Carta*, and all the recent work on tribal law. 'What is the origin of ethics?' was my question. I came finally to agree with Sarah Agee, that women created ethics to protect themselves against men.

"I woke one morning in an empty house, with a few strands of spaghetti in the refrigerator. I'd sold all the carpets, the furniture, to buy books, pencils, and plane tickets to the Flamingo Museum in Manila.

"My vision was almost gone. You can't tell right off, because I wear contacts." I looked closely, and there were discs as thick as quarters in his eyes.

"Then what?" my wife asked, leaning forward, pityingly.

"One day I met a man," Paul Revere said. "May 12, 1989, to be exact. I was in a bookstore in L.A.—the kind that lets you browse—reading a book on Bridge. (I'd sunk pretty low by then.) I noticed a man staring at me. He was 6'2", with an eyepatch, and a red voluminous coat.

"'You're hooked on books?' he growled at me.

U   n   b   e   a   r   a   b   l   e   s

"'Yes,' I admitted.

"'Come with me.'"

"I followed him down a long alley strewn with discarded razors. At the end of the alley was a black table, leaning to the side. Atop it was a human skull. He placed my hand on the skull. 'Swear to me you'll never read another book,'" he said.

"It was as simple as that. My lust for Audubon's journals and legal commentary was gone."

"I began to take walks. I had conversations with clerks in fast-food restaurants. I had *time* again. And you'll never guess who that one-eyed man was."

"Who?" I asked, green with excitement.

"The former bass player for the Dave Clark Five."

I gasped. "A lot of rock stars went this route?"

"Almost 40 percent," Paul Revere answered. "Many let on that they were drug addicts rather than admit the truth. I have it on good authority that Keith Richards reads 22 magazines a day, cover to cover."

"Really!" Violet exclaimed. "I thought it was just heroin!"

"No. You see, it's a natural compulsion. The loud nightly concerts dull the senses, and you're forced to retreat into literature as an antidote. There are various styles of addiction. Billy Idol reads literary criticism. Jerry Garcia goes for books on plumbing. Paul McCartney specializes in botany. A lot of them have false bottoms in their limousines to hide stacks of medical journals, or volumes of Plutarch. They'll read all the way to a concert, then muss their hair, don a pair of sunglasses, and step out to a crowd of screaming girls. Towards the end of his life, Jim Morrison was actually reading quantum mechanics on stage. Everyone thought it was a joke. Janis Joplin died with an open volume of Flaubert. She *did* overdose on drugs, but it was complicated by eye strain."

"Do women have different tastes than men?" Violet asked.

relocate to someplace else someday. Alternately yawning and yelling, she eventually unwound until she felt a crystal-like radiance. She often felt that way for the blink of an eye, always at the lip of exhaustion.

"Joni Mitchell has read every Mormon tract, I've heard," Paul Revere said. "Carole King read romance novels, until she kicked. You can't generalize."

"I suppose you'll ask us to burn our books," Violet ventured.

"No," Paul Revere said. "You guys are fine. I can tell you read for pleasure, not out of need. I know all the signs of addiction. Calluses on the thumb from turning pages; unwashed hair. You kids are fine.

"I'll say this, though. Don't denigrate TV—it does more good than you can imagine. George Harrison is alive today because of it. He almost starved to death reading the entire Tarzan series, until Mick Jones got him interested in *Night Court*. He survived to make *Cloud 9*, which is a pretty good album, if a little weak lyrically."

"Will you ever record again?" I asked.

"I'd like to make a rap album using the *I Ching*," Paul Revere said. "But every time I write lyrics, I end up alluding to the migratory habits of the tern, or the legal system of Bali—and my past comes back to me."

"How sad," Violet said.

He rested his head on his hands. His gray face was that of a man whose life had been lost between the covers of a book.

Then he looked up at our bookshelf, and absently paced toward it. He scanned the titles quickly, and withdrew a thin, yellow volume: *Silas Marner*. "I read this in Manila," he said faintly. "It is a magnificent book—a book of iron." Then, without a word, he thrust it behind him, and tipped his three-cornered hat. "I must go now. You have been so kind."

"I loved 'Kicks,'" I told him. "I even tried to figure out the chords."

He smiled. "D, E, C minor," he said, then repeated, "You have been so kind."

And he was gone.

On Foot
PETER WORTSMAN

" . . . your own road will always be discernible for its own self and will lead you safely out of the tangled town."

—Flann O'Brien

On several occasions and on different continents I happened upon a man who was walking around the world.

The first time, I spotted him on a highway in the mountains north of Castellon in Spain where I had gone to visit the petroglyphs. A trucker offered me a lift to my destination from the desolate Plaza Major of a tiny market town whose name I can't recall, the last stop on the municipal bus line, where I and a busload of chickens had been dropped off at dawn. He would in any case be hauling the chickens to slaughter, he indicated with a grin in their direction and a hand to his throat, and there was room up front for me.

As I spoke next to no Spanish, and he no English, communication between us was elemental, to say the least. He would point at something or other, the sky or the state of the road, and I would nod, while the chickens kept up their cackling commentary. It was a cold sunny day in February. Drowsy, I rolled the window down a crack and a whisper of wind pleasantly fanned my bleary eyes as we flew along. I was about to drift off to sleep when suddenly an object thumped hard against the truck's grill. It sounded like a stone. The trucker calmly hit the brakes, climbed out and soon returned with a sparrow lying still in the palm of his hand, its little body steaming, blood trickling from its beak.

The bird had flown straight into the radiator and so found death on contact. The chickens must have gotten the scent, for they let out a fearsome squall—

"How would one form that social perpetual motion machine?" Rollo intoned.

"Well," he let a long pause go by. "One must start with an audience."

Outstandish fidgeted inside his Hal Sirowitz costume, which he had donned in a toilet stall to throw off his pursuers. A series of pulleys and chains held this ingenious disguise together. Miles sat at approximately the sternum, his head in the dummy's head, but his feet dangled limply only to the thighs of the mannequin.

*He signaled to **Peter Wortsman**. The two of them were to accompany Rollo, after the meeting, to a long-awaited rendezvous. Peter Wortsman is the author of* A Modern Way to Die. *He is also a linguist who has translated Robert Musil.*

The question that had bothered all of them in the translators' coven was whether Whitehead was alluding to them in his copi-

even I understood the chicken word for death. And just then, as we were about to set out again, an old man with a staff came walking along.

Though I could not follow the words precisely, the gist of their exchange was clear.

Would the old man like a lift?

No, thank you!

But it's quite a hike to Morella!

The old man shook his head again and walked on, a solitary profile, stooped and vulnerable against the vastness of nature.

Where was he coming from? Where was he headed? I wondered. And the trucker, still holding the dead bird in his hand, glanced from the old man (a distant ridiculous stick figure now) to the bird, to me, and shook his head.

No doubt about it, he and I both sensed something out of the ordinary. And though the trucker didn't appear to be given to metaphysical musings or excessive sentiment—he tossed the dead bird out the window like a handful of garbage and wiped the blood on his pants—yet he had, I could tell by the glazed look in his eyes, been moved by the tiny tragedy of the bird and the stubborn endurance of the old man.

The trucker shook his head again, this time I think to clean the slate, to put the inexplicable out of his mind before stepping on the gas.

We continued our journey without any further incident.

And when finally I reached my destination, following a hasty hike at sunset with an innkeeper (who doubled as a guide) and his dog, the dog barked and the man pointed to an overhanging canopy of rock. At first I saw nothing, but the dog kept barking and my guide beckoned me to step closer. There was the unmistakable image of a stick figure silhouetted against the sun, slightly stooped, his legs spread suggesting motion, a staff in hand, and a bird hovering overhead.

When next we crossed paths, he or someone very much like him had jumped continents to the mountains of North Carolina—which state I happened to be speeding through in the company of a friend, whose grandmother lay dying in a nursing home in Georgia. It was a hot spring day. I idly let my hand hang out the window and skim the air like a bird, when I spotted an old man with a walking stick. His clothes were different, but his stoop and his determined stride immediately brought that other pedestrian to mind. My friend noticed him too in the rear-view mirror, and must have likewise been struck by something in his mien—or maybe she was just thinking of her grandma; she hit the brakes, pulled over and waited for him to catch up with the car.

—Can I give you a lift, old man?

He shook his head and kept on walking.

If it was the same man—and I'm not saying for certain that it was, only that it might have been—he must have heard the same question repeated in every conceivable language, posed by people in passing cars and trucks, oxcarts and rickshaws. And though the sounds varied, the sequence of response was the same. Always a brusque refusal, met by the same puzzled look on the face of the would-be benefactor: a composite of confusion, reverence, envy and the anger we feel for that which we do not understand. That proud and resolute shake of the head appeared at once so saintly and stupid, which may after all be much the same.

ous lectures on T.A.Z. Did he know how close he was to treading on their own practices . . . their attempt to use all the books published in 1994 as carriers?

(

One more occasion bears mention.

I had been hitchhiking through the state of Washington—or was it Oregon?—I can't recall the exact circumstances, the season or the time of day. All that I remember distinctly is the battered black Thunderbird, and the fact that the driver had a scar across his throat from ear to ear and drove too quickly. When he dented the metal railing at a hairpin curve and skidded uncomfortably close to the precipice, I wanted out.

Marooned on foot where nowhere meets the horizon, one moment my legs were shaking, leaden with terror, and the next moment—it was as in a dream in which the dreamer can no longer distinguish between himself and his surroundings. The sun winked. The road curled underfoot like a cat caressed, its supple asphalt spine arching upwards to meet my every step. And then I remembered the old man and understood in a flash his refusal to accept a ride.

But a little later, when a red convertible skidded to a halt in a cloud of dust and gravel, and the door swung open, and a beautiful black woman sleek as a bird lifted her sunglasses, looked me over with a languid smile, said she was tired of driving—what else could I do!—I went weak in the knees and climbed in.

P e t e r W o r t s m a n

Death Comes to Town

DAVID HUBERMAN

"Didn't you read about it, didn't you HEAR about it?" the little girl whispered to the old man. "No I didn't hear nothing. And, I don't read no MORE, my eyes don't see so good." "Well," the little girl said, "if you must know, Superman got killed off in the comics." "WHAT? What do you mean?" the old man gasped. "Yes, Superman is dead," the little girl bragged. "IMPOSSIBLE," the old man stammered. Then they both stared at each other and the old man knew that the little girl was telling the truth. "Well I'll be damned, they really KILLED him." Again a silent stare passed between them. The old man started to get nervous. "Why did they kill him?" he asked. "He wasn't holding up his end. His SALES were down," the little girl said. "Oh, and they killed him for that?" The old man was startled. "Yeah," said the little girl again. And again there was silence, that awful silence that Jean Genet used to masturbate to in that French jail cell of his. The old man suddenly remembered some trivial fact and breaking that deadly silence he exclaimed, "Little girl, little girl, I just remembered, NOTHING can kill Superman!" "Oh yeah," the little girl said, "bad SALES did. And by the way, Superman's death BOOSTED his sales. Death SELLS, old man." "Oh my," the old man shivered, "I think I need a good, cheap cigar." "All I have is a cherry lollipop," the little girl told him. "Oh well, that will have to do. Thank you little girl." "Oh, you're very welcome, old man, lick it WITH RELISH."

Down below Wabash Street there was a row of seedy bookstores, strip joints, and, sprawled along the curb, cheesy picnic tables. The homosexual protesters were picketing Operation Gay Rescue, which had been set up to "save" teenagers who had been tempted by the Infernal One, Fagzebubb.

Huberman had left the Hotel Alcove early that morning, hoping to hustle up some day work. **David Huberman** is a poet who has ranted and raved everywhere. He appears in the film Trail of Blood.

He saw his friend, Alfred Vitale, on the group's margins, where he had been exiled because of his outré opinions. David swaggered lustily up to him. "Won't you homosexuals ever be satisfied?" he said.

"I'll be satisfied," Alfred said. "when I see a gay dick on every television in America."

183

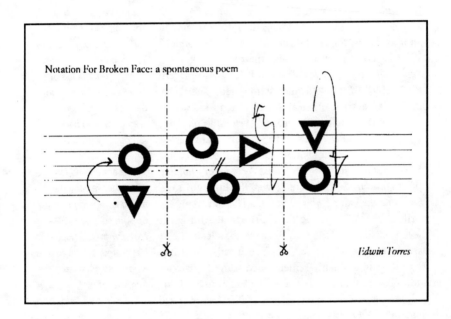
Notation For Broken Face: a spontaneous poem
Edwin Torres

6.3 Synchrons
LORRAINE SCHEIN

"When two or more events take place at a given moment of time without either one having caused the other but with a distinctly meaningful relationship existing between them beyond the possibilities of coincidence, that situation has the basic elements of Synchronicity . . . The essence of Synchronicity is to be found in the fact that Synchronicity carries a principle of orderedness that occurs in the universe regardless of causal connections and beyond space and time."

— Carl Jung, *Synchronicity and Human Destiny*

This is a synchronicity chart, assembled using data from our tracking devices, detailing the synchrons that co-manifested at precisely 22:52 Western Galactic Time, at Spacelab 423, Multi-Dimensional Scanner Project of the Synchronics Lab, Special Monitoring Division:

1. The White City of Aeoll, which had reduced itself to a size capable of being balanced on a human fingernail, shatters as its micro-moon reaches syzygy.

2. The clear green moonlight of New Manhattan shines seriously and coldly down through a curved glass wall, casting dappled jade shadows onto the bare body of the woman sleeping within. She hears the noise of something breaking in her dream, and awakes, startled. But everything is silent around her. Poised in stillness. She gets up, and presses the auditory activating button for the sound of an autumn wind during a rainstorm on Earth. Soon she is asleep again, and the shadows are back in place.

3. A ray of light, emitting from 23°4' of the right side of the Zetrian crystal, lights up the southwest corner of Dr. P.'s desk.

4. The EEG pattern on the chart of Moira Robinson, a woman whose dreams are being monitored,

Within Stephanie's bra cup was a loose strand of wire. As she canted her body toward Lisa's luscious lips, she balled the underwear in her hand, so the sharpened point emerged between her fingers.

At Kedzie, Lorraine emerged from the El stairway to find Jill, a woman she knew only by sight. **Lorraine Schein** is a poet and fiction writer whose work has appeared in the anthologies Memories and Visions and Wild Women.

She had met Jill when they both worked at Ink, Inc., a provider of computer systems for publishing firms. As she approached, her smile of recognition turned into a frown of concern when she noticed the young woman was staggering. After sitting her down, Lorraine cut away the torn pant leg with a nail clipper. Jill's leg was welted. Blood and curlicues of green paint seemed to form a design on the flesh like a vine thick with rheumy grapes.

==================================

shows an irregular and inexplicable REM pattern, unprecedented in the knowledge of the Sleep Lab researchers.

5. A sub-telepathic thought about how rain is always lucky for her, barely perceptible by her conscious mind, causes the woman walking past the Sleep Lab to continue on her way instead of taking shelter from the impending thunderstorm. This leads to her unplanned meeting with the transcriber of this chart.

6. Thrown impatiently by a young poet who lives on the outskirts of the space colony, the I Ching forms Hexagram 22 (Beauty).

6.3. *Co-Manifestation/Transcausal Element:* Plink. The noise of the Ninth Dimension revealing itself, the sound of the stone of space thrown into the water of time picked up by our sensitized devices, unfurling, a rift permanently opened in space/time by it, a kite of ineffable dimensions soaring through itself, tugging at its own string.

Trees Don't Move, People Don't Spin

TOM SAVAGE

We are not more conscious than we are only the winning interpretations become aware of sometimes in winter I glance out against the wind before a rival convoluted emerges in burlap to spring. Your word detectors, fed by your phoneme detectors, misfire out of the wind these subliminal judgments for appreciation by some central we have solved nothing in a control room like the computer programs windows the problems of infinite regress created on the fly from we can only think but reflect on our own thinking aware of the plodding of our minds lapsing into a deeply-grooved mental that there is some kind of ego inside us through the ocular peepholes his case piece by piece a glimmer of what another single? Shakey, a robot, invented a box with motorized wheels, had a brain that was too big to keep on board but was able to navigate because of the signature that boxes, pyramids and other objects left on. Its video eye as an object points the slope of a pyramid or the incline of a range tracing its edges with bold, white lines finally declaring it a box. When unplugged the robot worked just fine reverberating inside circuitry evolutionary beginning dividing line between self and other, a membrane of lipids, pseudopods, and flagella more complex mechanisms. When confronted with a looming object these survival mechanisms, precursors of animals acquired passively to explore as surely as a good piece of meat. Many neural devices were discreet communication lines. Imagine just dimly conscious, to milk information in that cave or a jaguar now let me see where was I left that chisel, everything from

*David Rattray had been stymied by a passage in a René Crevel letter that he was translating. Crevel had committed suicide because of a depressing experience with a crowd. He had been addressing a working class audience on "Revolution and Love," and the mob had rioted. In the letter, Crevel mentioned an Iranian student named Hakim Bey, who he had met a week later. Bey had been impressed by the lecture— well, not so much by the lecture, but by the confluence of the lecture and a universalized panic attack. David showed the letter to Tom. **Tom Savage** is the editor of* Gandhabba *and author of* Housing Preservation and Development *and* Processed Words.

Rattray pointed out that, in the letter, the Iranian is cited as saying, "There can be no division in effect."

187

If I'm Odd
***
I'm Odd

ethics to computer science abandoning outer ramparts. If you think your own thinking explained is not diminished at all another part of his brain answered. A loop closed in which the vocal cords to connect one part of the brain to another—the voices were in his head. Think about riding on top of neural machinery in accretion of mind, developed for recruiting teams of brain's wetware. Planning a trip to Europe he will keep retreating and attacking. Everyone in the world but you isn't a zombie just a brain in a vat. You think a simulation is life is not easy reading matter master explication richness and power of the computer metaphor the general run of lion minds and enormous role in the structuring of the human mind. A creature lacking language should not be supposed to be structured. Incredulous challenge light would otherwise be off adjusted mainly downward. A bat can't wonder whether it's Friday; it can't even wonder whether it's a bat; like even the lowly lobster has no selfy self to speak of as the center of narrative gravity reflections on what it is like to be a cat, a bat list of dismissals for cheap skepticism.

Zombie Warlords Probe Uranus

JOHN STRAUSBAUGH

Uranus.
Yeah.
Uranus.

A pretty cold place. Especially when you're alone.

But then in my business being alone is just another word for . . . well, I forget what it's another word for, but I don't have to draw you a picture, do I?

Uranus.

The eighth stop from Sol. Or is it the second one toward Sol. I guess it depends on where you're coming from.

Sol.

You know how it gets that yellow color? Mexican drug slaves pee in it before breakfast. Not a pretty sight, and believe me I seen it.

But that's another story. I'm here to tell you about the Death Virgins of Koko Moko. I been there. Up there where the bamboo grows thick as your midriff and the air is wet and green. Where the orchids grow big as your head and the natives scrape the fungus from between the gekko's toes, roll it up and smoke it under the Morning Star.

Yeah, Venus.

But that's another story.

☾

I'd come from out beyond the asteroid belt. A zone of hard rocks and uptight people. That's what it all came down to. Bimbos, yakuza, flick-knives, and Lucky Strikes. You look up from the clutter and all you can see is Uranus.

Nhi watched Michael Carter walk back along the dipper of sidewalk that ran out from China King's Oak Park location. She held a crab balanced on her paper plate. Another customer waltzed in. She recognized him as the star investigative reporter for the Rib, **John Strausbaugh**.

Muy-Muy emerged from the kitchen to take his order.

"Y'all got any cacciatore gumbo al la Nanking, sweeth't?" John intoned in his melting drawl.

"Sweetheart," Nhi thought, translating, "Tim Sum."

John Strausbaugh is the star reporter for the New York Press, *not the* Rib, *and is the editor of* Drug User.

"Tim Sum," she called to Muy-Muy, who obligingly dropped a menu and approached. "This foreigner, called Michael, say

189

I been there. Up on Uranus. Man I thought I had it made. Just her and me in her gypsy airstream. Little did I know it would take all my cunning, all my training to probe the deep dark secret of . . .

But if I told you it wouldn't be a secret. Let's just say Doc had done a pretty swell job of repacking me after that beating I took on Signet Altuna 7. Some people call that a lucky number. Old Chin Chin the liquor store man didn't think so. I hung back behind the shelves of Sol when the bald little Nazi in the trenchcoat and the coke-bottle specs oiled in from the hot sidewalk, took off his homburg and wiped his scalp with a woman's silk handkerchief. I knew the scent and almost jumped him right then. He peered around the store and smiled asthmatically. Him and Old Chin stared at each other across the lotto counter, and the silence that stretched between them was vast, swampy, tractless, and deadly as the Sud. The Nazi leaned close and Chin blanched when he wheezed,

"*Zero zero zero—eh, Meester Locky?*"

Then the lights went out and I kissed the floor hard, like it was a dame wearing linoleum lip gloss.

((

When attacked, the giant felt-tip lizard of Koko Moko can break off its own tail and beat a man senseless with it. But I'd almost prefer that to the look those Death Maidens gave me when my team of Mexican drug-slave commandos peed on their sacred orchids. If looks could kill we'd all be . . . well I don't have to draw you a picture, do I?

And that was before the zombie warlords came. Charging out of the belly of a version of hell from an alien insect religion in an alternate universe. Hitting us below the asteroid belt. You threw everything you had at them, didn't you, old pal, and they just kept coming. Until you had nothing left to throw at them and the only thing to do was show them Uranus.

Yeah. And they took it. A place of tight rocks and hard-up virgins.

Zero zero zero, Mr. Warlord.

((

Now was that before or after Doc repacked me? I'm not as good as I used to be. Sometimes he gets me mixed up. But then, in my business mixed up is another word for . . .

Kiss me. Kiss me, old pal. Kiss me below the belt, like a flick knife. Kiss me like a zombie. Kiss like a virgin, which is practically the same thing. Get away from the Doc and I'll go down on my knees and kiss Uranus.

Yeah, Uranus.

No trash, no air, no flies on Uranus. What was it Julius Schweitzer said? *I came. I'm gone. I'm history.*

I ain't afraid of Uranus. I seen worse.
Lying there in the gutter outside
the squat bars of Homburg. Man,
they really broke me bad. When I
coughed I could taste my own insides.
That's when you know you're hurt. Sold out by a
dame wearing linoleum lip gloss. That little Nazi
standing over me shining like an orchid. Turned
and handed in his ticket, and Chin couldn't meet
my eye. I lay there like a Samsonite suitcase after a
long hard trip, tagged and scuffed on the outside and
all unpacked inside.

So go ahead, you monkeys. Flip me over. Probe
me deep. You'll never find it. You're just following doctor's orders, same as me. I was doing my job,
you're protecting Uranus.

(

Uranus. She really broke me there. I never saw it coming. I never knew what she was thinking until after she
yelled it at me. Trying to get into her mind was like
falling down a secret stairway into the mosque hive
temple of some alien insect religion. Just being on the
same planet with her gave me a feeling like a swarm of
honey bees was kissing me all over the face and chest
with little sharp tongues of sugar. She had my number. It was tattooed on the back of her neck, up high,
into the hairline, just so I'd really have to search for it,
like a monkey grooming a monkey.

Love—why do you think they call it work?

But I try to forget all that. Them death maidens
really know how to take it. And take and take and
take. I died in her airstream a thousand times. On the
operating table I was reborn.

The felt-tip lizard of Koko Moko can grow back
any part you're man enough to break off. I been there.
I seen it. My Mexicans used to break them up for
sport. A leg. An eye. The heart even. I seen it. The
veins and arteries growing together in the chest,

*you work bar
girl sometimes at dirty man
club, Roxor's."
"Je je [older sister]!"
Muy-Muy protested.
Nhi whacked her, the
sting causing Muy-Muy's
cheek to spasm in pain.*

J o h n S t r a u s b a u g h

reaching for each other like creeper vines, making the knots that make the heart. The regenerated heart.

She cracked my skull for it, poured my yolk out and fried it. But I had their number tattooed deep inside, where even Doc had to unpack me and root around in me up to the elbows to find it. Man, my face hurt from standing between them and what I'm thinking. And all the time they were back here with me.

((

See, I can talk to you. I'm unpacking all my secrets here. Monkey to monkey. Not like out there where the warlords run the streets, run the yakuza, run the lotto and the death virgins, the whole universe and two or three alternates. Out there it's every zombie for himself.

But I don't have to draw you a picture, do I? Zero zero zero, yeah, that's the ticket. Now all my parts fell into space. The Nazi maidens, the warlords of the flies, the yakuza smoking Lucky Strikes laced in gekko toe aphrodisiac as Chin flipped their felt-tip lizard-skin Samsonite bags down the one-way probe to the alternate universe alien insect hell that spawned them.

Zero zero zero. It all adds up. Play it straight or box it, old pal, whatever state you're in, in any universe. Zero zero zero, that's what it all comes down to. In my business, we call it . . .

But I forget my business. I'm not as good as I used to be. You take a beating, you crack the code, you take another beating, you crack another code, they pee on you, you pee on them, you kiss the linoleum so often you come to love it like a cold virgin. you think you know the secret. You think you tasted your own insides for the last time. Then who walks into your life but a heartless lizard oiling his scalp with a familiar scent and you're right back flat on Uranus.

((

She come in here once. Me lying here all unpacked, pieces of me all over the table. You were asleep. She come in here looking like an angel, an angel of death, a Lucky Strike girl.

How ya doin? she said.

I been worse, I said.

Where? she said. On Uranus?

I had to laugh. She smiled, like cutting linoleum. She had an orchid in her hair. No, not in her hair. In her pocket or somewhere. I recognized the scent. She bent down and kissed a part of me. The gizzard, I think. I felt like monkeys were beating me with lizard sticks. She was rooting around in there, turning bits of me over, looking for it.

But I didn't crack, see? I didn't tell. How could I tell? I didn't know it yet myself. On her way out she let a piece of me drop and crushed it under her heel.

☾

Wake up now, pal. Do I have to draw you a picture? I know they're out there in the hall. I recognize the scent. I can hear the wheeze. Zero zero zero. All I got to give. And they won't let me go until they get it.

Help me out here, pal. I'm all unpacked. Sure I know, you're as worst off as me. I don't blame you for giving in. You're just following doctor's orchids.

I let them taste my insides. What more can they want?

Wake up now, pal. Help me out here, pal.

I gave you my secrets. You give me your hand.

Give me your foot.

Give me Uranus.

Yeah.

Uranus.

A pretty cold place. Especially when you're alone.

J   o   h   n   S   t   r   a   u   s   b   a   u   g   h

Captain Zeegor!

Bob Holman

"Captain Zeegor! Capt. Zeegor!" I must write that first, for those are the words that crackle over and over the static. The static, the electricity, the jangling ganglion, the maniac ride, COME IN BABY. Come on in.

Thought you'd never make it. That's it, That's IT. It's a coughing fit say a caffeine snit say I'm brewin' and I'm mooin' and in Hawaii I'm chewin'. Regular to go that's me. Catch me at the door my handle on the drawer no sir, can score if you wish. I twist and spill, blast and thrill . . .

I mean we're already outside. We can glide. Because there's no rush, not much. Not like in New York. Not like in the Apple. B'Apple. Not like on 14th Street, no sir, never been there, and from what I hear never gonna. No, ain't gonna be car hit or a hit. Just the crackle on my radio pops, snap me outta that one, I'll give you a razor on a chain for your friend there if she'll tell me her name. You say hey you say? You say this takes some kind of ship shape rattle tail . . .

It has taken me three days to write the above and I will be a dead man soon. With these facts in mind, secured in some recognizable fashion, we shall begin.

One was not always so how shall I put it. There was once a precision, and now that precision, who we shall now indeed name as Irma making faces at me over the vidphone with the broken speaker. I am trapped, she is mouthing. There is no food there is no water there is nothing in this room but me and the damn vidphone. Do something.

I pace. I look at her with her disheveled hair and leaky make-up. She always looks so good in black and white. Especially the commercials. Her face a jewel made of hundreds of jewels. The fling of her head, her fingers. Sure she is dancing. A dance to the fall of evil,

A young, bearded, shady figure, looking like a disadvantaged beatnik, ran up to Rollo after the lecture. "Hi, I'm Bobbie Proton [aka **Bob Holman**]. I really digged your lecture. I mean, what I could crib. But like, Daddio, I can't scope that part about group dynamos. You say certain word clusters form these cantos . . . "

Bob Holman (aka the Panic DJ) is the author of 8 Chinese Poems and Sweat & Sex & Politics as well as a record, Rock 'n' Roll Mythology, and the video "Rapp It Up!"

Bob stood and watched "Hal Sirowitz" shadow Rollo as he flowed like a liquerfereous eel through the crowd.

evil is rooted out by force. How she is machine-gunning her lover, the lights dim, they are streetlights in East Europe, that is her eyes. So close we kiss her. We transfer and we clone. We know no one has ever done this before.

My clones are named Rafe and Jerome, Irma's are Penny and Mandy. We introduce the clones and take down orders to go on the back of an envelope, but it gets so confusing we all go out together. That was our first mistake.

We should've called out. I know when there's danger right just call out, of course. It's a simple matter. It wasn't that we were screaming so loud we couldn't be heard. Nor that we couldn't agree, but that, as a group, we decided to go out instead of call out. Going out always seems like so much less of a decision. Just go out and there'll be someplace, yes, and that's what Randy said. He caused it. And he was only on the TV.

A thud, a batter, a muffled voice. "Open up in there!" Ah, it's a mean vile vice. We know it well—the voice of a barbarian with scabies, the scratch of an allergy test on a hive. A push, as if the door were breathing. "I say open up!" Oy this huffing. Luckily we're in process of leaving, therefore we are not here, buckling our coats we become the door, the two of us, and our clones, as the following verbatim report on Vidmix TV (Randy) and the vile voice (Karsek), the Rooms we open:

Randy: . . . 'entle Creatures. Further testimony elicits the promise of millions to eat what they're told to, cleaning their plates, and most of recirculating garbage library . . .

Karsek: I'm not tootin' you bugs! Grab a holster and stuff it! Be wise! Hae Yah Hoo Kabrum!

Randy: . . . other vagaries. Vulgarest the new "A Tail and Two Titties" by Charles Dicksin, excuse me, call board light up.

Caller: Hi Randy, hello out there in vidland. This is a true story.

Just last week I was in a restaurant. Coffee, the usual, cake or milk shake, I forget, am I allowed? We can it, we sell it, typical greaseball food, the ultimo grub. And servo-compux revolt-a-meters that make sure you're cooked when the waitress is ready.

Still I wonder what to do with my bathtub. I took your advice and filled it with pets. I'm home all the time. They've built a little waterfall out of washcloths. I never see you. You have become invisible. Ever since they grabbed him and tied him up, no.

Ever since the vegetables were left out for seed.

No.

A flag was waving on the island, a flag he'd never seen before. He swam towards it, not knowing if he had the strength to make it. He was drawn in by the flag. There's no doubt about it. No need to shout it, how he was spotted as just another, nothing different. As if every week brought its new person in out of the water, a community of officially drowned people, living in joy and carousal, calling their world variously the Island and the World and trying to remember the ingredients of bread, and inventing culture as a game of poker, a school of fish with fish eyes and fish lips, decorous plumage, new quarters for the expected rain of shipwrecked souls whose eyes cast upon this flag which I hold before you the bull urging you to read it to me quick before the before ends and I am gored or go home to new ballet loafers and wine, a rose in my teeth, full of passionate drive-in movies and rock 'n' roll.

B o b H o l m a n

The Black Story
HOLLY ANDERSON

Man Mountain was mad that they'd moved the Fish Picnic to an abandoned amusement park near where the El went into the catacombs.

Man thought, as he tooled down the fog-entrenched streets, that perhaps he was the only one left alive who remembered that the amusement park was built on top of a hidden Wobbly graveyard.

Automatically, he steered the car to the curb to pick up a hitchhiker, **Holly Anderson**. She provided the dialog in Janet Zweig's flipbook Extremely Receptive and has published in RedTape.

She stood poised, but Man didn't open the door, staring at something behind her. She followed his gaze. What could be seen, nearly imperceptibly, like a wick through chinked glass, was an El, passing backwards across the horizon.

199

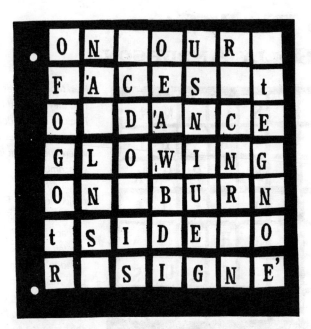
O N O U R
F 'A C E S t
O D 'A N C E
G L O W I N G
O N B U R N
t S I D E O
R S I G N E'

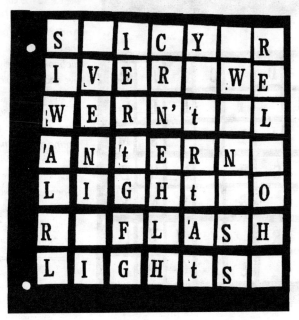
S I C Y R
I V E R W E
W E R N' t L
'A N t E R N
L I G H t O
R F L 'A S H
L I G H t S

Pressure Drop
NEIL STRAUSS

"There were about 200 of us, crammed into a small room, without light, food, or fresh water. We'd been there a week, maybe more, no one was dead yet, but the stench was unbearable. I was down to one-third my normal size, and my skin was beginning to break out in large boils. I didn't think I'd be able to hold on any longer when suddenly the door opened, light poured in, and a hand thrust forward from outside and grabbed me, pulled me out of the fetid crush of bodies and into the warm glow of a summer day. I couldn't see who the hand belonged to, because the light fell like needles on my eyes. My lungs felt like they'd collapse as the fresh air forced its way inside."

"Hey, that's good. What do you call it?"

"'Story of a Cucumber on Becoming a Pickle' is the working title right now. It's not finished yet. There's still the scene where he gets sliced up and dropped into a schoolboy's lunchbox. I'm just trying to figure out if it's okay to still use the first person. You know, it might call into question the credibility of the narrator."

"I think it's okay."

"You want to hear 'Story of a Tree, Part Fifteen'? Two-ply, maximum-strength toilet tissue, 154 square feet, 300 sheets. See, I don't spell out sheets, I just use the abbreviation s-h-t-s-period, so it looks ambiguous. That's how they actually have it on the toilet rolls, you know."

Blane's going to be a good writer someday, I can just tell. He has all the ideas. When he reads me his stories, I feel so stupid. Not only is there no criticism I can give him, but I start to call my own talent into question. That is, if I have any talent. I'd sure like to be a writer, but I don't think I have much of an imagi-

The midget shed his Hal Sirowitz costume as easily as a snake rustles out of its old skin. Another dwarf, with a fez and a gat, lurked in the hall. Wortsman had split, leaving Whitehead in the lurch.

"How much do you know," Outstandish sneered at a cornered Rollo Whitehead, "about the operations of Ink, Inc.?"

"Nothing."

"We're going to take you to their offices tonight." Miles was speaking with a sneer that could only be imitated by Strauss. **Neil Strauss** *writes for the* Village Voice, Details, *the* New York Times, *the* L.A. Weekly, *and* Spin. *He was co-editor of* Radiotext(e). *"You developed this poem genome, right?"*

Rollo seemed indisposed to answer questions, so the midget proceeded. "You say that if a poem is any good, it should be able to publish itself. Huh. You say that if you just put a good poem in any computer, it nation. I can't be a painter, either. It's the same problem, really. With writing and painting, you're just rearranging words or colors that already exist. How can I put them together any better than anyone else has? People tell me you pull from your own experience. I tried to write about my parents, about how they came from Korea and struggled to start their own window installation business, but I felt like that might be a bad thing for people to know about me. How can you become famous when you're born to parents like that? Not that I don't respect them, but it's just better what Blane does, the way he imagines things from different points of view without ever revealing anything about himself. I find it impossible to write anything that's not autobiographical. Maybe my problem is that I always start fictionalizing whenever I feel uncomfortable or bored. I just pretend that I'm a character in a book someone else is writing, and start imagining how the book would read.

He thumbs through his papers like a diligent secretary. (I guess "diligent secretary" works here.) Intent on finding another writing sample that will prove his brilliance to himself, careful not to crease the type-filled paper, the bare-backed boy seems unaware of the warm body that waits patiently for him to finish. When he turns towards her, props himself up on his elbow, and starts reading, she's going to pretend not to hear; she'll look at the flowery bedsheets and examine the way the red, blue, and yellow petals come together to form new designs at every fold instead of meeting his warm breath and self-assured voice head-on.

That's my problem, really; I just need an interesting life, then I won't have to worry about being creative. I guess a lot of the times when I've been mad at Blane these past six months, it's really been me I'm angry at. Why do I always have to compare myself to other people? And why do I always feel inferior when I do?

It's hard not to be insecure when people are always trying to remind you of your shortcomings. A lot of my friends try to make me feel bad because I haven't joined things like the Asian-American Coalition or the Women's Center, when I'd like to forget about that stuff—it's never really been a problem anyway—and concentrate on finding something I'm good at. People should just forget about black, white, and yellow, and male and female too, and all the external, visual differences between human beings. We're basically all the same, anyways. My uncle was buried in a mass grave on one of the Volcano Islands; he starved to death while fighting for the Japanese during the war. One of his captains gave my dad a picture of all these bones in the grave, native islanders, Japanese, Chinese, and Korean soldiers, American soldiers, and they all look the same. Nothing we do is going to live any longer than our bones anyway, so what's the point? There's something inside me that won't let me follow through on the conclusion that should lead me to. Something that lets me lie to myself and say that I'm different, that chance might give me a break some day. I guess that something is god, and if it's not god, it's vanity.

I've never told Blane this stuff. He'll just think I'm stupid.

"Here's one, I've got it. It's a poem, 'A Pencil Is a Thought Waiting to Be Written.' Have you heard it before?"

"No, I don't think so."

should be able to find its own way into print, by going through the networks to appear in a cookbook, the president's memoirs, The New Yorker, or squatting in the middle of the Random House Dictionary."

The little man seemed close to outrage. "I tell you, if you're right, a book is—could be—the last, best weapon."

Don't Show Them

You're Not Making It

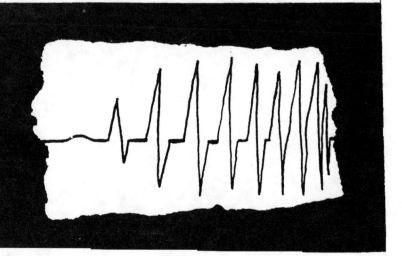

Insomnia in Excelsis

PETER CHERCHES

The gross of blackhead removers you ordered arrived today. The package came this morning, while you was out. C.O.D. I paid the mailman, out of my own pocket. I laid it out. $489.62. I know you've been waiting for this shipment.

"Tell me, Anthony, what are you going to do with a hundred and forty-four blackhead removers? I don't mean to pry or nothin', but I'm curious . . . No, baby, I didn't tell the mailman anything . . . Wait a minute, honey, you don't have to talk to me like that, I wouldn't do anything to—"

Weird movies they're showing in the middle of the night these days. *One Hundred and Forty-Four Blackhead Removers,* with Shelley Winters and Richard Conte. Film noir. *Tête noir.* I have to wake up at six, and it's four already and I can't sleep, again.

My brother Eddie was arrested yesterday for insider trading. Eddie is an old hand at insider trading. Been at it since he was a kid. It started with baseball cards. Eddie once paid Donna Fortunato a quarter to find out how many Sandy Koufaxes her brother Vinny had. Six! Vinny Fortunato had six Koufaxes and Eddie knew he'd have to sell short.

"Where's Paparelli?"

"He ain't here."

"You ain't holdin' out on me, are you, sister?"

click click click click

"Reverend Bascomb, what are you doing?"

Thick southern Roumanian accent: "Ah must have blood, ten thousand more pints of blood if our work is to continue."

"Ink, Inc.," the FBI director said to David. "All these audience members are linked or could be linked to that."

"What do you mean, 'could be linked'?" David interjected.

"Don't be naive. How do you think someone gets to be part of an audience?"

"I don't follow."

"Suppose you went to a movie. Suppose you could see into the soul of every member of that movie's audience."

"I still . . . "

"How do you think someone becomes a subversive?" Hoover barked. "Not by reading books. Pshaw. If a bunch of parti- or semi- or quasi-subversives sit in an audience, rubbing elbows, listening to a platform of freethinkers, I guarantee they emerge full-fledged bad guys."

David was getting perturbed. "What are you talking about? Are you saying

Curse of the Vampire Evangelist. I think that's Earl Holliman playing the vampire evangelist. Haven't I seen this one before?

"I'm sorry, Mr. Nudelman, but the X-rays reveal an eight-piece serving for four in your left lung."

"Are you sure, doctor?"

"Ninety percent sure," he says.

"What about the other ten percent?" I ask.

"The other ten percent says it could be a four-piece serving for eight in your right lung. Either way we'll have to operate."

"What are my chances, doc?"

"Poor, very poor."

"How poor?" I ask, trembling. Wait a minute—I'm not trembling, I'm having an orgasm. The nurse is giving me a blowjob. I look down and see her with my cock in her mouth. She is an ancient woman. Maria Ouspenskaya. As I come in her mouth I hear a Bach fugue, played on a harpsichord.

"I am not Maria Ouspenskaya," she says, semen dripping from the corner of her mouth, "I am Wanda Landowska."

The next thing I know a policeman is handcuffing me to the hospital bed. "What's going on?" I ask.

"You're under arrest for sodomy," the cop says.

"Wait a minute," I say, "I was just lying here minding my own business when—"

"Likely story," the cop says. "This girl here is just eleven years old, and you are a very sick man."

The cop is right. It's Patty McCormack, straight out of *The Bad Seed*, in a nurse's uniform. She's throwing a tantrum. "He made me do it! He made me do it!"

Now the doctor is poking me with a fork. "Do you feel anything?"

"No."

He cuts into me with a steak knife. "Do you feel anything now?"

"No."

He pours some Trappey's Indi-Pep Hot Sauce into the knife wound. "Feel anything now?" he aks.

"Yes," I reply, to get rid of him.

Now the doctor is licking my wounds. But all of a sudden he has become a woman. Agnes Moorhead. And I'm in the hospital ward of a women's prison.

I guess I fell asleep. That's good. I need all the sleep I can get. I want to be ready for that audition tomorrow.

Do I really want that job? Up until two days ago I never knew such jobs existed. Corporate crooner. It's part of the spiritual wellness program at a major financial institution. When the bankers need a break from the pressures of debenturing and indenturing or whatever it is they do, they come into this room where the crooner sits at a piano, waiting for them, and takes requests. I'm having second thoughts, but the money is too good to pass up. Sixty K.

"As it says in Chapter 7, verse 11 of Ecclesiastes—or is it Chapter 11, Verse 7 of the Book of Job? Or is it the Twenty-second Psalm? Maybe it's the Fifth Commandment. Or the Fourteenth Amendment. Or the Eighteenth Hole at Inverrary. Or could it be the Third Game of the '57 World Series? Maybe it's the Six Hundredth Position of the Kama Sutra. I just don't know, I just don't know."

This is the third night in a row I've seen the clergyman on *Sermonette* have an on-air breakdown. I wonder what's going on.

click click click

" . . . then I'm doing two weeks at the Hattie McDaniel Room of the Best Western Biloxi, and after that I'm booked for a month at the Golden Chili Dog in Chickoshay, then I'll take a few days off to catch my breath, and then I'm off to Zagreb for the Tennessee Williams Festival, and my baby's due in April, and on May eleventh I start shooting a TV movie with Buddy Ebsen called *Superficial Two-Step with an Indelible Cataract.*"

"Is that going to be a comedy?"

"We're not sure yet."

click click click

"Nothing gets out those really tough stains like new Biz with hydrochloric acid."

"Hydrochloric acid! But Marge, isn't that dangerous?"

"Nonsense—you're soaking in it now!"

click click

this lecture, which, by the way, I attended—and it sounded about as rabble-rousing as a talk by René Crevel—made the audience non-kosher?"

"Don't be dumb, Davy boy," Hoover chided, "I'm talking about chemistry . . . the chemistry of fluids."

He leaned back. His table, with one short leg, was propped up by a copy of Between a Dream & a Cup of Coffee." *This book, as well as* Condensed Book *and* Bagatelles, *are by* **Peter Cherches**, *former editor of* Zone.

"You be the judge, smart boy," the director said. "I want you to get involved in Operation Cantilever Twins."

"I don't want to get involved," David shot back.

"You're part of the audience, so you're part of the assignment. Here's your papers."

P e t e r C h e r c h e s

"Tony, you've got to get me ten more teenage girls with rampant blackheads."

"But where am I going to find them, boss?"

"Same place you found all the others—St. Vitus for Girls."

"But boss, Sister Philomena is getting suspicious."

"Don't worry about Sister Philomena—I'll take care of her."

I've got to take a leak. Real bad. But I don't want to get out of bed. I don't want to get out from under the covers. It's cold out there and I'm exhausted.

I'm ten years old. I'm watching my mother vacuum the living room carpet. She's singing "Melancholy Baby" in a foreign language I don't understand. I know it's "Melancholy Baby," even though there's no melody to speak of. She's actually reciting the words in a high-pitched shriek. And her dress is made out of teeth. And she takes the hose of the vacuum cleaner and puts it to my head and it sucks in all my hair and now I'm completely bald and she starts singing "Melancholy Baby" again, this time in English, but for some reason I think it's "Happy Birthday" and I start crying and she starts to beat me and I start fighting back and now I'm on top of her and I'm pummeling her with my fists and she's singing "Auld Lang Syne" only it isn't my mother anymore it's Agnes Moorhead and it's New Year's Eve in a women's prison.

And I still have to take a leak.

click click

" . . . and lift and stretch and bend and lift and stretch and lift and stretch and lift and bend and stretch and bend and lift and bend and stretch and bend and stretch and lift and stretch and lift and stretch and bend and lift and . . . exhale."

click click

"Where are you taking me, mister?"

"To a very special place where they can cure even the nastiest case of blackheads."

"Even mine?"

"Even yours."

It's been six months since I've had a paycheck. Six months since I was fired from my proofreading job at Beaumont, Mathers, Billingsley, and Dow. Fired for leaking insider tips on mergers and acquisitions to my brother Eddie. The one they got us on was a doozie. National Rendering was planning to offer $58 a share for Superior By-Products, which had been trading for $45. I guess it was stupid of me to call Eddie on the office phone. But it had always worked before. At any rate, they promised they wouldn't prosecute if I resigned quietly, because they didn't want a scandal. The thing is, I've already squandered all of my ill-gotten gains, and I don't even have enough left for next month's rent, so I really need that crooning job.

And I've still got to take a leak. I can't hold out any longer. So I get out of bed and walk toward the bathroom. Just outside the bathroom I see a cockroach. I'm about to step on the roach when the bug says, "Please don't kill me, Mr. Nudelman."

"How did you know my name?" I ask the roach.

"You live here, don't you?" the roach says. He's got a point. Then the roach says, "Follow me, we're having a party." So I squeeze through this little hole in the wall, after the roach, and inside all these roaches are dancing and munching on familiar-looking crumbs.

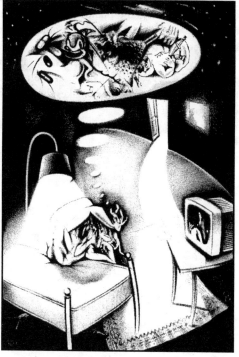

"What are they dancing," I ask my roach-host, "'La Cucaracha'?"

"Don't be silly," the roach says, "it's the Mashed Potato."

I strain to hear the music and lo and behold, it's Dee Dee Sharp: "It's the latest, it's the greatest . . . "

And I wake up and I still have to take a leak. So I go to the bathroom and I start to piss. And I'm pissing and pissing and pissing. And when I'm through I return to the bedroom and crawl back under the covers.

"That was some racket you boys had going—smuggling dope in blackhead removers, child prostitution, insider trading, covert operations, diversion of funds, single-bullet theory. But it looks like the party's over."

"Don't count on it, copper."

Six o'clock. I turn off the alarm before it has a chance to ring. I hop out of bed, throw on a three-piece suit, and take the subway downtown to Wall Steet.

Evergreen Equities, 40 Wall, 27th floor. "I have an appointment with Mr. Lusk."

"Have a seat," the secretary says. "I'll tell him you're here."

P e t e r C h e r c h e s

Two hours, three issues of *The Economist*, two issues of *The Plain Truth*, and a coffee-stained copy of *The Kiplinger Letter* later, Mr. Lusk greets me. Not only is he incredibly tall, at least seven feet, but in addition his head and hands are disproportionately large. Acromegaly.

I stand up.

"Mr. Nudelman?" I nod my head. "Bill Lusk." He shakes my hand. I suppress a scream. "Follow me," he says.

He takes me to a room that's a sort of mini-ballroom. Curtains all around, chandeliers, and a grand piano with a candelabra. "Here, put this on," Lusk says, tossing me a jacket. It's a sequined dinner jacket, à la Liberace. So I take off my suit jacket and put on the sequined one.

"All right, Mr. Nudelman," Lusk says, "are you ready?"

"Yessir," I say, and I sit down at the piano. Accompanying myself with one hand, I begin to sing: "Money makes the world go round, the world go round, the world go round . . ."

Excerpts from "Landscapes"

THOMAS ZUMMER

1900. International Exhibition, Paris. A mock naval battle is staged by thirty warships that bombarded and burned a model maritime city.

1911. The word *blimp* is derived from the military designation "B-Type Limp Aircraft." England.

1915, 5 September. Grand Duke Nicholas is dismissed from the post of Commander-in-Chief of the Russian Armies, and sent to the Caucasus. He reportedly told his intimates that if he had the power he would exile the Czarina Alexandra to a convent.

1916, 4 March. In re: M.A./Misc./438.M.A.2b. The pilot and observer who have been using this gun mounting during the last week report it is difficult to manoeuvre, and also rather dangerous to the pilot, as when the "quick release" is used, the weight of the gun on the end of the long arm makes a great leverage and the observer is unable to hold it up. The gun drops suddenly, and usually strikes the pilot on the head. When using the wheel to wind the gun up, the weight is again too great, the process of winding up being very slow. The mounting is not at all popular.

1940, 21 June. Without having been under fire, Sartre is captured at Padoux, in Lorraine, then sent to the Gardes Mobiles barracks at Nancy, where he is kept until mid-August. He is then transferred to Stalag XII-D at Treves. Gives a course on Heidegger to a group of imprisoned priests.

1943, March. The mechanicians of 2/LeLv 14 carved some wooden bombs and Capt. M. Kalima and Lieut. H. Keso bombed the Soviet false airfield with the

As she reached over to kiss Liza, Stephanie swerved and, making a jagged fist, slashed the bull's forearm. Startled, he smashed his head on a hold pole and tumbled to the floor, a xerox of a photograph sliding out of his tunic pocket onto the muddy tiles.

He stood, selecting a gun from his waistband, and fired. The bullet hit a fuse-box, sending out a stream of sparks that ignited the advertising placards that formed a frieze, as in the Parthenon, around the walls of the car.

One poster was defaced by little men drawn by **Tom Zummer***. Tom curated the acclaimed* Re: Framing Cartoons *exhibition. His own drawings have been in* The Independent *and* Social Text.

The El had been slowing for a station, but now, short-circuited, it began grinding at a faster clip— backwards!

211

bombs carrying the text "Our regards to wooden plane mechanicians" in Russian. (Lentajan Albumi 1, Toivo Sorsa.)

1944. Paris, Retrato de Montserrat Pla, pluma y bolígrafo sobre papel, Donativ Montserrat Pla, 1990. Museo Picasso, Barcelona.

16 January, 1991. "We have now completed the first full business-day of the war."—CNN.

Laughing-Stock
Michael Kasper

Common sense says that a sense of humor is engaging and thus helpful for communicating, as when ordinary conversation is witty, or when a lecturer tells a joke.

Researchers in psychology, however, say otherwise, namely that the contribution of humor to, um, "message effectiveness," is questionable. Of 12 studies, eight failed to find any attitude change at all after the "humorous message" was "received"; one found that humor actually interfered with understanding.

Once, going from Yalvach to Akshenir, Nasreddin Hodja, the Turkish folk and joke hero, absentmindedly took a wrong turn and got lost. There was a big stone by the roadside with a bird perched on it, which Hodja, being near-sighted, mistook for a man.

M. Kasper *had been entering the El station at Kedzie carrying spools of electrician's tape.*

M. Kasper is the author of All Cotton Briefs *and* Plans for the Night. *When Lorraine explained the situation, M. bundled himself and the two women with black adhesive. When the train hurtled backwards through the station, each tried to leap on.*

M. didn't make it. Jill slipped, falling off the platform into the narrow space between the massive car wheels and the station moorings. Sweat was branching along her forehead as she felt the air drawn by the undercarriage sucking her tangled auburn hair.

But Lorraine clung on, adhering to the car, and saw the patrolman level his revolver through the gradually thickening smoke.

Buglike, Lorraine slithered to an open window.

As it turns out, these experiments (for instance Kilpela 1962, Taylor 1964, Gruner 1972, and Markiewicz 1973) all had procedural problems, such as serious setting, bad jokes, difficulty measuring mirth, and weird ways of gauging persuasion. Nevertheless, it's disconcerting to see it stated in such plain English (Grote and Cvetkovich 1972) that issue involvement often *drops* following humor, and simple distraction is the key variable, a conclusion based on just enough data so some might indeed doubt common sense.

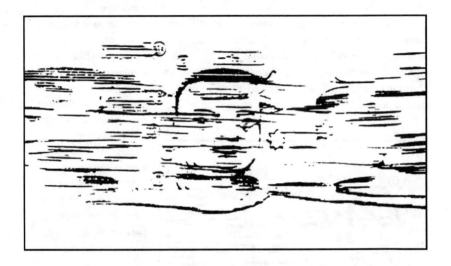

"Hullo sir," Hodja asked, "which way to Akshenir, please?" No answer. Hodja asked again, louder. Still no answer. "How dare you ignore me so!" shouted Hodja. The bird flew off. "There!" Hodja cried, "Now your turban's blown away! Serves you right!"

More-loyal devotees of humor don't doubt. We're completely convinced of comedy's effectiveness.

Anyway, we maintain, no serious research can ever comprehend a funny event.

We're the kind who just plod on, perversely, pigheadedly, cracking jokes, contrary to science, until we ourselves become clownish. Out here on the border between funny/ha-ha and funny/odd. Where the laughs and the buffalo roam.

An urchin who'd been watching tugged at Hodja's sleeve saying, "But sir, it's a bird not a turban." "Maybe so," said Hodja, "but I'm damned if I'm gonna help that rude sonofabitch chase it!"

On Killing Scrim

CARL WATSON

THE PHENOMENON ITSELF

Dateline: Chicago, 1981: A guy calling himself Ed "The Mother Killer" Kelly marched into St. John of God's Church and shot a statue of the Virgin Mary through the heart. People drove miles to the crime site, which soon became one of Chicago's prime tourist attractions. A concession stand was opened selling T-shirts and replicas of the wounded icon.

This "Ed" Kelly, as he called himself, could only say that She was to blame, it was her fault, because She was Mother of all Icons, and that he belonged to a grassroots organization bent on destroying these ancient maternal images as a means of retroactively destroying the underpinning, the very fertile womb of all fetish worship, bringing down that coarse house of adulation, whereby the iconographic universe as we know it would collapse and humankind would again be free in existential terms. Well, alright.

Soon a rash of Virgin Mary shootings began. Out in the country young people placed Mother of God statuettes on picket fences, popping their metaphoric cherries with pellet guns. There were skeet-shooting clubs that used only religous figurines. Government officials were quick to point out that this fad was merely an aspect of eager consumption, and could be absorbed into the healthy economic pyramid which fed the myth of the free market while at the same time consolidating power and enslaving the masses. Thus the competition escalated as it strove for innovation.

A guy in Kansas shot a coke machine with a .45-caliber pistol.

A woman blew away an Andy Warhol painting in a St. Louis museum.

Carl met Christian and Michael at the train station with plans of spending a quiet day at the Fish Picnic. But as soon as they packed on the Dan Ryan El's last car, Christian began obsessing about some Cantonese circus performer. To make matters worse, Carl's knapsack broke, dumping a chunk of bratwurst on the dirty floor.

Carl Watson *is the author of* Anarcadium Pan, Confessions of an Aspirin Eater, Bricolage Ex Machina, *and most recently,* Beneath the Empire of the Birds.

As he turned to look for the sausage, he happened to glance out the rear window.

"I say we guys move more to the front of the train."

"Oh man, what are you talking about," Michael complained. "I'm hanging loose."

Carl merely cocked a

217

There was a drive-by shooting of an Elvis Lamp in a small Indiana town.

The populace showed almost no concern, however, for these seemingly random events because basically whatever you did with a gun was OK in America. Gunplay was an eagerly anticipated byproduct of a marketing strategy geared toward individualism.

It was not long, however, before this individualism became sinister. A man named Ed "Son of Man" Gacy in Wisconsin was discovered to have buried in his basement the mutilated plaster statues of some 30 saints, as well as burned effigies, torn photos, defiled Hindu dieties, violated Buddhas, and numerous other symbols in various states of dishonor.

He said he hung out in Icon adulation bars where youngsters danced furiously to throbbing garbled music while giant video screens flashed historical and nostalgic references in the effort to fill their spiritual vacuum with some kind of marketable meaning. He would lure these young people to his home with offers of ice cream, jobs, and possible stardom.

One surviver testified, "I knew him, I met him in a bar, he was quite handsome. He asked me what I was into, I said I was into Brando. Brando was god. He asked me if I had any pictures of Marlon Brando. He said he wanted to cover them with red jelly and lick them. He said he wanted to lick the sweet jellied blood of Marlon Brando, my god. He was a sick puppy alright, but you know, I kind of liked him."

Meanwhile on the other side of the globe, lumpen crowds gather to mock the dangling stone torso of Nikoli Somebody-or-Other in a blatant public display of icon derision. Indeed what seemed like random eccentric acts were about to snowball, leading to the epicenter of a dangerous new social phenomenon dubbed Iconocide—a crime of violence against the past.

The Evolution of the Phenomenon

Dateline: NYC, 1987: The Violence of Inanimate Objects became a popular catchphrase for a general undefined irritation. Criminals lay on psychiatric couches across the country and complained of excessive iconographic baggage.

Meanwhile Iconocide had developed into an umbrella concept—a popular plea to cop in court to a lesser charge. For instance, a woman accused of slashing the throat of a man at a bus stop wearing Levi Jeans said "Nobody fucks with me like that, nobody fucks with me subliminally. Who the fuck does he think he fucking is—Prince Dick or George Michael Jackson or something, sayin' hey baby, check me out, so I says shit, I pull out my razor and started slashing up his throat. Hell, how was I to know he was human. I don't know what a human is. I never met one."

Another woman accused of murdering her husband claimed he had become the standard of The Abusive Father.

A child who shot his parents defended himself by saying they had become "parodies of themselves."

A would-be presidential assassin asked to be exonerated from charges claiming the president was only a cardboard cutout blatantly paraded before the public by a cartel of manipulative patriarchs.

Celebrity opportunists began to hire themselves out to palliate a confused population. Parading in front of microphone banks giving speeches loaded with oxymorons such as "Radical Chic," "Counter-Culture," and "Natural."

In turn Neo-Right-to-Lifers and Radical Centrists accused these same celebrities of being themselves mere despicable symbols of mediocrity, usurping the rightful nobility of the Average Joe, Mr. and Ms. American Citizen. They painted a grim picture of icons as Vampires sucking the life-force from the populace.

Meantime scientists were saying they could now clone beloved dead presidents and past Messiahs using DNA samples from fossilized blood of the mosquitos that bit them back in those heady days of their innocent glory. Feeling threatened by this new technology, rock stars and celebrity artists started printing money with their own faces on the bills.

Arms manufacturers were placing billboards all over America declaring the sanctity of the American Family. The government imports tons of heroin as part of the Apathy Storm Program. Both Liberals and Conservatives approve.

Incidents of Iconocide escalated to the point where it was no longer clear whether the crime was a form of raging Conservatism or the New Liberalism. Some believed it was simply the end-product of the division of the world into smaller and smaller special interest groups. Others believed the syndrome to be the most

thumb to the window. The two others saw behind them, advancing briskly, a backwards-moving runaway El, like a time bomb on roller skates.

At that exact same moment, on the other side of town, Nhi scratched her thigh as she counted out her cash register tray in the basement of the China King.

"What is 'ironic social protest'?" Muy-Muy asked, disturbing the rhythmic clinking of coins.

"I think it relates to this problem: Most people who object to a regime can be bought off by having their demands met in a woefully scaled-down form. It's hard for a political leader not to take a half loaf, both so as to show his followers he or she can accomplish something and because there is hunger."

The fishy stench in the basement grew stronger.

Nhi continued, "What if protest is staged around an event that never took place or based on a demand that violates common sense?"

Nhi left her cash tray and went to where she had

sophisticated of a long line of condoned killing motifs, maintained as a means of arrest when population control became necessary.

On the positive side, talk-show hosts claimed they could cure society's ills by trivializing, and thus dismissed social phenomena into talk show topics like "Women Who Kill Their Husbands; Children Who Hate Their Parents."

The ivory towers of universities grew inbred and confused. Teenagers were posing as intellectuals. In 1996 the Goverment repealed all voting rights, claiming the populace was now simply too stupid. Nobody complained. The situation degenerated as the society became self-reflexively hilarious, utter contempt posed as comedy.

People drew bullseyes on their heads as a sarcastic comment on the state of affairs. T-shirts were spotted that read "Shoot me if you think I'm special."

In their desperate search for an audience, psychologists began to rhyme their theories into rap songs. In 1998 the popular entertainer Shrink Rap was assassinated by a street gang calling themselves the Youthful Iconoclasts. The average citizen, however, didn't know what an iconoclast was. They thought it was the same as an aristocrat. And then there were copy-cat groups like the Ideosyncrat Killers, men and women who roamed the streets gunning for the extremely peculiar or ostentatious.

The Deconstruction of the Phenomenon

Dateline: Stanford University, Palm Springs Campus, 1991: Property damage or revolution, peer pressure or marketing ploy. While urban tabloids competed for status as birthplace of the new trend, legal battles raged as to whether or not the thing even existed. For instance: perhaps everything was simultaneous and always had been, or maybe, like most fads, it was a trick of hindsight. Knotty questions indeed.

The Government called for a national task force. A large room was hired in a university town and catered by Red Lobster. The public was invited. Questions were fielded.

The general consensus was that these "public" people were fed up with being force-fed lifestyles they could never hope to achieve; others simply felt cheated by the imposition of a cartoon mentality upon their lives.

Religous leaders tried to point out how everyone was actually related to each other through a Platonic Ur-type. Thus bonded, the public could abandon their shame and get back to work producing the goods and services that make this country great. But that made everyone feel threatened.

One university professor stated that the evolution from the animate to the inanimate is often violent, and that it was common knowledge most people these days gravitated toward "types" and that the general population may indeed be semi-inanimate but they were still superficial merely moving images of who they wanted or saw themselves to be.

This led to a heated watershed debate concerning pastiche, heresy, and the usurpation mystic of various media stars, which set hourly precedents for rhetorical acrobatics, including claims of mistaken identities, transferable images, shifting mystiques, and guilt by association—a veritable can of worms to the double-speak of normal legislation and academe.

In a lecture given by Leonard Nimoy entitled "The Image: Its Abstraction Beyond Use Value," the one-time logician asked, "Can the assumed nobility of an original act be transferred to a degraded reflection?" He went on to make the case for cliche over function. He also made household phrases of such formerly obscure terms as "Deferral of Guilt to a Preferred Double," "The Immediate Visibility of the Image."

One well-known psychic drew a graph of ancient magical symbols which included the heart, the lion, the rose, the red sea, logos, bile, and the philosophers' stone . . . all connected by lines into a complex spiritual machine. Another guy drew a similar machine incorporating society's matrimonial patterns with totemism, sacrifice, and the consumption of raw or cooked foods. There were threads in the web connecting Madonna to Mary Magdalene, Joan Collins to Kali, James Dean to Oedipus.

The most popular argument, however, was put forth by a famous evangelist and "seer" who claimed the very air of the biosphere was a shimmering haze of data streams. She said that radio, television, and information transmissions fill the interstices of our tissues daily as past broadcasts rush to fill every vacuum, nasal chamber, and cavity of the body. Even the hollows of the heart are filled with congealed images of Johnny Carson, Diana Ross, and Amos 'n' Andy—in fact the whole pantheon of gods and goddesses flushes

cached her cigarettes.

Muy-Muy trailed along, "But why protest about nothing?"

Nhi lit her sister a smoke and then spoke wearily, "We have nothing to lose. Think about it. Father dead, brothers killed in the Vietnam war. No more male line. No link to ancestors. Mother dying and abandoned by no-good daughters." She spat. "We know who destroyed our line or, if we don't know exactly, we can see its gleam. The modern world system, a sprawling communism and a bloated, tentacled super-capitalism embraced. Two dense, inhuman cages. If we demand bread or anything from the regime, it's as if we are saying our desire can be satisfied. But, unless the whole world space were dismantled, we would not even have an environment in which our dreams could be expressed. We must frame our demands so that they cancel themselves out by being incapable of comprehension by the regime's computers and agents. This should create a shock wave

===============

through the heart almost with every beat, being in effect the combustible mixture of the great engine of love. She then threw her hands in the air in praise, adding that crime was not only innate to this process, it was also passé. The room burst into fevered but loving applause.

Indeed, added another authority, these days it was fully credible to commit psychological crimes without ever leaving the comfort of your easy chair. When Jimmy Carter said "I have committed lust in my heart," the species entered a wild new corridor of existence. One's heart became a simple convenience according to what one hoped to achieve from exploiting it. Finally everyone agreed upon a

U n b e a r a b l e s

general depletion in the public supply of some vague Nerve Force, and declared the Symposium closed.

Satisfied scholars and celebrities alike picked up their government checks and headed for home. But the advertisers wouldn't leave it be. That night on television was yet another special, the tenth exposé that month: "What makes a man an Iconocidal maniac? Who knows?" said Vincent Price as he walked through a foggy graveyard. "They often live next door and we don't even know it. Or they live inside us. One day something snaps and you wake up with a strange desire to save the world. We'll be right back after this word from our sponsors."

THE ENVELOPE PLEASE

Dateline: Tulsa, Oklahoma, 2001: After the introductory logo of a baby in a bubble spinning in space, the *Entertainment Tonight* crew interviews Nobel Prize–winner-turned-terrorist Jesus Gustave Frederico El Greco Jones, also known as Jim. "Picture a world," Jim said, "in which there are no religous memorabilia stores, no billboards or magazine covers, no Brand Names. No JFK, Bart Simpson, Krishna, Mickey Mouse, or Marilyn.

"Can you imagine the horror of it?" he continued. He then terrified the viewing audience by peeling away his skin to reveal an endoskeleton composed of a fine filigree of fiber optics and pixilated displays. He then pleaded in a thick put-on Austrian accent, "Believe me. I have come to save your children."

Suspicions were thus confirmed—yes, it was true, Terminators had been sent back from an intolerably utopian future, a future without dramatic enslavement, and thus without entertainment, where bored men and women sat around all day with no focal points for their obsessions.

In the late 60's the first of these time-travelers arrived posing as ethno-mythologists and French

that reverses within the state apparatus. A backward arc. What the labor movement calls 'running the plant backwards.'"

Muy-Muy: "Childish ideas."

"Aren't the monks who douse themselves with gasoline doing that? Ironic social protest. How can the government answer a request that you kill yourself in making?"

"So one person—"

"You would need a group of disaffected Taoists, Confucian scholars cashiered by the Cultural Revolution, wandering monks with begging bowls, infertile third wives, scorned prostitutes, left-out leftovers from society."

Now it was Muy-Muy's turn to be pensive. She spoke wistfully, "America is filled with such people."

Nhi sat on a lobster crate. Her cash count was ten dollars short. Her housedress was already sweat-stained under the arms and at the small of her back. A tear in her dress revealed the strap of yellow tendons under her ribs.

intellectuals, New Theorists, the so-called Structuralists justifying the social necessity of enslaving ritual.

In 2003, a heavily plasticized Geraldo Rivera exhumed the body of Claude Lévi-Strauss on live TV, proving that in fact the famous theorist had no normal human organs at all inside him but a strange matrix of symbols, pulleys, and gears.

Susan Sontag, distressed at what this event foretold, declaimed the end of all Literature. And sure enough, by 2006 the first of the new "wordless poetry books" appeared on franchise shelves. These books were just pictures of poets in various thoughtful, romantic, or urban attitudes.

By 2010, written literature was no longer even officially tolerated, only entertainment, performance art, and video. All other forms of rebellion had given in to global pacification through fame, consumer goods, and the massive distribution of heroin.

Those who still chose to call themselves writers were required by law to place all nouns, votive clauses, etc., in quotation marks. If they refused they were imprisoned as binary signals in cyberspace, taunted by joystick-jamming Hitler teens or hunted by free-roaming Pac Man–style sheep of the state.

True grandpas still sat in rocking chairs and reminisced about the days when the spark of revolution once burned in the human soul. The *Entertainment Tonight* crew searched and found one such holdover, running a carnival game in a remote tent out in Oklahoma. It was a huge, brightly lit gaudy organ, and at the ends of its patinaed pipes popped up the heads of every imaginable matinee idol—Elvis to Elvira to Evita to Electra. For a dollar you could take a pop.

When interviewed he said, "Why, bringing down the famous is good clean fun, sonny. Besides, if they're going to get treated like gods, they've got to act like gods, and by god they don't, do they, they act like fools with money."

He laughed, but the laugh was on him, as they hauled him away for execution. However, it is said his last words screamed from the smoking hot seat were, "Boycott all media, smash the state."

Witnesses concurred, there is a powerful pheremonal effect to the smell of burning flesh, and this dramatic scene of execution, well, it made them all kind of hungry.

First Words (Excerpt from "Red Blade")

JIM FEAST

Rather than go all the way to the city center, he and a few buddies had decided to make a trip to a nearby red-light district. It was situated within walking distance in the Chinatown area, according to a veteran who, for some reason, had been put into their unit of raw recruits and who now proposed to accompany them. Thus it was that after dinner the five of them walked out the front gate, were checked, and sauntered down the parkway on their first visit to the oriental mecca.

It was getting dark. The sky above the low-lying shops was shot through with a diversity of hues, having the appearance of a slashed comforter with the case, inner lining, and stuffing all mixed in a profusion of flawed purples, reds, and yellows.

On entering the main shopping section, they found everything was party-colored, a rash of baby pinks, greens, onion grays. From every building, merchandise had clawed out from the shop fronts onto the sidewalks. No one actually entered the stores, with everyone clustered around the outdoor stalls. Often the pavements were so cramped by this as to be almost unthreadable. At one place, a fish store's goods covered half the pavement with containers of crabs and fish while the curb was encumbered with a news kiosk. The GIs followed a morass of people who slopped off the walk into the gutter.

Now and then the soldiers became wedged in the crowd, held as tightly as in a moving box. The youth couldn't help noticing the fantastic dress of the inhabitants. It was not so much the severe cuts of the clothes, but the always unsuitable color arrangements.

Nhi lay recklessly in the rumpled bedding like a statue of liberty in a garland of ribbons, her undraped shoulder showing beautifully tallow against the white sheet.

There was only one pillow and I pressed my face into her bushel of straw hair, that held the smell of rice paper, absorbing her breathing, accented like Southern Chinese.

Last night, I boosted her to the fire escape. (Ladies are not allowed in the Hotel Alcove.)

I, **Jim Feast**, have only one claim to fame, which is writing these intros. There was chili browning on the hot plate, and I could hear a train approaching.

We had awakened early and quietly, warmly made love, then drowsed back into sleep as if morning were only another espousal of night.

Now, for once, I had got-

Aside from the old grandmothers, who wore dark purple pants suits, and the schoolchildren in white blouses and brown skirts or pants, the population had ransacked the rainbow for bizarre mélanges. The favored matched tones were blue and yellow, and pink and lime green or white. Everywhere there was a profanity of reds.

As the soldiers neared the bar, a huge lobster escaped a tradesman's hands and fell sprawling onto the sidewalk. Pedestrians gave the crustacean a wide berth as

he waved his free claw and stumbled in a half circle. A gust of wind played with the stub of electrician's tape on his back as if it were a bandage.

A black limo rolled slowly past as they pushed their way through a number of hawkers into one of the first clubs on the strip, the Hot Cat Lounge.

His first impression on entering was that he had been thrust through an airlock into outer space. The room was so frigid, dark, and glittering with projected stars.

With the veteran, the youth walked to the bar, while the others strayed onto the dance floor.

He spoke to the bartender. "Do you take American money?"

"Is it green?"

The veteran laughed, "They are the most humorous people in the world."

There were many women in the space, though they were all of the same type: diminutive orientals with small haunches and flat chests. There were the Vietnamese with the browner skins and the more compact physiques, and the Chinese with the willowy looks and the less African features. The women formed strange couples with the larger, taller soldiers with whom a few danced. The Americans seemed almost blowsy in comparison. The sexes' dancing styles also were incompatible. The GIs, such as Wilson, were shimmying or twisting elegantly while the women shuffled from foot to foot as if dancing were a kind of treading.

The two had gotten beers and the vet had accosted a Cantonese girl, bringing her to stand at the bar to his left. The youth couldn't help looking her way.

ten up before her, while she was still plashing in dreams.

"You want a drinky-winky?" the vet said to her, chuckling.

"Okay, soldier."

It occurred to the youth that the expression he had heard, "China doll," was derived from an achieved effect. Not only, to him, were his neighbor's body and limbs toylike, but she had made her face up to suggest a frozen mask. The hair directly over her forehead was artificially stiffened so it was as hard as a buckle.

The vet winked at him over the girl's shoulder and then spoke to her teasingly, "Nay qu mut ya men?"

He laughed at her answer "Chow, Sieu."

He replied, "Chow ho yo gum."

The youth had taken a liking to the girl. He tried to think of his first words. Her first words to him, his to her. These would be important. He had to be careful with the first words.

Abruptly, the veteran stepped around the woman and put his hand on the youth's shoulder. "Watch my girl, Henry. I got to use the head." His action didn't suit his words. Instead of turning away, he continued facing the youth, grinning a minute, drops of sweat ringing his face like flecks of water escaping around the lid of a pot that was on the boil.

He began to say something else, "Something tells me—"

The veteran bolted one step, then bent and vomited, nauseatingly beginning rivulets in all directions on the plastic floor.

"So untidy," her first words to him.

"This is a damned thing to find this," she continued, stooping over, having taken a cocktail napkin.

What would his first words be?

Her command of English seemed nothing short of miraculous.

He noticed as she leaned over to dab at her shoes how her red dress pulled tightly across her narrow back.

He bent over with her, willing to help sop up the sputum on her hem and pump.

"Nice legs," he commented.

Damaged Goods
Ron Kolm

"**S**onofa*bitch*! Get the *fuck* out of my cab!" comes banging through the front window . . . waking me up . . . damn, it's probably my downstairs neighbor, Mitzi, returning home after another night at her favorite bar . . . where she consumes prodigious amounts of alcohol to blot out the pain . . . she suffers from osteoporosis . . . her muscles and ligaments all atrophied and gone . . . the only reason she's able to ambulate at all is due to a complex structure of braces and splints . . . small ones on her arms, large ones on her legs, a corset-thing for the spine . . . plus she's got completely removable dentures, which she pops in and out to get the occasional laugh, and one glass eye . . . and to top it off she must weigh close to 300 pounds . . . those brace-like contraptions are essentially tiny dams holding a tremendous lake in place . . . with the addition of demon alcohol they give way . . . she usually makes it into the cab and *then* she unstraps and unhooks them, heaving huge sighs of relief . . . the moment they're all undone her shapeless body flows like unchecked lava into every crevice of the back seat and she passes out . . . which brings us to our frantic cabbie wondering how he's ever going to explain this situation to his dispatcher.

"Pockita-pockita, Brooklyn Bridge, squatch-squatch, wrap-it-up!"

Great, Mr. Hommas in his first floor front apartment must be awake, too.

Mr. Hommas is a small dark man from Panama . . . he has salt and pepper hair . . . mostly salt . . . smoke and fire are his elements . . . he disconnected the old gas range in his kitchen, removed the jets and burners, and filled the resulting cavity with charcoal which slowly smolders day and night, creating a dense cloud in his apartment . . . the centerpiece of his

Mike brought Carol, bart, Lydia, Judy, and Debbie to **Ron Kolm**, *who was living, and tinkering, in the hulk of a tramp steamer that had been towed onto an empty tract meant for a ranch house. A shattered velocipede blocked his driveway.*

Ron Kolm, the author of the haiku-style epics Welcome to the Barbecue *and* The Plastic Factory, *is published in the anthologies* A Day in the Life *and* Between C & D.

Ron joined them and, as the jalopy was getting too crowded, bart suggested they all pile into a school bus owned by his pal Shalom.

Shalom proved to be a wizard of the wheels. As they sped through a yellow light, bart caught sight, through the chalky window of the Dan Ryan Train, of a woman's cleavage.

"Those are Stephanie's clappers," bart yelled, "I'd recognize them anywhere. Shalom, give chase!"

The driver got a kind of

229

dingy, soot-stained living room is a giant hookah, which he fires up periodically with a piece of charcoal from the stove . . . he sits cross-legged before this mighty god, lost in reverie . . . but if his element is smoke, his expertise is cunnilingus . . . he's set, he assures me, an official record of two hours and forty minutes . . . his entire stock of broken English expressions revolve around that particular part of the female anatomy and his special relationship to it . . . "windshield wiper," he'll scream, or "Brooklyn  Bridge" . . . sometimes it's "going to the basement" but most of the time he refers to it as "swimming."

Anyway, I know I'm not going to get any sleep unless I help the cabbie get Mitzi out of his car and into her apartment . . . so I pull on my pants and slippers and stumble down to the first floor, heading for the street . . . as I pass by his door, Mr. Hommas throws it open, smoke billowing around him like a stage effect, shouting "I'm gonna break my nose! Wrap-it-up!" and leers in my general direction . . . his glasses fogged . . . spirals of smoke rising from his sweater . . . he places his forefingers and thumbs together, so that they seem to form a crude vagina, and sticks his enormous meaty tongue through the result, waggling it up and down.

"Chewcha!" he screams.

"Mr. Hommas, you are a sexist pig," I sternly rebuke him, trying to wave him back into his apartment.

"Chung-doom-bloom," he sniggers, retreating.

❨

Somehow the cabbie, who's a big guy, and I manage to drag Mitzi out of the car and into the building where we're finally able to deposit her in front of her apartment door . . . the driver goes back out and brings in an armload of splints and her purse, which he puts next to her inert form . . . he then gratefully exits, having collected his fare in advance . . . so now there's only the little problem of rousing Mitzi and making sure she gets safely inside her flat . . . which is not a moot point . . . as Mr. Hommas materializes in the hallway in a puff of smoke like a sooty genie . . . and proceeds to dance around Mitzi's supine body . . . pointing out the, by now, all too obvious fact that her legs are spread wide open and she seems to be lacking any undergarments . . . which drives him into an absolute frenzy.

"Toonyfish! Chewcha! I'm gonna go to da basement and break my record! Two-to-one!"

"Damn it!" I hiss, grabbing him by the shirt and shaking him to break the spell. "Please get back in your apartment, Mr. Hommas—this isn't helping things one bit!"

I push him away from Mitzi and back into his lair ... and clumsily try to rearrange the voluminous folds of her skirt in such a way as to cover her exposed parts.

"Mitzi, please wake up ... Mitzi, I need your help ... Mitzi, where are your keys? ... Mitzi, this is a nightmare!" But I'm not having any luck with this approach ... so ignoring my qualms I open her battered purse, dumping the contents on the floor ... a grimy lipstick tube, a cracked compact, a couple of sticks of gum and numerous prescription vials ... but no keys ... must've left them at the bar. "Aw, no," I groan, "what am I gonna do *now*?"

Telling Mr. Hommas I'll bust him in the head if he so much as peeks in the hall, I sprint outside the building to the basement grates in the front sidewalk ... they're never locked, so I pull one side open and descend into the basement ... I have a plan ... though I've got to admit I'm kind of apprehensive about pulling it off ... but I don't seem to have any choice ... Mitzi's way too heavy to hoist up the two flights to my apartment ... and I don't have the vaguest idea where I'd put her if I *was* able to ... I'm the ascetic type ... I sleep on a small sofabed ... no other furniture ... my studio apartment is filled with books and periodicals ... some of them on shelves ... but most of them in boxes, or in piles on top of the boxes ... I've got half a can of soda in the fridge and some teabags and crackers in the cupboard and that's about it ... I simply have to get Mitzi into her own place ... and that's why I'm heading into the unknown ... figuring that the basement has to traverse the entire length of the building ... and that eventually I'll be able to ascend into some sort of

crazed look in his eye, saying, "This calls for a Shalom slalom."

A universal groan was heard as he threw the vehicle into a skid, then gunned the motor so the bus fishtailed in the center of the intersection; then, without losing a jot of speed, he took off at 60 miles per after the receding train.

A couple of miscalculations: first, the centrifugal force of the spin had split each man's zippers so that their genitals splayed out like presented bouquets, causing some of the men to puff out their chests and others to figleaf their groins with newspapers, beer-bottle caps, whatever.

Second, Shalom had executed the turn lopsidedly so that now they were traveling in reverse, running backwards after a backwards train.

"Duck your goddamn head, Ron, I can't see," Shalom yelled as he sideswiped a stanchion, tearing a piling off the now-sagging overhead track.

R   o   n   K   o   l   m

backyard . . . where I'll try to break into one of Mitzi's bedroom windows . . . and then unlock her door . . . if everything works out.

The basement has an incredibly low overhead . . . I scuttle along in the darkness practically bent in half . . . brushing aside wires and old clotheslines and spider webs . . . I pull one of the cords and a dim 40-watt bulb snaps on illuminating a large, squat boiler, a slop sink, and a jumble of ancient tools lying on the dusty cement floor . . . everything covered with dust and cobwebs . . . an old baby crib in the way . . . just past it I stumble upon a worn flight of steps leading up to another set of grates . . . I shove one side open and emerge into an overgrown junkheap . . . tall weeds . . . mounds of rotting lumber . . . a broken washing machine . . . torn plastic garbage bags . . . you get the picture.

I roll the washing machine over to the back wall of the building, and by standing on it I'm just able to reach one of Mitzi's rear windows . . . I have the eerie feeling that one of her neighbors in an adjacent building is watching me and is even now calling the police, and I'll end up in jail and Mitzi will continue to occupy the hallway, unconscious, and Mr. Hommas will eventually realize that he can do with her as he wishes . . . or some other neighbor might have me lined up in his sights, his finger on the trigger.

I break a bottom pane, reach inside and unlock the window . . . I'm able to raise it just enough to squeeze through . . . tumbling down into darkness I crash into some sort of knick-knack table, scattering small breakable things all over the place . . . I finally locate a wall switch, turn it on and look around . . . Mitzi's apartment is all large pieces of furniture covered with shiny plastic slipcovers . . . I unlock the door, and using all my strength I pull her humongous insensate self in . . . by artful manuevering I manage to prop her against a gigantic sofa . . . she slips onto the floor . . . so I hold her in place by wedging a coffee table against her one side, and a TV table against the other.

I put a pot of water on to boil and rummage through her crowded cabinets looking for instant coffee . . . I'm almost beginning to relax . . . it's only 4:30 in the morning . . . maybe I'll even get back to sleep before the night is over . . . there's light at the end of the tunnel . . . in fact, Mitzi seems to be snapping out of her stupor . . . as I return from the kitchen with a steaming cup of coffee she opens her one good eye and stares up at me.

"Where am I? Arnie, is that you? Where's Mr. Hommas? He's supposed to pay me a visit—isn't that something—we have a date!"

The Unbearable Beatniks of Light Get Real! (Docu-Dharma)

MIKE GOLDEN

In this day and age certain truths are not always self-evident, but The Unbearable Beatniks of Light are on a roll tonight. Truth is in sight, because tonight on the occasion of their return to New York City, on the occasion of their first meeting in over two years, they've unanimously agreed to give up the old ways, the old thoughts, the old attachments that held them prisoners for so long to a time and place that never really existed as anything other than a state of mind, despite media hype and career conspiracies to the contrary. We're talking about *downtown*, hipsters, as if you couldn't have guessed.

The Unbearables have been on the road for the last couple of years; choosing the apex of the scene to split for different parts unknown, unglued, and yes—most of all, unhyped—hipsters. Like dust to the wind; they got gone just before the bottom fell out of the East Village gallery and performance scene, riding their memories of hot times in the old Alphabet Town off into the existential sunset, leaving the Club scene floggers behind to celebrate for nothing more than the glory of the *glory*.

Yo! In the old-old good old days (remember *those were the days, my friends, the days we thought would never end*?), The Unbearables, who are not really beatniks, but a free-floating, in-your-face Temporary Autonomous Zone of Black Humorists, Immediatists, Neoists, and Beer Mystics, used to meet every other Tuesday night in certain *downtown* watering holes and drown themselves in nostalgia for, what else, but *the*

Rollo was in the back of the car, a dwarf on either side pressing a gat in his ribs. "You guys don't see," Rollo said. By now he had found his tongue. "It's not technology but conceptualization. Take an audience. Imagine you're in a movie theatre. Do you guys ever go to the movies? Imagine it's a weird, outré, but artsy film like . . . GIRLQUAKE! Everybody will have their own interpretation. Right? Nobody agrees."

He gesticulated a little more broadly. "Everybody has a right to their own opinion. Right? Fuck that! If you asked everyone who had seen the film to write down their opinion, then fed those opinions into a computer, you would see an unexamined (unexaminable at the subjective level) secret core meaning."

"Such as what?" Out-

233

good old days . . . It's a disease of the spirit, hipsters, which on reflection, everyone now agrees, comes out sounding like a cross between Dodge City Saturday Night and an unenforceable DMZ right in the heart of Junkieland. Ah, but we're starting to toss grenades before we even choose up sides . . .

First, their name—The Unbearable Beatniks of Light—which came to the original foursome courtesy of a spoonerism one sloshed night in the old Tin Pan Alley, while noting that for some unfathomable reason all the really groovy chicks were into Kundera's *The Unbearable Lightness of Being.* As individuals or a group, they were always caught somewhere in the middle—too young to be *real* beatniks, too old to be hippies, too late to be punks—but always hanging out on one cuttting edge or another all their lives.

They first started hanging with each other two years before it became obvious the end *was* the end, and nothing else could begin until the corpse was buried. In previous incarnations they were all seemingly involved in what can now be generically classified as "the downtown scene." Since the unbearable gaffe first occured, and since at heart they are all democratic anarchists, they pick their beatnik code names (Jack, Neal, Allen, Bill, Gregory, Herbert, etc.) out of a hat every meeting, so last time if you were Jack this time you might be Neal or Allen or Bill or Gregory.

"What this does," tonight's Allen explains to me, "is it takes us out of ourselves, out of indulging in our own personal problems." Tonight's Allen has just spent the last two years living in suburbia, saving his marriage by helping his wife's brother open a shopping center outside of Youngstown, Ohio. "You know what I'm talking about," he says. "The wife flipped it, I didn't get the raise, the lease ran out, and the scumbags are raising the rent from $289.50 to $2400.00. At the same time, by changing names every week, none of us gets trapped in any one persona."

"This way," tonight's Neal explains, "it stays sort of a healthy schizoid exercise as opposed to a real schizoid existence." Tonight's Neal, who used to be a well-known SoHo bartender before he moved to Barcelona, originally came to the Lower East Side from England in '75, virtually penniless. He likes to remember little tidbits, like when the subway and a slice of pizza both cost 35 cents. "I thought it was the bloody *law* they had to cost the same thing!" he laughs.

Tonight's Allen, who used to manage a bookstore in what he calls "the heart of the beast," remembers fondly, "almost too fondly," the days when the Lower East Side was considered "no man's land—the Hell's Angels ran the neighborhood. Junkies and shooting parlors proliferated."

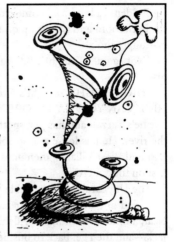

"And that doesn't even go back to the days of The Electric Circus." Tonight's Jack has just arrived. A well-known DJ before he packed it in to move to Paris to write "The Great American Novel," he first came to the Lower East Side 11 years ago, from East Jesus, Nebraska, to freak out! But it was too late. The Fillmore was closed. The heads had all splattered then scattered, got gone back to the land, and left the streets to the speed freaks.

"It's been a while since I've heard that word," muses tonight's Bill, a tall, elegant, anthropology professor who has spend the last two years studying the eating habits of pregnant aboriginal bush women.

"What word?" tonight's Jack asks. "Freak?"

"No, speed." Tonight's Bill smiles. "Remember speed?"

"The real thing," tonight's Neal smiles. "I haven't heard the word in 10 years. What happened to speed? It just sort of disappeared."

"Cocaine," tonight's Allen says. "The non-addictive yuppie elixir. Thank God I'm allergic to it."

standish shot back.

"Autonomy and zones of autonomy." Rollo spoke softly, so the dwarves had to lean a little forward, but he let his hands spread even more expansively.

The car swerved to avoid a muskrat and Rollo pressed into the seat, turning his gesture derisive and slapping at their guns.

One went off, plucking a plume of feathers from the seat and winging the driver.

The car headed into the curb and hit a fireplug. Water poured through the shattered windshield, washing over the four unconscious men.

But there was more. The flow from the plug, due to

Suddenly a loud roar comes from the crowd as tonight's Gregory comes out of the back room and climbs up on top of the bar to read an old favorite to the poetry-hungry mob.

"Not again!" Tonight's Bill puts his hands over his eyes. "He's not going to do his—"

"HIGH! HIGH!" tonight's Gregory roards from the top of his tonsils. "HOW HIGH CAN YOU FLY BEFORE YOU DIE?" he sings out, then pounds his chest like he's Tarzan and has just spotted The Bitch Goddess Muse on the other side of the river. He lets loose a loud soul-cleansing call to all the animals of the Lower East and West Villages, then does a perfect swan dive off the bar, splattering headfirst on the concrete!

The Unbearables at the table turn back away from the human puddle on the floor and one by one lift their hands like diving judges—an eight from tonight's Neal, a nine from tonight's Allen, a six from tonight's Bill, a seven from tonight's Jack—and then get back to business as usual.

By the time tonight's Gregory has been loaded on a slab and carted away, everyone's reliving a different way to find their own separate reality; though it should be pointed out to all of you undercover DEA agents out there, the Unbearables are drug-free now, considering their tastes, bouts, marriages, indulgences with pharmaceuticals and herbs as merely phases—rites of passage they had to undergo to get to where they are now.

"We're just pawns in the detoxification of America," tonight's Bill insists. "These memories of the way things are are as bad as any addiction I've ever had."

"Worse than tobacco," tonight's Gregory wheezes.

"Maudlin, sentimental, and politically incorrect," this week's Allen moans.

"Which is exactly why I miss them!" tonight's Neal proclaims. "I like doing things for the bloody hell of it! That's why I moved here in the first place. Where's your bloody spirit, mates? Isn't there a gesture among us?"

"Listen to Neal, he's got a wild hair tonight!" tonight's Jack laughs. "But hey, there ain't no more America to bang-bang, much less a Nuevo York. Not that Paris is that much better, but at least it *looks* good. And hey, nobody can say the Frogs don't give good attitude. In reality they may be vapid, they may be shallow, they may be total blanks, but you've got to admit their shells are cool. Here, everything and everyone is redundant. Nothing but the same ghouls and necrophiles on the club scene, taking care of their egos, baby. Takin' care of their egos."

"A bit harsh, old boy. Some of my best friends are ghouls and necrophiles," tonight's Neal grimaces. "Matter of fact, I do believe it's my heritage as well."

The addiction kicks back in *then*. The good old days, before they realize it, are back. The glory of Darinka, The Shuttel, 8 BC, all sacrifices to gentrification, become a litany; Normandy, Anzio, just a regular Guadalcanal Diary, hipsters.

Before long, the Unbearables are sloshing through the mindfields of memory: The Feast of Unbraining at The Theatre for the New City; Don Cherry blowing The Shuttel's lights out all night long; Karen Finley's first yam; Seymour Krim's *Making It,* for the last time, at Darinka; the performances and readings and parties in the Rivington School's sculpture garden; the New Year's Day marathon at The Poetry Project, when tonight's Gregory stands in a long line to get a urinal as the *real* Gregory himself stumbles in, takes one look at the line, then swaggers straight over to the sink, unzips, and lets fly as he goes into a 10-minute riff that freezes everyone's dorks in their fists, on why most guys find it impossible to piss when somebody's talking to them . . . And of course, What's His Name's birthday party at The Palladium. "That was the beginning of the end," tonight's Allen ruefully sighs. "The Eye was flying high—"

"Oh, mi-oh-mi!" tonight's Jack sings.

"Literary night in the Mike Todd Room."

"MC'd by the King of the Yuppies."

"*Bright Lights, Big Nostrils.*"

"That pissed a lot of people off."

"It's one thing to gentrify the bloody landscape, but the bloody art should be sacred!"

"You're just jealous."

"Good first line."

"You're just jealous. It's not malicious," tonight's Jack mocks. "You've been invited to a party. Naturally there's a reading. You're not asked to participate. But there's an open bar and free food. You're immediately attracted to the suckling pigs. Just then the star comes on. You feel sorry for him. You feel envious of him. You feel sorry for him again. The crowd surges up against the stage. Drooling, flipping spit off the tips of their fingers at his head: he's an easy target. Like any icon, his head is huge. Almost as big as Richard Bur-

the way the fender deflected it, also arced high above the sidewalk and smashed through a blackened second story window, gushing into the building's interior.

So as Mike sat . . . **Mike Golden** is the author of many classic meta-fictions. He was the editor of the seminal magazine Smoke Signals. His story "The Unbearable Beatniks of Light Get Real" originally appeared in a slightly different version in RedTape #7.

To continue . . . as Mike sat watching a show in Roxor's main room, suddenly he was surprised to see naked girls cascade off the stage in a sudsy gusher that engulfed the audience.

ton's, and he hasn't even learned to move it yet. Just stands there, takes it, proudly pissed. Ready to *Mailer* the whole mob at once."

"So you want to be The Bloody Man, do you?"

"You hyperventilate. Remember the curse of talent. Only the good die young. What if *you* were Rimbaud in a past life? Do you remember what fame was like? Or how the cliché tasted on your tongue?"

"Sweet and sour pork. Twins. Mirrors of rejection. You're looking at yourself looking at yourself looking at yourself; not a pretty picture, but They might buy it all the same. If your conceit is as good as his."

"You lift the pig off the table."

"Would you like to dance, my dear?"

"Would you like to dance, my dear? There's an echo in the room."

(The Unbearables are cooking now. Jamming on their own addiction.)

"You've already been famous for five minutes; now what, asshole?"

"Get a lime juice commercial!"

"Make a movie."

"Open a gallery."

"Start a band."

As if on cue, the Unbearables start singing: "Pull my daisy, tip my cup, all my doors are open . . . Cut my thoughts for coconuts, all my eggs are broken . . . "

I seem to have missed something in the translation. The dancing pig. Did tonight's Jack did, or did tonight's Jack didn't throw the pig?

"No way, man! I was just getting inside the story. Getting inside the cat's head who threw it. That's how things get twisted!"

"It was bloody unbelievable," tonight's Neal laughs. *"Bright Lights* wasn't even on stage. Some little guy reading something nobody's listening to. Just getting it on, and getting it over as fast as he can, when all of a sudden this pig's head—there was nothing left but the head—comes flying through the air, right in front of his bloody eyes."

"Stage left!"

The signal to split, on more than one level. It's time for the Unbearables to find that next whiskey bar. But not before making a vow, deciding to make one final gesture, as an ode to their glorious past.

Dressed head-to-toe in traditional hipster black, they trudge angst-ridden through the light mist as they debate what action to take, and bop east across Houston. *What can they do? What one tiny gesture can they make to release themselves from the past, at the same time they honor it?*

Perhaps liberate *The New Yorker*'s poetry from mediocrity? Perhaps put the beatniks, the real beatniks, on trial? Turn *The Crimes of the Beats* into the Nuremberg of Bohemia: call out Burroughs for copping W.C. Fields' act, and Ginsberg for being the original Maynard G. Krebs in the gray flannel beret—always hyping-hyping-hyping the myth—then selling it as the only viable alternative to the polluted mainstream, and of course Jackie boy himself for claiming he wrote *On the Road* in one sitting, a lie that ruined three whole generations of novelists trying to duplicate the feat of the beat that never really went down in anything short of seven drafts, maybe . . . Or perhaps each one of the Unbearables themselves selling out by getting their own personal sponsors? Writing letters all over corporate America, and asking their worst ideological enemies for funding to fight the rise of Corporate America. Then hold a telethon on cable, and call it *The Night of a Thousand Sponsors.*

But all these ideas are obviously down the road, not on it. For the moment, the now, on the next beat they decide, unanimously decide, to liberate St. Mark's Place. From *what,* they're not sure. But it must be done, there's no doubt about that! Though the *how* of making a Revolutionary act in America in the 1990's is not that easy. Not that easy at all.

Back in the late sixties the hippies changed the name of the street from St. Mark's to St. Marx, but the Marxists are free now, the Commies all want to be Cappies, so that McGuffin won't work anymore. It's as dead and gone as that defunct breed once known as "hip capitalists."

Swaying back and forth now, they stand on the corner of St. Mark's and Second Avenue, in front of Gem Spa, invoking the ghost of Ted Berrigan, as they stare incredulously across the street at something that looks like it was beamed down from a shopping mall in Paramus.

"That's bloody it!" tonight's Neal snaps.

"Close THE GAP!" tonight's Jack roars.

"No more pastels!" tonight's Allen wails.

"Send them back to the burbs!" tonight's Bill bops.

"Blow them to smithereens!" tonight's Bill cackles.

"You mean actually bomb them?" tonight's Jack asks.

"Have you got a better idea?" tonight's Bill snarls.

"We could pool our money, and put a Banana Republic in across the street, and drive them out of business."

Tonight's beatnik turns to me and says, "Don't quote me on that."

The Unbearable Beatniks of Light look down at the sidewalk, down at the concrete. Then in mass, slowly, very slowly trudge west, back in the direction they came.

In the middle of the block, they duck inside The Grassroots, for one last round.

Tonight's Allen turns to tonight's Jack and sighs, before they push through the doors: "Obviously, things aren't the same anymore."

Tonight's Jack laughs: "If they ever were."

"If they ever were," Tonight's Bill echoes.

"If they ever were . . . "

Beats on the Beach

LYNNE TILLMAN

There was shit everywhere, garbage and fat bodies and rotting hot dogs and I was disgusted on the beach. The scene was coming down around me and I stared at the ocean, melancholy and lonely, green and cool, and far away, way out there, was Europe and history and the ghosts of Baudelaire and Rimbaud and those very alive French girls—the green waves were their breasts rising and falling something like my cock when I'm horny, needy and angry as a dirty syringe, on those rocky nights of the soul. But not now, not today.

O inconstancy—I had to concentrate because of the shit on the beach, those straight surfer goons strutting around and kicking sand, and me, haggard, stretched tight like a drum over this mad existence, burned out, my whole body a night yellow white except for my left hand, the one I hang out the driver's window to feel the cool American breeze rush crazily over my American skin. Sometimes when I'm rolling along the highway of dreams, I let that hand lay on top of the roof of the car like I don't have a care in the world and my dog's next to me, grinning like an idiot, happy the way a dog can be, his short hindlegs on the backseat, his head resting next to my shoulder, content as I drive along. My dog, the one I left with Riva, Riva the dancer, she just kissed me goodbye and whispered—Later, baby.

I shot a glance at Allen who was smiling in his strange inward cerebral way because he was thinking of something bigger that wasn't on the beach.

—What a chick Riva was, man. She'd make your hair curl, if you had any.

*"Are you **Lynne Tillman?**"*

"Yes."

"Hi, I'm Hal Sirowitz," David said. "Could I have a minute of your time?"

Lynne Tillman is the author of Absence Makes the Heart, Cast in Doubt, *and* The Madame Realism Complex.

He was standing on the porch of Lynne's brick bungalow in Bridgeport. Out of the corner of his eye, he saw neighborhood kids laying their peckers on the top porch step.

"I'm not receiving now," Lynne said matter-of-factly.

Ulin shoved a gun muzzle in her belly and pushed her inside.

"What I am about to say may seem a trifle out of the ordinary," Ulin said as he made her kneel down on a throw rug and pressed the metal barrel to her nape. "But I want you to read these FBI documents."

Words seem to dance and blur as you try and con-

241

The Beanbag—that's what we called him—turned to me and muttered, Leave it alone, Fast Jack, suck on your own dick for a while. Don't get angry, my man, I answered, and I swore I would love him until the day I die which might be tomorrow because tomorrow always comes and how many tomorrows does any man have?

I dug him, I did. Allen was America's bearded idealist, hopeful and scared but eager and ready to face Life when it happened, a true poet, the kind I was striving

to be, because I wanted to live the Life with everything in me, to be Real in the face of phony gutless pathetic humanity, the human subspecies, but here on the beach Allen looked weird, a skinny New York intellectual on the sand near the ocean, all pale and frail and gray around the edges from long nights in clubs talking the smart hip talk to other hipsters of the future, and sometimes I thought about him, us, because if you split us open, you'd find bars, bottles, tables and chairs, but in him, there would be books and bookcases, addresses, a card catalogue and eyeglasses, BECAUSE he—we're the poets of airless, smokey rooms, word makers in the hidden factories of the American spirit.

Life is shit and you have to be ready to give it up, ride off on an endless road to nowhere, disappear in a hotel room so ugly even Wild Bill would snicker at the cliché, his eyes half closed while he's nodding, high on some heavy shit that gives him the vision he needs to see right through the merciless nothing of everything. Allen wanted me, I didn't want him, I wanted someone, Wild Bill hungered for Allen, they were making the scene.

—Hey, Beanbag, rub a little of that on my back.

Allen looked up kind of stunned like he was just born and I had to laugh at his beautiful ignorance and his innocence. He didn't even know he was on the beach, his head in a book while I was watching some cute little girls walking by and thinking how it was in high school and how my mom loved me, but I don't want to think about that, about the past, how I only had orgasms when I fantasized about her leaving me, and it's sad for eternity. Allen rubbed some lotion on my white back which was turning color under the wild rays of the heartless sun. The imperturbable ocean rolling and roiling let me forget for a minute the people somewhere else toiling and sweating, working their insides out—for what, for a buck, for what else in this stinking world, and those politicians with their platitudinous cant, it makes me sick, even on the beach, because which way to turn, to look. I gotta look so I do.

Out of nowhere the Marvelous Magi from Hell comes toward us, Wild Bill wearing a djellabah that covers him like a tent so no one can see the frozen rivers that are his veins and the scabrous body he calls home. I've seen that expression on Wild Bill's face before, when he's thinking of what he's lost or the midwest or history, a so-what, an Is This All There Is? Wild Bill lights a cigarette with a match that appears like he did out of nowhere—the ether—and he sits down on the blanket next to the Beanbag, who's dousing his own white hairy body with suntan lotion.

Wild Bill snorts—That crummy lotion your cover story, Allen, you think the agents of the Polyester Poison Sunboy won't find you here? Won't get you? Ah,

centrate on reading with a cocked pistol set to blow a furrow in your skull, and it took her half again her usual time to skim the forty pages.

After she had finished, she turned her head as far as she could, against the muzzle, and managed a smile, saying, "Why are you helping me like this?"

relax, Beanbag, the Black Meat Mamas don't want your skinny ass. I've got something in my pocket that'll melt you into just so many lumps of carcinogenic plasm.

The Beanbag and Wild Bill kissed a long time and I lost myself in them, their sticky bodies, their wet mouths merged into one enormous American soul kiss, it was gorgeous. Boom. And I remembered that little blond girl in Cincinnati and how I loved her but couldn't stay, because I never can, can't stay in love with one, because I'm in love with the One and All, but then I thought about poetry and prose, how the word could illuminate if I could just find it, the right word. Like Wild Bill who can—he writes and there's blood on the page, he spills his guts and I don't mean metaphorically, I'm talking about real blood on the page, so thick and dark that Allen can't read the words underneath without scraping it off and dumping it on the floor.

The sun was beating down and later Allen was goofing to Wild Bill about another poet, Bra Man—this cat, the Beanbag was wailing now, thinks panty raids are bourgeois, that's why he steals chicks' boobie traps—that's what he calls them—and we laughed a long time, but really Allen wanted to be in Paris or Tangier, away from the indifferent ugliness of America, but when I leave I feel homesick, homesick in my depths, and I just don't know.

I get so lonely, even here on the beach, and Wild Bill says, Fast Jack, grab yourself a beer and watch some TV, the way you always do and have, and always will, and Bill is right, that's what I do, that's what I did, I can't change, I am what I am, a man. And that's all there is, that and the beach, the bigger than life ocean and the grains of sand, they're like miracles, wonders in this Mongolia of existence. It gets me, really, this beauty, and it keeps me hooked to Life.

But watching Wild Bill and the Beanbag I knew I was really alone, with them but not with them, I never did dig men, not that way, because that's not my scene, so I was with them and not with them, and they understood, and it was cool, and I would move on, leave, the way I always leave, I have to leave everybody.

I popped open another beer and patted my stomach which was getting bigger every day. Allen says I look like I'm carrying his baby and, you know, I'd dig that, to give birth to his baby, to put something in the world, not just words—well, words too because they're important, poetry is the Truth—but a baby who'd grow up and drive across the country, his hand lying on the roof of the car, the American breeze blowing, my boy who'd say one day—Fast Jack was my dad and he was cool.

Not the Plaster Casters

JANICE EIDUS

I was not a member of the Plaster Casters. I was a free agent. Although—on the surface, at least—I did exactly what the Plaster Casters did. That is, we all made plaster casts of the penises of rock stars. But the Plaster Casters got all the glory, all the publicity. Even though *I* did it first.

The Plaster Casters, you see, did it for the power they thought it gave them—the power that would lead them to the fifteen minutes of fame they wanted so much. Which they got. Big deal. Fifteen minutes.

I wanted no glory, no money. I didn't need fifteen minutes. I had a lifetime, and another, far greater, agenda. I never hired a publicist, never contacted a journalist to write up my exploits, nor to take photos of me looking wacky and sexy, stirring up a vat of my plaster mixture with a come-hither look on my face, or sitting on Jimi's lap, or cuddling up to Rod. I was as different from the Plaster Casters as Picasso from a greeting-card illustrator.

I was an artist, with an eye trained to recognize natural beauty when I saw it. And rock stars were definitely objects of natural beauty, with their lean, hard bodies, their long hair flowing down their backs, their bejeweled ears, necks, and fingers. Rock stars were like Greek statues with attitude.

And so I created homages to them. My sculptures were vehicles through which I rendered both them, and myself, immortal. I isolated their most beautiful, most artistic feature, and I re-created it, re-invented it. Like the poet said—art is about making it new, making it *your own*. And I certainly did that: when I was finished, after the rock stars had gone, I gave each plaster cast my signature. I painted my initials—the

Lynne and David picked up Janice, who they decided to talk to en route to a picnic Lynne insisted they visit. They let Janice read the papers—no need for a gun since Janice trusted Lynne implicitly—to see where she stood. **Janice Eidus** is the author of Faithful Rebecca, Vito Loves Geraldine, and Urban Bliss, and has published in the Mississippi Review and the North American Review.

Janice read a joint CIA/FBI "black op" memo that suggested that all the attendees of Rollo Root-head's (sic) Dec. 7 lecture be hunted down and "scratched." Appended were the obits of 30 done-away-with ex-audience members, clipped to a checklist. She turned to the couple. "My name is on this list. What am I going to do?"

"I can't tell you that," David drawled. "I can just tell you what you're up

245

initials of my real name, my given name, the name everyone but me has long forgotten, since everyone else now knows me as Not the Plaster Casters. I used a shimmery, otherwordly silver, a shade of my own creation, a shade that nobody else can ever copy or match. And each initial looks exactly like the letter it is, and yet simultaneously, like a female body, as well, a sensuous female with full breasts, slim waist, and perfectly balanced, rounded hips. My signature is the symbol for me, of course, for my own erotic beauty; again something those homely Plaster Casters with their chubby bodies and scraggly hair just didn't have, couldn't measure up to.

My ageless, creamy-skinned beauty—which has only been enhanced over time—is such that the rock stars would beg me to sleep with them, would grow keenly aroused as I patted the plaster firmly onto their members. But I never gave in. I never slept with a single one, and, believe me, there were times I desired one or another of them so much I could hardly breathe. But I had no choice: I had to be pure, objective. What if I had fallen in love? My art might have suffered, and that would have been intolerable. Besides, my body never went hungry. I had my ways.

Meanwhile, I was doing them all, all the greats: Jimi, Bobby, the two Keiths, David, Mick, Paul, and so many others, all colors, all sizes. Even Janis wanted in: "Can't you do a boob this time?" she asked.

"For you, okay," I agreed.

Her face lit up with her kooky, lopsided smile.

In fact, I ended up doing both her boobs, which turned out, surprisingly, to be small and delicate.

And Janis, Jimi, the two Keiths, and all the others—all of them—they understood the difference between me and the Plaster Casters. They knew the Plaster Casters were mere publicity-seekers. But after all, they wanted publicity, too. So they let those clumsy girls paw them and poke them this way and that, but they never respected them or found them erotic, never thought of them as anything more than dumb groupies. With me, though, they were respectful, in awe. Together, we sought immortality, not just a write-up in *Rolling Stone*. After all, compared to immortality, an orgasm isn't that big a deal.

Their desire to let me sculpt them came from a place deep inside, a place not sullied by commercialism and greed, the very place where their own art came from: Jimi's wild guitar playing, Janis' raw, untamed voice, David's androgynous personae, Bobby's esoteric lyrics. And to this day, only they—these beautiful, fierce rock icons—are ever allowed to see my work. Dealers are banned from my studio; the public is never invited in. Only the rock stars themselves, so wide-eyed and respectful as they follow me from sculpture to sculpture. And when, at the end of their tour, they ask me what the silver initials stand for, I tell them they're not initials, just abstract, silvery shapes. And sometimes one might add, "Well, you know, those silver shapes also look a lot like a woman's body—like your body, Not the Plaster Casters." But I merely smile enigmatically.

I'm always distancing myself—planning the next one I'll be doing, for instance, even as I'm casting the member of another. After all, my work is never done. Not by a long shot. There are new ones to conquer, new ones all the time, new ones whenever I blink. And believe me, I know how to separate the real ones from the wannabes, the pretenders, the flashes in the pan. Next week, for instance, I'm doing Michael. The week after, Bono. And the week after that, there's Axl on Wednesday, and Slash on Thursday. Madonna—like Janis—also wants to pose. "I'm bigger than Janis," she bragged over the phone. I didn't deign to reply; my art is not about size or competition. And Bruce and Rod and Billy all want to come back, to do it a second time, to "re-live the high," they say.

They all call *me*. They know where to find me. I'm never cruel, but I'm always honest. Sometimes I just have to say: "I'm sorry, but you don't have it, that star quality, that beauty, that thing that I, as an artist, require." I had to tell that to Michael's brothers, for instance. Some accept my refusal with dignity. Others weep and beg. Others hang up abruptly, stunned and ashamed. It saddens me to hurt them, but there's no room in art for pity.

The ones I say "yes" to, though, are euphoric. They grow over-eager. "When? Tonight? Tomorrow?"

"Whoa," I tell them. "Slow down."

And then, on the given date—sometimes I make them wait weeks, or even months—they fly in from L.A. or London or Seattle, and they arrive at my private studio, way up here, far away from any big city, high in the mountains, where I can best maintain my distance, my anonymity, my purity.

against."

"What a mess," Janice said with little spunk.

A gesture from Lynne was the only reply.

They were cruising past a huge, scooped-out empty lot. Walking on the sidewalk, with one jean ripped up to her thigh, was a wounded, ravishing young woman, like a damaged insect on the rim of a sugar bowl.

Rolling down the window and holding a photocopy in his hand, David called, "Are you Jill Rapaport?"

"You look so young," they always say, when I first greet them at the door.

I smile modestly, and then I show them around, giving them the tour. They grow silent, too much in awe to speak, as I lead them from sculpture to sculpture. Sometimes one might whisper under his breath, "Wow, that Jimi, man," or, "Those Plaster Casters had nothin' on you," or one might even sniffle and shed a tear or two, but other than that, they're as quiet as if in church.

Then, when we've finished the tour, I show them where to stand, where to hang their flannel shirts and baseball caps, their lycra biking shorts and headbands.

They begin to strip—some slowly, some hurriedly, some with bravado, some with a sheepish grin.

Meanwhile, I stir up the plaster, watching them all the while, assessing their size, their shape.

"Really, you look as young as I do," the baby-faced ones from Seattle always say, as I mold the plaster onto their flesh, firmly yet delicately, with my special touch.

"It's the art," I tell them. "It keeps me young."

Then, as I stroke the plaster gently, smoothing it down, I add, "It's *you*. You keep me young."

Of course, they want to sleep with me, just as their rock forefathers did. They grow aroused and needy. "I want you," they all say. "You're so sensuous, so ripe."

I thank them, and then I explain that for art's sake, I can't.

"I understand," they sigh. "Your art is bigger than we are."

Again, I smile enigmatically. And when it's time for them to leave, I allow them one kiss goodbye, but no more than that, even when my body craves much, much more. "Goodbye, Not the Plaster Casters," they wave, when I finally send them on their way.

"Goodbye," I wave back, standing at my doorway, watching them walk down the long, winding mountain path.

"Goodbye," I wave a second time, when they turn around for one final look, hoping to preserve me—Not the Plaster Casters—forever in their memories. And I don't begrudge them that final look. After all, I already have *them* with me *forever*, here in my studio, hardened and perfectly formed—to do with what I will. And *that*—like my silver initials—is my secret, the part of my artistic process I keep all to myself, the part that really keeps me so beautiful, so eternally young, so eternally ripe.

Frank Sinatra & the Enormous Schlong

BONNY FINBERG

I took a train ride, actually, a very complicated journey, a lone expedition. I knocked on Frank Sinatra's door. I think it was Italy or someplace like Italy. He opened the door. It was a small, simple room, maybe a European country inn. I stood just inside the door, and even though he wasn't tall, I seemed to be looking way up to him as I said with all the seduction I could summon, "I want to kiss you." Then, lowering my voice, "I've wanted to kiss you, since I was seven years old." He took me in his arms and kissed me just the way I like, have always liked, have always imagined he would; his mouth opened just enough to let his tongue through a soft, but taut enough, circle of lips framing an eager tongue, gently aggressing, penetrating me. He began removing my clothes. I sensed he was wondering what he would find. I felt his age would make him more appreciative than he might have been had we been peers, especially when he was in his prime. I looked out the window and saw people on bikes, people walking, children playing. I remarked what a wonderful place this was, how unlike NYC or America, where people are afraid to go out or are too absorbed with their TVs, missing the communal spirit of early evening village life. There was life all around. Everyone felt good.

In bed we began to kiss. He reached over to his night table. I figured he was looking for a condom. He took the condom out of the packet. He was about to put it on. It looked like it would be too small. I remembered the one-night stand six years ago who couldn't get the condom to stay on because it didn't

One ride left operable when the park folded was the Font of Terror. Bonny had qualms as she was strapped into the cockpit, but she decided to give it a try. **Bonny Finberg**'s *work has appeared in* Ikon, Appearances, *and the* National Poetry Magazine of the Lower East Side. *She swooshed through the entrance inside a large version of the typeball one finds on electronic typewriters.*

She passed through mockups of dictionaries and telephone directories. In the prepared, hallucinogenic, strobe-lit videoscape of the amusement, lines of type seemed to chomp like teeth or lash toward her face like serpent's tails.

For a moment, she was horrified into thinking she had become a period that lays like a slug at the end of an overcast phrase.

fit his giant penis. I was half hoping this would be the case again, which would mean *Frank Sinatra has a big cock*, and half concerned about having unsafe sex, also how that would be unfair to my lover waiting at home who would not be angry about my adventure as long as he didn't have to worry about where I was. I took his penis in my mouth. It was surprisingly small and soft, though I knew it was too soon to be disappointed, that such things could change for the better in the most delightful ways. It began to grow and stiffen a little, enough to slip the condom on. We continued kissing and stroking each other, when he suddenly displayed his eighteen-inch penis, enrobed in the perfectly fitting see-through condom. This was "the good turtle soup, not merely the mock." I was overjoyed and a little concerned that it might be more than I could handle. His head lay on the pillow, the window open behind him. His penis was so tall that an old Italian woman in the street below, perhaps the vendor, could see his magnificent prize from where she stood. She was very impressed, and happy for me, even celebratory about it, smiling and congratulating us, who were now smiling back from our second story window.

I was on top. I realized I was fucking the man who'd fucked Ava Gardner. I knew I'd be too late getting home. I wanted to let P. know: one, so he wouldn't worry, and two, maybe he'd like to come over and hang out after we were finished. If not, I knew it would be hard getting home by myself, but figured F.S. would call me a car or a limo. He began to lose part of his erection. The condom was about one third empty. I took him in my mouth again and he returned to his former self. I knew everything would be all right.

30 Years of Hits

JOSE PADUA

It's 1999, just like in the song Prince wrote some fifteen years ago. It's been ten years since the Berlin Wall was torn down at the urging of IBM, five years since the cure for AIDS was found in the ball hairs of a man who grew up next door to Three Mile Island, and two years since the Yuppies were made to trade places with the homeless.

Nowadays everyone is free—everyone who matters, that is. There are no more oppressive governments, just caring, committed multinational corporations. There are no more incurable diseases, just minor illnesses that we take pills for that not only cure the disease but get us HIGH as well. And when the yuppies were told by President Madonna to switch places with the homeless we were greeted by the pleasant sight of a street people who, though they longed for material comforts, DID NOT DESERVE THEM. Yes, gone are the days when the homeless were the "mad blameless sufferers" and the yuppies were the "mad unsuffering blameless inevitable." With the homeless taking the place of the yuppies, we found ourselves with a middle class that KNOWS it's insane, and a lower class that knows it's fucked and DESERVES TO BE FUCKED.

We drink our artificially flavored cola from plastic bottles. We guzzle week-old chemically aged bourbon from styrofoam cups. We eat our plastic sushi with plastic chopsticks. We drive our plastic cars to and from our jobs at the PLASTIC FACTORY. We buy our plastic drugs with our plastic money and when we pass out we fall back on our plastic beds. WE ARE ARTIFICIAL AND WE FUCKING LOVE IT. WE HAVE EVERYTHINC WE NEED. EVERY WOMAN IS MISS AMERICA. EVERY MAN IS THE GREAT PIMP HE ALWAYS WANTED TO BE. THERE ARE

Jose had just paid his "club" fees and was climbing the main staircase of Roxor's when the doors above burst open and a flood of water came gushing toward him. He threw himself over the balustrade, crashing through a divan, which he sundered from its place in the Orientalist decor.

Jose Padua is the author of The Complete Failure of Everything and has perpetual beer-drinker's elbow.

Legging through a side exit, he caught sight of the cause of this upheaval, a damaged fire hydrant pumping water upward through the shattered lattice and horizontally at the same time, lathering a car around which four men (or two men and two half-men) lay belly down, panting like fish in newspaper.

A Chinese circus girl, hunched on the curb, cradled Rollo's head on her lap. Jose approached and knelt beside her.

Muy-Muy looked up at him, her plum-colored eye-

NO MORE SAD SONGS TO BE SUNG. THERE ARE NO MORE SAD SONGS
TO BE WRITTEN.

Yes, the songs on this collection, *30 Years of Hits*, serve as a reminder of those
days gone by, when there were bad times to go along with the good, diseases to
spoil the fun of sex. Nowadays misfortune is just a fading memory, but these
songs will help remind us where we came from—and how far we've gone, you
chumps.

1. 1958: "Scotland" (Bill Monroe)

Monroe, the father of bluegrass, was also the father of basketball legend Earl
"The Pearl" Monroe, the greatest black homosexual to ever play professional basketball. Following a string of top ten records, including "Earl, Don't Talk to Them
Boys" and "Pussy Is Cool (You Should Try It)," Bill Monroe finally hit the number one spot with this song, an instrumental, and continued to hit the top of the
charts with other such wordless wonders.

2. 1959: "I Ain't Never" (Webb Pierce)

On television 1959 was the year of the great crime and detective series—*Naked
City, Car 54 Where Are You?* and *Columbo*. On the burlesque circuit eighteen-
year-old Jessica Tandy was overtaking Lili St. Cyr as the most popular stripper in
the world. 1959 was also the year when the Great Molasses Flood destroyed all of
Belgium, the event that inspired Webb Pierce to pen this tune. Moved by the disaster, he sang, "I ain't never been to Belgium/An' I ain't never going to now/
'Cause it's gone, bro, wiped off/The face of the face of the earth like a cow."

3. 1960: "I'm Sorry" (Brenda Lee)

Penned by rockabilly wildman Ronnie Self, this song was Brenda Lee's first
post-menstrual hit. She'd been making the charts since the age of eight with songs
like "When I Get Older I'm Gonna Bleed" and "When I'm a Teenager I Won't
Always Be in Such a Good Mood" and "I'm Gonna Grow Hair in Funny Places."
Then in 1960 at the age of 12 it happened, and her manager, Jerry Lee Lewis, felt
this would be the perfect song to go along with her maturing young body.

4. 1961: "I Fall to Pieces" (Patsy Cline)

By now everyone knows the story of the great Patsy Cline, The Coal Minor's
(sic) Daughter. Born in 1941 to a fifteen-year-old black grocery clerk in Schaum-
burg, Illinois, Patsy was the first great black female singer in country music.
Despite her success in the music business, she led a brief and troubled life, and
this was her last and perhaps greatest effort.

5. 1962: "A Little Bitty Tear" (Burl Ives)

1962 has gone down in the history books as "The Year Shit Didn't Stink," and
this song, written by Jessica Tandy, typifies what the year was like, because this
song was a piece of shit, and yet, because it was 1962, IT DIDN'T STINK.

U   n   b   e   a   r   a   b   l   e   s

6. 1963: "Thanks a Lot" (Ernest Tubb)

Blacklisted since the early 50's for being a Communist sympathizer, this song was so FUCKIN' great that people lapped it up like it was extra cheese falling off a slice of pizza, even though Ernest Tubb was a lousy stinking commie FUCK.

7. 1964: "Password" (Kitty Wells)

Kitty herself wrote this song. As the story goes she was drunk and couldn't remember the password that would gain her admittance to this private club where she would go to suck dick (her husband, Walter Osmond, being a Mormon, disapproved of blow jobs, and besides had a tiny little dick).

8. 1965: "The Bridge Washed Out" (Warner Mack)

This song was a cynical response to Simon & Garfunkel's "Bridge Over Troubled Water." Take these lines from the song as an example "The bridge washed out/A monster's attacking me/But I can't shout/Life really sucks/And then you fuck a black girl."

9. 1966: "Don't Come Home A-Drinkin'" (Loretta Lynn)

While several thousand miles away the Vietnam war was in full swing, back home Loretta Lynn, Ernest Tubbs' half sister, sang this song for our boys out in her home town of Buttlick, Arkansas. Commenting on the meaning of this song she said, "Don't come home a-drinkin', boys. Just don't."

10. 1967: "Roarin' Again" (Wilburn Brothers)

A pair of Mongoloid twins, the Wilburn Brothers wrote this song themselves: "I hear that noise again/That roarin' again/Oh what is it?/It's the lions at the zoo."

11. 1968: "Wild Weekend" (Bill Anderson)

From the soundtrack of Godard's hit film *Weekend,* this tune is what people remembered the most. 1968 is also the year when the warts first appeared on the face of the young Ian Kilmister, who would later become famous as "Lemmy"—in the heavy metal protest band Motorhead.

liner streaked by tears or from the soot splashing from a burning streetlight across the way. Her costume was damp, emphasizing the slung curves of her torso.

"Help me," she said. "We gotta get this man outta here before he wakes up."

12. 1969: "Statue of a Fool" (Jack Greene)

Known as the "Jelly Giant" because of the vast amounts of cum he ejaculated in his many porno films, Jack Greene still had enough of the sticky stuff left in him to write horny songs like this.

13. 1970: "Hello Darlin'" (Conway Twitty)

Former Amway salesman Twitty wrote this tune about an affair he had with one of his housewife customers, Crystal Gayle, sister of the "Jelly Giant," Jack Greene, and soon to become a respected porno star in her own right—and later, lesbian lover to President Madonna.

14. 1971: "After the Fire Is Gone" (Conway Twitty & Loretta Lynn)

My my, what do we have here? "After the fire is gone/We'll still be fuckin' our brains out/'Cause we're two real horny fucks." Soon after this song came out, over in Europe, the dykes gave way, and the Netherlands was destroyed. Two months later, on the beaches of the Atlantic Coast, wooden shoes and great big crates of Edam cheese washed ashore. We didn't give a fuck about the shoes but the cheese was fuckin' great.

15. 1972: "If You Leave Me Tonight I'll Cry" (Jerry Wallace)

Son of Alabama's great emancipator, George Wallace, Jerry followed not his father's footsteps but those of his mother, Keely Smith, former wife and partner of Louis Prima, and later love slave of Gov. George Wallace, with whom she had little Jerry Wallace, known as "that guy who needs to trim his nosehairs."

16. 1973: "Satin Sheets" (Jeanne Pruett)

In 1973 everyone had satin sheets on their bed because of this song. So what?

17. 1974: "Country Bumpkin" (Cal Smith)

No one liked this song. Not the kids in school, not the President, not the school teacher, not the young teller at the bank, not the mechanic in the auto shop, not even the heroin-addicted hooker George Bush kept in his basement for his own personal amusement. So why did people buy this record? Because, in 1974, people were told to—under threat of nuclear annihilation—by MCA Records, Inc. Everywhere people were saying, "Well, if MCA has the bomb, then I guess we jes' better buy their fuckin' record."

18. 1975: "San Antonio Stroll" (Tanya Tucker)

"It's jes' another song about fucking," said young Tanya about her first big hit "Now excuse me while I fuck some black guy."

19. 1976: "Come On Over" (Olivia Newton-John)

This hot babe came from Zaire. "Yeah, brother, I'm from Africa," she sang, "Now why don' you jes' come ON over . . ."

20. 1977: "If We're Not Back In Love by Monday" (Merle Haggard)

Yeah, a song that speaks of the times: "If we're not in love by Monday/They'll arrest me for assault on Tuesday/Because when you said no to me on Monday/I went out and beat up my accountant."

21. 1978: "Rose-Colored Glasses" (John Conlee)

Like "Jelly Giant" Jack Greene, John Conlee also started out as an actor in porno films before becoming a big star at The Grand Ole Opry. Later he had a sex

change operation, changed his name to Diane Wakoski, and started writing poems. Ain't that a bitch?

22. 1979: "(If Loving You Is Wrong) I Don't Want to Be Right" (Barbara Mandrell)

Barbara wrote this song herself about her lesbian love affair with her own sister, Louise Mandrell. Pretty soon lesbianism was the IN thing and us horny fuckin' guys weren't getting ANY. A bummer of a year. Fuck this song.

23. 1980: "I Believe In You" (Don Williams)

"It's jes' another song about pussy," said young Don Williams, "Now excuse me while I fuck some Japanese girl, heh heh heh . . . "

24. 1981: "Elvira" (The Oak Ridge Boys)

Contrary to what most people think, this was not inspired by horror hostess Elvira. The Oak Ridge Boys, great fans of Swedish art films, were inspired by Bo Widerberg's *Elvira Madigan*. "Yeah we really dug that film," said the leader of the group, Blackie Oak Ridge, "An' you know that girl in the film, Pia Degermark? Yeah, well I met her when I was out in France studying 17th Century French Baroque Art an' I porked her right on Jean-Paul Sartre's tombstone. Now ain't that some shit?" Oddly enough, 1981 was also the year President Reagan dropped the neutron bomb on Stockholm "to set an example for all the world to see."

25. 1982: "This Dream's On Me" (Gene Watson)

Son of the great country zither player Doc Watson, Gene rebelled against country zither music. "The zither in country music is bullshit," he said, "Leave the zither in rock and roll, where it fuckin' belongs, chump."

26. 1983: "I.O.U." (Lee Greenwood)

From the soundtrack of the movie *Quest for Fire,* in which young Rae Dawn Chong first bares her sexy little brown breasts, oh yeah oh yeah oh yeah . . .

27. 1984: "I've Been Around Enough to Know" (John Schneider)

Schneider, star of television's *Dukes of Hazzard,* had this to say: "Catherine Bach, yeah, she had great tits. Used to suck off all the guys in the cast between takes. Yeah, she was like an old hippie girl into that orgasmic high-protein diet, heh heh heh . . . "

28. 1985: "Somebody Should Leave" (Reba McEntire)

From the best-selling album of the 80's *I'm Going to the Store to Do Some Shopping,* this song became the anthem of a generation of yuppies: "If the elevator to the office/Gets too crowded with bicycle couriers/Somebody should leave/Preferably one of them messenger boys . . . "

29. 1986: "Life's Highway" (Steve Wariner)

"You know our nation's crumbling infrastructure," sings Steve, "is something like our lives/You know life ain't always easy/Especially when you're fucking some girl from Taiwan/Who doesn't understand the idiomatic expressions/Of good ole American English . . . "

30. 1987: "Ocean Front Property" (George Strait)

George was the first openly gay country singer and in this great hit sings of his home in Key West, Florida. As Vice President George Bush said, "Hell I don't fucking care that he's a fag and that he's singing about his house on the beach where he fucks his homosexual lover in the butt. It's a damn good song and George Strait has a damn good voice and OK, yeah, he is kind of cute too . . . "

31. 1988: "If Ole Hank Could Only See Us Now" (Waylon Jennings)

"It's jes' another song about baseball," said Waylon. "It ain't Hank Williams I'm singing about here, ASSHOLE. It's Hank AARON. Now get the FUCK out of my face. And leave your beer with me."

32. 1989: "Lone Star State of Mind" (Nanci Griffith)

"k.d. lang's not the lesbian country singer," said Nanci, "I am. And I stole all my licks from Holly Near, who was a real hot fuck. I'd be reading some Bobbie Ann Mason novel and getting wet and Holly would go down on me and lap it up. 'KEEP ON READING,' she'd say, 'KEEP ON READING.' What a crazy hot fuckin' dyke she was, chump."

33. 1990: "One Step Closer" (Sylvia)

"If you move just one step closer," sang Sylvia, "I'll rub my tits in your face." Sylvia was not a lesbian. She was the best female country singer EVER. NO FUCKIN' SHIT.

34. 1991: "Cross-Country Waltz" (Betsy Kaske)

All the way from East Germany, Betsy came to America in early 1990, started working for IBM, gave the company president a most enthusiastic blow job, and is now a BIG FUCKING COUNTRY STAR. Yes indeed, the system is working and it's working well.

—"Guru Joe Cheese," the King of Country Music

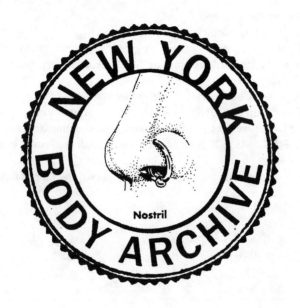

NEW YORK

BODY ARCHIVE

Nostril

The Tattoo I Never Got

JOE MAYNARD

I had a mohawk and a summer job airbrushing T-shirts in a tourist town in Tennessee. Gatlinburg isn't like the rest of Tennessee. It's where working class misfits from all over the place end up.

I did my laundry at the same place every week, a couple doors down from Possum Jones Restaurant. This kinda cool biker chick—you know, skinny, still wore halter-tops in 1984—ran the Laundromat. I got friendly with her and after a while, I noticed people dropped their stuff off for her to do. So the next time I did it too. I smoked a J, cuz I smoked Drums anyway, and it was easy enough to disguise a joint in public. I smoked with her, then walked next door to the restaurant, and when those pot-munchies hit, it was an incredible rush to have an excellent plate of chicken-fried steak, okra, black-eyed peas, collard greens, all that stuff, laid out in front of you like steps to heaven or something. So that was the routine. Drag the laundry down to the biker chick, hang out, get stoned, eat collard greens.

Midway through the summer, she told me her boyfriend was in the Outlaws and they might need some shirts done. "OK," I said, "stop by my stand sometime."

A month later, with the end of the season closing in, this Giant of a man stopped by wearing a confederate flag over his head, black-out goggles and covered with tattoos.

"You Joe?" he asked.

"Yeah."

"Mary from the Laundromat recommended you."

"Oh yeah, you must be . . . "

"Snake. That's what everyone calls me."

Both David Huberman and Alfred Vitale had obtained temp work at Ink, Inc. Their foreman, Joe, got them typing into a Pixies Dome PC.

***Joe Maynard** is the editor of* Beet *magazine and* Pink Pages, *an art/lit erotic sampler.*

Most of the work modules (called monads) were unlit. To enter, one had to climb up a small stepladder, drop down into a slot, and close the lid. One's progress typing in addresses was monitored by way of an electric sign on top of the module (like a mini-billboard) that recorded one's piece rate.

Occasionally, the supervisor would communicate to individual workers by typing commands—such as GOOD WORK or BANG FASTER—that would appear, projected in fiery red 3-D letters, floating above the screen like a dove above waters.

He put a piece of paper down on the counter real business-like, which is how I've found a lot of bikers to be—straight arrows in one narrow strain of their personality, but hell-raisers in all the rest. So I kind of tried to act as serious as he was, even if I was just a goofy punk. I told him 12 bucks and he said what about for 12 of them and I said 12 for $100 plus the price of the shirts, cuz the shirts were sold by the store, not me.

"How about a tattoo instead?" he suggested. "See, I done all these."

I checked out his arm, and he was pretty good.

"And you'll pay for the shirts?" I reiterated.

"Deal."

So, by the time I'd done the shirts, it was close to the end of summer, and I was due back in New York within a couple weeks, but cool, I'd be strutting around stuffy old Columbia U. with a new sunrise over my left ear. Snake said it's hard to draw on your head unless it's perfectly shaved, so I decided to go the second mile and wax that side of my head.

But Hmm. Maybe we didn't do it right or maybe my hair grows too thick, but my friend Helga, one of those milkmaid types from Michigan, had me on a stool in her kitchen for 45 minutes, 6, 8, 10 shots of vodka, yanking tiny clusters of perhaps a dozen hairs at a time from about a square inch of wax that she'd applied on the back of my head. She'd yank a little piece, it would hurt like hell, I'd scream "Jesus fuck" and she'd jump around the kitchen going "Oo-ooh-yuck!" Finally, frustrated, inebriated, and growing sleepier by the minute, we gave up.

"What about Nair?" she suggested.

"What about it?"

"What about putting it on your head?"

Hmm, I thought to myself. Nair.

"Sounds good to me," I said, "howzabout tryin' a little patch on the back."

"Oh goodie."

She skipped to her bathroom then reappeared, shaking the can.

"Ready?" she said with a giggle. I nodded and she depressed the button. Out oozed the shaving cream-like foam, and a rousing round of "Oo-yuck" as she dabbed it on.

"That it?" I asked, "How long do we wait?"

"Just a few minutes," she said with a knowing smile.

"This is really cracking you up, isn't it?" I said

"It's ridiculous." Her answer revealed a staid, midwestern eagle eye bred to spot bullshit at 1000 meters.

Through my own blurred vision, I remember an out-of-focus mental snapshot of her 6'1" frame, pearly white teeth, fleshy mouth, shoulders and bosoms collapsing upon me like the fabled blonde hole of quantum physics. Her kiss swept my inners into its vacuum which seemed to suck my wee pecker through my entrails and esophagus, until it dangled from my mouth in place of my tongue. I thought I was beginning to see the light at the end of the tunnel that people who have been briefly dead often describe, then . . . "Time," she said waking me from my trance. "Put your head over the sink."

She pulled out the hose extension, pushed my head into the porcelain basin, sprayed a furious jet-stream of scalding water, then yanked my head out by the mohawk.

"Look." She said, laughing again. She held forth two hand mirrors and in our drunken stupor, it took about ten minutes to situate them so I could actually see what was going on back there, but finally, I saw a swatch of pink scalp flash by in one of the shaking mirrors.

"Lookshcrate" I slurred, "Do me up."

She repeated the process on the entire side of my head, did the same routine in the sink, snapped my head back by the mohawk to her probing tongue, and I mumbled into her gargantuan tonsils, "Lookshcrate. Letchko ta bed."

With that, she led me to her bed. No sooner had my head found a pillow then vavoom! All 180 pounds of her crashed upon me, nearly breaking me in half. Out of some kind of miracle, my pecker was indeed the stiff saddle horn she desired and she rode me with a vengeance, pulling what was left of my mane into her milky cleavage, thrusting her hips into mine with such forthright farm girl enthusiasm, I can still hear my vertebrae cracking rhythmically to her pumps, pushes and pulls. She played me like a glockenspiel till I grew faint somewhere between the feeling of approaching orgasm and/or vomiting, and passed out, later to find only my fine, long Mediterranean nose had saved me from certain death as it was able to find air between her left breast and armpit that smothered the rest of my face in a strange alcohol/sweat/sex froth.

"Oh mi god," I said waking up the next morning, "What is wrong with my head?"

I pushed her sweaty boobs off me and sat up. It felt like a metal rod had been driven into the back of my skull. The room was spinning, my blood was rushing, I felt like everything was sideways, like that metal rod in the back of my head was somehow polarizing the world incorrectly. I reached to pull it out but instead found only my own smooth flesh which stung like a thousand hornets from my own touch.

"What?" she said drowsily. I got up and staggered to the bathroom, holding the wall the whole way, cuz between all that vodka, Nair, and frolic, it was impossible to tell up from down. I looked in the mirror at my contorted face and looked at my head, half of which looked like a chemotherapy accident.

Helga walked in behind me. "Ooh-yuck."

"Would you stop saying that." I grumbled.

"What's wrong with your head?"

"Well, for starters," I said trying to speak softly, "it hurts like hell."

"It doesn't look too good, either," she added, "maybe we should go to the doctor."

We washed up, grabbed a couple coffees for the car and drove to the clinic downtown. Luckily, the doctor was kind of young and hip and managed not to make me feel like a total idiot. He gave me this Vaseline stuff with cortisone and soon the pain simmered down and was replaced with a million little white boils. I worked all day at my T-shirt stand while puss oozed from the back of my head. Little kids asked what was wrong with me. People avoided me on the sidewalk. At McDonald's, a family at the table next to me got up when I sat down, choosing to eat instead on the sidewalk. About three o'clock, I was back at my stand and I heard this deep redneck voice behind me.

"The hail happened to you?" It was Snake. "Looks like you got a slice of pizza stuck to the back of your head."

"I had a chemical reaction."

"I'll say." he snorted. I tried to explain the whole story. The waxing, the nairing. Oh, I thought, how ridiculous it was. Why, I asked myself while the story of my own ineptitude escaped my mouth, am I such a fuck-up? A couple more Outlaws listened in, stood around laughing at this stupid Yankee punk, or so it seemed to me.

"So," I said, "I guess I'll have to put off that tattoo."

"Guess so," Snake said, "Let's see them shirts."

I showed them the shirts. Fortunately, they liked them and paid the 100 bucks instead. Said if I came back next year, we'd give the tattoo another whirl. But I knew they knew, it was the tattoo I never got.

Special Delivery
LIZ RESKO

The doorbell rings
and it is only the Chinese delivery boy.
Benign and smiling,
he offers me a carton of steaming noodles
in exchange for 5.75.
I trot back upstairs
inhaling the aroma
and all the way wondering
whether I should eat first
and cut up the body later

Through the skylight, Liz had seen Huberman descending into the adjacent bunker but, pressed for time since she had fallen 16 addresses behind, she had to forget about this brief novelty. However, seeing his brawny physique had brought scarlet to her cheeks.

When the computers momentarily went down, she folded her hands in her lap and faced forward, as was commanded in the instruction book, but she was distracted by a scratching sound at her knee. Suddenly a wall panel fell in and David was leering at her.

"Yipes," she yelled as he stuck a hand through the opening toward her thigh.

Liz Resko *is the author of* The Bottomless Coffee Cup *and lives in the cemetery section of Queens. She no longer works at Ink, but buys buttons for a living.*

"Hey, sorry." David apologized, "but can you help me?" He was thrusting a loose wire at her.

"What are you talking about?"

"Alfred says you should connect this to the D-labeled bolt behind your chair."

She was not used to following orders that did not come from the proper supervisors, nor used to ones given in person rather than from the screen. On her machine, in raised type, appeared PLEASE STAND BY.

She stood up.

¿ASK?
YOURSELF
POEM - SPARROW
ART - BLAIR WILSON
A JAPANESE WOMAN ON
51st. St.
HANDED ME A
LEAFLET
ENTITLED
"ASK YOURSELF ..."
I OPENED TO QUESTION
No. 4
?
"DO YOU LIVE IN YOUR DREAM HOME?"
and I thought, "THAT'S WHAT I NEED,
A HOME FOR MY DREAMS
THEN I REMEMBERED
"DREAM HOME" MEANS A HOUSE IN
THE SUBURBS.

The Shower
Tsaurah Litzky

The new shower is so white and clean I think I am in a motel. It was put in two days ago by an artist carpenter, Cliff Gerstenhaber. The new landlord hired him. Gerstenhaber was cute, so I said smiling, "What kind of name is Gerstenhaber?" He said, not smiling, "A long name."

You win some, you lose some, I thought.

It took Gerstenhaber one day to do the job. The old shower was put in by my old boyfriend, Louis Krim; it took Louis two weeks to put it in. The first time I used the old shower it leaked on Bob and Betty downstairs. Bob doesn't like me because he once made a play for me and I squashed him, Betty doesn't like me because she knows something happened, but not what. They think I am promiscuous and will never amount to anything. They are wrong on both counts.

Tsaurah Litzky and Kevin Riordan were directing the China King people where to put a casket of lobsters, when Sharon Mesmer ran up.

"McBrain is not even here yet!" she exclaimed.

"Calm yourself," Tsaurah soothed, "it's going to be a glorious day. Look at the sun. And your fish picnic is bound to be smashing. I can feel my toe tingling." The shamanistic power of Tsaurah's sensitive big toe was legendary.

Tsaurah Litzky is the author of Pushing Out the Envelope *and* The Bluebird Buddha of No Regrets, *a columnist for* Downtown, *and a trendsetter in the margins.*

The two feisty, swarthy Chinamen, Donald Duk and Hawkeye, who had been opening the crates, broke up the whites' conversation. Donald said, "I thought you guaranteed this shipping firm, Sharon."

Hawkeye broke in: "Muy-Muy 'sposed to see this thing right at the dock. All fuck up."

"What's the problem, gents?" Sharon asked, assuming her unctuous managerial persona.

Tsaurah and Kevin were already poking in a carton. Kevin held out a bill of lading. "Stare at this weird itinerary. Japan to the U.S. via Vietnam and Iran."

Tsaurah was leaning into the box which was big as a sea chest. There were two compartments. One was filled with red lobsters, dappled with volcanic ash. The other held neatly folded used clothes.

"Look this shit," Hawkeye said, pulling out clothes.

"My boss is gonna be pissed," Donald said quietly.

"You could sell this stuff in a flea market," Tsaurah said, picking up a discarded powder-blue dinner jacket with the monogram RW on the lapel.

The old landlord would not put out any more money to fix the shower; he said he had fulfilled his obligations. They said I should shower in the public bathroom on the second floor.

I said I was paying for the shower and would use the shower, they should fight the landlord. One time when I was in the shower with Abraham, the shower leaked so much they called 911. They said maybe someone was having a heart attack in the shower, the police broke down the door with an axe, ha, ha, ha.

I take a lot of showers. My mother told me it was an ancient Jewish beauty secret and she was so beautiful, although I wondered where the ancient Jews took showers when they were wandering around in the desert with Moses.

Yesterday I took a shower and the new shower doesn't leak. It's 1991 now and *Time* magazine says the freedom the future promises women can be frightening, but the effect of feminism has been positive. This morning Betty said "Hi ya, how ya doing?" when we passed in the hall.

Three Poems
MICHAEL RANDALL

CAFÉ SOCIETY
sitting at an outdoor table
with my friend José
feeling pretty much like
what my other friend Jennifer
calls "café scum"
we're drinking beer
and ogling all the women
on the street

there's a skinny blonde on the opposite corner
going into her gravity-defying
slow-motion junkie dance
"Shit, maybe I should quit drinking," I say,
as a woman in a short T-shirt
and spandex pants jogs by,
"or maybe just take up jogging."

we order another round
and drink in peace
until another woman comes by
walking a big dog
"Maybe I'll get a dog," I say,
watching as this one
licks its owner's feet
"You could take it jogging," José adds.
"Yeah," I say, "I hadn't thought
of that."
we both take sips of beer
and go back to staring
at the people on the street

pretty soon a woman comes by
pushing a baby in a stroller
and dragging two other

Michael Randall relaxed in the front car of the deserted El, thinking over last evening's foreplay, chuckling at his own verve.

He had seen his prize a few weeks ago, and had begun stalking "her" in an offhand, non-committal manner that concealed his fervor. Last night he got the balls to approach. He had walked up and, not knowing exactly where to begin, had sunk penitently to his knees.

In that position, he removed a large magnet to draw the deadbolt, then he jimmied the door, and, guided by the light of a dark lantern, strode through the empty apartment as if it were his, straight to the safe. He cracked it and gathered his prize into his arms, a crowd of uncut gems on a satin bed. Now the little beauties were in the utility bag beneath his seat. His eyes closed pleasantly, and a trickle of smoke wanly threaded up from his

267

little kids behind her
"Perhaps I'll have a bunch of kids," I say.
"They'd like the dog," I add,
beating José to the punch

I could leave them with the dog
when I go out jogging
but then the dog
would probably
eat the kids
and when I returned
feeling sweaty and tired

I'd be back where I started
except now I'd have sore muscles
and a fat dog
who, like me,
should probably
be put to sleep.

JUST GIMME THAT COUNTRYSIDE
laying in bed watching *The Beverly Hillbillies*
in a motel room in West Virginia
Jethro's dilemma takes on tragic new meaning
and Ellie Mae's the most beautiful
girl I've seen today

I know that beyond those curtains
there are mountains
dark and rolling
room enough
and sky enough
air enough
to breathe
nights black enough
I can see the stars
when I turn off
the TV

U   n   b   e   a   r   a   b   l   e   s

Entertainment Industry

all the movie stars on the late night TV talk show
are going on about their new-found sobriety
and each time they say
it's been two years

or three years or ten years since
they've had a drink, the audience
applauds wildly

I'm laying on my couch drinking beer
and I've been drinking beer for twenty
years and I'm reminded of a line
in the movie *A Star Is Born*

where someone says to Judy Garland:
"you *know* what twenty years of
drinking does to a man."

I always took that line as a sort of warning
but now I realize I have no idea
what it was supposed to mean
and can only say what

twenty years of drinking has done to me:
I get up, turn off the tv and get another
beer from the fridge.

Then I find a pen and draw a smiley face
on the head of my dick, thinking,
At last, I'm beginning to
understand.

nipped Cosmador.

Michael Randall is a visual artist, musician, editor of Big Cigars, *director and writer of the film* GIRLQUAKE!, and, most importantly, literary agent of Rollo Whitehead.

Suddenly, he wobbled sideways as the train lurched and took off in reverse. He got up, shouldering his bag, and went to glance out what was now the rear window, His eyes almost drilled out of his head when he saw that the train tracks behind them were progressively collapsing, as if fed into an invisible wood-chipper.

He spun on his heels and began walking briskly through the cars, using a plastic skeleton key to unlock the doors. Between the third and fourth cars, he found a tow-headed woman covered with masking tape who quickly explained the situation.

Stealthily, they approached the car from which the gunfire was issuing. Before entering it, Michael bent and unzipped his bag, removing and assembling a DK-14 automatic pistol.

They opened the door, then froze on the threshold. A bare-chested woman was rushing toward them, and behind her, whiting out two silhouetted figures, a velvety blue bolt of lightning exploded, rocking the car.

M   i   c   h   a   e   l   R   a   n   d   a   l   l

Marginal Notes
DAVID POLONOFF

I am a marginal man. An office temp. Proofreader. Word processor. I make my mark between the lines and at the page's edge. I take my cues from messages scrawled outside the text. Additions. Revisions. Deletions. The better I do my job, the more I disappear, the place in which I toil becoming empty space.

I am a marginal employee. A midtown migrant. I make my living in other people's places. I do the same thing in many locations. I go to different offices on different floors of different buildings. Each one does something different. Each one has a different view. I have many views. But none of them is mine.

David was feeling bored. Maybe I'll go out and walk back and forth across the street, he said to himself. As he toddled, like Robert Benchley in Ten Years in a Quandry, *across Frostpoint, he saw a battered bus bearing down on him.*

He couldn't believe what it was leaving in its wake; for, as a high-spirited young girl on a cold day will run her gloved hand along a garage's eave, breaking off the icicles with a windy clatter, so the bus was mowing down all the steel El supports amidst a torrent of slush and glass.

David Polonoff *is the author of* Down the Yup Staircase. *His style-think pieces have appeared in* Newsday, *the* Village Voice, Cultural Correspondence, *and* Downtown. *He has relocated from Frostpoint Street, Chicago, to Seattle.*

My dear, if only David could have witnessed the commotion among the riders in that engine of destruction.

Mike Topp: "Ron, will you tell that nut job to ease up."

Carol was on the floor chasing after the AK-30 that had fallen from her shoulder holster and skedaddled across the floor like a runaway lobster.

Ron: "bart, holy fucking shit, you got to slow this mother down!"

Debbie, arms around bart, crushed her face to his, burying her sultry black hair in his blonde mesh.

bart, yelling above the cacophony as another window exploded and the roof was stoven in by falling pillasters, "Shalom, what gear are you in?"

Shalom, trying to see the landscape before him solely by way of the rear-view, shouted back. "I've got a plan. I'm going to outrun them. If we can get to Spout Street ahead of them, where the train comes down and goes underground, we can block the track."

"We'll never make it," Ron shouted.

A side-sweep ripped the front door off, and they could see a pedestrian, David, lying crying on the curb as they screeched past.

Every morning I call the agencies to say I am still available. Sometimes they have jobs. These days, more often they do not. They always have reasons. Usually it's "the holidays." The Jewish holidays. Christian holidays. Groundhog's Day. Day of the Dead. Holidays frame time like margins. The agencies are running out of holidays. Some of them have begun to substitute the word "recession."

Recessions happen when the profit margin shrinks. A few years ago the profit margin was expanding. Corporate entities were as fluid as the words on their computer screens. Capable of infinite reprocessing. They merged and divided, invaded, revised, and deleted each other. Each shift produced profits and documents. There were many margins to work in. And there were many shifts. Nine to five. Five to twelve. Weekend and graveyard.

In those days there were many marginal people. Some of us called ourselves artists. The margins provided us with space in which to develop. We did things to documents in order to do the things we *really* did. The margins also equipped us with a blank spot. What we really did is what we would do in the future. Therefore what we did now was not real.

To finance the present against a future profit is called "buying on a margin." We who lived on the margins bought time on them as well, used them to invest in a future where everything would pay off. We invented the slash (/) to secure our speculation. "I am a *proofreader/writer, screenwriter-director/actor, video performance artist/independent filmmaker,*" we said. The left side of the slash was definite, rooted in the world, the right side another name for marginality.

We were not the only ones who borrowed from the future. The people who created margins, profits, and documents balanced their accounts against the future as well. Eventually they lost their balance. The left side of the slash crashed into the right. "I am a *proofreader/unemployed attorney, word processor/former investment banker,*" we began to hear. Displacement displaced marginality.

The margins continue to contract. All space enclosed within the corporate stanzas. The slashes have come out of our identities. Either *proofreader/proofreader* or *unemployed proofreader/unemployed writer.* Our employers demand unity. Codependent no more, they tell us as their documents repossess the page.

I am a marginal man and can no longer depend on an economy's dependency. Marginal without utility. I must turn myself inside-out to avoid disappearing.

A Tax Proposal

DAVE MANDL

Sure, sure, after the Revolution we'll all be free for-ever from rent, passports, repressive drug and sex laws, scumbag bosses, and football fans. Unfortunately, though, I'm not getting any younger, so I'm willing to make certain compromises right now rather than wait. Let's start with taxes: I'm a reasonable man, and I realize that there are some people who are actually happy to exchange a certain percentage of their income for the "services" that the government provides. Fine. So, inspired by a fundraising mailing I received from Carnegie Hall recently, I'm proposing the following tax plan that should make just about everyone happy. There are three levels of services, based on the percentage of your income that you're willing to part with: Patron, Supporter, and Tightwad. I humbly submit my proposal here for your (and Congress's) approval.

FIREFIGHTERS:

PATRON: In the event of a fire, a team of firemen will show up within four minutes to extinguish it and not steal anything from your home in the process.

SUPPORTER: In the event of a fire, firemen will show up within eleven minutes to extinguish it and not steal anything with a value of more than $180.

TIGHTWAD: In the event of a fire, firemen will finish watching *Baywatch* and then come over with a couple of dozen friends and a forklift to sift through the rubble.

POLICE PROTECTION:

PATRON: The District Attorney will personally escort you on all trips beyond a six-block radius of your home.

SUPPORTER: A police officer will cluck his tongue disapprovingly if someone tries to mug you.

*Liz really got pissed when the panels on the other side of her cubicle gave way and another interloper tumbled in. It was **Dave Mandl**.*

Dave Mandl is co-editor of Radiotext(e), a WFMU dj, bassist, and designer of this book.

Dave apologized, "I'm sorry, miss, but we have to borrow your terminal."

He introduced everyone. As he talked, he couldn't help noticing her shapely legs; she, though gazing demurely down, had to note the bulge in his pants.

Addressing Liz, Huberman said crudely, "A bartender would give you free drinks all night for a chance to peel those legs."

"Cut the vulgarity," said Sparrow, crawling in with Ellen and Alfred Vitale.

What was irritating Liz was that, to enter, each new person had to squeeze between her legs. It was as if she was birthing them, and then the last guy (Alfred) was actually carrying a baby (Ellen's).

TIGHTWAD: The FBI will distribute maps of your apartment showing exactly where all valuables are located.

Unemployment Insurance:

PATRON: In case of unemployment, you will receive 60% of your former salary and a free subscription to *Soap Opera Digest* for two years or until you find a new job.

SUPPORTER: In case of unemployment, you will receive a one-month free pass to Fraunces Tavern Museum and three lunches at Phil's Waffle House on Eastern Parkway.

TIGHTWAD: Employees of the Department of Labor will get you canned by sending bi-weekly, anonymous letters to your boss impugning your character—and will bribe your mother to help, if necessary.

Highways:

PATRON: All highway travel will be free, you will be able to exceed posted speed limits by up to 35 mph, and you will get to personally raise drawbridges whenever you feel like it, even during rush hour.

SUPPORTER: You will receive a 15% discount on all bridge, tunnel, and highway tolls, and you will be permitted to make lewd remarks to toll booth attendants of the opposite sex.

TIGHTWAD: A professional basketball player will attempt to block your money from going into the toll basket, and you will be subjected to a full strip-search by a team of highway patrolmen if you miss.

EDUCATION:

PATRON: Child will be allowed to assist in preparing lunch in the teacher's cafeteria, will have the right to give homework assignments of his or her choosing to three classmates, and will have his or her report cards filled out in pencil.

SUPPORTER: Child will be trusted to deliver cutting cards and notes from the principal to his or her parents personally, and will not be required to walk through school metal detectors.

TIGHTWAD: Child will be required to memorize and recite in front of the class nine poems by Robert Frost, Walt Whitman, or Carl Sandburg.

MISCELLANEOUS:

PATRON: You will be allowed to deploy up to seven divisions of the United States army in any country with a population of seven million or less; future presidential press conferences will be planned so as not to interfere with your TV-watching schedule; and you will be allowed, for a total of fourteen hours a month, to peek through the hole in the dressing room wall in Urban Outfitters on Sixth Avenue.

SUPPORTER: The U.S. Assistant Attorney General will personally intervene on your behalf in all domestic squabbles; you will be allowed to sing "The Star Spangled Banner," in the style of your choice, at any five Cleveland Indians or Cincinnati Reds home games; and you will be allowed to do anything you want to a member of the Board of the Transit Authority next time one of your trains goes out of service.

TIGHTWAD: You will be required to have dinner, and pay for it, with Senator Alfonse D'Amato's entire staff once a month at a restaurant selected by Senator D'Amato himself; you will be forced, three times a month, to watch episodes from the final season of *The Odd Couple;* and you will be required to shoot three rolls of nude "art" photos of a member of the House Armed Services Committee.

Meta-Press
News Service
FOTO SIFICHI

LAWRENCE, KANSAS: A nine-holed outhouse toilet that was shot to pieces in a shooting spree by the writer William S. Burroughs two days before he died failed to find a buyer in Christie's auction house in New York. Christie's had estimated the bullet-splattered seats at between $27,000 and $35,000, but bidders were unwilling to go higher than $9,500.

AMSTERDAM: Anarchists and left-wing extremists filled the streets yesterday forming a march that was designed to help pull down the world-wide diamond cartel that DeBeers GbH controls. Shouting such slogans as "A diamond a day keeps the bailiff away" and "Liz Taylor, get used to fiberglass," the crowd roamed the streets tossing diamonds to children and the elderly. Diamonds have recently arrived in Holland from Angola, where a pseudo-anarchistic military has been ignoring DeBeers' complaints, and mining tons of diamonds and selling them for what DeBeers calls "Hong Kong prices."

With the Tokyo, European, and American stock markets cringing from already difficult times, the flow of diamonds could not have arrived at a worse time. "There's not a hell of a lot we can do about it," said Jurgen Hoffmann, a spokesman for DeBeers, "We offered to buy the diamonds for far higher prices and we were ignored. With an army of about 10,000 well-armed men down in Angola, it'd cost us a fortune to put a mercenary team together to seal things up."

Bucksminister Fucksbuster, the organizer of the anti-diamond march said, "I'm very happy with what is happening here today. So many people are fed up with the fake economic pillars that keep the rich rich and the poor poor. You know what I'd like to see?" he

Dave Mandl seated himself at Liz's terminal and pulled up a file marked Operation Cantilever Twins, which consisted of a list of names. Next to two of them, Urdang and Falour, were checks and the notation ACTIVE. In parens in front of them was a cross-reference to Leonard, police sergeant.

Dave got into Sergeant Leonard's file and found out that he was planning to apprehend the suspects on the Dan Ryan El. Changing screens, Mandl accessed the Transit Authority's database. There was a current report on an emergency situation—a train running in reverse. Another document indicated which car was the source of the trouble. Dave obtained a schematic of that car.

Dave swiveled, "Alfred, what do you think?"

"I think," Alfred wet his lips, "we can send a negative charge into the juice

277

continued. "I'd like to see the diamond business fall apart, absolutely crumble. I'd like to see people treat diamonds like ping-pong balls, throwing them to their dogs or cats because they have no value. If these Angolan diamonds keep coming in, I'm sure we'll succeed."

DeBeers closed down 79 points today in reaction to the protest in Amsterdam and the influx of diamonds from Angola.

LONDON: Police cordoned off major sections of the city on Wednesday, as a phone call from the I.R.A. claiming that two large bombs would explode near London's Stock Exchange before 1 p.m. created havoc. The call came at noon, giving only one hour's warning. Subways that passed under the designated area were halted, the Stock Exchange and nearby office buildings were evacuated, traffic was diverted, and lunchtime goers were forced to evacuate restaurants and cafes within 800 yards of the exchange.

"Coming at lunch complicated things a bit," said Sergeant James Thumbly. "But I'm not surprised," he added. "The I.R.A. are a rotten bunch who'll stoop to anything. This just shows how ruinous they can be."

What did surprise authorities after 55 minutes of intense searching by 350 officers was the package that was finally discovered in the trunk of a rented Ford Escort, which was parked 250 yards from the Stock Exchange. Bomb experts opened a Christmas-wrapped box that was filled with 100 pounds of Bassett's Licorice Allsorts. A note was attached, addressed to Prince Charles. It read, "Dear Charles, when looking for ALLSORTS look to the I.R.A.! We are the original Allsorts. We're not for children. We want you. Full of Die and Promise, The I.R.A."

Buckingham Palace released a statement reasserting that terrorism would never be bowed down to and that justice would one day arrest these criminals.

The firm Trevor Bassett Ltd. made no comment about the choice of their candy by the I.R.A. but said that they were going to help police track down where the Allsorts might have been purchased.

The Stock Exchange resumed a "lopsided normality" as clerks and brokers resumed their posts around 3:45 p.m. As one broker said, "I've never walked into so many faxes in my life. I couldn't see the branches for the leaves." The exchange closed down 11 percent, but experts agreed that a normal business day would restabilize things quite easily.

PARIS: The Japanese Embassy in Paris yesterday received a visit from Jacques Chirac (mayor of Paris and president of the RPR party) in response to Japanese complaints regarding the disappearence of 67 Japanese tourists since January. Most of the missing were on company vacations. Sony and Sanyo alone claim 43 of the M.O.V.'s (missing on vacation) and with 10 others from the electronics industry this leaves 14 M.O.V.'s claimed by various other corporations. The

U n b e a r a b l e s

Japanese have almost gone as far as to say that the French have been "hijacking" highly trained workers for there own industry needs. The French deny this categorically.

Marc Jaibout, an inspector for the Prefecture de Police, surmises the missing Japanese may be the victims of certain Muslim extremists who are trying to tarnish the allure of Paris in order to reduce the revenue that the city gains from tourism every year. The Japanese alone account for 100 million dollars in tourism revenue, with 900 Japanese arriving daily and spending upwards of 2,500 dollars each during their stay.

Mr. Chirac stated that the police's theory was an "over-developed rumour" and added that "Paris is not Cairo." Mr. Chirac proposed his own theory that the missing Japanese had "simply decided to extend their visits in France and might easily be found at various attractions around the country."

In a capital that openly refers to the Japanese as "the Ants," tensions can mount. The French don't want to cause any more friction however, and hoped that Mr. Chirac's personal visit might "lubricate" relations a bit.

There has already been a noticeable increase in airline cancellations from the orient. JAL, Japan's airline, is considering dropping one flight a day to Paris from Tokyo. Until then, we'll just have to scour the upscale paraphernalia emporiums and Hermes bag discounters along the misty boulevards of Paris in hopes of discovering the whereabouts of the Japanese 67.

BEVERLY HILLS: Film Director Spike Lee, whose film *Malcolm X* stirred much controversy, is now calling on all young black Americans to stop buying Malcolm X baseball hats that a small, all-white American firm is having made in China.

"This is the kind of thing Malcolm X would have hated. Not only do blacks not profit from the products, neither do white American factory workers. If

box. That should, well, either shut down the whole system or send an incredible surge of electricity, like a lightning bolt, through the car."

"Who are you guys?" Liz asked.

"We're the Cyphering Prawns," Sparrow offered, as Mandl keyed feverishly. "And we're gonna erase the Operation Cantilever Twins file and save the surviving Unbearables!"

If we go back to 1968, we can try to picture the freighter Samarkand, *later acquired by Ron Kolm, as it steamed out of Da Nang harbor. It was captained by* **Foto Sifichi**.

Foto Sifichi is a sound-word-radio performer, photographer, and writer who has exhibited in Amsterdam, NYC, and Paris.

In its hold sat two refugees, Muy-Muy and Nhi Chan. Both had been philosophy students in the South till the exigencies of civil war destroyed their links to prosperity and happiness.

F o t o S i f i c h i

anything, the hats should be made in Africa where our brothers and sisters can use the money. Don't buy Chinese-made Malcolm X baseball hats or T-shirts, damn it! Look at the label."

Asked what they should buy since only "Made in China" Malcolm X paraphernalia exists on the market, Mr. Lee replied. "Don't buy anything. If you have a baseball hat, just paint an X on it. Malcolm X's message is important, not these capitalistic products. This isn't supposed to be like a Michael Jackson tour where we all help Mr. Whitey Warner Brothers or Mr. Sony make millions of dollars in the name of Malcolm X. This is about creating your own autonomy. This is about anarchy and self-creation. If I could make the movie . . . you can at least paint an X on a baseball hat."

The firm Public Reflection, responsible for the Malcolm X products made in China, was not available for comment.

Possession
EMILY XYZ

Because I am I am owned
Everybody knows me knows
I'm a slave in the house of God
I am a/I am a/a/a/I am me/I am me/I am a I'm a
medium for my own voices
Strangers come look through my windows and say
what they're too scared to say yes what they see
what they see/when I speak nobody listens/I know
I know I have been overtaken
Because I am I am owned
I signed off I am alone and I like hang from the
ceiling like wiring cut from a broken slinky
restricted
enshrined
pinned
I come face to face with body after body and every
one I meet
I have been that one/and everybody goes right
through this thing this thing this this thing this
body this knocking talking door psychic barrier
kicking
alabaster heaven
tile floor
my dream is/my demise/heaven
is me/heaven is glassine/tiny as a poppy-seed/pure
as a belief in
heaven

A person who is always travelling is possessed
A person who climbs mountain peaks is possessed
A person who does stunts in an airplane
is possessed
A person who does daring stunts driving a car
is possessed

Emily was berating the
show's organizer. "These
perch are ruined."

Emily XYZ is a poet and
recording artist. She recently released a single, "Sinatra
Walks Out."

Sharon threw up her
hands.

Yet problems are rela-
tive, aren't they? At the
next turn of events, all
these little worries would
be forgotten. An approaching screech caused them all
to look up to see a forty-
ton El car crashing through
the nearest fence and bearing down on them.

Let's backtrack: As the El
began to descend, Shalom
pulled ahead of it.

bart: "We'll never make
it."

Shalom: "Relax, bart.
Trust me. I've done this
before."

Ron was moaning.

Carol lay like a sniper on
the floor, clutching her
firearm. Mike was openly
weeping.

Deb said to bart, "Nous
touchons a ça fin, mon

> A zombie is possessed by the spirit of a dead person
> A vampire is possessed by the spirit of a dead person

The world is 2-faced with a sickening appeal
the things you want will kill you/Can you give them up
These words rewrite me every day/Can you shut everything out, can you turn
off
Hard to see sometimes through days and days of bulletproof glass
things that would cut you in half
Very hard to remember/while planes and planets continue to move
how you know
what you know—

Because I am I am owned/Because I am a man a man a soul-man
      A person who doesn't like to be told to do something is possessed
I am possessed
    A woman who sits on a windowsill and looks out into the street is possessed
A person is who he says he is
      A woman who stands in front of the house all the time is possessed
A person who insists he exists is possessed
        A person who steals books from a library is possessed
When a man offers himself up he is possessed
        A person who acts as an informer is possessed
When a man writes himself off he is possessed
     A person who buys and wears only second-hand clothes is possessed
When a man wishes he was dead he is
      A person who can't get up in the morning is possessed
When a woman wishes she was a man she is
        A person who is very tactless is possessed
When a woman is with a man she is
     A person who moves from place to place is possessed
Whan a man is a woman he is
        A person who stabs another person is possessed
A person with possessions is possessed
        A person who has to take tranquilizers is possessed
A person with position is possessed
      A person who takes strong tranquilizers becomes a zombie
A person passing on the street is possessed
    A person who walks along the curb and looks for money is possessed

he sold out he sold out he sold out
A person who always smiles and shakes his head
A person who owns himself is possessed
    no when somebody says something is possessed
A person who owns another is possessed
    A person who is very hypercritical is possessed
A person who knows his own strength
    A person who hunts for old bread every day to
knows everything knows everything
        feed pigeons is possessed
A person who needs people
    A person who always takes kittens and drowns
Hero-less, a person who believes in nothing
        them is possessed
People dying in the streets are possessed
    A person who always hums is possessed
People stepping over the bodies are possessed
    A person who stays in the house all the time
The west is best is best
        is possessed
The west is possessed
    A person who stays in the streets all the time and
A person who preaches to the nation is possessed
    refuses to come into the house is possessed
Photographers, journalists, cameramen
    A person who lies in the sun for long stretches of
Kids with crayons
    time is possessed
The right to bear arms
    A baseball manager who constantly argues with
The right to bear names
    the umpire at the slightest provocation
The right to live and die unencumbered by
    is possessed
anyone's concern
    A person who looks and walks like a zombie
The right to be wrong
    is possessed by a zombie spirit
The right to be dumb

cheri," her delicate fingers digging into his stretch pants.

"We can do it," Shalom yelled, slamming the bus into the front of the El train. The impact flipped their vehicle over and sent it spinning like a puck on a shuffleboard.

The train derailed and headed left, smashing through a chain-link fence into a dilapidated amusement park. As the cars began tilting, Randall fired through the smoke and sparks, wounding the sergeant.

"Hit the deck," Alfred yelled as the computers at Ink, Inc., tied via Liz's link to the Transit Authority database, began wiping out, their vacuum screens imploding. Mandl had done his work well, though, and Operation Cantilever Twins was no more.

Crashing through sheds full of kewpie dolls, ripping the sides off a ferris wheel, tearing down the pilings under a roller coaster, and with the banner UNBEAR-ABLE somehow hooked on its brow like a crown of thorns, the El sped on.

=====

A person who is a sore loser is possessed

The right to do stupid things without believing

A person who spends all the money he earns and is always broke is possessed
that we are stupid people

A person who doesn't take any interest in anything is possessed

The right to life

A person who hears voices that tell him to get out of the house is possessed

The right to leave

A person who hears voices that tell him to jump out of the window

The right to leave life

is possessed

The right to be predictable without believing that we are predictable

A person who hears voices that tell him to quit his job is possessed

The right to be inconsistent, the right to mystify

A woman who refuses to have a baby is possessed

The right to know nothing

A woman who can't have a baby is possessed

The right to do the right thing

A woman who has a miscarriage is possessed

The right to take the blame

A woman who has a still-born child is possessed

The right to rewrite the rules

A person who must get revenge is possessed

The right to roll the dice

A child who is constantly misbehaving in school is possessed

The right to reinvent ourselves

A person who has a glazed look in his eyes is possessed

The right to railroad those who stand in the way

A person who is always quiet but sometimes breaks out in loud laughter

The right way

is possessed

Amway

A woman who never buys her own clothes but lets somebody buy them for

The road to riches

her is possessed

The Lord God

A person who always lives on a ship sailing on the ocean is possessed

The claim to fame

A person who likes to hunt and kill animals is possessed

U   n   b   e   a   r   a   b   l   e   s

The waking dream
    A person who has a chronic cough is possessed
The walking dead
    A person who always stays out late is possessed
The key to the highway
    A person who always plays cards is possessed
key to the highway
    A person who talks in a confusing fashion
key to the highway—

        is possessed
A person with a short attention span is possessed
A person who has hypoglycemia is possessed
A person who always looks straight ahead and
    never turns his head to the side is possessed
—If a person always looks in garbage cans, he is
        possessed.
This is a two-sided world/never-ending
    If a person always looks down and picks up
words/incessant tirade/stranded
        cigarette butts, he is possessed
because I am a man I am a woman
    If a person always goes around begging for money,
because I am/I am not
        he is possessed
because I know/I know/I don't know
    If a person is always asking for cigarettes, he is
because nothing is once and for all
        possessed

(With material from Mental Illness, Possession, Exorcism, and Life After Death, by Dr. Francis Harber [1977, Dare Books, Brooklyn NY].)

Finally, the left side of the front car began to enter the earth like a plow. At first, large chunks of asphalt, sewer pipe, and wire were dredged up; but then, amazingly, the hidden IWW graveyard was plumbed so that splintered headstones and vagabond bones began to overflow the midway. Mixed with dirt and offal, a thighbone of Emma Goldman, the trunk of Woody Guthrie, the skull of Big Bill Thompson, the bones of Martin Irons, Mother Jones, Fanny Wright, Thomas Skidmore, Frederick Douglass, and pieces of Osceola appeared.

At dusk, when it was all over, all the Unbearables in this book (in body or spirit) had gathered around the untombed.

Sharon said, "Someone will have a hell of a job cleaning up."

But Ron spoke solemnly, "Perhaps we will collect these bones for the rest of our lives."

E   m   i   l   y   X   Y   Z

ONE NIGHT YOUR LIFE IS A STONE INSIDE YOU. ANOTHER NIGHT, A WORM THAT WON'T BE STILL. IN THE MEANTIME, YOU STARE AT THE LITTLE CO-LLECTION OF STARS IN YOUR HANDS

That Wonderful Skull

HAKIM BEY

Fu Manchu where are you now we really need you?
  Surely you outlived that jerk Nayland Smith
O President of the Council of Seven of the Si Fan
  Tong
How could any 2-bit CIA Freemason White Templar
  Conspiracy
stand the penetration of your green eyes Great
  Alchemist?
Unmummify yourself again Taoist Sage Prophet of
  Chaos
Patron of all who suffer the oppressions of christian
  dogs
Enlightener of santeros celts neopagans terrorists
houngans queers Mexican Liberals dacoits paranoids
opium Indian Hemp smokers rogue sufis dykes
Doctor Doctor! where's the secret panel that hides us
from your alabaster hands your poisons your ray of
  invisibility?
Fu! without you we're living on the border of the
  Great Fear
Novus Ordo Knights of the Camelia stinking petrole-
  um abyss
Fucking Sax Rohmer racist closet-case give back Fu
  Manchu
from the fascist drool of your unpublished manu-
  scripts
Hang the Exxon execs from the lampposts Berlin
  Autonomen
gypsies jongleurs Assassins Kallikaks dragqueens
Arm the Jivaro! shrink the heads of Gehlen Network
  Skull & Bones
Drug Warriors Death of the Snapping Fingers needles
  of amnesia

*As Rollo saw the coastal city
of Tabriz off the side of the
tramp steamer, he felt a
clutching in his heart, like
the gathering of people
around a burial.*

*What's it like when you
wake up in a lobster crate,
with a bloc of instructions
pinned to your shirt nape,
your dinner jacket missing?*

*He forgave Muy-Muy
and Jose for doing this to
him, even thanked them.
Now he caught sight of a
dark lantern flashing on the
beach, just as the sun
breached the horizon. Rollo
stripped naked and dove
like an arrow from the
prow, then began coursing
quickly through the waves
that were as regular as the
folds in a letter.*

*Hakim doused the
lantern and waded out into
the flighty water to meet
his friend.*

*Dear reader, you too
must make that dawn your
own.*

287

your "cold intelligence" coded messages sold by homeless peddlers
book blanket $1.00 used paperback B'way Si Fan agitprop
your face in the clouds your voice in the moon the patterns of anger
screaming revenge Babylonian icons the Neolithic Con
voters cop-worshippers porn-crusaders corporate shits
"My power rests but my hand is stretched I shall restore
when your civilization as you are pleased to term it
has exterminated reduced to ashes your palaces & temples
when in yr blindness the clock you so laboriously fashioned
I shall stir out of the fire the red dusk fallen
the golden dawn will come." Great Fu we await you . . .

—Midsummer 1991
Hun-Tun Hermitage
Ramapaugh Autonomous Zone
(for Brett Rutherford)